"ARE YOU UNABLE TO STAY WITH ONE WOMAN?"

"No, Anne." Tim shook his head. "That's not what I'm saying."

"Then what are you saying?" she pleaded.

He didn't answer at once. He was staring down at his hands, and Anne sensed that he wanted to reach out to her as much as she wanted him to. She moved toward him, not even realizing what she was doing, and was startled when he recoiled.

"Please, Anne," he said, his voice thick. "Don't make it more difficult for us than it is already."

She shook her head, puzzled. "I don't understand you, Tim. Why...."

"Why don't I take you in my arms and make love to you right now, when that's what we both want so desperately?" he asked, his torment tangible. "I'm not free to love you, Anne. It's as simple as that."

Books by Meg Hudson

HARLEQUIN SUPERROMANCES

HARLEQUIN AMERICAN ROMANCES

These books may be available at your local bookseller.

For a free catalog listing all titles currently available, send your name and address to:

Harlequin Reader Service
P.O. Box 52040, Phoenix, AZ 85072-2040
Canadian address: Stratford. Ontario N5A 6W2

Meg Hudson
THE RISING ROAD

Harlequin Books

TORONTO • NEW YORK • LONDON
AMSTERDAM • PARIS • SYDNEY • HAMBURG
STOCKHOLM • ATHENS • TOKYO • MILAN

For Russ Haddleton and Cathie Gordon,
great experts, both,
in their respective fields.

My special thanks to Stephen Hudson Koehler, my primary
editor and consultant on the romance novels I write, for his
valuable contribution to this book, especially the added
atmosphere and color he injected to enhance both the Boston
and Irish segments of the story.

My appreciation, also, to Joan Ennis of the Irish Tourist Board in
New York City, who is forever helpful in sharing her
knowledge of her native land.

Published March 1984

First printing January 1984

ISBN 0-373-70106-3

CHAPTER ONE

ANNE PAUSED on the threshold to let her eyes adjust from bright daylight to a dimness she found unsavory at this early hour. Then, frowning slightly, she made her way through the crowded tavern toward the bar. Small patches of silence trailed in her wake as she passed tables where only seconds before the conversation had been boisterous. She was acutely aware of this and knew that she was being scrutinized, assessed, and she had no doubt that curiosity was stirring as a result—not at all the kind of curiosity she wanted to attract!

She was an intruder, and she certainly was being made to feel like one. She resented that. She had not walked into the Harp and Shamrock Pub because she'd wanted to. It had seemed her only choice at the moment.

As she neared the bar, several men standing in front of it moved aside to let her through. But there was no friendliness in their attitude, and Anne felt as if they were watching her with a mixture of leering interest and antagonism.

Tight-lipped, having run the gauntlet, she moved to stand directly in front of the bar's scarred oak surface, which came well above her waist. Then, even as she started to speak to the burly red-faced man who obviously was the bartender, she stopped short, her eyes widening with surprise.

He was dispensing beer from large glass pitchers into frosted mugs. At least Anne assumed it was beer—a frothy head came to top each mug as it was filled. But the liquid was as green as the crepe paper festooning the tavern and the huge cardboard shamrocks hanging from the ceiling.

The bartender was watching her with an interest that was disconcerting. Anne was accustomed to seeing admiration in men's eyes, whether or not she wanted it. If anything, she played down her own looks, usually subduing her makeup and choosing colors that were not attention getters, saving the deep rich colors she loved for off-business hours. Nevertheless, her innate sense of fashion made it next to impossible for her to escape notice. At that moment she wished she'd worn old jeans and a loose-fitting jersey. Then maybe she could have passed through this crowd unnoticed.

As it was, she was wearing a full skirt in a rust-and-dark-green plaid, with an ivory tuxedo-necked blouse. Her brown suede jacket was exquisitely tailored, and her buff-colored suede boots offered a subtle color contrast.

Slightly under average height—she was exactly five feet four—Anne favored fairly high heels, such as those on the boots she was wearing, to make her seem a bit taller. This illusion of height was furthered by her long slim legs. She'd been a serious cross-country runner during her college days and still enjoyed a variety of sports, which helped keep her in shape.

Anne was not vain, but it would have been ridiculous to ignore the message she saw in her mirror every time she stole a glance in its direction. Maybe the mirror didn't infer that she was the fairest of them all, but it did show that she was lovely, with cameo features set into a face slightly more square than oval, light gray eyes framed by dark lashes and brows, and very dark brown hair, which she wore shoulder length, parted on the left. Her hair had a deep natural wave, further accentuated by tendril curls around the hairline, which tended to escape much too easily. They were escaping now, she knew, and she brushed them back with an impatient gesture as the bartender asked, "Yes, miss? You wanted something?"

His tone made it clear that he wasn't going to solicit an unfamiliar customer, not on this mid-March Sunday at any rate, and Anne's resentment mounted. It was with an effort that she kept her voice level to say, "I've had trouble with my car, and I wondered if you might give me the name of a garage I could call for assistance."

"Well, now," a jocular voice said, just to her left, and she looked up to see a dark-haired man beaming down at her, his smile almost a smirk. "So it is help the young lady is needing, is it? Perhaps we can be giving it to her, eh, fellows?"

He was addressing a group of men just behind him, Anne saw, and they grinned knowingly. "You're not apt to find a mechanic who'll come running today, pretty face,'' the man went on. ''Or maybe you don't know where you are?''

There was a chorus of laughter at this, but before Anne could respond, the dark-haired man boomed to the room at large, ''Yer in the heart of Southie, darlin', and the parade's about to start any minute!''

A hearty roar followed, beer mugs clinked loudly, and Anne stood rooted to the spot, both stunned and chagrined.

''There's no chance of your getting anyone hereabouts out on a road call today,'' the bartender agreed, having gone back to his task of filling mugs with green beer. ''He's right about that, miss. You'd best leave your car and get back to it later.''

''But that's impossible!'' Anne sputtered.

''Nothing is impossible when you are dealing with true sons of Erin,'' the dark-haired man put in, and this time he reached out to clasp Anne's arm with a large and definitely muscular hand.

Anne tried to draw back from him, but his grip only tightened. ''We'll take a look at your car after a time, lass,'' he promised silkily, and despite the rather early hour—it was just after noon—Anne realized that he'd already had too much to drink. The smell of whiskey on his breath was overpowering as he urged, ''Why not come and sit for a spell and drink some of Mike's good Irish beer!''

''Thank you, no,'' Anne said firmly

''Too good for the likes of us, is that it?'' the man asked. But there was something a bit too quiet about the tone in which he voiced the question, and Anne felt a prick of fear.

She shivered. "It isn't that..." she began, only to be quickly interrupted.

"Well, so there you are!" another masculine voice observed, and someone tall and broad shouldered forced himself into the almost nonexistent space on Anne's right side, moving so close to her that she was conscious of the pressure of his thigh— a taut firm thigh—against her leg. He leaned close to her and he, too, reeked of beer. Green beer, she amended sullenly.

"I was wondering what had held you up," the stranger went on conversationally, and it took her a moment to realize that he really was speaking to her. "Car trouble, did you say?"

Anne found herself answering him despite herself. "I had a flat...just outside," she told him, looking up, then up further until she met eyes that were green enough to belong in the heart of Erin.

Those intensely green eyes were embedded in a face that Anne knew, even in that very first instant, would not be easy to forget. He wasn't handsome in a conventional sense, this man, yet he was diabolically attractive—despite the fact that he badly needed a shave. His features were craggy, as if they'd been hewn from stone but without a final smoothing. He was tall, standing head and shoulders over Anne. *He must be well over six feet,* she surmised, and although he was dressed atrociously—she winced as she took in a pale lime slightly soiled T-shirt with a vivid green map of Ireland emblazoned across the front— there was a decidedly sensuous blend of masculine strength and masculine grace to his physique.

Anne averted her eyes from his snug-fitting faded jeans, which left nothing at all to the imagination, and stammered slightly as she started to tell this man that he was mistaking her for someone else. But he was already saying to the bartender, "Two green ones, if you please, Mike," and as Mike handed back two frothing mugs to him, he in turn passed one to her.

Anne had to take it. She was certain that if she didn't the mug would crash to the floor between them. Then her free arm was being gripped by the stranger, and she was aware that the other man had released her and turned away and was busy talking in a low voice to his friends.

"This way," her rescuer told her. Oddly, that was the word that sprang into her mind in connection with him. "I must possess the luck of the Irish after all because I spot a table for two over there in the corner."

A minute later they were settled at the table and it was only then Anne realized her knees were trembling. Her companion reached out his frost-covered mug, clinked it with hers and said agreeably, "May the roads rise with you and the wind be always at your back, and may the Lord keep you in the hollow of his hand."

"What's that supposed to mean?" she asked.

"An old Irish toast," he told her imperturbably.

Anne stared at him, and despite the dim light in the tavern she could see a distinct glint of dark copper in his hair. A redheaded green-eyed Irishman, no less! Perhaps a leprechaun transformed into a full-sized man? She smiled inwardly at the thought and was unaware that her lips had also curved until her rescuer said, "May I share the joke?"

"What joke?"

"Something surely struck your funny bone just now, which I find reassuring. I was wondering if you possessed a sense of humor . . . you looked so frozen there at the bar. At this point," he added, "I imagine you must think Southie a most unfriendly place."

"I . . . I'm not sure."

"Well, to an outsider it must seem that way. But it's not, really. A bit insular, perhaps, and the people do tend to look after their own first. But they are good hardworking people for the most part." He paused thoughtfully, then went on, "Southie . . . it's a place to itself, you see. A separate entity— emotionally, at least—from the rest of Boston. You, I would say, have stumbled into the wrong neighborhood."

Anne had no ready answer to this. As a child she'd been plagued with a slight stammer, a hindrance that came on whenever she was excited or upset. It was something she thought she'd gotten over years ago, yet she'd caught a hint of it in her voice only a few minutes ago and was sure she couldn't possibly get a word out in one piece just then, no matter how hard she tried.

"What's the matter?" the disturbing man sitting across from her asked. "Cat got your tongue?"

"P-please. . . ." Anne began.

"Don't look so upset, *mavourneen*. May I ask what you are doing in here?"

"I...I told the bartender," Anne managed, avoiding those discerning green eyes as she spoke. "I had a flat, just outside. I was able to pull over to the curb—"

"Not in front of one of the parade reviewing stands, I hope," he interrupted.

"No, there was nothing there. That is...yes, I think there was s-something there. A fire hydrant." The stammer was coming back.

"So on top of it all you've broken the law, have you?" the stranger demanded, but there was a hint of laughter in his voice, and Anne couldn't repress a half smile.

"That's better," he said encouragingly. "The world is not about to come to an end. In fact, this is a great day! A great day for the Irish, in any event. But then, you're not Irish, are you?"

"No, I'm not."

"English, maybe?"

"American," Anne told him flatly.

"Aye, and so am I American," he replied, generously emphasizing the word. "Except at this time of the year. Now, everyone with a touch of the old sod in his ancestry is a son of Erin, at least in South Boston. You must know that you've stumbled into one of the biggest Irish strongholds in all the United States?"

"I know that a lot of Irish people live in South Boston...."

"You're right," he cut in quickly. "But Southie isn't an Irish enclave, not totally. We still predominate here, 'tis true, but we also have our Poles and our Lithuanians, our Albanians and quite a number of others. But on this day they are all Irish, do you see what I mean?''

"This isn't Saint Patrick's Day,'' Anne protested mildly.

"Aye,'' he agreed, raising his mug and taking a hefty swallow. "It is the Sunday before Saint Patrick's Day.''

"So why is everyone—''

"Because, lass, a number of years ago it was decided, for practical purposes, to hold the parade on the Sunday nearest to the seventeenth of March.'' He peered across at the big plastic clock revolving slowly over the bar, part of a beer advertisement. Then he frowned. "The parade will have started,'' he said. "It begins at Andrew Square and then wends its way around Thomas Park and through the various streets till it starts back down East Broadway—which is where you are now, in case you don't know it. Then it proceeds along West Broadway to Broadway Station.'' He laughed at the expression on Anne's face. "All of that means nothing to you, does it?'' he suggested.

Anne shook her head. "Not much, I'm afraid,'' she admitted. "I haven't been in Boston for…a long time. I was quite young when I left, actually.''

"When you left?'' he interposed, one dark copper eyebrow arching interrogatively.

"I was born in Boston,'' Anne answered, and then wondered why she'd told him such a thing.

There was a wry twist to his grin. "But not in Southie, that's plain enough!''

She ignored this and asked instead, "What about you? Were you born in. . .in Southie?"

She was unprepared for the expression that crept into his eyes, nor could she define it. He looked at her as if she'd trespassed on something, and for a long moment there was an oddly shuttered appearance to his face, a face that until now had been very expressive.

He said abruptly, "It doesn't really matter," then added, as if getting a hold on himself, "Anyway, my name's Timothy Flanagan."

He waited, and there was nothing to do but answer him. "I'm Anne Clarendon," she said a bit ungraciously.

She felt herself impelled to look directly into those green eyes as she spoke, and it was a surprising relief to find them friendly again. In fact, Timothy Flanagan held her gaze as he said, "Hello, Anne Clarendon," and reached out to click his mug with hers again. Then he observed, faintly disapproving, "You've hardly touched your beer. You don't like beer?"

"I don't drink it very often," she confessed.

"Yes, I would say you are much more the champagne type," he told her, a definite hint of mockery in his voice.

"It isn't that," she protested, trying not to stammer again. "Beer's fine. It's just that this beer is. . .green!"

"Made so by the addition of some food coloring, which we shall trust is not dangerous to the health in this day of chemical additives!"

As he spoke, Anne was suddenly struck by the sound of his voice. It was low and mellow, its tones unusually rich. There was a flow to the way he used words. He spoke like a person who'd had voice training. An actor, perhaps?

Yes, it would be easy enough to imagine him as an actor if he shaved and put something decent on. She wrinkled her nose. That T-shirt really was dreadful! she thought to herself. But then, as if afraid that he might be fey enough to read her mind, she lowered her eyes and took a sip of the beer—and found that it wasn't bad at all.

"How did you happen to drive into Southie?" he questioned, startling her thoroughly because her thoughts had strayed. In fact, she was thinking about *him*, wondering about him, her curiosity piqued. He'd shut her off completely when she'd asked if he'd been born here in South Boston. Why? He'd just been asking similar questions about her.

"What?" she demanded, then shook herself and answered before he could repeat the question, "Well, the traffic on the expressway was terrible."

He nodded. "Yes, but it's pretty bad here. too. and on this of all days. . . ."

"I didn't realize that," she pointed out reasonably.

"Where were you coming from?"

"New York. I left just after breakfast this morning. The traffic's always bad getting out of the city on a Sunday, but it was mild in comparison to what I encountered as I neared Boston. I got into the wrong lane, and there was nothing I could do but go off at the South Boston exit. Then the next thing I knew there was this noise—a thump, I guess you'd call it—and it didn't take too much imagination to know that I had a flat tire. So I pulled over as quickly as I could and found I was right at the door of...this place. There were people all over the sidewalk and curb, waiting for the parade you mentioned, I guess. The entire scene was so...so overpowering I really didn't care whether I pulled up by a fire hydrant or not. I wasn't even conscious of the fact.''

"Do you always panic so easily?''

"I don't call that panic, Mr...." Anne sought for the name he'd just given her, "Mr. Flanagan," she finished defiantly.

He laughed. "Sure, and you must have a touch of Irish in you after all," he told her, in the mock brogue he'd been affecting now and then. "At least, you do tend to get your back up quickly, a character trait attributed often enough to the Irish, whether or not 'tis rightful to do so.''

To her surprise he stood up, and she could not prevent her eyes from traveling the full length of him. She felt an odd little clutching sensation, followed by a brief but intense pang of something she recognized quite clearly. This man had a decidedly sensual impact on her that could not be denied. Anne felt her awareness of him spread treacherously through her body like a warm current, a potentially dangerous current, she knew instinctively. Yet, on the other hand, such a current could also be delicious.

"I'll go take a look at your car," he said, "and if there's a neighborhood cop around, as there should be, I'll explain your predicament. Don't wander off with anyone else, there's a good girl," he called back as a parting admonition, and Anne felt herself flushing because she knew that some of the people at nearby tables had heard him. They were laughing, and she had the feeling that it could well be at her expense!

They probably knew Timothy Flanagan a lot better than she did, she reminded herself, feeling more uncomfortable than ever.

She watched him move through the crowded room, stopping now and then to greet someone, and fancied she could hear his laughter above the din, even though the Harp and Shamrock was a decidedly noisy place. But then Timothy Flanagan would stand out in any crowd.

Anne sighed. She'd planned to be in Chestnut Hill by now. Glancing around, she wondered where she might find a pay phone so she could call her Aunt Muriel. But it was impossible to see anything other than people and green streamers and green shamrocks. Well, Aunt Muriel had told her to take her time. In fact, she'd been insistent about it. And anyway, Anne reassured herself when she got to Chestnut Hill, the story of her escapade in South Boston would make good conversation. It might serve to relieve some of the tension that had been much too obvious in Muriel's voice lately.

Muriel Clarendon had a weak heart. Anne knew

her aunt had already had two episodes that had been classified as warnings.

If we can get through this whole unhappy business without her having another one it will be something of a miracle, Anne told herself unhappily, then picked up her mug of green beer and drained it without even realizing she'd done so.

These past few months had been traumatic enough even for a person with a good heart. Anne's mouth twisted as she remembered the lunchtime phone call from Palm Beach just after Thanksgiving, with the tragic word that her father had been killed in a boating accident that morning while deep-sea fishing.

Forbes Clarendon, in his fifties, had been young for his age, at least ostensibly. Perhaps this was due in part to the fact that he had married a woman not much older than his own daughter, Anne thought, not without bitterness. She'd turned twenty-seven this October, and Laura was just over the edge of thirty.

Anne's parents had divorced when she was only five, and she had moved from Boston to New York, where she and her mother had lived for years in an apartment on West End Avenue. She'd visited her father during the holidays, spent at the family home in Chestnut Hill. It was a mansion of a place, crammed full of heirlooms that only served to create an oppressive atmosphere for a child who was torn in her loyalties between two parents, both of whom she loved.

Her father had always taken her back to the West

End Avenue apartment, and she remembered that her mother had always asked him in for a cup of tea or a glass of sherry. And—always—he had politely refused, but there had been an expression in his eyes as he'd looked at her mother, and Anne had felt convinced in her heart that the two of them still loved each other.

Then, while she was attending a private girls' school in the city, her mother had married a stockbroker. He'd since retired, and he and her mother now lived in Arizona. Once in a while Anne managed to visit them, and it was pleasant enough. But of late she'd taken advantage of the fact that her career in banking was becoming more and more demanding, and her trips west had decreased proportionately.

Her father had waited for a good two years after her mother's remarriage before he'd married Laura. Anne was in her first year of college. He had already moved to Florida by then, since his architectural firm had a number of interests in the Miami area. Laura had been his secretary, a rather sultry brunette who was an extremely attractive young woman.

Initially Anne and Laura had gotten along quite well and had pledged to treat each other like the sister neither of them had ever had. But despite this initial resolve, Anne had sensed less and less of a welcome—and felt less and less rapport with her stepmother—each time she'd visited the beautiful, Spanish-style home her father had built in Miami for his young wife. So here, too, she'd taken refuge in the fact that her career required most of her time and attention, which was more true than false.

After her father's death she'd felt many a twinge of guilt about this. He'd been such a healthy virile man, and she'd expected he'd be alive for years and years to come.

With Aunt Muriel, though, the situation was different. Muriel had made it plain that she had no great illusions about her own life expectancy, and that was why she'd been so insistent Anne come to Chestnut Hill right away.

"It's your inheritance we're dealing with, darling," she had reminded her niece over the phone. "Also, I couldn't possibly fight Laura for my own sake. But with you in the ring with me...."

A voice broke in upon Anne's thoughts. A deep mellow masculine voice, quite wonderful to hear.

"You look as if you've lost your last friend," Timothy Flanagan said, sliding into the seat beside her.

"Not quite," she assured him calmly.

"Another beer?" he suggested, noting her empty mug.

"Thank you, but I couldn't possibly." She became aware that people were getting up and moving toward the front of the tavern, some of them still clutching mugs of green beer.

"The parade," he said succinctly. "Will you deign to watch it, Queen Anne?" He was smiling down at her as he said this, but there was a sardonic touch to his words that served to put her on the defensive.

She stood, bumping the table as she did so in the confining space, and staggered slightly.

"My, my!" Timothy Flanagan observed with considerable amusement. "Don't tell me the green beer has had a real effect on you!"

"It wasn't the beer!" Anne snapped. "Please, will you move out of the way?" He was blocking the path of any possible progress on her part.

He nodded and whispered in her ear, "Come along, but stay close. There's no way you're going to be able to get anywhere until the parade is over and the crowd starts to thin out. So you might as well accept my invitation to come back in here once the bands have gone by and share a lunch of corned beef and cabbage."

Although Anne couldn't fully understand her own reaction, she found his smile infuriating at that moment. "It would seem," he finished complacently, "that for the present, anyway, you're stuck with me!"

OUTSIDE THE HARP AND SHAMROCK Anne soon realized that there was indeed such a thing as wall-to-wall humanity. She'd never been in such a crowd, even in New York, although to be truthful about it she'd studiously avoided ever being trapped in anything like this.

Still, there was an excitement that caught her. It was an insidious form of excitement, and she found herself unexpectedly stirred by the sight of the American flag waving in the breeze as the first units in the parade came marching down the street.

The spectators were almost as much fun to watch as the paraders themselves. One man wore huge sunglasses with green shamrocks painted in the center of each lens. Girls had shimmering shamrocks glued to their cheeks, and there were green bowlers to be seen in abundance, green carnations pinned to lapels, and huge kelly-green bow ties. In comparison, Timothy Flanagan's T-shirt seemed very understated.

It was cold, and there was a steady wind adding to the chill factor. Anne wished she'd worn something warmer than her suede jacket and marveled that Timothy Flanagan seemed quite comfortable with no coat on at all.

Vendors were hawking green heart-shaped balloons and Timothy Flanagan asked laconically, "Want one?"

"No, thank you," Anne said promptly, and he grinned.

"At the moment," he said, "you look as excited as anyone here. And as pretty," he added.

"Blarney," she scoffed, but she was laughing.

The parade swept by, unit after unit, band after band. There were military bands, bands from area schools. All sorts of organizations were represented, each bringing the cheers of the crowd to a new crescendo. And there were people everywhere— people on the rooftops, Anne saw now, and people leaning out of every available window, as well as the masses that thronged the sidewalks.

Finally it was over, and some of the surplus crowd spilled into the street. During the course of the proceedings Anne realized there had been people sitting on top of her Mazda. Under ordinary circumstances she would have been quick to protest, but on this particular Sunday afternoon in March it had hardly seemed to matter.

She saw that Timothy Flanagan was eyeing the car. "That really is some flat you have there," he said. "You must have gone over a chunk of glass or a jagged iron pipe or something. I'd suggest I change it for you myself, but there wouldn't be much elbow room." He hesitated. "After we've had our corned beef and cabbage, I'll take you wherever you're going. They won't tow your car, and tomorrow will be time enough for you to worry about it."

Anne thought about this for a moment and nodded. "I suppose you're right," she said, "but I wouldn't think of having you drive me. And I really can't stay for lunch with you. I'm already very late where...where I'm expected. Do you think I could simply find a cab?"

"Well, it won't be easy," Timothy warned. "Unless...."

"Yes?"

He was looking down the street, a quizzical expression on his face. Then, as she watched, he stepped closer to the curb and raised a commanding hand. As if by magic a yellow cab came to stop almost in front of them.

"It would seem as if you're in luck," he told her, but there was a strangely reluctant note in his voice. "And that would make it seem, *mavourneen*, as if the Irish aren't always so lucky at St. Paddy's time

after all, or surely there would not have been a cab to
be found for the next two hours...and you would
have had to take advantage of my offer of a ride."

He was standing very close to her, and suddenly he
pressed something into her hand. She clutched it involuntarily, but before she could even look to see
what it was he was ushering her toward the cab.

He opened the back door for her with exag-
gerated politeness and executed the parody of a
bow. Then, before Anne could even move, he was
bending over her, and in another instant he was
pressing his mouth against hers, his warm lips so in-
vasive where her senses were concerned, that she
felt herself rocking on her feet.

Involuntarily she found herself returning his kiss,
and for a tantalizing instant there was a fusion between them so tangible that Anne felt as if she'd
been welded to this tall redheaded stranger.

It was he who broke the bond, helping her into
the cab and then stepping back to wave a hand in
farewell.

The driver asked her where she wanted to go, and
Anne's voice trembled as she answered him. Only
then did she stare down at the object Timothy Flanagan had thrust into her hand.

It was one of a number of souvenir items the vendors had been selling during the parade, a big white
button with Kiss Me, I'm Irish emblazoned on it in
brilliant green.

A reluctant smile curved Anne's lips. She had
granted Timothy Flanagan's request even before
she knew he was making it of her.

CHAPTER TWO

ANNE DID NOT REDISCOVER the Irish button until she was getting ready for bed that night. She found it as she was fishing around in her handbag for a small bottle of aspirin.

It was only ten o'clock, yet the day had been long and tiring, and she had a headache. The drive up from New York had been difficult, the incident at the Harp and Shamrock Pub totally unexpected, and the reunion with Aunt Muriel depressing in a variety of ways.

Muriel Clarendon had a lot of stamina, but Laura's legal threats were taking a toll on her. As it was, Laura had inherited the beautiful house in Miami. Now she wanted the Chestnut Hill home as well, plus a considerable share of the Clarendon family heirlooms.

Anne knew it was difficult for her aunt to understand this sort of greed. She couldn't comprehend it herself. And ever since she'd arrived she'd been wondering if there was not some way she could approach Laura alone. They'd had a rapport of sorts, when they'd first known each other, and this whole affair seemed so needless. Laura had changed over the years, true. But even so. . . .

At this point in her train of thought, Anne had started searching in her handbag for the aspirin. As her fingers closed over something round and metallic, she momentarily forgot about her headache. She pressed the white button flat against the palm of her hand, her lips curving in a smile as she read its bright green message.

Kiss Me, I'm Irish. To Anne, the words conjured up a vivid impression not only of Timothy Flanagan's ruggedly handsome face, but of his farewell kiss, and she brushed her lips with exploring fingers as if to reawaken the sensations he'd evoked in her. He had branded her in an explicit way with that kiss. Each year as Saint Patrick's Day loomed near, or whenever she saw or heard anything Irish, she knew she would be reminded of the redheaded stranger who had rescued her from a potentially unpleasant experience in a South Boston bar.

Yes, Timothy Flanagan was unforgettable. Too unforgettable. Anne was mentally reviewing every word he'd said to her and every glance he'd given her as she swallowed her aspirin and climbed into bed. As she snuggled down under an old patchwork quilt she was wondering if there was a chance she might encounter him again when she went back to South Boston the next morning to redeem her car.

As it turned out, the trek to South Boston involved considerable logistical planning. Muriel Clarendon had a car, but for the most part it stayed in the big garage at the back of the Chestnut Hill property. She rarely got behind the wheel these days, admitting freely that contemporary Boston traffic was more than she could handle.

Anne suspected that Muriel's friends disliked driving in the city as much as Muriel herself did, as Muriel neglected to suggest any of them make the trip to Southie with her niece. Taking a taxi seemed the only solution to the transportation problem, Anne decided, but it left a little to be desired. She would have preferred to have had someone with her at the scene while the tire on her car was being changed. Someone she knew.

She was contemplating all of this as she went downstairs Monday morning. The house was very quiet, and although Anne now appreciated the family heirlooms much more than she had as a child, she still found something oppressive about being surrounded by so many antiques. The possibility of enjoying an object's individual beauty was lost in this en masse setting. It might improve the decor, she thought ruefully, if Laura was to be given half of the Clarendon possessions as a placebo.

Sounds of pans clattering drew her to the kitchen, but it was not her Aunt Muriel whom she found setting a kettle of water firmly down on the stove. The woman who turned to greet her was short and plump with a round smooth face and graying hair drawn back in a tight little bun at the nape of her neck. She wore a flowered cotton dress with a white apron tied around her middle, and a somewhat frayed yellow sweater.

Memory stirred. "You're Bridget Malone!" Anne ventured.

The woman smiled, obviously pleased. "I didn't think you'd remember, Anne," she admitted. "You were a little bit of a thing, last time you were here."

Anne bit back the words, "And you must have been only in your teens then," because that would mean Bridget could not be much over forty now. Yet she looked considerably older, despite the smoothness of her skin. Anne sensed that in the years since she'd last seen Bridget Malone the other woman had done a lot of living, and she suspected that not much of it had been easy.

Bridget answered her unspoken conjecture. "I was fourteen when I came to work for your aunt afternoons after school," she said, smiling wistfully. "That was a long time ago." Then she shrugged as if casting off the past, and straightened her shoulders. "I'll have coffee in a minute, Anne," she promised. "Or maybe it should be Miss Clarendon, now that you're a New York banker and all!"

Anne laughed. "Anne will do just fine."

"Well then, Anne, what else would you like for breakfast?"

"To tell you the truth, Bridget, I usually skip it," Anne said. "There never seems to be time to fix anything before I have to leave for the office."

"Well, that surely isn't the case now. How about some scrambled eggs and sausages?"

"I wouldn't be able to move if I ate that much first thing in the morning," Anne protested. "A piece of toast will be fine. Maybe with some marmalade, if you have any."

Bridget nodded and started setting out china and

silver. Then, unexpectedly, she asked, "Do you still sing?"

Anne was startled. Singing was something she'd relegated to the past, because there had stopped being time for that, too, once she'd become immersed in her career. True, she still sang once in a while when she was by herself. Thinking about this, she smiled ruefully. "I guess most of the singing I do these days is in the shower," she confided.

Bridget shook her head disapprovingly. "That's not right," she stated firmly. "God gave you a gift, and when He gives gifts they're meant to be used, if you ask me."

Anne was surprised at the seriousness of the woman's tone. Nor could she help but feel she'd been put slightly on the defensive.

"I couldn't make a quick living out of singing, Bridget," she said slowly, wondering why she felt the need to explain herself. Yet she did.

Maybe what I'm really doing is explaining it to myself, she conceded. *It's been a long time since I've dared to think about it at all.*

"Your father could have helped you," Bridget pointed out.

"I suppose so," Anne agreed. "But...he'd remarried by the time I'd ordinarily have been going to a conservatory for voice lessons. You know that. Anyway...well, I didn't want to ask him, that's all. I knew that I'd have years of study ahead of me before I could really hope to do anything—anything that would reap financial rewards, that is." She paused, then added, "Nor did I want to ask my mother for help. She'd made her own life, too.''

"Your Aunt Muriel would have helped you," Bridget insisted stubbornly.

"Yes, I'm sure she would have," Anne nodded. "But... the fact of the matter is that I wanted very much to be independent. As it was, it was through a friend of the family's that I was offered my first bank job. I still worked very hard, though, to make it on my own. After that, well, after that I went on to all sorts of other things."

"And you're happy with what you're doing?"

"Very happy," Anne said truthfully. "Bridget, I have a fascinating job...."

"You also have the voice of an angel. At least you did have. You used to go around singing when you visited here—why, you were just a little girl! I remember a friend of your aunt's who was married to a man connected with the Boston Symphony Orchestra. She had her husband come over to hear you one day. I remember him saying, 'That child has real talent!' Yes, I remember it as clearly as if it was yesterday."

"That actually happened?" Anne asked, surprised.

Bridget nodded solemnly, then put a plate of toast on the table with butter and a jar of orange marmalade, followed by a large cup of steaming hot coffee.

Anne, stirring cream into the coffee, felt oddly disturbed by this conversation. She hadn't realized that the subject of singing was still such a sensitive one with her. Until late in her teens, when she had graduated from a private girls' school in Westchester, she had always dreamed of the day when she'd sing on the concert stage. She'd had a mental vision of bowing gracefully as people applauded her, and then of stepping forward and accepting a huge sheath of red roses.

It had been a childhood fantasy, and in due course she had recognized it as such. But by then her desire to be a singer had become more serious, and finally she'd had to face the decision of either going on to college and studying something practical, or trying to convince her family that she should go to a conservatory and pursue what came to her naturally. She had opted in favor of college and a career in business, and her musical interests had, out of necessity, been relegated to the background.

She tried to tell herself now that there was the chance her voice hadn't been as good as people had insisted. Friends could be prejudiced in one's favor, she knew. Yet there was something else involved, and Anne winced at the memory of it.

Giving up her music in favor of business had caused the breakup between Ken Phillips and herself, and that still ranked as one of the more traumatic episodes in a life that had been anything but free of emotional trauma.

Bridget said suddenly, "I didn't mean to stir up a can of worms for you, Anne."

She forced a smile. "You didn't. It's just been a while since I've thought about how much I used to want to be a singer, that's all."

"Well, I suppose I was grinding my own ax, in a way," Bridget told her.

"What do you mean?"

"I'm not Malone anymore," the woman replied, as if this was part of her explanation. "My married name is Kincaid. I have a daughter Katharine. She's eighteen, getting out of high school this June. And...she's got a voice. When she sings, Anne, she reminds me of you! That's why I got onto this subject in the first place, I guess. I think she should study. Lord knows, I think I owe it to her! But," she finished dryly, "her father says she should go on and take business courses so she can get a good job as a secretary."

Bridget's round face creased into a scowl, an obvious indication of how much the question of her daughter's future was concerning her.

"Bridget..." Anne began, but the older woman shook her head.

"You've got enough problems of your own with that stepmother of yours about to sue and everything," she said softly, her tone comforting and familiar to Anne. "Matter-of-fact, I think your aunt wants you to go into town and see her lawyer today."

"I've got to do something about my car first," Anne said ruefully, then briefly outlined her adventure of the day before.

Bridget chuckled. "To think of you stuck in South Boston in the middle of a St. Paddy's Day parade!" she managed, much amused. "Let's see now, you'll need someone to drive you over there."

"I thought I'd just call a cab."

"No," Bridget contradicted. "Suppose the police have hauled your car away after all. I know what that redheaded Irishman told you, but there's no saying they didn't tow it later in the day. Anyway," she continued, "we can certainly find someone to go along with you."

"Do you think so?"

"I know so," Bridget said, after giving the matter a full moment's thought. "I'll call Peter Dwyer. He's working nights just now, and if I remember right he doesn't have any classes on Mondays."

Before Anne could ask who Peter Dwyer was, Bridget had turned to the wall phone and was dialing. The conversation that followed was brief, and Bridget turned back to say, "He'll be over in an hour. It's chilly out, Anne. Make sure you put on something warm."

Anne finished her coffee and stood up, prepared to do exactly that. But before she left the kitchen she asked, "Who is Peter Dwyer?"

"A friend of Katharine's," Bridget replied somewhat evasively. "He's a nice boy, really, and as it happens he's also a good mechanic. If your car is still parked down on East Broadway I think he can probably change the tire for you himself."

AMAZINGLY, THE MAZDA was still parked in front of the Harp and Shamrock Pub. Peter Dwyer easily handled the flat tire just as Bridget had thought he could.

Straightening, the task completed, he wiped his

hands on an old rag and smiled across at Anne. "She should be all set to go," he told her. "I still can't believe there isn't a ticket tucked under your windshield wiper, though."

Anne was finding that difficult enough to believe herself. It made it seem as if Timothy Flanagan must have quite a bit of influence with the police, for she felt sure that her car wouldn't have been allowed to remain parked on a main South Boston thoroughfare for the better part of twenty-four hours, were this not the case.

Either that, or it could merely have been the luck of the Irish—in this case his luck rubbing off on her, she thought whimsically. He certainly hadn't looked like an influential person. Not with that stubble of dark copper beard on his chin and that atrocious T-shirt straining across his broad chest.

The vision of this tormenting man that came to haunt Anne now was entirely too vivid. Dimly she knew that Peter Dwyer was looking at her curiously.

"Something wrong?" he asked.

"No, n-nothing at all," she said hastily. "Really, Peter, thanks so much. I certainly could never have managed any of this without you."

"I'm glad I was free," he said. "Would you like a cup of coffee before we head back to Chestnut Hill?"

Bridget had been right. Peter was nice, very nice. But although he might seem a boy to the older woman, he was not that much younger than Anne. She guessed that he must be twenty-three or twenty-four, several years older than Katharine Kincaid, Bridget's daughter. In fact, the age gap between Katharine and Peter, Anne decided, was undoubtedly a bit wider than the gap between Peter and herself.

He was a friend of Katharine's, nevertheless, and Anne was only too well aware of the wide gamut of relationships the word *friend* currently included. Regardless, she had no wish to encourage Peter Dwyer, even though he was definitely an attractive young man. Of average height, he had a slender athletic build, hair a bit darker than Anne's own, and dark blue eyes fringed by lashes any woman would have envied.

Anne, though, had become more accustomed to dealing with older men. Most of the men she met in business, most of the men she dated in New York, were older than she was. They were all sophisticated types, sometimes almost too urbane and worldly wise. Whether for winter or summer vacations, they went to the right resorts at the right time, wore the right kind of clothes, and donned the right kind of manners.

Thinking this, she flinched slightly. These past few years she had increasingly followed that sort of pattern herself. Only the week before she'd returned from a ski trip in Aspen, and already she'd planned a sailing venture for June with friends who had a place on Martha's Vineyard—and their own beautiful yawl.

Beautiful places, beautiful people, beautiful clothes.

Beautiful clothes! Anne laughed shortly to herself. That morning she had not followed her usual sense of fashion. She'd wanted to be as inconspicuous as possible on this return trip to South Boston and had chosen to wear jeans, a knit blouse and a bulky white sweater that had seen better days. She'd stuffed these clothes into her suitcase at the last minute as she was packing in New York.

She realized that her present garb made her look younger. She'd also simply brushed her hair that morning, not bothering to arrange it in any particular style, and had put on very little makeup. At the moment she didn't look any older than Peter Dwyer.

He repeated his question. "Want to stop for some coffee, Anne?"

"I don't think so, thanks, Peter," she said. "I had a second cup just before I started out with you."

That was true. She'd gone back down to the kitchen after getting ready to meet Peter and had accepted a second cup of coffee from Bridget, sitting down at the round kitchen table to drink it. She'd wanted to talk to Bridget about Aunt Muriel. If she remembered correctly, Muriel had always been an early riser. But there had been no sign of her that morning, and Anne hesitated to disturb her.

Bridget verified the fact that most of the time Muriel tended to "sleep in," as Bridget put it. "But she needs her rest," the woman had added, as if defending her employer.

Anne supposed that was so. Still, it was yet another change in her aunt that she found disturbing.

Now she said to Peter, "Thanks again for helping me like this. I really appreciate it."

He waved his hand deprecatingly, seeming faintly embarrassed by her praise. "Look, no problem," he assured her. "I work as a mechanic at a garage near Coolidge Corner. Nights, just now, which is fine with me because I'm going to college part-time."

"What are you studying?"

"Engineering and electronics mostly, with a good dose of computer science thrown in. Computers are into everything these days, and I'd like to keep up with the times."

"Wise of you," Anne agreed. "I know computers have become such an integral part of banking it's hard to imagine how we ever managed without them."

"Bridget tells me you've got quite the job in New York," Peter observed.

"A very interesting one, yes."

"I'd like to talk to you about it sometime. Anne. Maybe if you're free one evening. . . ."

"Call me," she told him, somewhat unwillingly. But there didn't seem to be anything else she could say.

Peter suggested she follow him back to Chestnut Hill, or at least try to, "It depends how bad the traffic is," he explained. But sliding behind the wheel of the Mazda, Anne had an odd reluctance to pull away from this South Boston curb.

The cleanup job in the wake of the previous day's festivities hadn't been completed yet. Green paper streamers littered the gutters along with the usual trash and broken glass, and in addition to this ugly assortment Anne also saw several battered green cardboard bowlers.

She glanced toward the entrance of the Harp and Shamrock. The tavern looked especially dim—there weren't even any lights on inside, as far as she could see. Chances were they hadn't opened yet. But as she stared at the grungy front door she found herself being transported back in time. She imagined herself again making her way to the bar, where a tall copper-haired man greeted her as if he'd been expecting her for a long, long time....

She shivered, wishing she had the power to conjure up Timothy Flanagan in the flesh.

Maybe he really was a giant-sized leprechaun! she told herself wryly, pulling out onto the street after Peter, who had already started down East Broadway ahead of her.

OVER THE NEXT FEW DAYS Anne did not find it easy to put Timothy Flanagan out of her mind. She found herself imagining she saw him wherever she went, and was annoyed with herself for acting like a romantic adolescent. But the man seemed to have cast a spell on her!

Maybe, she finally decided, Boston simply had more than its share of tall redheaded Irishmen. When shopping in Bloomingdale's at the Chestnut Hill Mall, she nearly called the name Timothy aloud as she rounded the end of an aisle and saw a man walking along some twenty feet in front of her.

Then the man turned, and blue eyes, not emerald green ones, appraised her appreciatively. Anne flushed and turned away hastily. It was only too easy to imagine how expectant the look on her face must have been.

Later in the week she persuaded Muriel to dine with her at a small neighborhood French restaurant. Glancing up from the menu, she found herself staring across the room at a man sitting at a table for two, his face etched by the light of the single candle flickering between him and his companion.

"Timothy!" The name came to her lips and she knew she must have spoken it aloud, for her aunt paused in her perusal of the menu to look up and ask, "What did you say, dear?"

"I think I'll have the vichyssoise," Anne said hastily. But then her gaze drifted across the room again to find dark eyes meeting her gray ones with a steadiness that was much too disconcerting. Certainly that was not Timothy! Fingers trembling, she dropped her napkin, then was grateful for the distraction provided by having to pick it up.

Anne had taken a two-week leave of absence from her job with the understanding that if she didn't need this much time in which to settle her family affairs she would return to New York earlier. But as day followed day, she began to wonder if two weeks were going to be enough.

Aunt Muriel had tried to make an appointment for her to meet with the attorney the day after her arrival, only to learn that he was in Chicago on business and would not be back until the beginning of the following week.

When Peter Dwyer telephoned on Saturday, Anne was tempted to agree to go out with him. Muriel Clarendon was keeping a low profile and maintaining a slow pace these days, and time sometimes hung heavily in the Chestnut Hill house. Nevertheless, Anne resolved not to see Peter until she'd first delved a bit further into the matter of his relationship with Bridget's daughter. Bridget did not work on either Saturday or Sunday, so that meant waiting till at least the first of the week for this, too, and from the sound of his voice, Anne gathered that Peter did not especially appreciate being stalled.

On Monday morning the attorney's office called to suggest a meeting at three that afternoon. Anne had hoped her aunt would go with her for this initial encounter with the lawyer, for Oscar Wechsler, she knew, had been representing the Clarendon family interests for many years. As it happened, though, Muriel had awakened late with the hint of a cold, and it was raining out.

"I hate to be such a sissy about things," she told her niece. "It wouldn't do, though, if I really came down with something!"

"Don't worry about it," Anne consoled. "It would have been nice to have you along, needless to say. I was looking forward to taking you to the Copley Plaza for tea once we got out of the lawyer's office. But I'll give you a rain check, okay?"

Muriel had come downstairs for lunch, and they were just getting up from the table when this conversation occurred. She paused by the dining-room window, gazing out at the steadily falling rain that spattered the street.

"I suppose it'll help the flowers and the trees to get started," she allowed. "Miserable day, though. I wish you didn't have to go out in it, Anne."

"I don't mind, Aunt Muriel."

"Take a cab, why don't you, dear? It's impossible to find a parking place downtown, especially in weather like this."

"Agreed," Anne told her. "Now go on up and take a nap and don't worry about a thing."

"It's difficult not to worry," Muriel replied sadly, moving toward the front-hall staircase. "I'm terribly afraid that Laura really has something up her sleeve. I don't trust her at all. But we've got Oscar to help us with all of that," she finished, managing a smile.

Anne nodded. After her aunt had gone up to her room, she sat in the living room for a time thumbing through a couple of magazines. Then she went to her own room and looked over her wardrobe with a calculating eye. It was necessary to take the weather into account, but she still wanted to be very chic for this first meeting with her aunt's attorney. Finally she selected a gray-flannel walking suit, which combined beautifully tailored trousers with a straight jacket. With this she wore a teal-green angora turtleneck and, as a final touch, a gray wool brimmed hat with a contrasting deep teal ribbon.

Short black suede boots, which had been carefully weatherproofed, completed the outfit.

She paid careful attention to her makeup, and a discreet application of her favorite perfume, Flora Danica, gave the perfect final touch.

There was a porte cochere in front of the Chestnut Hill house so Anne had no need initially for the umbrella Bridget had thrust into her hand as she was leaving, an old black bumbershoot that usually resided in the front-hall closet. She was glad she had it, though, when the cab, unable to pull up directly in front of the office building near Government Center where the law offices of Simon and Wechsler were located, had to let her off on Cambridge Street, a bit further down the block.

The building was relatively new, done in a stark contemporary style of architecture that was surprisingly effective, given that its neighbors were the Old State House and King's chapel, two beautifully preserved structures of Boston's colonial days. Anne entered a mirror-paneled elevator and was whisked to the fourteenth floor. She found the law offices down a carpeted corridor to her right.

A silver-haired receptionist greeted her, but as soon as Anne had identified herself the woman's words were apologetic.

"I'm so sorry, Miss Clarendon," she said. "We tried to reach you, but you'd already left Chestnut Hill. Mr. Wechsler has met with an accident and...."

"Not serious, I hope," Anne interrupted, shocked.

The receptionist hesitated. "He tripped on an escalator out at the airport and took quite a fall," she confided. "The first report is that he's probably broken his left leg, so...."

"I've been asked to stand in for Mr. Wechsler, if you don't object," a deep masculine voice said just behind Anne.

She closed her eyes tightly. Her imagination was taking over again. Lots of men in the world had melodious voices like Timothy Flanagan's. Lots of men around Boston must also have that telltale hint of the city's accent, with its distinctive way of pronouncing the letter *a*.

"Miss Clarendon," the man urged, and swinging around awkwardly Anne found herself confronting the oversized leprechaun who had been haunting her ever since that Sunday before Saint Patrick's Day!

She blinked. Very clearly he was flesh and blood...but she couldn't believe what she was seeing. Timothy Flanagan could well have been posing as a male fashion model.

He was wearing a dark green wool-blend suit, a pale yellow shirt with a button-down collar, and a knit tie that picked up both colors precisely. His dark copper hair was perfectly styled and combed. In fact, there was none of the unruliness to it that had been so evident that day in Southie, the unruliness that had made her want to run her fingers through it.

His face was close shaven, the scent of the rather spicy lotion he used wafting across Anne's nostrils as if to verify this. Only those very green eyes were the same, gazing at her now just as penetratingly as they had during that first encounter.

"Miss Clarendon," the receptionist said hastily. "This is Mr. Flanagan, a partner in the firm."

Timothy Flanagan nodded. "Miss Clarendon and I have met," he said smoothly while Anne stood before him still speechless.

"Now, Miss Clarendon," he added with a poise she only wished she could match, "if you'd care to come into my office...."

CHAPTER THREE

AS SHE FOLLOWED Timothy Flanagan down a long corridor thickly carpeted in deep blue, Anne was reminded of the old nursery rhyme invitation of the spider to the fly: "Won't you come into my parlor?"

He led her into a large corner office furnished in an ultracontemporary style that mixed light beige with the same blue in the corridor rug, plus splashes of clear lime. Abstract prints on the walls picked up these same color notes, but Anne passed them over quickly for her attention was instantly drawn to the spectacular view of Boston offered through several huge windows, each bordered by lime-and-beige drapes.

Below her, the shining golden dome of the State House seemed almost surrealistically near, and beyond this the Boston Common and the Public Gardens were magical scenes in miniature. Further on, Anne's eyes caught the rays of the sun and a picture of Back Bay townhouses reflected in the mirrored facade of the Hancock Building.

"Impressive, isn't it," Timothy Flanagan said indifferently as he motioned her to a chair in front of the massive teakwood desk that dominated one side of the room and gave its occupant a clear view of the Boston skyline.

Anne nodded, not trying to answer him. Since that day she'd met this man in South Boston, there'd been hardly a hint of her girlhood stammer, but now she felt as if it were about to return, bringing with it a terrible sense of awkwardness.

She was glad to sit down. Doing so, she warned herself she must get control of herself—and keep it.

That was easier said than done, though. Anne had never been much of a believer in the long arm of coincidence, and it seemed impossible to her that Timothy Flanagan could be an attorney in the firm that had long handled the Clarendon family affairs.

If he had not himself told the receptionist that they'd met before, she would have almost been willing to accept the fact that this urbane stranger she was facing was an identical twin of the man she'd met in Southie. But the resemblance was solely physical. She could see nothing of the redheaded Irishman wearing an outrageous T-shirt and sipping green beer in this rather austere individual who was glancing through the contents of a file folder on his desk.

Then he looked up at her, and she was rocked by a sharp sense of familiarity. Yes, those green eyes were indeed the same. Her pulse quickened. No other man could have eyes quite like his. And just now there was a knowing gleam in their depths. Anne was struck with the sudden suspicion that although this encounter was a surprise to her—a total shock, in fact—Timothy Flanagan hadn't been surprised in the least by their meeting.

This suspicion only made her feel even more at a disadvantage, and she was unprepared for it when he said, "Oscar Wechsler is going to be laid up for a while. The hospital called just before I came out to meet you, and the fracture has been confirmed. Oscar isn't young. It's going to take a while for him to heal."

Timothy Flanagan smiled faintly. "He'll probably insist on hobbling in here cast and all as soon as the doctors let him loose," he conceded. "As a matter-of-fact, though, he'd already suggested I take over the Clarendon file."

"Oh?"

A single eyebrow rose in a way that again reminded her of their first encounter in South Boston, and Anne caught her breath. She found she was trying very hard not to remember the last moment of that meeting, the moment when Tim Flanagan had kissed her so thoroughly. But it was impossible to keep her eyes from straying to his full, sensuously shaped mouth.

I've got to stop this! she thought dismally.

"You sound displeased," he was saying, surveying her with a directness that wasn't any easier to handle. "Do you have any objections to my taking over?"

Anne found her voice. "I think it should be up to my aunt to answer that," she told him stiffly. "I'm merely here as her representative."

Briefly he glanced back at the file folder. Then he

said, his tone impersonal, "You seem to be the person primarily concerned in all of this, Miss Clarendon. As I understand it, your aunt is an elderly woman, and she's worried that if your stepmother contests your father's will you are going to be cut out of your rightful inheritance."

"Aunt Muriel isn't old!" Anne protested. "Oh, I suppose she must be in her late sixties. She may even be seventy, so in years. . . ."

"Yes?"

"What I'm t-trying to say is that she's young in spirit," Anne persisted, despite the annoying stammer that threatened to return.

"And that's what counts? Is that what you're trying to tell me?" His smile was absolutely supercilious, she decided, and this nettled her.

"I think it is, yes," she answered coldly.

Timothy Flanagan grinned. "I agree," he said. "Let's take you, for instance. Despite that cool facade you tend to present to the world, Miss Clarendon, I detect a spirit of eternal youth in you."

"Please!" she objected.

He shrugged. "Sorry, my mistake. For a moment I forgot this is a legal conference we're involved in here."

Anne bristled and couldn't resist the question. "Are you really a lawyer?" she demanded.

Immediately she was reminded of the moment when she'd asked him if he'd been born in South Boston, and there was a decided edge of frostiness to his voice as he replied, "Do you doubt I could be?"

"It...isn't that," she floundered. "It's just that...."

"Perhaps you shouldn't always be so quick to judge a book by its cover," he suggested. "Or is it simply that you like to cast people in molds, and I've slipped out of the mold you cast for me?"

"No," Anne managed, shaking her head. Then she added, sounding much more helpless than she would have wished, "I don't know."

Timothy Flanagan folded his hands and leaned back, his face quite expressionless. "Well, Miss Clarendon," he said, "I *am* an attorney. I've been with Simon and Wechsler for several years, and just recently I became a full partner in the firm. In fact, we're in the process of changing the name to Simon, Wechsler and Flanagan. Perhaps when you see the new letterhead you'll have more confidence in me."

"Please—"

"You asked for it, Anne!"

Her heart thumped at the use of her first name. She could feel its thud against the wall of her chest.

Taking a deep breath, she said, "You knew I was coming here today, didn't you?"

Again that interrogative eyebrow rose. "Of course I knew," he said equably. "I do keep an appointment calendar, Anne. It's a business necessity."

"That isn't what I mean. You knew that...it was me."

His mouth twisted, and he picked up a slim brass letter opener, turning it around in his fingers. "I wondered about it the moment you told me what your name was. Clarendon is not a common name, but then it isn't all that unusual, either. After I had your license plate checked, though. . . ."

Anne sat forward on the seat of the chair. "You *what*?" she demanded.

"I had the police run a check on your license plate," he told her calmly. "Then, when I came in here the next morning I verified the fact that Muriel Clarendon had a niece named Anne. Of course there was still a chance there could be two Anne Clarendons."

"Stop it!" she ordered.

"Why?" he asked, looking across at her quizzically.

"Because you knew damned well it was me!"

"No, I didn't," Timothy contradicted gently. "Let's just say I hoped it would be."

A moment of silence drifted between them and Anne felt as if it were etched in pastel pink, delicate and very fragile. He, too, seemed at a momentary loss for words.

Whatever we say to each other next could make a lot of difference, she thought apprehensively.

It was a blessing when a buzzer on his desk sounded. Frowning, he pressed an intercom and didn't try to suppress his irritation as he asked, "What is it, Mrs. Hammond? I believe I told you to hold all calls."

"I'm sorry, Mr. Flanagan," the receptionist's voice echoed. "It's Mr. Wechsler calling from his hospital bed. I thought you'd want to talk to him."

"So soon," Timothy muttered under his breath.

But aloud he said, "Yes, of course." A second later his voice was hearty as he picked up the receiver. "Oscar? What the hell are you doing making phone calls? You should still be under anesthesia!"

As the telephone conversation continued, swiftly getting into legal complexities that made very little sense to her, Anne stood and walked over to the window, once again savoring the view. She watched a huge jet, glistening white against the deep blue sky, majestically ascend toward the west. There would be safety, she thought, in being on that jet just then. A lot more safety—as far as her personal equilibrium was concerned—than being in this office with Timothy Flanagan.

She heard the click of the receiver and, turning quickly, surprised an expression on his face that she hadn't expected to see there. For a single revealing instant she felt as if she was watching a small boy peering into a candy store window, a window full of delectable things he knew he couldn't have. A poor boy, wearing threadbare corduroy pants, a boy looking sad and cold. Imagining this, Anne felt herself wishing she could comfort him.

Had Timothy Flanagan been a poor little boy? Where, for that matter, had he been born? And why was he so defensive about it?

While these questions plummeted through Anne's mind, the man across from her gained visible control of himself and said with a touch of humor, "Oscar really doesn't know when to let up. They have his leg in traction, but even if it were his arms he'd still manage to use a phone. He'd just hold the receiver with his teeth!"

"Then, Mr. Wechsler is going to be all right?" Anne asked, truly concerned.

"It would certainly seem so," he told her. Then he added more seriously, "He's asked me to take especially good care of you...and of your aunt, too, of course. And I've assured him that I will."

With this statement he became all business, and as he went over the contents of the Clarendon file with her, Anne gained a new respect for him. He assimilated facts with a speed she found impressive, and although he was young—in his early thirties, she guessed—she didn't wonder that he'd been promoted to a full partner in one of Boston's leading law firms.

It had been pretty brash of her to ask him if he actually was a lawyer, she told herself dully. It was a wonder he had remained as polite about it as he had.

He'd been polite, yes. But, once again, he'd also been oddly defensive.

Anne's own career in banking was demanding. Concerned with promoting her bank's image via public relations and training programs, she was used to handling new information in an effective and efficient manner. She followed Timothy with relative ease as he went over facts and figures with her. When they came to something she didn't fully understand she felt comfortable in telling him so and appreciated his careful explanations.

Finally he put the folder aside and said, "To tell

you the truth, Anne, we're faced with a messy situation. Contesting a will is never pleasant, and if your stepmother goes to court with this a lot of bitterness will surface. It can't be anything but ugly.''

"My aunt and I don't want to go to court," she pointed out. "Laura's the one who started this whole thing brewing, after all."

"True. And you have to wonder at her motivation," Timothy said, shaking his head. "It would seem that your father left her very well fixed. She's also a young woman. Chances are she'll marry again." He picked up a pencil and tapped it against the file folder as if making a point. "I'm going to talk with her attorney in the next day or two, and I hope she'll agree to a meeting."

"With me?" Anne asked, aghast at the thought of this. She didn't think she could possibly face Laura until a lot more time had passed. Laura had been so cutting at her father's funeral. She hadn't seemed at all like a woman suddenly bereaved of the man she loved. Anne, on the other hand, had been steeped in grief. She hadn't been prepared to deal with Laura—a sharp-eyed caustic woman who seemed quite unlike the young woman who had married her father not all that long ago.

Anne searched her memory trying to recall exactly how many years it had been. She'd been in college, she'd been almost nineteen. So it was eight years, going on nine.

"Would you object?" Timothy's question came in the middle of her calculations and she looked up at him blankly.

"What?"

"Would you be agreeable to a meeting with Laura and her attorney?"

"I don't know," Anne admitted.

"So the animosity isn't entirely one-sided, then?" he remarked, sounding faintly triumphant.

"I'm not sure I know what you mean."

"Anne, it's necessary for you to level with your attorney, though you may not always want to," Timothy said patiently. "It seems to me you don't like your stepmother any more than she apparently likes you. Am I mistaken?"

Anne considered this. From her work she'd grown accustomed to thinking things through without giving hasty answers. She said carefully, "Yes, I think you are mistaken. At least, I don't dislike Laura. I've felt less and less rapport with her as time has passed, true. But I've regretted this." She paused and took a deep breath. "I...I loved my father. And when I finally realized there was no hope of my parents reconciling and they both remarried, my prime desire was for them to be happy."

"I see. And you don't think your father was happy with Laura?"

Anne hedged. "In the beginning, yes."

"But not for very long?"

"I can't answer that, really. I don't have any facts to give you, only impressions. My own impressions, garnered whenever I visited them in Miami. As it was, I made fewer and fewer trips down these last couple of years."

"Because of Laura?"

"I . . . suppose so," she said reluctantly.

"Then I think it could be said that at the time of your father's death you and your stepmother didn't have a very good relationship, isn't that so?"

Anne tightened her lips. "You make me feel as if I'm on a witness stand," she said bitterly.

"I'm sorry, but it's essential that I know just how you feel and where you stand, if I'm to represent you successfully," Timothy Flanagan told her formally. "There's nothing personal in my questions."

"I didn't say there was."

"Well, you might come to that conclusion," he replied mildly. "Now, to get down to exactly what's at stake here. As I understand it, your father actually held title to the Chestnut Hill house. Your Aunt Muriel merely has a life tenancy in it."

"I didn't know that," Anne said, perturbed by this bit of information. "My aunt has spoken to me about some of this, of course, but she's been rather vague when it comes to any particulars."

"Your aunt is a woman with a great sense of family," Timothy remarked. There was an odd note to the way he said this, and Anne looked across at him sharply. Once again she had the feeling they were treading on the brink of forbidden ground, at least where he was concerned. But then they weren't even talking about him.

"The house in Chestnut Hill has been in the Clarendon family for a long time," he continued. "I haven't seen it myself, but I understand it's a beautiful piece of property and very valuable. Besides the land and an old carriage house that's been converted into a garage, I gather there is a literal fortune in antiques.''

"The house is stuffed with them," Anne blurted out unthinkingly.

"You don't like family heirlooms?"

"It isn't that I don't like family heirlooms," she told him quickly. "It's just that I've always felt... oppressed by so many of them, do you know what I'm saying? Family-related objects, it's like...like ancestor worship! Please, don't get me wrong. It's great to have roots and I'm proud of my family, but...." She trailed off because again his face had gone blank.

He said impassively, "The house your father built for his second wife was new, of course, and furnished from scratch. Evidently Laura wants some of the family heritage. Some tangible aspects of it, anyway. She feels the Chestnut Hill house should be hers, and the heirlooms it contains should be divided down the middle between the two of you by an objective appraiser agreeable to both parties. No sentiment involved, obviously.''

"Laura could hardly be expected to be sentimental about the Clarendon family heirlooms!"

Timothy Flanagan ignored this. "She has a sharp eye for value, though, or it would certainly seem so," he assured her, shifting his position slightly. "Okay, next question," he said looking out the window. "You're not married by any chance, are you?"

"No, I'm not. And I should think you'd know that, seeing as my name is Clarendon."

"A lot of businesswomen retain their maiden name," he pointed out. "Are you engaged?"

Anne frowned. "I don't see what this has to do with Laura's lawsuit."

"It's necessary background," Timothy said calmly. "If we do have to go to court on this, I wouldn't want to run into any surprises concerning my own client."

"Then I'm not engaged, no."

"Living with anyone?" he persisted.

"Look, Mr. Flanagan," Anne began hotly.

"Are you living with anyone, Miss Clarendon?"

"No."

"So in other words, the field is clear?"

"What? What's that supposed to mean?"

"It means that I don't think you realize how much money is involved in the Chestnut Hill house and its contents," he told her and added infuriatingly, "If Laura's suit fails you could be quite a catch for someone."

She laughed shortly. "Are you suggesting that I protect myself against fortune seekers?"

"It might not be a bad idea." He grinned, and briefly Anne glimpsed her South Boston rescuer, the tantalizing man who might well have been a figment of her imagination.

Which is the real Timothy Flanagan? she asked herself. *The lawyer. . . or the leprechaun?*

There wasn't time to think about an answer to the question, for unexpectedly he said, "I think I've put you through enough for today." Then he pushed back his desk chair and stood up.

Anne was again aware of his height and of the latent strength about him, not hidden in the least by the proper business clothes he was wearing. No, he was just as sensuous in a suit that probably came out of Brooks Brothers as he'd been in an old T-shirt with the map of Ireland stretched across his chest.

He remained standing behind the desk, looking decidedly professional and bearing no resemblance to a life-sized leprechaun at all as he said, "Thanks for coming in. I think we both have a good concept of what's going on here. My hope is that we can come to a settlement without going to court. I'm going to check over everything thoroughly, and then I'll talk to Laura's attorney. After I've done that, I'll be in touch."

He nodded, not even offering her a handshake, so Anne only nodded in return. "Thank you," she mumbled, and made her way to the door as quickly as she could without stumbling over her own feet. She felt as if his eyes were boring a hole in her back, but she repressed the strong urge to turn around. Then, with the door closed behind her, she sagged, leaning up against the nearby wall for support.

She felt as if all the breath had been taken out of her. It was a long moment before she could walk down the corridor steadily and say goodbye to the receptionist. In the interim she was terrified that Timothy Flanagan might suddenly come plummeting out of his office and run right into her. If so, she knew he'd guess the reason for her weakness. It was *him*! And she knew she couldn't face another en-

counter with him until she'd regained complete control of her senses.

As it happened. three days passed before Anne
heard from Timothy Flanagan again. She was just
finishing her breakfast when she heard the phone
ring in the kitchen, and Bridget answered it. There
was a pause, then Bridget, who seemed in her own
world and obviously had troubles on her mind,
came into the dining room and said, "It's the
lawyer, Anne. . . for you."

"Thanks, Bridget," she managed, but her pulse
started racing as she neared the dangling receiver. It
was a wall phone, and feeling her legs turning rub-
bery she realized there was no place to sit down.

"Anne?" his resonant voice queried, "Tim Flanagan. You don't mind if I call you Anne, do you?"

"I. . . didn't object before."

"Good. Could you meet me for lunch today?"

"Well, I—" she began, but he swiftly interrupted
her.

"Listen, I reached Laura Clarendon's attorney
yesterday," he said. "And I've also been to the hospital and conferred with Oscar. You and I need to
talk."

"Wouldn't it be better if I came to your office?"

"I don't think so. At least, I thought it would be
more pleasant if we could talk someplace else.
Don't you agree?"

To disagree would have been to admit a lot more
to him than Anne had any intention of doing.

"Where shall I meet you?" she asked him.

"I thought you might like Friday's," he suggested. "It's noisy, but strangely relaxing. Shall we say twelve-thirty?"

"All right."

"You'd better take a taxi," he told her. "It's the devil in disguise finding a parking space over there!"

"That's what I planned to do," Anne answered a bit testily, for she was used to making her own decisions about such matters.

She dressed for her luncheon engagement with Timothy Flanagan as if she were going out on her first date. After considering and then dismissing several items in her wardrobe she settled on a jade-green suede suit. With it she wore a beautiful cashmere turtleneck in a soft ivory tone. Nubby gold earrings and a gold chain with a matching motif proved to be perfect accessories. She touched her eyes with mauve shadow and used a pearly peach lipstick, which glistened delightfully. She'd washed her hair the night before and it responded to only a few flicks of her styling brush. A touch of Flora Danica seemed like an actual whiff of courage, but as she ran down the stairs into the living room, where her aunt was reading in a comfortable armchair, she had the satisfaction of knowing that she looked good.

Muriel Clarendon complimented her niece generously, then added, "I do feel that I'm putting a great deal on your shoulders, dear. Perhaps one evening this young lawyer could come out to dinner and brief both of us."

"That might be a good idea," Anne agreed easily, but she wasn't going to suggest such a rendezvous to Timothy Flanagan unless it became absolutely necessary. For one thing, she wanted to spare Muriel all she could just now. Mostly, though, the very idea of that close an association with Timothy Flanagan was extremely disturbing. And yet she couldn't remember ever looking forward to a luncheon engagement as much as this one!

He was waiting for her on the steps outside the restaurant's entrance, and once again her heart played tricks on her as she looked at him.

He was dressed as correctly as a man could be dressed, in a three-piece, dark gray pinstriped suit. His shirt was pale lavender, his tie black, and he wore black Gucci loafers. Yet for all of this propriety Anne sensed a kind of unleashed energy about him. He could play the part of a proper lawyer, true. But she suspected this was only one of many roles he was capable of portraying.

It was tantalizing to know so little about him. As they were led under Tiffany-type lamps to a table that overlooked the entire eye-catching interior of the restaurant—a fascinating collection of bric-a-brac cluttered the walls attractively—Anne found herself wishing she could find a reason to ask Timothy Flanagan the same kind of personal questions he'd asked her during their interview on Monday. But she already knew he would retreat very quickly if it came to talking about himself.

Why did certain subjects cause a kind of veil to descend over him? she asked herself curiously. She would have to take it a step at a time with him.

He was holding out a chair for her, and as Anne squeezed by him he managed to mutter in her ear, "Did anyone happen to tell you that you must be the most beautiful woman in Boston?"

It was a casual comment, so much conversational fluff, she warned herself, yet she knew that the color surging into her cheeks must be apparent. The amused gleam in those green eyes verified this.

"You look even lovelier when you blush," he told her audaciously, taking the seat across from her.

"Mr. Flanagan..." she began.

He laughed. "I thought we agreed that we're on a first-name basis. By the way, did you have any problems with your car?"

It was such an abrupt change of subject that Anne was momentarily thrown by it, and the stammer came back as she said, "N-no. A friend helped. A young man who happened to be free."

She saw Timothy's eyes narrow slightly and was about to explain that it wasn't a friend of hers she was talking about. Not that Peter Dwyer didn't seem more than willing to become a friend of hers, she thought. He was a bit too persistent in suggesting they get together, and she still hadn't had the chance to talk to Bridget about him.

Before she could say anything further, though, her escort picked up a menu and asked, "Something to drink first?"

"Dubonnet, perhaps," Anne ventured.

"Dubonnet for the lady, and a Harp's ale for me," Timothy told the waitress. Turning back to

Anne, he said to her distress, "We might as well get directly down to business. Laura Clarendon's attorney is a man named Lance Bigelow, based in New York. Thus far we've only spoken on the phone, but sometime soon either he will fly to Boston or I'll go to New York so that we can have a face-to-face conference."

"I see," Anne said, but she wasn't really listening. It seemed to her that Tim Flanagan was as changeable as a chameleon, and she couldn't hope to keep pace with the fluctuations in his mood.

One would have to know him very well to even begin to understand him, she found herself thinking, and she wondered if she ever would.

CHAPTER FOUR

As SHE SIPPED her Dubonnet, Anne tried listening to Timothy, but she couldn't keep her mind on the things he was telling her. She was far more interested in the man himself, as puzzling as he was.

She'd been told she had a normally sympathetic ear and an innate knack for drawing people out of themselves. Yet she knew instinctively she would have to be extremely subtle to get behind Timothy Flanagan's facade once that blank aloofness took over. And this knowledge only caused her curiosity about him to mount.

There had to be some kind of skeleton in his past, she found herself thinking, and then decided she was jumping to conclusions. Tim Flanagan might be something of an anachronism, but that didn't mean there was anything dark and mysterious in his background. He was, after all, a very successful attorney and highly respected, or he wouldn't have been chosen a partner in the firm of Simon and Wechsler.

The subject of her speculations suddenly smiled, a smile that lit up his face and was so replete with charm Anne was emotionally staggered by its brilliance.

"You haven't heard a word I've said to you, have you?" he accused teasingly.

"Of course I have..." she began, but his laugh cut her short.

"I just told you there's a horse named Irish Laughter running at Suffolk Downs today. The odds on him are fifty to one...and I asked you if you thought we should place a bet on him. You just nodded back at me. You didn't even bat an eyelash. What could be occupying your thoughts to such an extent?" he asked, amusement making him sound very indulgent.

Anne stared across at him. She could hardly tell him that he had caused her mental wanderings. Feeling helpless, she tried to think of something to say, knowing that it would have to be good. Timothy was not a man one could easily dissemble with—she didn't have to be told that. He was obviously very sharp.

"I'm sorry," she said lamely. "I guess I've been woolgathering."

"Then my dialogue must have sounded pretty boring," he joked, adding, "Seriously, I suppose it is rather wearing getting into all these details about your stepmother's aspirations toward acquiring possessions that rightfully belong to you and your aunt."

"Frankly, it is. I just hate to think of Laura having become so...grasping!"

"People *can* change, Anne. And not always for the better."

"Yes, I suppose so," she said absently. "But I

really think we should go over all of this with my aunt. I don't feel I should make any decisions involving these family matters by myself." She hesitated, then said carefully, "As it happens, Aunt Muriel suggested that you come out to the house one evening. For dinner, perhaps?"

Timothy's eyes held hers. "And you're agreeable to that?"

"Yes. Yes, of course."

"Very well, then. What night would you prefer?"

"How about next M—Monday?" she answered, swallowing the lump that threatened to fill her throat. "I'm sure Monday would be okay with Aunt Muriel. She isn't keeping much of a social schedule these days."

"Monday. . . ." Timothy seemed annoyed as he said, "I'm sorry, but I'm tied up Monday evening. What about Tuesday? Would that still be convenient for you?"

"Tuesday would be fine."

"Tuesday it is," he nodded. "And let's agree to say nothing more about your family legal matters until then."

He'd ordered for both of them, and the waitress appeared then with an array of succulent seafood that engaged their attention for the next few minutes. There was a delicious lobster bisque, followed by tiny bay scallops broiled with crisp slices of bacon.

"These are fantastic!" Anne said appreciatively.

"Delicious," her companion agreed.

"I think New England has the best seafood one can find anywhere," she went on. "So fresh and all...." She paused, aware of the fact she was babbling—and that Timothy knew it.

She was prepared for almost any sort of comment from him. Despite that professional veneer of his—and he was coated with it today—there was a quality of unexpectedness about him. She had the feeling he would never cease to surprise her. Nor did he now, saying in a gentle tone, "Tell me about yourself, Anne."

It was dangerous ground, and forcing a little laugh she hedged, "What do you want to know?"

He paused, sipping the excellent white wine he'd chosen to go with the scallops. Then he said, "The obvious answer to that would be 'everything,' wouldn't it? Which is more than I can expect. After all, we don't know each other very well...yet. For beginners, though, where do you live in New York?"

Anne took a sip of the wine herself. "I have a small apartment in the East Sixties," she said.

"No roommates?" he asked quizzically, and Anne felt herself flushing as she recalled his earlier question as to whether she was living with anyone.

"No," she said hastily. "It's just a studio apartment, really. I live alone. I prefer my privacy."

That annoying gleam of amusement was back again as he asked, "And you really are a banker?"

Anne stiffened. "Do you find that so hard to believe?" she countered, then wished she hadn't. It was too leading a question.

"Naturally, I find it hard to believe," he told her bluntly. "You don't look like a woman who would be happy living with computers and calculators. Unless I'm very much mistaken. . . and you do have an electronic adding machine for a heart!"

"Do I detect a hint of chauvinism here?" Anne parried, slightly amused by his concept of women in banking.

"More than a hint," Timothy told her. "I should think it would be hellishly difficult for the people who work with you to keep their statistics straight!"

"They really don't have to," she said, laughing. "I'm sure you know there are many different career areas within banking."

"Yes?"

"Well, like many people I started out as a teller, but then I found my talents really lay in a different direction. I've been in creative services for quite some time now."

"Creative services? In a bank?"

"Yes, in a bank," Anne said, warming to the subject. This was something about which she was very enthusiastic. "Creative services involve a lot of things. For example, bankers are well aware that they too often tend to have a plastic image. Just recently one bank president told me he'd come to realize the need to get rid of his 'stiff celluloid collar.' That's what my job involves. Lately I've been working on training films and following them up with personalized instruction."

Timothy's eyebrows shot upward. "How do you choose your students?" he queried.

"I don't," Anne told him. "They're chosen for me, and then I train them in what we call 'a new mode of behavior.' I work with personnel from all departments, from tellers right up to the chairman of the board."

"And they all wind up being gracious and charming?" he asked skeptically.

"They wind up with a different concept of customer relations," Anne said firmly. "Our program teaches the banker to first presume there's a strong chance the customer may be right when he comes into the bank with a complaint. The old adage, of course, was that the bank could do no wrong. That it would be impossible, for instance, for the bank to make a mistake in tabulating your balance. The people who work at our bank are taught to agree with the customer first, using a positive approach to a problem. Then, if the customer is proved wrong, he's much more ready to accept it than if he'd had an initial negative experience."

"It sounds like a new sort of con game," Timothy observed. Anne looked up quickly, but his green eyes were dancing with a mischievous light.

"Do you ever accept lawyers as pupils?" he asked.

Anne's lips quirked with amusement. "I work for a bank, Mr. Flanagan," she reminded him. "Consolidated Empire, to be precise."

"You did pick a big one," he nodded. "With tentacles all over the country, I'd say. Do you do much traveling?"

"Not really," she answered. "My home base is

New York, and most of my work is there, though once in a while I'm sent to affiliated banks in other cities—if they've specifically requested our training program.''

"And you are part of the package deal?"

"I certainly wouldn't put it that way!"

"Ah, don't get your back up so fast, *mavourneen*," he cajoled, with that touch of mock brogue she remembered so well from their first encounter. "Who could blame a man if he asked to have you as his teacher?"

Anne was spared an answer to this by the appearance of the waitress, this time bringing them an outrageously delicious Grand Marnier mousse followed by small cups of cappuccino.

As they were sipping their coffees, Timothy said, "I suppose your office is located right in the heart of Manhattan?"

"The lower tip of Manhattan," Anne corrected. "We're in the World Trade Center. The eighty-ninth floor. I literally look out at the torch in the Statue of Liberty's hand, which is a rather unnerving experience until you get used to it."

"I get to New York on business occasionally," he told her, "but I've never had time to really get to know the city. And Boston, of course, is such a small town in comparison."

"Maybe," Anne agreed, "but Boston is unique—like no place else, really. There's such a blend of the new and the old, and it's amazing how they merge so compatibly. To tell you the truth I'd wondered if Boston would be. .well, stuffy...

being so hidebound to old New England, that is. And I'll have to admit I thought it would lack the vitality New York has. Obviously, though," she finished, looking around the crowded restaurant, "Boston has a terrific charm all its own."

"So you like us," Timothy stated.

"Yes," Anne answered. "I like you very much."

She looked up as she said this, feeling drawn as if by a magnet to his clear green gaze. Their eyes locked, and it was with a real effort that she finally looked away, feeling as breathless as if she'd just run up a steep flight of stairs.

"That is one of the better things I've heard in quite some time," he told her as he signaled the waitress to bring their check.

They parted outside the restaurant, Timothy finding a cab for Anne after telling her he was going to walk back to his office.

"It's only a mile," he added, "but when you're involved in the often sedentary practice of law you need all the exercise you can get."

As he held the cab door open for her, Anne found herself wishing that history would repeat itself, and imagined Timothy Flanagan once again bending down to claim her with his kiss. For that was what it had been. A clear-cut claim.

But he merely said, "Thanks so much, Anne. I enjoyed it, and I'll look forward to Tuesday."

As the cab slowly pulled away from the curb, Anne turned and watched him striding down the sidewalk. The cool March breeze was ruffling his dark copper hair slightly, so that it looked more as it had that first time in South Boston.

Still, she thought dreamily, he couldn't possibly look more attractive than he did right then. Or more fit! She doubted his need for the exercise that walking back to his office would give him.

Then he was lost from her sight, and feeling a sudden sense of loss Anne shivered. It had been a long, long time since a man had even begun to stir her as much as Timothy Flanagan did!

THE BALANCE OF THE WEEK passed slowly. Anne called New York and after explaining her situation to her boss was granted an additional two weeks' leave of absence. Her first fortnight in Boston was skimming by, and there was still so much to be determined in connection with her father's will and Laura.

Anne also sidestepped an invitation to go out with Peter Dwyer and resolved to ask Bridget about him and his friendship with Bridget's daughter Katharine the first thing Monday morning.

Then Monday morning arrived and Bridget's husband phoned to say she was sick and couldn't make it to work. "Some sort of flu bug," he explained to Anne, who had taken the call. "I doubt she'll be able to make it tomorrow, either."

This was unfortunate. Muriel Clarendon had been delighted to hear that Timothy Flanagan was coming to dinner and had planned to ask Bridget if she could stay on to cook and serve the meal, as she usually did when Muriel entertained.

At the breakfast table later that morning, she said chagrined. "It isn't just the dinner I'm concerned about, though, Anne. It's poor Bridget. She hasn't seemed like herself lately. I'm afraid the problem may be more than a flu bug."

"Something does seem to be troubling her," Anne agreed. "But don't worry about tomorrow night, Aunt Muriel. I like to cook and seldom have much time to. It'll be fun to see what I can come up with to surprise you!"

Tuesday morning Anne went shopping. Then, after she'd given Muriel a lunch of soup and rolls and sent her upstairs to take a rest, she set about getting things ready for dinner.

She'd decided to make a chicken dish that was one of her specialties. It required long slow baking, but it was foolproof and absolutely ambrosial. Boneless breasts of chicken were rolled with bacon then placed on a bed of shredded sliced corned beef. Topped with a mixture of mushroom soup and sour cream, the chicken rolls were baked for three hours. The result was a superb blend of flavors few people could resist.

In addition to the chicken, Anne chose to serve wild rice, glazed baby carrots and a fresh spinach salad liberally laced with sunflower seeds. She opted for a light Portuguese rosé wine to go with the meal and planned a pineapple sherbet with thin lace cookies for dessert.

It was fun to set the beautiful old walnut table in the dining room with linen embroidered with the family initials. She brought out the family heirloom sterling, too, and gave the knives, forks and spoons a quick polish so they gleamed. Haviland china with a small rose pattern and stemmed crystal goblets completed the setting, but at the last minute Anne realized she didn't have anything for a centerpiece. She solved this problem easily by borrowing a pink azalea that was blooming on a window in the library, camouflaging the pot with foil, then flanking the attractive plant with tall silver candlesticks holding pink tapers.

The effect was quite lovely—and very proper Bostonian, Anne decided, chuckling slightly as she surveyed her work before going upstairs to dress.

As chief cook, she didn't want to be too fancy in her attire, yet she definitely wanted to look good. She decided upon a cream-colored knit dress with long sleeves and a lace collar that framed her face beautifully. She wore it with a thin gold belt, gold earrings and two different gold chains as accessories, and complemented the dress with slim gold kid pumps.

Her cheeks were so flushed—from the energy spent in cooking or from excitement at the thought of seeing Tim Flanagan again? she wondered wryly—that she didn't need any blush. Instead she used just a touch of lipstick and the merest hint of eyeshadow, then took a last satisfied look in the mirror before going downstairs.

The front door chimes rang promptly at seven, just as Muriel Clarendon was descending the stairs. Anne nervously opened the door—and, once again, seeing Timothy Flanagan had the oddest effect on her. She felt herself clutching at the poise she usually possessed and was only too glad to keep their greeting brief before turning to introduce him to her aunt.

Muriel had dressed in a royal blue silk that had seen better days but was still quite impressive, and she'd decided to wear some of the family jewels. A sapphire-and-diamond ring adorned one thin hand, diamonds sparkled at her ears, and an heirloom pearl necklace with a lovely diamond center drop encircled her throat.

Anne served whiskey sours in the living room and pastry cheese twists sprinkled with paprika, deliberately going light on the hors d'oeuvres so appetites wouldn't be ruined for the dinner she was proud of.

Timothy, dressed in a discreet dark blue suit with a crisp white shirt and maroon necktie, looked not only devastatingly handsome but quite austere. His manners were faultless. Anne could see Muriel being visibly captivated by his charm and she couldn't blame her. Yet, she kept telling herself, this wasn't the real Timothy Flanagan at all. This urbane young man could have been any ascending Boston attorney who had gone to all the proper schools, moved in the proper circles and was accustomed to doing all the proper things. That Irishness she'd found so delightful could have been a figment of her own imagination, for now his accent was pure Bostonian without the slightest trace of Erin—either true or make-believe.

He'd be a fantastic actor, Anne found herself thinking.

Over dinner they spoke about Laura Clarendon and the possible lawsuit. Timothy sketched out the progress to date for Muriel, then told her that he and Laura's attorney expected to be conferring shortly.

"Then we'll be in a much better position to map out our own course of action," he finished.

At this Muriel Clarendon frowned. "Does Laura really have a legal leg to stand on?" she asked directly.

"She may have," Timothy evaded. "As your brother's widow she does have definite rights. And his will was drawn in Florida, so there's a question, possibly, of which jurisdiction we may have to deal with."

Muriel leaned forward, her fine-featured face strained. "Mr. Flanagan, I can't bear the thought of that woman inheriting so much as a blade of grass from this property, to say nothing of things that have been in my family for generations! I don't mean to sound like a snob, but the fact of the matter is...she's simply not our kind! My brother was mesmerized by her, true. But I can't believe he was hoodwinked to the point of allowing some kind of legal loophole in his will that would keep his daughter from her eventual, just inheritance. When I go, this place and everything in it should belong to Anne. That's the way we've always understood it, and that's the way it must be. To suddenly have this outsider come in and...."

She paused for breath, and Anne leaned forward anxiously. "Stop it, Aunt Muriel," she cautioned.

"You're getting yourself worked up needlessly. Tim will take care of it all."

"I'm sure if anyone can, he can," Muriel agreed, subsiding. "Very well, my dear, let's talk of something more pleasant, shall we? Are you a native of Boston, Mr. Flanagan?"

Why was it that the question seemed to thud between them? Anne was almost afraid to look as she heard him say, in a voice quite without emotion, "Yes."

No amplification, just, "Yes."

"You attended school here?"

"Boston University undergraduate and Harvard Law School," Tim said evenly.

"One can tell," Muriel said succinctly, bestowing a benevolent smile on him. He returned the smile, but Anne felt sure that her aunt did not notice the touch of frost edging it. The questions put to him had been answered without hesitation, yet she felt sure that Muriel had been treading on forbidden ground where Timothy Flanagan was concerned.

Why should that be?

Tim complimented Anne lavishly on her culinary achievements, and after dinner she led the way back into the living room for coffee. Not long afterward Muriel asked that they excuse her.

"Doctor's orders," she told Timothy reluctantly. "I do have to get my rest."

He walked to the foot of the staircase with her, and there was something very appealing about the way he took her hand and said, "Good night, and sleep well. And thank you for having me here."

"It has been my pleasure," Muriel assured him, and there was no doubt that she meant it.

Anne, who had trailed after them, walked back into the living room ahead of him and reached for the silver coffee pot on the low table. "More?" she asked.

"Thanks, but I don't think so," he said, and there was something in his tone of voice that made her look across at him swiftly. Once again she surprised an expression in his eyes that she hadn't expected to see there. He looked miserable.

The question came inadvertently. "Is something wrong?"

A wistful smile curved his lips. "So many things, *mavourneen*," he said with that hint of brogue.

Anne poured some coffee for herself and sat down on the nearest couch. "Sometimes, Tim," she ventured, "it helps to talk about things."

"Oh?"

"I keep feeling there's something you...." she began, then faltered.

"Something I what?" he prompted.

"I don't know how to phrase it. I suppose it would be simple to say that I have this feeling there's something you're hiding, but that wouldn't make sense, would it?"

"Why wouldn't it, Anne?"

"Because," she said, trying very hard not to say the wrong thing, "you're so...obviously everything you say you are."

He laughed shortly. "On the contrary," he told her. "I'm a fraud." Then he sat down at the opposite end of the couch, stretching out his long legs and staring at his black wing tips reflectively.

Anne put her coffee cup down. "That's ridiculous," she said levelly. "Are you saying you didn't go to Harvard Law School and—"

"Oh, I went to Harvard, all right," he interrupted. "Yes, I was born in Boston and went to Boston University undergraduate and then on to Harvard Law School. That much is true. But even the truth can come in a variety of shapes, Anne. One finds, in the practice of law, that there are all sorts of nuances in truth. And as for me... believe me, I *am* a fraud, Anne, and your aunt would certainly think so if I were to tell her very much more about myself. Maybe one of these days I'll tell you... but not tonight. I have only one thing on my mind tonight, and unless I've been misreading my signals you share it with me."

He had moved next to her before she realized what he was about to do, and in another instant his arms were around her, drawing her toward him. Anne froze for only a moment. Then, as the look in his green eyes sent emotion spiraling through her, instinct brushed logic aside, and her natural caution went with it.

Tenderly he cupped her face between his palms, then slowly, deliberately, his mouth descended to claim her lips, and Anne felt as if she'd been swimming in shallow water only to have the bottom suddenly drop off beneath her feet. She was shaken by a wave of emotion that started at her toes and crested at the top of her head. She was moved by this man. Profoundly moved by his strength, his sweetness and the sheer sensual impact of him. And, as his kiss deepened, the fire within her was kindled again, the fire that had been simmering since the first time she'd met him.

Their kiss became a voyage of exploration, their tongues probing, discovering, exulting. Timothy trailed his mouth along the curve of her neck and across the hollow of her throat while his hands began to roam, sculpting the contours of her lovely body. And she in turn began to touch him, shyly at first, then with more boldness. His strength became manifest under her fingers, and she felt the width of his shoulders, the thrust of the muscles in his arms, and the way his chest tapered to a tight slim waist.

At the waist, she hesitated. Simultaneously he paused briefly. Then he began unfastening the buttons on the front of her dress, his fingers gentle. He'd taken off his coat—she couldn't even remember when—and now she saw him unbuckle his belt before, once again, he drew her close to him. His hands, strong warm hands, came to cup her breasts, then he lowered his head and she moaned helplessly as his tongue encircled first one nipple and then the other.

Again she moved toward him, her hands fluttering from his shoulder down to his waist. It was only when she arrived at the unfastened belt buckle that she realized the full extent of his arousal.

He said huskily, "Don't stop! I've wanted this since I first set eyes on you."

Anne could not have later said what it was that

gave her the strength—if that is what it should have been called—to draw away from him. She was gasping, she could hear the shallow echo of her own breathing, and she knew precisely what the agony of being unfulfilled could be like. Yet something within her halted her as surely as if she'd been stopped by a firm hand on her shoulder.

She said, her voice little more than a whisper, "Tim...it's too soon."

He sank back against the couch, his own breathing coming raggedly. Then after a moment he asked, "What do you mean...too soon?"

Shaking inwardly, Anne pulled away from him. She could only hope he would not make a move toward her just now because she knew she could not possibly resist him a second time. She began to button her dress, her fingers feeling cold and awkward. The stammer back once more, she said, "I...I'm sorry."

Timothy had gained control of himself. She sensed this at once. His tone was entirely normal as he said, "You've nothing to be sorry about. I'd like to know what you mean by 'too soon,' that's all."

"I feel that I have to k-know you better," Anne told him. "It hasn't anything to do with the length of time we've k-known each other. It's just...the *way* we know each other. Can you understand what I'm saying?"

"Yes," he said. "I think I can."

He stood, looking very tall and somehow very distant. "I'm the one who's sorry. It wasn't my intention to try to seduce you the first time I got you alone."

"Tim...."

His smile was crooked. "Don't protest so much, Anne," he cautioned. "I can see your point. I think what you're telling me is that this isn't a casual thing with you, so let me tell you that it isn't with me, either."

"Tim...."

"No, Anne. Don't answer that." He straightened his tie. "I don't think I could handle it if you told me I was wrong!"

CHAPTER FIVE

Anne was still shaking when she went to bed. Timothy, rallying with what seemed to her remarkable ease, had offered to help her with the dishes, but she'd declined, telling him that she'd put the food away and Bridget would handle the rest in the morning.

Having said this, she realized there was a good chance that Bridget would not yet be well enough to come to work. Still, she couldn't face up to the kind of intimacy that would be involved even in something as normal and mundane as washing dishes with Tim.

He bade her good-night politely, thanking her for the excellent dinner. Murmuring the right replies, Anne couldn't help feeling that once again he'd become a total stranger to her. When he'd gone, she plunged up to her elbows in soapsuds, scouring pans with a vengeance while calling herself all sorts of a fool.

I am not a child, she reminded herself acidly. *I am twenty-seven years old.*

Nor was she inexperienced. Although basically her morals tended to hew surprisingly to the old New England line—a line laced with propriety, she thought ruefully—she *was* human. She and Ken Phillips had lived together for six weeks during that summer before she'd made her final decision in favor of banking over a possible career in music. Ken had not understood this decision, and his total failure to see her point of view had put such a strain on their relationship that they'd broken it off after a final angry scene.

She hadn't seen Ken since, but she'd read a great deal about him. He'd gone on with his music—he was a promising concert violinist—and was already making an international reputation for himself.

Anne stashed away a frying pan and sighed. It was impossible not to wonder sometimes what might have happened if she'd had the courage to go on to a conservatory with the goal of becoming a concert singer, or possibly even of singing in opera. She'd gotten over Ken a long time ago, the bitterness had faded, and she could understand now that they'd both been young, their visions of each other confined to youth's narrow scope. But she'd never entirely gotten over wanting to sing. There had been a freedom to letting her voice soar, a wonderful fulfillment, a creativity.

And as for tonight.... Anne paused in the act of drying a crystal goblet and stared down into the sparkling glass, seeing her own reflection mirrored inside its surface.

Why did I stop? she asked herself. *I wanted Tim as much as he wanted me. And after all, we are two adults! Our feeling was genuine enough. Even thinking about him now....*

She put the goblet aside to be carried back into the dining room later and carefully placed with the others on a shelf in the corner cabinet. It was only now occurring to her that Timothy had held a definite advantage over her that night. He'd had her precisely where he'd wanted her, and she was sure he'd known it. Looking back on it, it seemed to her that he'd let her go very easily. He had drawn a few ragged breaths, true, but he'd regained his composure a lot faster than she had hers. Was he really so disciplined? So in control of himself that he could turn passion on and off as if he was flicking a light switch?

Her task finished, Anne went slowly upstairs and got ready for bed. And tonight that empty bed seemed especially bleak and solitary. She felt lost in it and very much alone.

SHE AWAKENED to the sound of rain on the roof. Early April rain, she thought, remembering the old adage about April showers bringing May flowers. But well before she would see any of those flowers blooming in Boston she'd be back in New York, she reminded herself.

What of Timothy Flanagan? Once she left Boston was there a chance she'd ever see him again? Might he call her on one of his sporadic business trips to Manhattan?

Anne shook her head in self-reproof. *What am I asking for?* she demanded silently. *The man's as dangerous as a firecracker with an unspent fuse— and just as unpredictable!*

Bridget did not show up that rainy morning, which in a way was just as well, because her absence gave Anne something to do. She fixed breakfast for Muriel and herself, made their beds, and even gave the living room an unnecessary dusting.

These tasks soon petered out, though. Normally she would have enjoyed the chance to catch up on her reading or to work on one of the jigsaw puzzles Muriel always kept on a card table in the study. But such passive activities did not appeal today, nor was it any day to plunge outdoors into something more physically demanding. Anne liked walking in the rain. . . but not alone. One needed a companion.

Thursday morning arrived, and Bridget did come back to work. She looked a bit paler than usual and she still seemed preoccupied. Going out to the kitchen for a second cup of coffee, Anne found her cleaning out a canned-goods pantry that really didn't need cleaning at all. She took advantage of the situation, though, to pull up a chair and sit down at the kitchen table, and after some preliminary conversation decided to ask Bridget about Peter Dwyer.

To her surprise, Bridget pressed her lips together tightly at the sound of his name and said tersely, "I don't know what's to become of him!"

"What do you mean?" Anne asked, puzzled.

"If Katharine insists. . ." she began, but her voice broke. "Oh, it's all a very mixed-up affair, Anne," she managed, steadying herself, "and it has me worried sick! I think that's what's the matter with me, not a virus or any sort of bug. And Katharine's father has become as hard about the whole thing as a piece of Connemara marble."

"About what whole thing, Bridget?"

"He's dead set against Katharine going on with voice lessons," Bridget said miserably. "And it is a real crime, let me tell you. Just as it was a crime in your case, I might add," she persisted darkly. "But Katharine is equally stubborn and says she will not be a secretary. She has no talent for business, she says, so she has decided on another solution. She is going to enter a convent and become a nun!"

Anne stared across at the plump cleaning woman, feeling totally confused. She would have thought someone of Bridget's religious convictions would have been thrilled at having a daughter who'd decided to enter a religious order. But Bridget looked as if her whole world were about to collapse.

She interpreted Anne's bewilderment correctly. "Don't misunderstand me," she said quickly. "I think it would be as wonderful as anything could possibly be, Katharine's marrying herself to the Church—*if* that was her rightful vocation. I cannot think of a higher calling for a woman. But in Katharine's case it would be entirely wrong, and Ben, my husband, agrees with me. She would be entering the convent out of a sense of spite. I'm not saying she's not a religious girl, because she is. But this is a different thing, if I am making any sense to you at all."

"Yes, I'm sure it is," Anne mused. "But Bridget...."

"Yes?"

"Where does Peter Dwyer fit into this? I presume he's in love with Katharine?"

"Very much so, I would say," Bridget agreed.

"But she doesn't love him?"

"I think Katharine's too mixed up to know what her real feelings are," Bridget said bluntly. "She's as stubborn as her father and he's as stubborn as she. . . and I can't see how it isn't going to be a black time for all of us. I must say my heart goes out to Peter. He's a good boy, ambitious and a hard worker. He stands by Katharine with her music, too. He says he'd give every penny he could ever make if she could become a singer, because that's what she's meant to be."

"And Katharine refuses to stand up to her father about this?"

"You don't know Ben," Bridget said direly. "I should have stood up to him years ago, but I didn't. He's a strong man, a good man, and. . . he's Irish to the core. He believes the man is head of the house, period. That's the way it is. The man handles the money, he handles the affairs of the household, and there's no talking back to him. I'm supposed to give him my earnings when I get home every day, because he thinks he can take better care of the money than I could." Bridget paused, as if repressing a hint of laughter. Then she added with an oddly appealing touch of slyness, "I don't give it all to him, you know. Not all of it. Your aunt, bless her, knows my problem and always pays me in cash. I've kept a bit aside ever since I realized Katharine had a voice. If I hadn't been doing that, there never would have been any singing lessons for her."

"Doesn't your husband suspect anything?"

Bridget smiled. "He thinks she's gotten them free at school," she confessed. "On that, at least, Katharine has kept mum. The lessons have meant that much to her."

"Hasn't your husband ever heard her sing?"

"Ben doesn't listen. Katharine's soloed in church a number of times, but Ben, for all of his upbringing, isn't a churchgoing man. I suppose he thinks it's something the women in the house can handle for the whole family. Lord knows I can't remember when he last went to mass with me."

"It seems to me," Anne said slowly, "that if he could just hear her—"

"Ben's not about to change," Bridget said flatly.

Anne searched the sad face looking across at her. "There's something else, Bridget . . ." she began.

"Yes?"

"Peter Dwyer knows I've been involved with computers in my work at the bank and . . . he wants to talk to me. I think he's probably just putting out feelers about job opportunities, things like that. I gather he's very much into computer science and other areas of electronics."

"That's what he's studying for a degree in," Bridget nodded.

"Yes, he told me as much when he helped with my car. But . . . well, he's called me a couple of times, and I didn't want to make a date with him until I talked to you."

"Go right ahead, next time he asks," Bridget said, a determined thrust to her chin. "And **don't** worry about word of it getting back to Katharine. It would do her good to have a little competition!''

That afternoon Peter Dwyer did call, and Anne agreed to have a drink with him that evening. Muriel was reading in the living room when he came by just before nine o'clock. She seemed a bit surprised, but was her usual gracious self in greeting him. Good manners were so ingrained in her aunt, Anne decided, that she'd probably be polite to a man she caught robbing the family silver!

They went to a small lounge in nearby Brighton that featured Mexican food, and snacked on nacho chips and hot sauce as they sipped margaritas. Peter was as attractive as Anne had remembered him from their first meeting and had an eager, inquiring mind. To her surprise she found they had a lot to talk about, and they were both startled when they heard the last call for drinks being announced by the raspy-voiced young waitress.

At the Chestnut Hill house Peter walked Anne to the door, and it seemed quite natural to have him bend and kiss her good-night. She returned the kiss, but this was as a sister might kiss a brother. There was no surge of feeling, no sense of having been cut adrift into a caldron seething with hard-to-handle emotions. And when Peter told her he hoped they could repeat the evening soon, Anne nodded agreement, deciding, as she unlocked the door and entered the house, that Katharine Kincaid was a rather foolish young woman. There were, unfortunately, not too many Peter Dwyers in the world.

She shrugged off the light all-weather coat she'd

been wearing and tossed it over a chair in the foyer. She was about to start up the stairs when her eyes were distracted by a slip of paper prominently displayed on a silver calling-card tray.

Muriel had written:

Timothy Flanagan has phoned several times for you during the evening. He seems anxious to get in touch with you. He asked if you'd give him a call at his office when you wake up in the morning.

When I wake up in the morning! Anne could imagine Tim's arched eyebrow and the tone of his voice when he'd made this request, and she wondered if Muriel had caught what must have been a cynical note.

She was certainly aware of that edge of sarcasm when she spoke with him the next morning, after being put through immediately to his private phone by the receptionist.

"Only nine-thirty," he said, greeting her. "It would seem you don't need much sleep."

"I wasn't out that late," Anne answered, then told herself she shouldn't respond to his taunts so quickly. She should be faster to realize when he was baiting her, which was obviously what he was doing now.

"Well," Timothy said somewhat obliquely, "you're beautiful enough anyway. In other words, you don't have to worry about catching up on your sleep." He paused, then continued with the air of a man getting down to business. "Now, Anne. There have been a couple of new developments. I've been in touch with your stepmother's attorney again. Giles Winslow, who is a junior partner here, will be in New York the first of the week, so I felt that we could, in effect, kill two birds with one stone if he meets with Bigelow while he's there. As it happens, he's just the right man for your case."

"Oh?" she questioned.

"I'll fill you in on the reasons for that when I see you," Tim said. "Look, Anne, I'm tied up with conferences all day today, so I wondered if we might get together tomorrow."

She couldn't resist posing the question. "You work on Saturdays?"

"When necessary," he told her coolly. "Actually, I plan to drive down to the Cape tomorrow. There's a cottage in the Wellfleet area I want to look at. I'm thinking of renting it this summer if . . . well, if certain things work out. Anyway, I hope I can persuade you to come along for the ride. The weather promises to be beautiful and . . . ."

A warning bell rang somewhere in Anne's mind. "I don't know, Tim," she began cautiously, then was halted by the sound of her aunt's voice.

Muriel was standing in the doorway, wearing a rose-colored housecoat that should have lent a touch of color to her cheeks but didn't. Looking across at her, Anne realized that she didn't look well at all.

"Excuse me a minute," she said into the receiver, then cupped her palm over it and turned to her aunt. "Did you want me, Aunt Muriel?" she asked gently.

"Is that Timothy Flanagan you're speaking to, Anne?" Muriel queried.

"Yes, it is."

"I was hoping you'd see the note I left for you," Muriel said with satisfaction. "He mentioned to me that he has to drive down to Cape Cod tomorrow— and he hoped you'd be free to go along with him. He said he wanted to talk to you about some new developments involving Laura. . . ."

"Yes, I know," Anne said a bit grimly.

"I just wanted to assure you not to hesitate on my account," Muriel told her. "A couple of old friends have asked me to lunch with them, and I've agreed to go. It has been quite a while since I've gotten out of the house, and now that the weather's getting better. . . ."

Muriel waited expectantly, and with reluctance Anne turned her attention back to the telephone. "It seems," she said, "that Aunt Muriel thinks it would be an excellent idea for me to go along to the Cape with you."

"A wise woman, your aunt," Timothy chuckled, then added, "I'll pick you up at ten."

ALTHOUGH SPRING tended to be a latecomer in New England and there was apt to be a lingering chill to April, this particular Saturday, the first one of the month, gave more than a promise of the lovely weather soon to come.

"One really gets the sense of rebirth this time of

year,'' Muriel observed as she stood at the living-room window looking out at the spacious lawn that stretched down to the elm-lined street. ''The grass is actually becoming green again, and there's a tinge of green gold to the willows. Before we know it, the crocuses will bloom, and then comes the forsythia.''

''You sound absolutely poetic,'' Anne teased, laughing.

But her aunt had her mind on other things. ''Here he comes,'' she said expectantly. ''I suspected he might drive a nice car. What is that, anyway? Oh, no matter. Whatever it is, it's green, which suits him all the more!''

Tim's mesmerized her, too, Anne thought as she went to open the door for him. Yet gazing up the long length of him she had to concede that it would be hard for any woman to ignore the nerve-tingling impact he made.

He wore jeans, a sport shirt in a soft apricot shade and a suede jacket that was almost the same dark copper tone as his hair. And his handmade cordovan boots, which were banded in an attractive, tooled pattern, would be the envy of any cowboy.

Anne had given her own outfit a western touch. She, too, was wearing jeans, with a bright blue overblouse and a vividly patterned hand-quilted vest. She'd draped a variety of Indian turquoise beads around her neck for a final splash of color. The turquoise was reflected in the length of wool she'd used to tie her hair back in a ponytail, and she wore almost no makeup, just a touch of lip gloss.

Tim eyed her appreciatively as he walked into the house to greet her aunt. He talked for several minutes with the older woman in a casual manner that was most disarming. Nor was there any doubt about Muriel's response to him!

He was good with older people, Anne found herself thinking. Even if it was an act one couldn't fault him...he was making Muriel feel absolutely marvelous.

And he'd be good with children, too!

The thought came unbidden, bringing with it an odd twinge. She could imagine having children that would look like Timothy—leprechauns, all of them, a whole batch of fey little boys and girls. She could imagine him playing with them, a mischievous light glinting in his green eyes. He'd be stern when necessary, somehow she was certain of that. Timothy Flanagan would not spoil his children. But there would always be an understanding shoulder for them to lean on....

Anne gulped, and at that instant looked across the room to meet his eyes, feeling again as if he'd managed to read her mind. But there was no levity in his expression. The look he gave her was long and intent, leaving her feeling as if she were standing on a threshold, with no idea at all of what might lie just beyond the door. Yet, strangely, she wasn't afraid to take the next step with him.

Reality returned, and while Anne kissed her aunt goodbye, Timothy promised to get her back at a reasonable hour. Muriel said lightly not to worry about it, because she wasn't going to wait up for them.

"Just be careful driving," she cautioned, and Tim grinned.

"You may be sure that I will be," he said gallantly, "with such precious cargo in my car!"

Anne preceded him out the door, her cheeks burning. But once they'd started out, driving toward downtown Boston with the Southeast Expressway their initial goal, she discovered that Tim was not at all in a flirting mood, as she'd suspected might be the case.

Instead he got down to business very quickly as he competently wove his way through the late-morning traffic.

"We've finally discovered exactly what sort of ace it is your stepmother thinks she holds over you and your aunt," he told Anne.

"You have?" She stirred restlessly, facing up to the knowledge that just now she didn't want to talk business with Tim Flanagan. Not in the least. For that matter, it hadn't occurred to her that he'd really intended to talk about her legal affairs on their drive down to Cape Cod.

Maybe I've been flattering myself, she thought dismally, *and there isn't anything romantic simmering between us. Maybe this is only one more instance where he's shown me that I don't really know him at all!*

"Laura claims she has a holograph will," he went on, evidently not noticing Anne's reactions. "And although we're not certain about this yet, it may be considerably more valid than such documents usually are."

"A holograph will?" Anne asked. "What does that mean?"

"Legally speaking, a holograph is a document written in an individual's own hand," Timothy told her. "In this case we're talking about a will. But the writing of such a will would have to have been witnessed, otherwise it would be invalid in both Florida and Massachusetts."

"Then what is there to worry about?"

"Well, the situation here may be a little more complicated," Timothy replied. "But until Giles has been to New York and consulted with Lance Bigelow there's no need to get into the details with you. I only wanted you to know what we're dealing with so that you'd be prepared for what could be a nasty contest."

"You think Laura really has another will?" Anne persisted. "One written at a later date than the one my aunt and I know about?"

"Truthfully, I don't know," Tim said cautiously. "But there is no reason to think that she would bring this up unless she did have, and I don't think her attorney—who, by the way, is a reputable man—would become involved unless there was something definite on which he could base his argument."

"What does he say about it?"

"He hasn't said anything about it, specifically," Tim answered, his patience a bit too obvious. "We only know that your stepmother evidently alleges your father wrote a holograph will about two months before his death. We understand that she claims she has medical evidence to support the fact he was mentally competent at the time, and that the will was witnessed by two individuals, as required by law.''

"And in this will I suppose my father left the house and everything in it, to Laura," Anne surmised bitterly.

"We don't know that," Tim told her.

She flared at this. "Don't be such. . . such a l-lawyer," she sputtered. "You know damned well, Tim, that Laura would never have started all this unless she felt she could back it up. She isn't a fool!"

"Evidently not," he agreed with infuriating calmness.

"It's easy enough for you!" Anne plunged on. "It isn't your family home at stake, or things that have been in your family for generations."

She started to say that it wasn't herself she was concerned about—it was Aunt Muriel. She could imagine what it would do to Muriel at this point in her life if Laura were able legally, to take her house away from under her, and a fair share of the family heirlooms with it.

Tim's voice stopped her, though. He said, "Believe me, Anne, I know what your heritage means to you."

Despite the softness of his tone there was an edge of frost to it, and she turned toward him despondently. No doubt about it, the veil had fallen again, and he'd retreated behind it. Invisible and gossamer though it was, Anne still felt the full force of this barrier he could put between them so easily.

She stared helplessly at the rugged profile turned toward her. Ostensibly Tim was concentrating on the highway ahead of him, giving his full attention to driving. And there was nothing about his face—or what she could see of it—to give her the slightest clue as to what he was really thinking.

Tentatively she fingered the leather upholstery at the edge of the seat she was sitting on, a rich ivory that perfectly complemented the exterior color of the car, a new Saab Turbo. Timothy Flanagan had a beautiful car, excellent taste in clothes, was successful in his profession, and possessed faultless manners—at least when he wanted to.

What, then, was his hang-up? A woman, perhaps? Had there been a woman in his life who had treated him in a way that had soured him on all women?

Anne dismissed this. She felt certain there had been a woman, many women, she imagined, in Tim's life, but she doubted he was so narrow in viewpoint that he would blame the whole female sex for one unfortunate experience, no matter how much he had been burned by it at the time. And certainly he appreciated women. He appreciated her. He had shown that by his actions from almost the first moment they'd met.

She had the sudden wish they could go back to Southie together, back to the Harp and Shamrock Pub, where they'd had that first encounter. She wished they could start all over again, and told herself that she would handle matters very differently were she given a second chance.

She should have accepted his invitation that afternoon, she thought whimsically, and joined him back inside the pub for that corned beef and cabbage feast.

Picturing this, she chuckled out loud.

"What's so funny?" Tim queried, glancing across at her sharply.

"I was remembering the day I met you in South Boston," Anne admitted. "I still have that button you gave me. I . . . keep it as a lucky piece."

She saw his lips twist into a smile and felt an incredibly triumphant stab of victory. She'd ruffled the veil, at least.

"Well, now, *mavourneen*," he said, that brogue back in his voice again, the lilt of laughter that went with it as refreshing to Anne as the salt breeze drifting through the car windows. "You might try being a wise lass, don't you think, and heed its message?"

CHAPTER SIX

ANNE, SURPRISINGLY, had never been to Cape Cod before, so she was unprepared for the beauty of the curving canal that separated the armlike peninsula from mainland Massachusetts. As they drove across the arcing Sagamore Bridge she glimpsed swirling blue water far beneath her and saw a single white-hulled yawl.

Timothy Flanagan said laconically, "There's a stiff current in the canal. I tried swimming it once on a dare when I was in college."

"What happened?" Anne asked, struck by the thought that this was one of the few things he'd volunteered about himself.

"Oh, I got across," he said. "But I was beat, let me tell you. I ended up several hundred yards further down toward the bay, with more than a few scrapes to show for it! Those rocks along the edge are great for striped bass, but...."

"You must be quite a swimmer," she observed.

"I've always loved the water," he said. "Swimming, waterskiing, sailing. What about you?"

"I'm an indifferent swimmer," she replied honestly. "I've never tried waterskiing, and I'd probably only end up capsizing a sailboat if I were at the helm. Still, I love the water, too. Maybe as more of a spectator, though. I could stand on an ocean beach and watch the waves forever.''

''You could spend a lifetime on different beaches around the Cape doing exactly that,'' Tim told her. ''Got any other interests?'' he asked then, unexpectedly.

''Well, I like to run,'' Anne said slowly, ''although I haven't kept it up as I should have. I used to run on the cross-country team at school, but it's just not the same being in New York. A lot of people jog in Central Park, but I'm not that crazy about it unless I can get out early in the morning.''

''Traffic hazards?''

''That's part of it, yes.''

''Boston isn't too bad for runners,'' Timothy said then. ''Anyway, you see people jogging almost everywhere. Chestnut Hill Reservoir, right near you, has a path going all the way around. And Jamaica Pond, nearby, is even better. You should try them sometime. I'd even join you, though my knees wouldn't exactly thank me.''

''Oh?''

''I get my exercise doing other things,'' he said evasively.

What did he mean by that? Anne thought.

He'd turned off the main highway shortly after crossing the bridge onto the Cape, and now they were driving along a picturesque winding road lined with trees just beginning to show a touch of green.

''The back way,'' Timothy told her as they passed several stately old homes. ''It takes a little longer, but the drive is much more enjoyable. Anyway, we're not in a hurry, are we?"

"I'm in no hurry at all," Anne answered, stretching as if to prove it.

"I thought we'd stop for lunch at a place in Barnstable," Tim continued, "just across from the county courthouse. I was down here on a case last fall and a couple of the other lawyers took me there. Good food, nice atmosphere...."

"Sounds wonderful," she agreed, nodding.

Her mood was becoming downright euphoric, Anne decided whimsically, feeling inspired by this man at her side. Timothy Flanagan had the power to mellow a woman as well as excite her. A dangerous combination, Anne warned herself, then knew this was a warning she wasn't at all sure she wanted to heed.

The restaurant was comfortably homespun, its back windows offering a glimpse of marshes leading down to Cape Cod Bay. It was furnished in rustic pine with copper accents and bright blue curtains in a nautical print. Sitting down opposite her, Timothy suggested, "They make a wicked whiskey sour. Want to try one?"

"Why not?" Anne told him, a heady sense of freedom overtaking her.

They sipped the tart drinks appreciatively, and then ate richly flavored clam chowder served in heavy porcelain bowls. When they finally finished off with grapenut-custard pudding topped with whipped cream, an old Cape Cod favorite, Anne felt as if she were melting in a very pleasant sort of

way. Tim Flanagan could be excellent company—
when he wanted to be, she qualified.

As they started out in the car again, she said,
"That was terrific."

"Glad you liked it," he told her. Then, lowering
his voice slightly, he added, "It's wonderful,
Anne... having you with me today. I thought
you'd probably have made plans."

"No," she said quietly.

"After the other night I was afraid you might not
want to see me again," he finished wryly. "At
least... not alone."

She hadn't expected him to bring up the incident,
and thinking about it, her throat tightened. "That's
f-foolish, Tim," she stammered.

"Is it, Anne?" he questioned. "Hell, I don't
know what came over me!"

"Tim...."

"Wait, that's not true," he corrected. "I *do*
know what came over me. But I should have had
enough self-restraint not to move in on you like
an—"

"P-please," she interrupted. "Let's not talk
about it."

He shot her a quick glance blending surprise with
something she couldn't identify. "Why not?" he
demanded.

"It h-happened," Anne began lamely. "It was as
much my fault as it was yours. I mean, I could
have...."

"You could have what?" he asked slowly,
amusement surfacing. "Tried to rebuff me?"

"Yes, but I. . . ."

"But you didn't!" He paused, then added more softly, "So that makes two of us."

"That's what I've been t-trying to tell you," Anne managed valiantly.

At this, a tense silence threatened to loom between them, but Tim brushed it aside. He said simply, "Thank you."

"For what?" Anne asked, chagrined.

"For being so honest," he told her. "And maybe for accepting this. . . feeling between us. It started in Southie, didn't it, Anne?"

Suddenly she felt herself floundering. Once again she was wading into potentially deep water, where at any minute the bottom could drop off under her feet. Even with Timothy behind the wheel, she knew she wasn't emotionally safe.

His laugh was short. "Am I being too blunt?" he asked, and for a terrible minute Anne thought the veil was going to descend again—that he was going to shut her off. But he only smiled rather ruefully.

"Let's talk about Cape Cod," he said abruptly. "It's a fascinating part of the country, as you probably already know. More history per square inch than just about anyplace else I can think of, except maybe downtown Boston."

Anne decided her wisest course would be to pursue this, and said quickly, "I don't really know very much about the Cape."

Tim grinned impishly, obviously sensing her relief at the change of subject. "Well, then," he began, "the *Mayflower* anchored first in Province-town Harbor. Did you know that?"

"I'm afraid I didn't," Anne conceded.

"In fact, she stayed there for a month," he went on. "During that time some of the crew members explored up and down the coast in their shallop and even had their first meeting with the local Indians. This happened in Eastham, the town we'll be passing through just before we get to Wellfleet."

"Really?"

"Aye, sure and I'll be giving you a lesson in American history!" Timothy teased. "Anyway, the Mayflower Company nearly made the decision to settle on the Cape. But winter was coming on fast, and deciding they'd better find a more protected location for a village, the pilgrims sailed across the bay and established themselves at Plymouth. Not too long afterward, others followed from England and began settlements on the Cape. So today there are fifteen towns stretching from Sandwich out to the tip at Provincetown, a distance of about sixty-five miles."

"Funny," Anne mused. "I always thought of the Cape as one big resort area."

"An oversized sandbar?" he suggested. "Well, as you can see for yourself, it's a lot more than that."

"I never expected to find hills here, or so many large trees," Anne agreed.

"True. This was the main road until the Mid-Cape Highway was built after World War II," Tim nodded. "A stagecoach route, in much older days. The towns along the bay shore are my favorites."

"These old homes are really lovely."

"Yes, they are," Tim said. "Sometimes I think in a few years I'd like to give up practicing law in Boston and move down here and buy one of them. There would be plenty of work for an attorney on the Cape, and the pace would be so much more relaxed."

"You'd have time for all those water sports!" she teased.

Tim looked across at her, his intensely green eyes suddenly serious. "Yes. . . among other things," he said. "Like everyone else, I have my dreams. Not that I'm so naive as to expect all of them to come true."

She took the risk. "What are your dreams, Tim?" she dared to ask him.

"That would be telling!" he retorted, smiling.

With that he returned his attention to driving, leaving their conversation hanging. But at least the veil didn't descend again—a consolation as far as Anne was concerned.

At Orleans the "old road" ended, so they drove Route 6 the rest of the distance, turning off when they reached the sign for Wellfleet Center. Tim bypassed the tiny business section of town and continued on past the town pier, where the masts of several fishing trawlers jutted awkwardly into the sky. Sand spilled across the pavement all along the winding coastal road they were following, and Anne glimpsed Wellfleet Harbor and one deserted summer cottage after the next. Finally, after crossing over a narrow inlet, they arrived at what seemed a terminal parking lot.

Tim stopped the car. "That's Great Island to the left there," he said, "and this is called Chequessett Neck. Thank goodness most of this land lies within the boundaries of the National Seashore Park. It will be preserved rather than developed like so much of the Cape. That's a wonderful thing to know."

"Yes," Anne told him. "So much beauty."

"So much beauty," he nodded, speaking very softly.

Glancing up, she saw him looking at her once again with that expression of a little boy peering through a candy-store window at forbidden delights, and a wave of surprisingly intense emotion swept over her.

I want to draw him near me! This self-revelation was astonishing. *I want to hold him in my arms and assure him.* . . .

She broke off her thoughts, annoyed at herself. How could she possibly imagine Timothy Flanagan needing assurance. Still. . . .

"What is it, Anne?" he asked perceptively.

"N-nothing," she evaded.

"Come on, now. You have to be thinking something!"

"Well, it's just that you look so. . . ."

"Yes?"

"So. . . forlorn, sometimes," she told him, and then was horrified at what she had said. Her tongue seemed to trip over itself as she plunged on, "P-please. Before you start. . . ."

"Before I start what?"

"Before you shut me out again," she said distinctly, desperately wanting to get the words out.

Silence came between them, a total silence as if they'd been suspended in a clear glass ball. Then it fragmented, as he laughed. But she knew it was a laugh forced from him, and that it had taken all the acting ability he had to manage it.

"What an imagination you have!" he commented lightly, starting the car again. "Why would I want to shut you out?"

"Tim...."

"On the contrary, I want you close to me. Very close to me."

"Timothy...."

"Timothy!" he mocked. "Darling, you are so utterly beautiful when you get flustered. And I love that little stammer of yours. It's like an emotional barometer, though. You must realize that. It's a dead giveaway."

"P-please," Anne managed, turning away from him.

He didn't answer this. Instead he began driving down a very rutty sand road, a road Anne hadn't even noticed, angled off the end of the parking lot. Then he veered onto a second one, a sandy driveway skirted by scrub pines and beach-plum bushes. Ahead of them Anne saw a gray shingled house sitting atop a rise. *Our destination,* she decided, and a second later was proved right as Tim drove up at the side of the house, then, with an expansive wave, said, "Take a look at that."

They were at the edge of a bluff, the beautiful, cerulean bay below them. There was a serenity to the water, the deep blue seeming to go almost forever until at the horizon it was met by the lighter blue of the sky. Offshore to her right she saw a trawler moving along slowly. Nearer to land, gulls circled lazily. She could hear their cries and it seemed to her they echoed the sound of the sea itself.

At her side Timothy said, "Incredible, isn't it? Can you believe there could be so much peace anywhere?"

"No," Anne answered, in little more than a whisper. "No. . . I can't."

She felt his arm touching her. "Anne. . ." he said huskily.

Tears came to her eyes, though she couldn't understand why she felt like crying. It was such a beautiful moment, such a beautiful place. And Timothy was with her to share it.

"Darling," he whispered. Then his lips moved upon hers, without the slightest trace of haste. He kissed her slowly, tenderly, the kiss deepening exquisitely.

Anne felt as if every last vestige of tension was leaving her body, and that all her restraint would follow. But it was he who ended the embrace.

"Hey!" he said, laughing shakily. "Let's get out of the car. I want to show you the beach."

He walked around to her side of the car, and taking her arm led her to the edge of the bluff. A long flight of weathered wooden steps led downward, and when she got to the bottom of them Anne felt a bit breathless.

"I think you need to get more exercise!" Tim joked.

"I do," she admitted ruefully. "When I get back to the city maybe I'd better retrieve my running suit from the mothballs and try out Central Park after all."

When I get back to the city. The phrase seemed to thud between them, and Timothy's face darpened. "When do you have to go back?" he asked.

"A week from tomorrow. I...I've already extended my leave of absence by two weeks. I was in Boston a full week before...I had the chance to meet with you."

"Yes," he cut in, frowning. "There was a lot of time lost—all the way around."

What did he mean by that? she wondered, then watched as he reached down, picked up a flat stone, and skimmed it out over the water. It skipped across the surface gracefully, leaving circular ripples in its trail. Then it turned on its edge, plopped and sank.

"Quite a trick," she complimented.

"That?" he asked impishly. "That's easy!" Pointing at their feet, he added, "These stones were left by the glaciers. They passed over this area thousands of years ago, melting on the way. There are dozens of fresh-water lakes on the Cape that people call ponds, but many of them are actually glacial potholes, surprisingly deep. The glaciers contoured the whole peninsula, and the rubble they left in their wake will probably keep surfacing forever."

He'd picked up another stone as he spoke and

stood staring down at it, a very set expression on his face. "It's good to think some things may go on forever," he said expressionlessly.

"Tim...." she began, then caught her breath.

"I'm not pretending that we could go on forever, Anne," he said, looking at her directly. "But... there's one thing I've learned. Life is made up of hours, minutes and seconds. And once we've let them go by there's no snatching them back. Today is our space in time. Right now, Anne. Do you know what I'm saying?"

There was a certain edge to his tone, an edge of desperation. Yet why should he feel so desperate? Anne asked herself, knowing there was no ready answer for this. Living for the moment was an old overused line. But this was what he was suggesting to her, though it had a different meaning as he voiced it. He wasn't using an expedient ruse. She was sure of that. He was as much as saying that this was their only chance, the only moment they would ever have together....

The question came straight out of her subconscious. "Are you married, Tim?" she asked him.

He stared at her incredulously. "How can you even ask me such a thing?" he demanded.

"Because...."

"Because what?" he snapped, and there was no doubt at all that the edge of desperation—if that's what it had been—had changed to clear-cut anger. "Do you think if I were married I'd be here now, with you?" he said, his voice suddenly hoarse. "No, Anne. I'm not married. I've never been married, nor will I ever be married! Does that answer your question?''

It more than answered her question. And, inevitably, it paved the way for all sorts of other questions that came tumbling into her mind.

Why did he say he would never be married? That was the first of them.

"Tim," she ventured slowly, "I only w-wondered—"

"Wondered what?" he sneered, plainly not mollified.

"Why you speak as though we have...only t-today.''

"Because that's all I'm sure we'll ever have," he told her bluntly. "Come on. Let's go back and take a look at the cottage.''

He started up the stairs and Anne followed him silently, wondering how she was going to handle the rest of the day with him.

Better to ask, she told herself then, how he was going to handle it with her. Was he merely going to survey this cottage he was evidently thinking of renting, then head back to Boston, having thoroughly retreated into that shell of his again?

She was tense as she watched Timothy take a key out of his coat pocket. Then, as he was about to insert it in the lock, he paused and turned to face her.

"Let's not spoil it, okay?" he asked, smiling that sweet-sad smile that twisted Anne's heart. Then he added, with that touch of brogue, "I should have had the sense not to say anything down there, *mavourneen*." He gestured toward the beach. "I should have known better than to tamper with magic."

With this, he turned his attention to opening the door. It squeaked as he pushed, and grinning he told her, "Were the circumstances a wee bit different I would carry you over the threshold. As it is...."

He bowed mockingly and motioned Anne to precede him.

The cottage was delightful. Anne's pleasure was audible as she looked across a living room furnished in antique maple to a wall of windows facing directly out on the bay.

The colors used in interior decoration picked up the outdoors, combining the blues and greens of the water with sand beige. Touches of olive green—a shade almost exactly matching that of the beach grass—added an unexpectedly effective contrast.

The living room had a big stone fireplace, and Anne could imagine sitting before it with rain spattering outside, feeling as protected and snug as one could anywhere in the world—provided that Timothy Flanagan were there, too.

She quickly tried to suppress such thoughts. They were so potentially treacherous. But when she and Tim moved on to survey the adjoining bedroom other dangerous thoughts came unbidden. There was something so inviting about the huge double bed that centered one wall. Impossible not to imagine what it would be like living here with Timothy and, when night came, sharing that bed....

Anne turned so abruptly she bumped right into him.

"Sorry," she choked. "I didn't realize you were so close...."

He was watching her intently, and she had the uncomfortable feeling that once again he was reading her mind. "I like being close to you, Anne," he said. "I'd like to be much closer."

"The view," Anne said, trying to distract both of them. "The owners have really taken advantage of it. Imagine, this bedroom has both a picture window and a fireplace all its own!"

"Yes."

"Is there another bedroom?"

"Yes. A smaller one for guests. There is also a kitchen. And a bathroom. Do you really want to look at them right now?"

He was standing in front of her as he said this, so near that she took an involuntary step backward and almost lost her balance. A strong hand quickly grasped her shoulder, and Timothy said gently, "Anne. For heaven's sake, you act as if you're afraid of me."

"Afraid of you?" She shook her head. "No... I'm not."

"What, then? Afraid of yourself?"

Her clear gray eyes seemed enormous as she looked up at him. "Yes," she said. "Yes, perhaps I am afraid of myself."

"So afraid of letting go, Anne?"

"It isn't that, exactly."

"Then what is it, exactly?" he mocked, but there was affection in his tone.

"I don't know," she said, and never had she felt more ineffectual.

"I would never do anything you didn't want me to do. You do know that, don't you?"

"Yes. Yes, I do know that, Tim."

"As I said before, this is our time, Anne. It's ours, all ours. No people, no telephones, no distractions. Just total beauty, total peace. Darling...I want you so much!"

She tightened at this, and noting her reaction, he dropped his hand from her shoulder and stood back. He said softly, "It has to be mutual, you know. I had the crazy feeling it was mutual. Was I mistaken, Anne?"

She couldn't lie to him. She said, her voice catching, "N-no. No, you weren't mistaken."

"You've already told me you're not married, not involved with anyone. And I...believe me, I am as free as a man could be, Anne. No ties. No ties at all. I'm thirty-four, you're twenty-seven. We've both...lived. And there is no one to be hurt by anything we might do." He paused, then said, "Is there?"

"No one I would be hurting," she said, in little more than a whisper.

"Darling, let me just hold you," Timothy implored. "Let me just feel your closeness, knowing that this time is entirely ours. The other night—"

"I wish you'd stop talking about the other night, Tim."

"It was a bad move on my part, that's all," he said. "This is different, darling. The wanting is the same but...it's much deeper. Do you know what I'm saying? Every minute I've spent with you today has been like a precious thread to be woven into a tapestry I'll always keep with me. I want to complete that tapestry, Anne.''

She stood before him and knew that everything she was feeling in her heart was mirrored in her eyes for him to see. He looked deep into those eyes and sighed raggedly.

''You're so lovely,'' he said. ''I want to know you, Anne. I want to know all of you. . . .''

Incredibly, she saw his green eyes glisten. So he could be moved to tears. . . even as she could be. And he was not ashamed of letting her see them.

This tangible evidence of his vulnerability did something to her. She moved into his embrace of her own accord, and as his arms folded around her she felt as if she'd reached an ultimate destination.

They kissed, slowly, tantalizingly at first, for—as he had said—there was no reason to hurry. *We have the rest of the day,* Anne found herself thinking. *We have forever.*

If only they had forever.

Even thinking about it caused her own urgency to increase. She found herself certain that she must hold onto Timothy, that she must never let him go, and her kisses held a touch of frenzy as they trailed across his throat. She didn't have to be told that it was she who had pushed them past a point of no return.

He carried her across to the bed, depositing her gently on a thick quilt handmade by someone with painstaking care. She sank into its softness, then instinctively held out her arms to Tim, and in an instant he was by her side.

She moved into his embrace, and this time he drew her so close to him that the contours of her body blended with his as if nature had designed them for this moment. There was an intimacy, despite the fact they still had their clothes on. Tim's arousal became obvious. She could feel the masculine core of him thrusting against her thigh, and it was a reflex action older than time that made her part her legs as if to allow him admittance.

He raised himself up on one elbow, gazing down at her quizzically. "I do want to be sure I'm getting the right message," he teased, and the huskiness in his voice told its own tale.

Then his green eyes darkened and became the color of malachite. Gently he moved her so that she was lying on her back, and then slowly, with exquisite care, he undressed her, doing so with a deliberateness that was very, very sensuous.

His lips followed the path of his progress until he had left trails of kisses all across Anne...and it seemed to her that she could feel the lingering warmth of every one of them. Finally she lay nude before him, and he moved back to survey her like a sculptor admiring his work. Time began to telescope.

Tim did not rush, but he did move faster. He did not wait for her to undress him but divested himself of his own clothes. She watched him, and it was as if she was memorizing every line of his wonderfully masculine body. When he lay down beside her again she was ready to touch him, to let her fingers explore him with a kind of familiarity that was entirely new for her.

After a long moment he laughed, a short little laugh that hinted more than anything else could have at the effort control was causing him.

"Not too much more, darling," he warned. "I'm not a superman!"

Anne laughed too, a low throaty little laugh she didn't even recognize. And she knew that only now was she fully ready for him to claim her—ready for the first thrust that would be the beginning of their union.

They blended, Tim filling her with his manhood while she gasped at the sweet-sharp pleasure he was giving her, soon to become an upward surge of unabated ecstasy. And when, at last, they reached love's most sensuous pinnacle, Anne sensed the emotional totality that encompassed them.

She had given herself to Tim, and he had given himself to her. It was this that was so devastating.

I am complete with him, she found herself thinking as she lay within the circle of his arms, her pulse finally coming back to a steady beat.

And I'll never be the same without him!

CHAPTER SEVEN

ANNE AWAKENED SLOWLY, and for a moment was completely disoriented. She was still lying on the thick patchwork quilt, but a blanket had been drawn over her. As she rubbed her eyes, the room swung into focus. It was bathed in a golden glow as if it had been painted, the walls and furniture burnished by the setting sun.

Immediately she realized she was alone, and a sharp sense of loss possessed her. She knew that she'd drifted off to sleep after their lovemaking, and she would have thought that Tim might have done the same thing—or at least that he would have stayed beside her.

She stood up groggily, wishing she had a robe to slip on. She felt impelled to find Tim without wasting any time. Instead, she had to pause to dress, her hands fumbling at the task. Then, running agitated fingers through her hair and not even bothering to check herself in the mirror, she hurried out the bedroom door.

Why did she feel so bereft?

Maybe I'm afraid he's deserted me and has gone back to Boston, she told herself. *But he wouldn't do that! Would he?*

Questions and doubts vied with each other as Anne went into the living room only to see that it was empty. She checked the kitchen and the bathroom. Then she peered into the little guest room. No sign of Tim!

Fighting down a sense of panic, she went to the living room and moved across to the picture window. For a moment she found distraction in the spectacular panorama that met her eyes. The golden rim of the sun was just touching down on the waters of Cape Cod Bay, now the palest shade of shimmering turquoise. Ribbons of rose and apricot and mauve radiated from the horizon across the water, and it seemed to Anne they were spiraling in her direction, making her feel as if she should be able to reach out and grasp their beauty.

Then her eyes fell on something else—a man walking along the beachfront. His head was down, his hands thrust deep into the pockets of the jacket he was wearing, and there was something about his silhouetted figure that made Anne wince. She seemed to be sharing the pain she was certain he was feeling. For there was something very stark about Timothy Flanagan as he walked alone along the sand, not even pausing to gaze toward the awesome magnificence of the sunset.

Anne had never seen a more lonely looking figure.

More than ever she yearned to know more about him—everything about him. She longed to find a way of reaching him. More than ever her heart ached for him. She didn't know what his problem was, but she did know she wanted to share it.

Trembling as she watched him, a frightening new knowledge possessed her. She was on the verge of falling in love with Timothy Flanagan, dangerous though that might be. For she knew that this mysterious yet wonderful man was without doubt the most unpredictable person she'd ever met. There was no telling whether or not he would ever truly return her feelings.

By the time Timothy returned to the house, Anne had washed her face, repaired her makeup and combed her hair. She was prepared to deal with him as she never had before.

She moved toward him, greeted him with a radiant smile, and hoped he would take her in his arms and kiss her. But he didn't.

"Well," he said, returning her smile, yet seeming strangely aloof. "I see the sleeping beauty finally realized she'd be too beautiful for human eyes if she didn't decide to wake up!"

"Oh, come on!" Anne protested, then she hesitated. She had been about to tell him that she'd seen him walking along the beach and had wished he'd waited for her to go with him. But as she thought of him silhouetted against the sunset, so solitary, so remote, the words caught in her throat before she could utter them.

"We'd better be going," he told her. "I don't want to get you home too late. It might upset your aunt."

"Aunt Muriel certainly won't be sitting up waiting for me," Anne pointed out. "After all, she knows I'm with you."

"What's that supposed to mean?"

"She has confidence in you."

"Misplaced, perhaps?"

Anne was surprised at the bleakness of his expression. Surprised, and also a little annoyed. It didn't seem to her that there was any good reason for this sort of attitude on his part.

"Look," she blurted. "If you're thinking of s-saying anything about this...this afternoon, please don't...unless it's positive! I'd hate to think you r-regretted it," she finished, adding valiantly, "because I don't!"

He shot a sharp glance at her. "I would hardly say I *regretted* it, Anne," he said, his voice tense. Then he added more gently, "I'd be lying if I said that. Making love with you was probably the most... well, the most beautiful thing that has ever happened to me."

Hope surged, but Anne soon learned it was premature hope. He shrugged as if casting away the memory of their time together, and said, "Come on. There's no heat turned on in here, and it's getting chilly."

In Anne's opinion the temperature inside the cottage was only slightly cool, but she wasn't about to argue. Picking up her handbag and vest, she started out the door ahead of him, though not without a strong sense of reluctance. The cottage had quickly become a special place to her, and she didn't want to face the thought that she might never see it again.

"Who owns it, Tim?" she managed softly.

Locking the door, he asked a bit irritably, "Who owns what?"

"This cottage."

"One of the lawyers in the firm," he told her, shoving the key in his pocket. "At least his wife does. She inherited it a couple of years ago. They're both mountain people, though. They have another place on a lake in New Hampshire, which they think offers the best of all worlds. Swimming and boating in summer, skiing in winter. So they've decided to unload this place."

"You mean they're going to sell it?" The mere idea was a shock. It made the cottage seem like any ordinary piece of real estate.

"Yes, although they're willing to rent it to me for the summer, first—if I decide it's what I need," Tim said. "If I take it, they'll wait until fall before they put it up for sale. If I don't, they'll put it on the market now."

She couldn't repress the question. "Are you going to rent it, Tim?"

They were at the car and opening the door for her, he smiled crookedly. "You're full of questions, aren't you?" he observed.

The comment stung. "I didn't mean to pry," Anne said stiffly. "I . . . I was interested, that's all."

"I guess I'm not used to having people interested in what I'm going to do or not do," he said, sliding behind the wheel. He turned the key in the ignition switch.

"I find that hard to believe."

"Do you? Well, I suppose that's because you met me at what was a very garrulous moment, for me."

She was thinking back to that day in Southie, and she knew he was, too. "Well, you certainly weren't what I'd call shy. You were quaffing down a mug of green beer and. ..."

"Yes, go on."

"I've often wondered, Tim, what did you do on Saint Patrick's Day?"

There was an oddly strained note in his voice as he answered, "I didn't do much of anything. The big celebration this year was the week before, after all. Anyway, what did you think I'd be doing? Consuming vast quantities of corned beef and cabbage?"

"Corned beef and cabbage is American," Anne said unexpectedly.

"What do you mean by that?"

"Corned beef and cabbage isn't the national dish of Ireland, that's all. It happens to be American. And chop suey isn't Chinese, either. Nor do the Mexicans put beans in with chili. People in Texas started that."

"My, my," Tim said chuckling as he steered the car over a sandy bump in the road. "Aren't you the walking encyclopedia! How do you happen to know so much about cooking?"

"Cooking is something of a hobby with me," Anne retorted. "Ethnic cooking, especially. It gives you the chance to learn a lot about the background of America."

"How so?" Tim asked.

"Well, people immigrating here from other countries have always brought their favorite national dishes with them. Of course they change over the years. So...corned beef and cabbage isn't really Irish at all. It's an American adaptation of cabbage and boiled bacon."

"What?"

"Why so surprised, Tim?" she asked him. "You've been to Ireland, haven't you?"

"No. Why would you think that?"

She laughed. "Because you seem so...Irish," she told him. "Your birthday should be on Saint Patrick's Day!"

"It is," he said.

"Are you serious?"

"For all intents and purposes, my birthday is on Saint Patrick's Day," he said levelly.

"For all intents and purposes? What does that mean?"

They had traversed the last of the sand lanes and were back at the parking lot. Tim started down the paved road, and for a moment he didn't answer her. Then he said, "Look, let's skip it, shall we, Anne? I don't feel like being analyzed."

She was dumbfounded by his response and more than a bit affronted. "I didn't mean to pry, Timothy," she said coldly.

He glanced across at her. "I've come to realize that when you're annoyed with me you call me Timothy," he observed with a faint smile. "The rest of the time you call me Tim." He paused and took a deep breath. "Okay, Anne, I deserve your annoyance. And...I'm sorry. Sometimes I bark too quickly. I guess you could call it Irish temper.''

You call it Irish temper, she told him silently. *That wasn't temper, Timothy Flanagan! It was that crazy complex you've got about anyone finding out very much about you!*

What have you got to hide?

TIMOTHY SEEMED TOTALLY PREOCCUPIED for the first part of the drive back to Boston. He switched on the car stereo as if to discourage conversation, and soon Anne found herself responding to the beautiful music enveloping her.

After a station break the soft strains of "Stardust" sifted through the air and, unconsciously Anne began to sing. "Stardust" was such a plaintive, nostalgic song, the melody a haunting perennial.

The music ended, and Timothy abruptly switched off the radio. Into the ensuing silence he said, quietly, "I had no idea you could sing like that."

It took a minute for his words to sink in. "It's something...I've always loved," she told him.

"It should be a hell of a lot more than that!" he said bluntly. "What is someone with a voice like yours doing in banking?"

Anne's lips tightened. It was all right for him to post No Trespassing signs where his privacy was concerned and insist they be obeyed. In contrast, she felt as if she'd been an open book to him. She'd wanted him to know her. She'd wanted that dreadful veil of his to disappear....

Suddenly she became defensive. Singing was her Pandora's box, and she had no desire to open it—for anyone. She had no desire to relive bitter memories. Long since she'd gotten over Ken Phillips, but the memory of his disgust with her still lingered. It still hurt.

He hadn't been able to comprehend her decision to give up singing. He'd accused her of defecting to a "world peopled by robots." That last scene between them, when he'd been so openly contemptuous, had been unforgettably traumatic.

"Well?" Tim asked patiently.

"That's something I'd rather not t-talk about," Anne evaded.

He disregarded this. "Why not?" he demanded.

"Tim...there's an awful lot about yourself you seem unwilling to discuss, and I...I've respected that. Just this time, could you afford me the same courtesy?"

"To hell with courtesy! You have the voice of an angel! Obviously you've studied. Anyone could tell that."

"Tim...."

"I have no musical talent myself," he continued. "But, Anne...I love music. I don't think there's an Irishman living who doesn't love music. And I know what I was hearing when you were singing just now."

"P-please. Can't we change the subject?"

"No, we cannot change the subject," he frowned. "I want to know why you didn't choose music for a career. And why, if you couldn't make the necessary sacrifices, you didn't keep up with it anyway, as an avocation? You say you love singing. Well, I have a feeling it's been a lot more than that to you. Am I right?''

Anne couldn't answer him immediately, but it struck her as ironic that their roles had been reversed.

Then, carefully, she said, ''When I made the decision not to go on with singing, Tim, my personal life was seriously affected. Very seriously affected.''

''Was there a man involved?''

''Yes.''

''Did it matter so much to him? What you did, I mean?''

''Yes, it did. He was a musician himself—a very talented musician. And he couldn't understand anyone abandoning what he considered a God-given gift.''

''Then that makes two of us,'' Tim said stubbornly.

''There were many other things to consider. I . . . I had to make my own way.''

His laugh was derisive. ''Oh, come off it!'' he scoffed. ''You, having to make your own way? With a family as loaded as yours? You could have studied at any conservatory in the world if you'd wanted to.''

Anne had never thought of her family as being ''loaded.'' They had never wanted for anything financially, she admitted, but she realized she had no idea of the Clarendon family's true monetary worth. Her Aunt Muriel, she knew, was independently wealthy. She continued to live in the Chestnut Hill house under the terms of the life tenancy given to her by her brother because she loved it, not because of necessity.

Anne knew that her father, too, had never lacked for money. For that matter, her mother had always had an independent income. As she thought of it now, Anne admitted she'd never considered her family's ability to pay for her musical education when she'd made her career decision. She'd thought only of doing something that would assure her personal freedom.

She wanted to explain this to Tim with an urgency that surprised her. "Tim," she began, "I wanted to do something entirely on my own."

His smile was wry. "That seems to be a standard ploy for little rich girls," he said sarcastically.

She didn't like his tone of voice.

"I don't consider myself a 'little rich girl,'" she told him coolly. "You must understand that when I had to make my decision between singing or banking, my mother had remarried, my father had remarried, and I didn't want to be a burden to either one of them."

"A burden?" Tim queried. His eyebrows arched skeptically. "What kind of a burden could you have been?"

"A f-financial burden," Anne said seriously.

"You've got to be kidding! As I've just told you, you could have frittered away years in studying without even putting a dent in your family's fortune."

"I don't think you get my point," Anne said steadily. "I wanted to be my own person."

"To do your own thing, is that it?" he taunted.

"Yes," she said, flushing. "Is that so difficult for you to understand?"

"It's pathetic, maybe," he told her, "but not difficult."

She found herself edging away from him, huddling into the far corner of the car.

She refused to look at him, but she could feel the glance aimed in her direction and knew those green eyes were raking her, assessing her much too acutely.

He said softly, "I'm sorry, sweetheart. That wasn't a very decent way to put it. Look, you're right, I shouldn't have pried." He exhaled a long sigh. "How about a change of pace?" he suggested. "I know a place in Duxbury where they make terrific fried clams. Could you go for some?"

She nodded, surprised to realize she was hungry, and a moment later was startled when he reached out and clasped her hand.

IT WAS AFTER TEN O'CLOCK when Tim let her out in front of the Chestnut Hill house. As a matter of politeness she asked if he'd like to come in for coffee or a drink but was relieved when he refused. They had tried to get back on an even keel with each other during the respite in the Duxbury restaurant, but there'd been a lingering tension between them that had lasted through the rest of the drive.

Muriel had already gone to bed. Anne, suddenly

weary herself, switched off the downstairs lights and went upstairs, but once in her own bed she couldn't get to sleep. She didn't want to review the day she'd just lived through. There had been too much to it. Too many conflicting emotions, ranging from rapture to total discouragement. She found it impossible, though, not to go over it mentally step by step, and her emotions became almost too heavy to handle when she got to that consummating scene in the cottage between Tim and herself.

She still could not believe she'd gone to bed with a man she'd known so briefly. Yet she also knew that time didn't count where she and Tim were concerned. Their knowledge of each other went beyond the calendar.

Finally, exhausted, Anne drifted off into a sleep that was plagued by disturbing dreams. Fortunately she couldn't remember the content of any of them when she awakened.

She put on a pale yellow lounging robe and went downstairs to find that Muriel was ahead of her and had already made coffee. Nor was she able to side-step her aunt when it came to giving some sort of recital about her day on Cape Cod with Tim Flanagan. She tried to stick to business in detailing it, going into the matter of the holograph will, and when the conversation was finally interrupted by a phone call, she was glad to escape on the pretense of having letters to write.

She expected Timothy to call her that Sunday, but he didn't. And when bedtime came again, she couldn't quite believe this. She was sure that he hadn't been any more able to forget the previous day than she had. Yet he was an entirely different type of person than she was—only now was she beginning to realize that thoroughly. He was a lot tougher, for one thing. A lot more able, perhaps, to shrug off emotion and involvement, if neither fit in with his plans.

To Anne's growing astonishment, Monday passed, too, without her hearing from him. At this point anger began to stake its claim. It was impossible not to feel that she'd been used, even though honesty compelled her to admit that Tim's conquest had been made with her full compliance. She could not possibly ever pretend that she hadn't wanted him fully as much as he'd wanted her.

Perhaps, she told herself, as she lay in bed that Monday night unable to sleep, there really was an elemental difference between men and women when it came to the philosophy of making love.

Anne remembered a quote she'd read once—attributed to Lord Bryon, she thought, though she wasn't entirely sure. It had been something to the effect that "love to a man is a thing apart, but 'tis woman's whole existence."

She knew she'd been very much in danger of letting Timothy Flanagan become her whole existence, and, thinking this, she took a firm emotional grip on herself.

"From here in," she promised, speaking the words aloud, "things are going to be different!"

TIMOTHY CALLED late Tuesday morning. Anne was in the library with her aunt, watching a TV special broadcast from the United Nations, when Bridget called her to the phone.

When she heard Tim's voice her knees went weak, and she sank down onto the nearest chair.

"How have you been?" he asked politely.

"Fine, thank you," she answered, adding automatically, "And you?"

"Busy," he told her. "I went with Giles to New York yesterday. He handled the session with Bigelow, as I had another matter to attend to. Anyway, it required my doing homework all day Sunday. . . or I'd have been in touch."

Anne felt like telling him that he didn't need to explain his lack of communication to her. She didn't think he was doing a very good job of it, at that. If he'd really wanted to get in touch he could have managed, regardless of his work load.

"Anne?"

"Yes," she replied sweetly, determined to keep the conversation on a level plane.

"If you and your aunt will be free tonight, Giles and I would like to stop by. We'd rather talk about his meeting with Lance Bigelow in person, with both of you. It's difficult to discuss things like this over the phone, and I don't want to ask your aunt to come into our office."

"That's thoughtful of you," Anne said sincerely. "We'll be here."

"Would eight o'clock be all right?"

"Fine," she agreed.

For the rest of the day, the hands on the clock moved with excruciating slowness. Anne and Muriel had an early dinner, and at the last minute Anne debated as to whether or not she should change her clothes. She was wearing beige corduroy trousers and an oversized floppy sweater in a deeper shade. It was an attractive outfit, and to dress it up further would be a bit more obvious than she wanted to be just now. She satisfied herself by running upstairs and putting on some copper earrings and touching her lips with a copper-toned gloss.

Dressed in brown herringbone tweed, Tim was very much the proper lawyer that evening. It was impossible for Anne to believe this was the same man who had made love to her so ardently only the previous Saturday.

Giles Winslow was tall, blond and very handsome. He had classic features, deep blue eyes and a charming personality. Inevitably he and Muriel got onto the subject of ancestors. The Winslow and Clarendon families had both been around a long, long time.

"If we search out the family tree sufficiently we'll probably find we're cousins," Giles laughed.

Anne interrupted their genealogical discourse to ask if the men would care for coffee or would prefer something to drink. Both opted in favor of Scotch and soda, and Muriel allowed that she'd indulge in a glass of cream sherry.

To her distress, when she started out to the kitchen to get the drinks, Timothy immediately suggested he help her. He did not accept Anne's swift retort when she said, "Thanks just the same. I can manage."

Once in the kitchen, though, he sat down on a straight-backed chair and surveyed her morosely as she got out ice cubes and the other drink makings.

"Listening to your aunt and Giles makes me feel like a displaced person," he confessed.

"Why?" Anne asked over her shoulder, busy measuring out the Scotch.

"I suppose because I already know I don't belong and that sort of thing just hammers it home."

Anne was almost afraid to look at him. This was the most revealing statement he'd ever made about himself, and she yearned to pursue the subject, yet caution made her proceed very slowly.

"I think you have a thing about heritage, Tim," she said carefully. "Especially so-called old New England heritage."

"Am I that obvious?"

"No, but you've made a few...similar comments before," Anne said, still moving gingerly in her dialogue with him. "Anyway, your attitude does seem a little out-of-date to me. I thought we'd gotten beyond all that."

"I don't believe you, Anne," he said flatly.

"What is there to believe?" she asked him.

"Your background means as much to you as it does to your aunt. She's been around longer, that's all, so one is more aware of it with her. But you have the same self-confidence, the same unshakable poise."

Unshakable poise! It seemed to Anne that much of the time she'd been around Tim her poise had been anything but unshakable!

"It's a basic thing," Tim told her. "Something you can't get if you haven't got it. It isn't for sale...as so many things are in today's world. I remember a psychologist once telling me that a person is either born with self-esteem or without it. For those unlucky enough to be born without it there can be compensation, to a point. Education, achievement...things like that. But there will never be that innate sense of breeding, of belonging, that you have. You don't have to explain yourself to anyone, Anne. You know who you are."

His tone was deadly serious as he spoke, so serious it made her uncomfortable. She looked across at him as she set the glasses with their drinks on a chased silver tray.

"Are you saying you don't know who you are, Tim?" she asked teasingly, striving to lighten things between them.

His reaction shocked her. She saw his jaw clench, a muscle at its side working as a veiled expression came over his features. She saw him become a stranger before her eyes, and his fight for self-control was visible. But although he was outwardly calm by the time he answered her question, his voice was choked with emotion.

"No, Anne," he told her. "As a matter of fact, I don't know who I am!"

CHAPTER EIGHT

GILES WINSLOW stood in the door of the kitchen, his blue eyes dancing with a merriment he didn't try to suppress.

"Your aunt said she's getting thirsty," he told Anne, then added, "Here, let me take that for you."

Before she could answer he crossed the room and picked up the tray. He smiled at her as he balanced it, and she didn't dare look at Tim. She could feel the tension crackling between them, and it seemed amazing that Giles was unaware of it.

Anne suspected, though, that Giles was a relatively simple young man. Or perhaps, she thought bitterly, it was only that he came from a background similar to hers and so, if Timothy was right in his analysis, had no need to prove himself. Tim, on the other hand, seemed to be suffering from a staggering identity crisis.

I don't know who I am!

The words came to echo in Anne's mind. They had a double meaning, she felt sure. He was speaking of knowing himself in an abstract sense, yet his major obsession, she was convinced now, had to do with the matter of family, of heritage.

Maybe he was from a poor family, and was ashamed of it. That would be so wrong, she thought. Timothy's heritage must have a good side! One had only to look at him to know that he came from special people.

He asked indifferently, "Shall we join the others, Anne?"

"Of course," she told him hastily, and was glad for the refuge the company of her aunt and Giles Winslow offered. She wasn't up to another session of misunderstandings with Tim.

She soon discovered that though Giles might be relatively simple insofar as comparing his personality to Timothy's, he was a very astute lawyer. He detailed his meeting with Laura's attorney in clear-cut concise language, adding ruefully at the end of his account, "As I've told Tim, it does look as if she has a fairly firm leg to stand on. That doesn't mean I don't think we should wage our own battle. We should, and we will! We're going to get into every possible angle involving holograph wills, and we're going to be sticklers when it comes to her proving that the will in question was witnessed as it should have been."

"But she does have a case?" Muriel asked anxiously.

"Yes, I'm afraid so, Miss Clarendon," Giles admitted. "This isn't something that's going to be settled quickly, though. It will take time, and there's a lot of groundwork to accomplish first. Tim and I will be going over everything thoroughly during the next few days. Meanwhile, we wanted to update you...."

Tim had said nothing at all while his associate spoke. Now he answered a couple of the questions Muriel put to him directly as briefly and politely as he could. But when Muriel glanced at the clock and then told the two men it was getting past her bedtime and she'd have to say good-night, Anne sensed that Tim would be glad to get away.

While both he and Giles were talking to her aunt, she found the opportunity to study his face. He looked tired, there were dark circles of fatigue beneath his eyes, and he seemed very tense. She wondered if he and Giles would linger or if they'd leave once Muriel had gone upstairs, and she discovered that she, too, was relieved when Timothy took the initiative and both lawyers departed.

It had been a tormenting evening so far as Anne was concerned. Now that it was over it seemed that an added distance had been put between Timothy and herself. They certainly hadn't become any closer, and she felt as if she must have dreamed everything that had taken place between them in the cottage on Cape Cod—a cottage that she would forever think of as enchanted.

It was Giles who made the next move. He called on Thursday and asked Anne if she'd be free to have lunch the next day. He kept the invitation in a business context by adding that there were a few papers for her to sign in connection with the administration of her father's estate, which was also being handled by the firm of Simon and Wechsler. Soon to be the firm of Simon, Wechsler and Flanagan, Anne amended.

Giles took her to a popular restaurant in the Quincy Market complex, and their lunch together was a pleasant interlude, something Anne needed. The fact that she'd be leaving Boston in just a couple more days was becoming oppressive, and it had nothing to do with Laura or holograph wills. No matter how she tried to get control of her emotions, she felt in a constant state of inner chaos, all due to Timothy Flanagan. And it seemed impossible to her to think of simply leaving—or of him letting her leave—under these conditions.

He didn't seem to have any intention of suggesting she might stay longer, or that he might come to New York to see her, or that they might ever meet again. Anne was thinking about this as she and Giles walked back up State Street toward the building where Simon and Wechsler's offices were located. In fact she was literally lost in thought and was completely unprepared for it when they bumped into the subject of her dilemma in the downstairs lobby.

On his way out of the building, Timothy stopped short when he saw them, and Anne knew at once that he'd had no idea she'd been invited to lunch with his co-worker. Her first thought was that this was rather dirty pool on Giles's part, but then she swiftly reversed her opinion.

Why should Giles have thought anything about making a date with her, business or otherwise? she asked herself. Surely he knew nothing of the relationship between Timothy and her...if it could even be called that!

She saw a quizzical reddish eyebrow rise, then Tim said unconvincingly, "Well, now. What a surprise!"

He was trying to be genial about it, which only made matters worse. Looking up at him, Anne had the urge to throttle him.

"Haven't you had lunch yet, Tim?" Giles asked, slightly taken aback.

Timothy shook his head. "Got held up with a long-distance call," he replied, "so I'm going to have to settle for a snack. I won't be gone long," he added, glancing at his thin gold wristwatch. "I have an appointment with a client in forty-five minutes. Was there anything you wanted me to do for you, Anne?"

The question threatened to throw her off completely. She stared at him, knowing that if she were to attempt an answer she would stammer hopelessly.

She was spared the necessity of saying anything when Giles remarked cheerfully, "I want Anne to sign a couple of things, that's all. Strictly routine."

"Very well, then," Tim nodded.

For a heartstopping moment Anne had the feeling he was reaching out to her. It was a very intangible thing, yet she could feel an emotional tug toward him, and it was all she could do not to reach out and grasp his hand.

He turned to her and said slowly, "I take it you're heading back to New York this weekend."

Anne swallowed hard. "I'm flying down Sunday morning," she managed. "I'm to be back at work Monday, so...."

"Well, if I don't see you again, take care," Tim told her.

Anne could feel her throat burning, and tears that were going to be shed sooner or later seemed to be storing themselves behind her eyes. She said bravely, "You too."

That was all. He walked away, and it was all she could do not to swing around and watch him go. Without even looking, though, she was aware of his presence as he crossed the lobby and went out the front door. And she knew at once when he was gone.

Giles had paused to buy a newspaper from a vending stand in the lobby, and he'd been gazing at the headlines during the last bit of her conversation with Timothy. Now he looked up. "Ready, Anne?" he asked, and gestured toward a waiting elevator.

"Yes," she told him, anxious to put her signature wherever it was required so that she could get away from the law office, the building and, as soon as possible, from Boston itself.

Giles Winslow was in no hurry, though. Once they were settled in his office—two doors down the hall from Tim's office, Anne noted—he moved with a slowness that set her completely on edge.

He riffled through the file folder on his desk page by page, and before he asked Anne to sign anything he went into a series of explanations about the various matters they were dealing with in a legal jargon that didn't make full sense to her. Perhaps, she conceded, she would have understood the nuances of what he was saying to her under more normal circumstances. But she was attuned to the knowledge that in only a few minutes Tim Flanagan would be returning to his office, and there was the chance that she might bump into him in the hall on her way out.

Do I want that to happen, or don't I? Anne asked herself. It was a simple question, impossible to answer. Everything in her cried out with the desire to see Timothy again. Yet he certainly had rebuffed her. He seemed so cold. She couldn't understand why—she couldn't understand him!—but she knew her pride should be strong enough to make her want to avoid him. She'd always had almost too much pride.

What's happened to me? she asked herself so intently she nearly posed the question aloud.

Giles said patiently, "Anne? Would you sign here, please?"

She sensed he was repeating himself, and she responded eagerly. Thank goodness he was at last thrusting a document in her direction.

Finally, having signed everything he wanted her to sign, Anne was free to go. Giles walked her to the elevator, and she stiffened as they passed Timothy's door. It was closed, and the walls were so soundproof she couldn't even hear the echo of his voice if he was in there.

At the elevator Giles asked, "Could you use a ride to Logan on Sunday?"

Anne had planned to ask Peter Dwyer if he might be free to take her to the airport. If not, she could easily call a taxi. She had decided to leave her car at her aunt's for the summer. She didn't use it that often in New York, and she would probably be returning to Boston when there were further developments concerning her father's estate. Yet at Giles's offer she hesitated.

"That's awfully nice of you, Giles," she said. "But . . . well, I wouldn't want to put you out."

"You'd be doing me a favor, Anne," he told her, his voice low. "It would give me a chance to see you again." As he spoke, his blue eyes were caressing her in an unexpected way.

Anne sighed. The last thing in the world she wanted at the moment was a romantic complication with Giles Winslow, regardless of how much of a charmer he might be.

"Just tell me when I should meet you," he urged.

"All right," Anne conceded. Then, realizing her own abruptness, added, "It really is very nice of you to offer, Giles. My plane leaves in the early afternoon, and you probably know better than I how much time should be allowed for traffic and all."

"I'll pick you up at eleven, Anne," he promised.

SUNDAY MORNING Giles arrived exactly at eleven. Peter Dwyer had stopped by earlier to say goodbye to Anne over coffee and danishes, so she was late in getting her packing finished.

This was something of a blessing, actually. Since her departure was of necessity done in a rush, neither she nor Muriel had the time to become unduly sentimental. They did hug, though, their embrace one of deep affection. And Anne's voice was shaky as she said, "Now, take care of yourself, do you hear?"

"I will, dear," Muriel promised. "It . . . it's been so wonderful having you here."

Anne was wiping away a tear as Giles's car pulled away from the curb. He said sympathetically, "She's a great old girl."

"Yes, she is," Anne agreed, and added vehemently, "And she didn't need all this unpleasantness with Laura on her plate! Aunt Muriel has such a strong sense of family—she's a Clarendon to the bone. The mere thought of giving Laura so much as one monogrammed silver spoon. . . ."

"I know," Giles told her seriously. "I have an Aunt Muriel of my own. I think she even has a framed copy of our family tree. It's great, of course, but sometimes it's. . . ."

"Oppressive?" she suggested.

"Exactly. Sometimes I wonder how I would have made out if I hadn't had my family to back me up. No one to introduce me to the right people, push the right buttons—"

"Like Tim Flanagan?" Anne interposed, her own question surprising her.

"Yes, I suppose you could say that," Giles agreed easily. "I doubt Tim has ever had any doors opened for him. He's had to unlock them and then push them in himself."

"Have you known him very long?"

"We were classmates at Harvard Law School," Giles told her, and this surprised Anne too. The thought flashed that Tim was a senior partner in the lawn firm and Giles was still a junior partner. Yet it was Giles who'd had all the right connections, the best opportunities.

Anne decided to continue with her inquiry as long as she could do so and remain seemingly casual. "Do you know Timothy's family?" she ventured.

"I don't think he has any," Giles said. "No close relatives, anyway. If he does, he never mentions them."

"Strange," she mused.

Giles frowned. "I suppose it is, in a way. And I'm not saying that I've never wondered about Tim, because I have. But he's a total loner. That's what I put it down to, anyway. Some people are like that. Very...private. I'd say Tim is an extremely private person."

"Don't the two of you ever go out together?" Anne persisted. "Socially, I mean."

Giles shook his head. "No, we never have. At school Tim kept to himself. I'm sure you can imagine that anyone has to do his share of studying to get through Harvard, but Tim did more than his share. He also worked."

"Worked?"

"To help pay his tuition, I guess," Giles said, and it was apparent to Anne that Giles had never even had to think about such practicalities.

"Funny," he said. "I never thought too much about it, but I'd say that about the only thing Tim does outside of practicing law these days involves his kids."

"What?" Anne blurted, totally shaken. Timothy Flanagan had told her that he'd never been married, that he . . . .

Her throat went dry as she stammered, "H-how many does he h-have?"

Giles glanced across at her, then laughed. "He doesn't look like the fatherly type to you, is that it?" he teased. "Well, I'm not speaking of Tim's own kids, Anne. As far as I know he doesn't have any. He's involved with a group at a boys' club, that's all. About a dozen youngsters who come from broken homes or have had it rough one way or another. Today, for instance, you'd probably find him out on some sandlot organizing a baseball game. Matter of fact, I'd bet on it. That's the way he spends most of his Sundays—doing things with the kids. Monday nights, too. Each Monday night, year-round—unless he's away from Boston, of course—he takes the kids to a movie or to some sort of sporting event. Or the circus, when it's in town, or the Ice Capades. All sorts of things like that."

"He told you about this?"

"No, he didn't. I was visiting the Kennedy Library out on Columbia Point a couple of weeks ago, and I spotted Tim with a bunch of youngsters. They were staging a model-rocket meet with Tim in command. And I do mean in command. You would have thought he was in charge of a launch at Cape Canaveral!"

Giles grinned. "I've got to admit it was pretty exciting," he admitted. "The people I was with started getting restless or I would have hung around all afternoon. Those rockets really go up with a roar, let me tell you. It was quite a thrill to watch them. The kids made them from kits, and they were painted all sorts of different colors. Anyway, everyone around was stopping to watch. I told Tim I thought he must have paid off the cops or he would never have gotten away with it!''

Memory flashed again. Tim had "taken care" of having her car left at curbside in South Boston, too. Tim was simply a person who could handle things effectively when he wanted to. Probably because he'd had to so often in his life. As Giles had said, Timothy Flanagan had needed to unlock most of his own doors, and then push them open in the bargain.

They were approaching the airport, and soon Giles became involved in the stream of traffic heading for the various airline terminals. He found a temporary parking space near the Eastern terminal and insisted on seeing Anne right to the checkpoint before her gate. Then, at the last moment he bent and kissed her as she had known he would. His kiss was warm and tender, an affectionate promise of what could be, if she wanted it. But all she wanted right at that moment was the ability to wash the memories of Timothy Flanagan from her system.

THEY HAD MISSED ANNE at the bank. Work had piled up for her, and before she knew it she was involved in the production of a new training film. Voluntarily she put in long days, returning exhausted to her apartment in the East Sixties each night, ready to fall into bed and sleep. For the moment, this was for the best.

She hadn't realized until she got back into her familiar work and living surroundings how very much a tall redheaded Irishman had upset the pattern of her life—a pattern that had been more calculated than she would have cared to admit.

It was not pleasant to think that she'd been putting herself in a rut. Anne had never thought of her life—and especially her career—in such terms. She was certainly not in a rut as far as her career was concerned. Her work was challenging, creative, lucrative, and the opportunities endless. She thrived on what she was doing. . .or, she amended, she *had* thrived on it. Now there was something lacking in her working day, an emptiness she didn't seem able to fill. But this was nothing compared to the void in her personal life.

Anne had never been at a loss for invitations. Her phone had begun ringing as soon as people found out she was back in town, but at first she sidestepped the invitations, using the excuse that she had a lot to catch up on, which was true enough. But there was another reason, too. She had needed time alone, time in which to think. . .and to wait for Timothy to contact her.

It had seemed to her, once she was away from Boston and could look back at everything that had happened between Timothy and herself with at least some degree of objectivity, that he would get in touch with her. Unless she was very much mistaken about him, he wasn't that casual a person. They'd had a transcending experience that day on Cape Cod. She couldn't simply put it down to the execution of an age-old response between a man and a woman. She'd meant something to him that day, just as he had to her.

Anne was convinced of this. And, she told herself, if she were right he would get in touch. Getting in touch would become more important than giving in to his mysterious idiosyncrasies.

A week passed, then two weeks, then a month, and suddenly Anne knew she was wrong. She faced this fact on a beautiful May evening after she'd gotten off the subway and was walking the several remaining blocks to her apartment. Before her the street was bathed in a golden glow, an echo from the sun, which was currently performing its nightly drama beyond the Hudson River, sinking in magnificent splendor behind the Palisades. There seemed a sweetness to the air even here in the middle of Manhattan, and the slender trees along the sidewalk had leafed out, their color the bright new green born with the spring.

There were several town houses on her block with window boxes outside their first floors. The boxes had been filled with jonquils and tulips sometime that day. Anne was sure they hadn't been there when she left for work in the morning. She paused, drinking in their colors, and a swift stab of nostalgia assailed her.

She wanted to be with Tim. She wanted to be with him so much she didn't think she could bear it. There was a softness to this young evening, a promise to be executed. It was a time for friends to share, a time for lovers to love.

Anne broke off her thoughts sharply as if snapping a twig and went into her own apartment house. But by the time the small, slow self-operated elevator had groaned its way to her floor, she knew that Timothy Flanagan was not going to get in touch with her at all, and the pain of the knowledge was overwhelming.

She nearly called him that night. She was thankful she didn't have his home telephone number at hand or she might have succumbed to temptation. As it was, the detour of having to ask information for his number was enough to stay her. It was enough to summon up that Clarendon pride.

In the morning, after a restless night's sleep, she felt both older and a little bit wiser. But there was still a terrible hollow inside her, and as she started out for work even the beauty of the spring day failed to fulfill her. She wondered, in fact, if anything would ever again happen to fill her out emotionally.

That day was an especially busy one. Anne was scheduled in the morning to give a training lecture to new tellers from a number of branch offices affiliated with her bank, and in the afternoon she was to be interviewed by a local New York paper for a feature article on women in banking.

Knowing that she would probably be photographed in connection with the feature, she had dressed with added care. Her turquoise-colored skirt with a matching lacy sweater heightened her lovely coloring, and she'd found a stretch belt that matched perfectly, centered with a colorful buckle that looked like a sculptured rose. With this she wore a string of pearls that had belonged to her mother, and matching earrings. Had there not been a lingering ache in the region of her heart, she would have been quite satisfied with herself.

As it was, she had to struggle inwardly to get through both the lecture and the subsequent interview. By the time the interview was over she felt totally drained. Outwardly, though, she was as poised as ever.

Camouflage, she thought, alone in her office at the end of the day. *I'm becoming so camouflaged that pretty soon I'll just be a shell with nothing inside at all!*

The thought was interrupted by a knock on her door, and looking up she automatically called, "Come in."

It was Stuart Miller who entered, and Anne smiled at the sight of him. Stuart, one of the younger bank vice-presidents, was just the type of person she needed to be with right now. Recently divorced, Stuart had gone through his own traumas while his marriage was breaking up, but in Anne's opinion he had emerged a better person. He was fun loving, he had an excellent if slightly caustic sense of humor, and he obviously didn't want an involvement any more than she did.

"You're much too dressed up today to go home all by yourself, beautiful," he said. "How about a drink somewhere, and then dinner up at that little French place on Fifty-sixth we both like?''

"You're on," Anne told him without hesitation. "Give me fifteen minutes.''

"Fifteen hours, if you like," Stuart assured her wickedly, and she found herself making a face at him.

It was the first invitation Anne had accepted since coming back from Boston, aside from an occasional business luncheon, and it was good to be out with someone again, especially a companion as pleasant and witty as Stuart.

They taxied uptown, stopping at an intimate bar just off Fifth Avenue for a drink, and then walked the rest of the way to the French restaurant Stuart had mentioned.

It was a beautiful evening. A new moon slashed the sky, which still held some of daytime's blueness, and the city seemed wrapped in a special sort of magic. Stuart took her hand as they walked, and Anne trembled slightly at his touch—it reminded her of someone else's hands, someone else's strong fingers. . . .

She forced these thoughts away. She was not going to let Timothy Flanagan spoil her evening, she decided. As if determined to prove this to herself, she said something light and merry to Stuart, which provoked a smile from him in return.

Then, only a moment later, Anne froze. They were just a few doors down from the awning that graced the restuarant's entrance when, looking ahead, she saw a tall redheaded man come out the same door she and Stuart would shortly be entering.

It was Timothy Flanagan. The lights from the marquee illuminated him distinctly, and there could be no mistake—*it was Timothy Flanagan*! Nor was there any chance of mistaking the woman by his side.

Laura Clarendon was dressed in a stunning ivory outfit that highlighted her dramatic dark coloring. She looked as beautiful as Anne remembered her, and she was laughing up at Timothy.

She doesn't look in the least like a bereaved widow! Anne thought viciously.

Timothy was smiling down at her appreciatively. Even from this distance, it seemed to Anne there was a tenderness in his smile.

She stopped short, unable to suppress an audible gasp.

At once Stuart asked, "What is it?"

"S-something in my eye, I th-think," she flubbed.

"Come over closer to the streetlamp and let me look," he urged.

She obeyed, glad to be shielded by him as he bent over her, having first taken a clean white handkerchief out of his pocket. The last thing in the world she wanted was to be recognized by Tim.

Stuart probed gently, then shook his head. "Can't see anything," he said.

"I think m-maybe it...washed out," Anne managed, glad for an excuse to let tears fill her eyes.

She was aware that Stuart was looking at her with

a rather perplexed expression on his face. "Are you all right?" he asked, bewilderment edging his tone.

Anne stole a glance down the street and saw Tim help Laura into a taxi and then climb in behind her.

"Yes," she said, looking back at Stuart as the cab pulled away into traffic. "Yes, I'm quite all right."

But she wasn't. She wasn't at all.

CHAPTER NINE

ANNE STAYED LATE at her office the first Tuesday evening in September, scanning the preliminary script for a new training film that would soon be going into production.

The dog days of August had lingered through the Labor Day weekend, and she had remained in the city over the holiday, catching up on a variety of odds and ends in her apartment. As the summer had passed, she'd become more and more consumed by her job purely of her own volition. She hadn't wanted any spare time on her hands, time when her memories could plague her, and the result was that she was forever behind in everything from the mundane matters of washing and ironing to catching up on personal correspondence.

This past weekend, though, she'd had the strong feeling she should go to Boston and see her Aunt Muriel. In fact, she'd nearly yielded to the idea. It would have been a simple matter to catch a shuttle flight and take a cab out to the Chestnut Hill house, and a surprise visit would have been a tonic for Muriel. But on the verge of doing this, Anne had lost her nerve.

There was the chance that Tim might be out at

the house, conferring with her aunt, and she couldn't face seeing him again.

The lawyers were still dickering back and forth about the holograph will in Laura's possession. Muriel had told Anne on the phone recently that Tim Flanagan felt they were making progress, but it seemed slow.

Anne had bitten back a swift, caustic retort, not wanting to upset her aunt. She had been gravely troubled about Tim and his part in handling her family affairs ever since the night she'd seen him coming out of the French restaurant on West Fifty-sixth Street with Laura.

As she tried to read through the script before her, Anne found herself brooding about her personal lack of courage where the matter of reencountering Timothy Flanagan was concerned. She was also annoyed at herself because she hadn't come right out and told Muriel that Timothy had seen Laura, and that she was very much afraid he was playing both sides in the case. She hadn't wanted to upset Muriel, and she knew that casting aspersions of any sort on Tim would do exactly that.

Muriel had quite taken to him. She often mentioned him in the letters she wrote Anne, and it was seldom that they could get through a phone conversation without her bringing up his name.

Yes, Anne thought frowning, as she slashed her red marker pen through an offending word in the script, there was no doubt at all that Timothy had completely won over her aunt. And since that night she'd seen him with Laura, Anne's worry had been that he must be conning Muriel, though she couldn't understand what his reason for doing so would be. His firm stood to make out very well insofar as fees were concerned, no matter who won the case of the disputed will.

Timothy, though, for reasons she also couldn't understand, had spent a lot of time over the summer out at the Chestnut Hill house, according to Muriel's reports. It seemed as if he couldn't be solicitous enough where the elderly woman was concerned.

A guilty conscience? Anne mused. Was that what he was suffering from? Maybe he had become infatuated with Laura, and was having qualms about the fact that he'd compromised himself—professionally, at least.

Would Timothy ever compromise himself professionally? Anne had to admit to herself that this was doubtful. She knew he'd worked very hard to get to his present pinnacle in the legal profession, and she doubted that he'd let someone like Laura put his career in jeopardy.

She slammed the red pen down on her desk angrily. Every time she thought about Timothy—which was as seldom as possible, for she usually forced herself to fight off such intrusions—she found herself completely adrift where her work was concerned. But now that she'd been distracted by him, there was no point in trying to do any more on the script.

She was the last person left in the office, and was alone in the elevator on the long trip down to the first floor, which only heightened the feeling of isolation. The day had not gone well, and this was especially discouraging to Anne because she'd always felt that the day after Labor Day was a perfect time to make a new beginning.

It hadn't worked that way, though, and she was feeling tired and dejected as she stepped out onto the sidewalk into a blast of heat that felt like a furnace after ten hours spent in the air-conditioned office building. She quickly found a cab and discouraged the efforts of the driver to make conversation on the way uptown. Then, in her little apartment, she slipped out of her clothes, showered and put on a cool terry shift. She made herself a tall glass of iced tea and then impatiently turned on the TV set, hoping she could find something—anything—that would be distracting. But before she could settle on a program, the telephone began to ring.

Anne didn't believe in premonitions, but she did have a strange, almost sick feeling as she picked up the receiver. She said "hello" nervously, and the moment she heard the man's response at the other end of the wire her knees went weak.

"Anne?" It was Timothy. No one else in the world said her name quite that way.

"Y-yes," she said, sitting down quickly.

"Anne... I'm afraid I have bad news for you."

"Aunt Muriel?" The name came unbidden, and just speaking it was like a confirmation of her fears. All weekend Muriel had been at the back of her mind.

"Yes," Tim said gravely. "It was just...about an hour ago, Anne. I came out to have some supper with her earlier tonight. Afterward she complained of some pain in her chest, but she insisted it wasn't bad. I...I called the ambulance, anyway. We took her to the hospital...."

"Yes?"

"It was all over very quickly, Anne," he said, the words catching with unconcealed emotion. "There wasn't time to contact you."

"I'll leave for Boston as soon as I can get a plane," Anne said automatically. "Tell her—"

"Anne, she's gone!" Tim said, and she was struck by the hopelessness in his voice. "Look, sweetheart, there's no point in you flying up here tonight. Morning will be time enough. I've taken care of things. Quite some time ago your aunt gave me an envelope and said I was to open it if anything happened to her. It contained her wishes about... about the final arrangements, the way she wanted things done...."

"You might have informed me about that," Anne heard herself say coldly through the increasing haze of her own grief. Tim's words were just beginning to register.

"She didn't want you to know how sick she really was," Tim said. "She was afraid you'd give up your job and move up here with her and...."

He broke off. "This is no time to talk about it," he said abruptly. "Do you have any sleeping pills?"

"No, why should I—"

"Is there anyone there with you, Anne?" he interrupted.

"No!" she blurted, the mere question irritating her. *He knows perfectly well that I live alone!* she thought to herself angrily.

"Look, is there a friend you could call who'd come over and stay with you tonight?"

"I don't want anyone with me," Anne said stubbornly.

"Then at least take a good shot of something, will you do that?" Tim urged. "I...I'll give you my number. Write it down, will you?"

Reluctantly Anne reached for the pen by the phone and jotted down the number. "After you've booked a plane reservation for the morning, call me back and give me your flight details."

"There's no need—" she began, but he cut in on her.

"There's every need," he told her tensely, and with that he hung up.

Anne slowly replaced the phone receiver and then sat very still. Dusk was merging into darkness, and with night creeping over the city the stillness was intense. Even the traffic noises seemed to have abated.

She sighed. Tim was right—she did need someone with her. But although she had dozens of friends in New York, she didn't feel close to anyone. Not close enough, at least, to want them around at the moment.

She went to the small corner cabinet where she kept a modest liquor supply, and drawing out a bottle of bourbon, she poured herself a liberal shot. She mixed the amber liquid with a little water, then walked across to the window, holding the glass carefully because she was afraid that if she didn't it would drop right out of her fingers.

She sat down in a chair by the window and looked out at the slender tree growing at the edge of the sidewalk across the street. It was in full leaf, as lush and green as it would ever be. But soon its leaves would begin to turn color. Then they'd wither and die, and once again the life cycle would have been completed. Birth to death.

"Muriel!" Her aunt's name was wrung from her aloud, and hearing it, scalding tears came to fill Anne's eyes. Then they dripped down her cheeks, and clutching the glass of whiskey more firmly in her hands, she began to cry in earnest. For a long time she cried, not moving from the chair by the window.

"ANNE!"

Anne was walking up the long corridor leading to the airport lobby when she heard Tim call her. She stopped in her tracks, rocking back on her heels.

He was beside her in an instant, reaching down to take the small overnight case she was carrying out of her suddenly stiffened fingers. Then he hooked his arm in hers, urging her on.

She was afraid to look up at him. His appearance was a shock, for she hadn't expected him to come to the airport to meet her. She didn't know why, but she'd been sure he would send Giles. Giles had filled

in for him during those final days she'd spent in
Boston last spring. And Timothy had made no attempt to contact her himself in the interim until last
night. The implication had been plain enough. He
hadn't wanted to see her. So it seemed logical that
he would have sent Giles now.

But he hadn't done that. He had come to the airport himself.

These thoughts tumbled over one another inside
Anne's tormented mind. And her mind *was* tormented. She hadn't slept at all, she'd been unable to
eat, and though normally a good traveler, she'd felt
slightly sick on the plane during the short flight to
Boston.

Timothy asked abruptly, "Do you want a
drink?"

"No. No, thank you."

"Then we'll go straight out to Chestnut Hill. I
managed to latch onto a thirty-minute parking
place right outside."

He was walking a shade too fast for her, and
Anne had to make an effort to keep up with him. At
least this kept other thoughts from infiltrating. She
had to concentrate on what she was doing for fear
of falling down, her eyes not even straying in his direction.

She recognized the green Saab immediately and
felt herself being washed by memory. Cape Cod.
That glorious early April day when she and Tim had
driven to Wellfleet. The magnificent view of the
bay, the sand roads, the cottage on the bluff. . . .

An agonized voice deep within her cried, *"No!"*

and she heeded it. But some sound must have escaped through her tightly compressed lips for Timothy asked, anxiously, "What is it, Anne?"

"N-nothing."

"You gave a little cry, as if something hurt you."

Something did hurt me. Something hurt me very much. You hurt me. Anne said these things, but she said them silently. Aloud she only voiced the mono-syllable "no" once again, but this time it was not a small sliver of emotional agony.

He held the door for her and she got into the car. For a moment she was stunned, then she realized Tim was opening the trunk and stashing her suitcase in it. She heard the lid slam and saw him come around to slide in behind the wheel next to her.

He was much too close. The scent of his after-shave lotion drifted across her nostrils, and she winced. She couldn't handle being so close to him. She couldn't handle being with him at all.

"Anne," he said gently. "Anne, look at me."

Slowly she turned her head and felt as if she were being swallowed up by his green eyes. They were caressing her face with such a...hunger. Thinking this, she shook her head. It didn't make sense. Why was he looking at her this way, feasting his eyes on her, when....

"You look so tired, darling," he said.

Darling! Last night on the phone he had called her sweetheart. Yet they hadn't been in touch since April, and in the interim she'd seen him smiling down into someone else's eyes—Laura's! The memory was white hot like a hornet's sting.

She saw his jaw tighten. He slid the key in the ignition switcn, and she heard the motor purr. Sights, sounds, seemed heightened just now. Feelings. She didn't want to feel this much.

Timothy pulled away from the curb, and they circled out into the main line of traffic leaving the airport. He said slowly, "I'm very sorry, Anne. She was a terrific person. I found that out over the course of the summer, I guess you'd say. What I'm trying to tell you is that I. . . also loved her, Anne."

"How could you. . ." she began, then saw him swallow hard.

"How could I possibly have had any real rapport with someone like your Aunt Muriel?" he asked. His voice was soft as he spoke, too soft. Dangerously soft.

"I didn't mean that, Timothy. It's just that. . . ."

"You don't have to explain," he told her. "I get the meaning. That's one thing about the Irish, you know. We don't usually need to have things spelled out for us. Not things like this, anyway."

"Timothy, please," Anne said wearily. "I don't want to argue with you."

"I'm sorry," he repeated, then added with a clearly deliberate change of subject, "Bridget is at the house. So is her daughter, Katharine. Bridget suggested it might be a good idea to have Katharine stay with you, and I agreed. I hope you don't object."

Anne could not help but wonder why Tim had taken over as he evidently had. Was it normal procedure for one's lawyer to do this in times of tragedy? She couldn't remember her father's lawyer being around at all when she'd gone down to Florida for the funeral. Laura had been there, and a brother of Laura's. His name was Harold, and she remembered she hadn't especially liked him at their first encounter. Then she'd liked him even less when he'd tried to flirt with her.

"Your aunt wanted a memorial service at Trinity Church in Copley Square, because the Clarendons have been connected with that church for a very long time," Timothy said. "It has been arranged for tomorrow afternoon. She wanted the traditional Episcopal service read, no eulogy." He was staring straight ahead as he spoke, his profile hard and unyielding, his tone very formal. "I went ahead with the plans. I saw no reason to wait till you got here because I was sure that you would want to follow her wishes."

"Of course," Anne replied, equally formal.

"Bridget said there will probably be quite a number of people calling at the house after the service," he went on. "She asked if it would be all right for her to get a caterer to help with food and beverages, and I agreed. You don't object, do you?"

"No," Anne answered tersely, the tension within her mounting so dangerously she felt she would scream from its pressure. "No, of course not."

"I don't think there's very much else for the moment."

Anne got a firm grip on herself. "Thank you, Tim," she said, forcing the phrase out.

"Thank me? For what?"

"For t-taking care of these things," she told him, and was angry at herself for stammering.

"I'm here to help you in any way I possibly can, Anne," he said seriously. She caught a note of regret in his voice she didn't quite understand, but there was no doubting his sincerity.

She started to answer him, then realized they were on the edge of exchanging a whole series of platitudes. Instead, she took refuge in silence, only beginning to notice how much her head had begun to ache.

It was very difficult to enter the big old house. At the last moment Anne was overcome by the feeling that Muriel would be standing right inside the door, ready to greet her with an affectionate kiss. Only there was, of course, no Muriel. Muriel would never again be standing in the doorway. She would never again beckon her niece with the warm smile that had been all her own.

It was only now that a real sense of loss came to strike Anne, and it was impossible not to cry when Bridget emerged from the kitchen to enfold Anne in ample arms, her plump body raked with sobs of her own.

After a time Briget led her out to the kitchen and introduced her to Katharine. The girl had a wistful elfin beauty, with long lovely copper hair. She was too thin, though, too pale. Hadn't she ever been out in the sun this summer? Anne wondered. And her eyes, as green as Timothy's, were enormous. There was something very appealing about her, even though just now she looked terrified.

It was difficult to be thrust into the situation of staying with a stranger under circumstances like these, Anne conceded, and resolved that one of her first tasks would be to put Katharine at ease.

Bridget said, "Go along into the library, now, and have a drink."

Anne smiled faintly. "It isn't even noon," she pointed out.

"No matter," Bridget said staunchly. "There are times when a bit of the bottle does some good. And certainly this is one of them."

Timothy had already gone into the library, Anne guessed, but as she crossed the highly polished foyer floor she was surprised to hear another voice. A masculine voice.

She frowned. She was not in the mood for visitors yet, and she would have thought that Timothy might have realized this. Then, as she stepped across the threshold and saw the tall blond man standing next to Timothy, her mood changed.

"Giles!" she exclaimed. The name rang out joyously because she was very glad to see him. She needed someone likes Giles right now, someone who would stand as a buffer between Timothy and herself.

He turned, a smile lighting his blue eyes, and held out his arms. Without further thought Anne rushed across the room and went into them directly. Only at the last instant, when it was too late to draw back, did she glance at Timothy Flanagan—and was shocked by the expression on his face.

Never had she seen a man look so tortured, so hopeless and so hurt.

FOR THE REST of the week both Giles and Timothy were pillars of strength for Anne. She got through the memorial service in something of a daze, and afterward received a stream of callers that seemed never ending.

Bridget stayed late each evening and prepared dinner, and Giles and Timothy found time after work to be with her, too. Anne insisted Katharine join them at the table, which obviously pleased Bridget. She also insisted that Bridget leave the dishes to her, which took some convincing, and was glad that Katharine helped with the washing up once the men had left.

During the course of the week she didn't find herself alone with Timothy for even one second. It became obvious to her that he was keeping things this way, making very sure there was no chance for a dialogue.

Their personal conflict aside, Anne felt this was curious. She knew there were going to be many legal affairs to untangle in connection with both the holograph will and Muriel's estate. She imagined she would frequently be consulting with someone from the firm of Simon and Wechsler. Who would that someone be? Would Oscar Wechsler, who was getting around quite well again according to Giles, decide to handle the Clarendon family interests himself? Would Timothy? Or would matters be turned over to Giles?

Anne had taken an emergency leave of absence from the bank, and now she began to realize she was going to need time in which to put things together. There were so many things to be decided.

Her own future, for one, she thought rather dismally, as she went downstairs on Saturday morning after another poor night's sleep. If she didn't get some rest soon, she wouldn't be able to cope with any of this.

Bridget had come to work despite Anne's protests that it wasn't necessary, and she was baking muffins as Anne walked into the kitchen.

"Mr. Winslow phoned," she informed Anne breezily. "He's on his way out. He said he has a couple of things for you to sign."

"He always seems to have me signing something," Anne said morosely, sitting down at the kitchen table. She accepted the cup of coffee Bridget poured for her with a mumbled "Thanks," and stirred cream into it absently.

"Katharine went over to the house to get her music," Bridget said. "She has a singing lesson this afternoon."

"I've wanted to talk to you about Katharine," Anne allowed, glad to have the chance to get onto a different subject. "She's such a lovely girl, Bridget."

Bridget flushed with pleasure. "She's the apple of my eye, Katharine is," she said, unabashed. "But I have to admit I'm more than a little bit prejudiced where she's concerned."

"Is she still seeing Peter Dwyer?" Anne had heard nothing of Peter since her return, and it surprised her that he hadn't called to offer his condolences.

Bridget sobered. "Peter had a chance to get a job with a logging company up in Maine for the summer," she said. "He'll be down tomorrow, though, for a day or two. He and Katharine... well, I don't know what's going to happen. Ben was as stubborn as ever about Katharine going to secretarial school, so finally she registered. She's supposed to start classes the middle of the month. But I get the feeling when the day comes she may just not show up."

"Is she still thinking about going into the convent?"

"Yes," Bridget nodded. "And I even got her to have a talk with our parish priest about it. He's a sensible man and he knows as well as I do that she doesn't have the vocation. It would be wrong for her to enter the convent. He came right out and told her so."

"How did Katharine respond to that?"

"She went into her shell, that's all," Bridget reported. "She wouldn't say much about it. When Katharine doesn't want to talk about something, she doesn't want to talk about it, period! I...I was hoping that maybe with you...."

Anne smiled rather sadly. "Don't expect miracles, Bridget," she cautioned. "When it comes to affairs of the heart, I'm no expert. And when it comes to Katharine I think that both

Peter and singing could be called affairs of the heart.''

"Anne. . ." Bridget began with an air of determination that caused Anne to look up swiftly.

"Yes?"

"I've been wanting to tell you that your Timothy Flanagan—"

"He is not 'my' Timothy Flanagan, Bridget!" Anne blurted involuntarily.

"Well. . .whatever," Bridget said, taking the muffins out of the oven. "What I want to tell you is how kind he was to your aunt this past summer. He'd come out in the evening sometimes and take her for a drive. Other times he'd take her out in the country to an old inn for dinner. She loved things like that, you know. She became very fond of him, your Aunt Muriel did.''

"That's nice," Anne said stiffly.

"She told Mr. Flanagan there was no need for him to do those things, but it had nothing to do with their business affairs," Bridget went on. "She said he was a fine young man, a very unusual young man in this day and age. She hoped the two of you had taken a liking to each other.''

The old-fashioned phrase made Anne want to burst into hysterical laughter. The quicksilver emotion she'd felt for Timothy far transcended "taking a liking" to him. She'd been catapulted into an emotional caldron so tumultuous she'd nearly drowned in it!

In fact, I did drown in it, Anne thought. And the ache that suddenly possessed her now was so bittersweet that her lips twisted and her eyes filled with tears.

Appalled, Bridget said hastily, "Anne, I didn't mean to pry."

"It's all right, Bridget," she managed thickly. But it wasn't, and she was too heartsick to rally quickly.

"No, it isn't," Bridget insisted. "Anne, dear, I know it's none of my business, but...well, you're like family to me. You and your aunt...." Bridget was in danger, Anne saw, of dissolving into tears herself, and had to pause for a minute. Then she went on, "I've seen the way he looks at you, with his heart in his eyes. Like he thinks you're the most beautiful, the most wonderful thing on earth, and way beyond."

Anne shook her head. "You're misreading him, Bridget," she said.

"If I didn't know that you always scoff at such things I'd suggest we turn out some tea leaves," Bridget told her. "I'd be willing to wager I'd find him right there in your cup!"

Anne smiled. "Because you'd put him there, Bridget," she countered, trying to inject a light touch into their conversation.

The sound of the doorbell was a reprieve.

"That must be Giles," she said quickly, and started toward the hall before Bridget could get ahead of her.

I've seen the way he looks at you, with his heart in his eyes. Bridget's words echoed as Anne pulled the heavy front door open.

Then her own heart leapt, not into her eyes but into her mouth. For it wasn't Giles Winslow who was standing on the threshold looking down at her. It was Timothy.

CHAPTER TEN

TIME STOPPED. Anne stood statue still. It would have been impossible for her to move an inch just then. Outwardly she was composed, her lovely face revealing nothing at all of the emotions that were surging inside her with tidal-wave strength. Only her eyes were a giveaway. They devoured Timothy, taking in every line of his beloved face. And they did not like what they saw.

He looked tired and strained, his tension manifest in the tautness of his jaw. Fatigue's dark shadows had brushed his eyes, and his lips were compressed in a tight line. For a moment he was as unable to speak as she was.

Then he said abruptly, his voice sounding unnaturally gruff, "Hello, Anne." Before she could respond to this greeting, he added, "Giles sends apologies. He made the mistake of leaving the papers he wanted you to sign at the office, so he had to stop by for them this morning. He immediately got waylaid by a desperate client who'd driven in from Worcester on urgent business. He said to tell you he'll call you as soon as he's free. In the meantime...."

Anne realized she was blocking the doorway, and

she stood back. But Tim hesitated and did not immediately cross the threshold.

"Giles knew I was coming out this way so he asked me to bring the papers along for your signature," he said lamely.

So he had not come to see her of his own volition.

A sliver of sharp pain needled Anne at this. Stiffening, she had to force herself to remember her manners.

"Come in, won't you?" she invited.

"This shouldn't take a minute," Timothy promised, equally stiff.

Anne wanted to shake him. Why was he behaving like this? After all, they were adults, she reminded herself. They should be able to meet and conduct business without becoming embroiled in the past.

But Timothy wasn't acting like an adult in the least. Anne felt sure his self-control was straining at its seams. As she started across the foyer toward the living room, she tried to put a few mental pieces together. She tried to reach a conclusion as to when it had become like this between them, when being with him had become so impossible.

Looking across the living room gave her the answer. In an instant of revelation, she had a flashback of the day she'd come back to the house, the day after Muriel had died. Giles had been waiting in the library, and she had flown into his outstretched arms. Those arms had represented sanctuary to her at the time, a release from the tension that had been mounting during the drive from the airport with Tim.

Giles had been a sanctuary of sorts ever since. He was easy to be with, he made no demands. He and she came from similar backgrounds.

Similar backgrounds. Anne put a period to her thoughts and turned to face the tall copper-haired man who was looking down at her gravely.

"Tim. . ." she began, not certain of what she was going to say to him, yet knowing she must say something if they were to get back to any semblance of rapport. But Bridget Kincaid's voice interrupted her.

"Ah, Mr. Flanagan," she said, a distinctly Irish lilt to her tone, "I thought it was you I heard."

Bridget was standing in the doorway looking plumper than ever in a vivid pink cotton dress, her voluminous flowered apron tied tightly around her ample waist. She was beaming. One didn't have to be particularly astute, Anne thought, to know that Bridget was overjoyed at the sight of Timothy Flanagan.

"Bridget!" he exclaimed, a note of relief to his voice. It was as if he'd suddenly been reprieved, Anne decided ironically.

"I've just made a fresh pot of coffee and some cranberry muffins," Bridget confided. "I'll fetch them for you in a wink."

Anne bit her lip, and glancing at Timothy knew that he'd noted this gesture, as he noted most things.

"I'm sorry," he said. "I didn't intend to linger, believe me." There was nothing apologetic in his tone. It was a statement of fact. He was making it

Say Hello to Yesterday
Holly Weston had done it all alone.

She had raised her small son and worked her way up to features writer for a major newspaper. Still the bitterness of the the past seven years lingered.

She had been very young when she married Nick Falconer—but old enough to lose her heart completely when he left. Despite her success in her new life, her old one haunted her.

But it was over and done with—until an assignment in Greece brought her face to face with Nick, and all she was trying to forget. . . .

Time of the Temptress
The game must be played his way!

Rebellion against a cushioned, controlled life had landed Eve Tarrant in Africa. Now only the tough mercenary Wade O'Mara stood between her and possible death in the wild, revolution-torn jungle.

But the real danger was Wade himself—he had made Eve aware of herself as a woman.

"I saved your neck, so you feel you owe me something," Wade said. "But you don't owe me a thing, Eve. Get away from me." She knew she could make him lose his head if she tried. But that wouldn't solve anything. . . .

Your Romantic Adventure Starts Here.

Born Out of Love
It had to be coincidence!

Charlotte stared at the man through a mist of confusion. It was Logan. An older Logan, of course, but unmistakably the man who had ravaged her emotions and then abandoned her all those years ago.

She ought to feel angry. She ought to feel resentful and cheated. Instead, she was apprehensive—terrified at the complications he could create.

"We are not through, Charlotte," he told her flatly. "I sometimes think we haven't even begun."

Man's World
Kate was finished with love for good.

Kate's new boss, features editor Eliot Holman, might have devastating charms—but Kate couldn't care less, even if it was obvious that he was interested in her.

Everyone, including Eliot, thought Kate was grieving over the loss of her husband, Toby. She kept it a carefully guarded secret just how cruelly Toby had treated her and how terrified she was of trusting men again.

But Eliot refused to leave her alone, which only served to infuriate her. He was no different from any other man. . . or was he?

These FOUR free Harlequin Presents novels allow you to enter the world of romance, love and desire. As a member of the Harlequin Home Subscription Plan, you can continue to experience all the moods of love. You'll be inspired by moments so real...so moving...you won't want them to end. So start your own Harlequin Presents adventure by returning the reply card below. <u>DO IT TODAY!</u>

clear that he didn't want to be there any more than she wanted to have him there.

But I do want him here! Anne admitted. *I've wanted him here all along!* The situation was totally frustrating to her, and she tossed her head impatiently.

"What is it, Anne?" Timothy asked quickly.

She didn't hedge. "I...I'd like to know what's happened," she asked him directly.

He didn't pretend to misunderstand her. He said slowly, "A variety of things, I suppose."

Suddenly Anne experienced another flashback. This time she was seeing Timothy coming out of the French restaurant in New York with Laura at his side. She felt something inside her go cold, as if her emotions had been plunged into a deep freeze.

There could be a perfectly logical explanation for his having been with Laura, she knew this. Their dinner engagement could have been a business one, in connection with the will situation.

All she had to do to find out, Anne told herself, was to ask Timothy. And now she wished she'd done exactly that, long ago. The passage of time had made the posing of such a question unbelievably difficult. Was this because she was afraid to hear his answer?

He'd walked over to the big picture window and was staring across the lawn toward the street. "A couple of the maples are beginning to change color," he said absently. "Have you ever gone up into the mountains in New England at foliage time, Anne?"

Was that an invitation, she wondered, and at once was sure it wasn't. She shook her head, dumbfounded at the change of subject. "No," she said levelly, "I haven't."

"It can be beautiful beyond belief," Timothy told her softly. "Many things are beautiful beyond belief. Intangible things. Things we reach out for... only to find they're beyond our grasp."

What is he trying to tell me? Anne asked herself wildly.

She came as close to asking him this as she dared. "Have you reached out for a beautiful intangible lately, Tim, only to find it beyond your grasp?" she queried, her tone a bit more taunting than she intended.

Timothy turned his back to the window, his face shadowed so she couldn't see his features clearly. "Don't tease, Anne. It doesn't become you."

His bluntness took her by surprise. "I w-wasn't trying to tease..." she began, but broke off because this wasn't entirely true.

He walked away from her and over to the polished grand piano that dominated the far corner of the room. Touching the dark wood gently he said unexpectedly, "I miss your aunt."

Tears Anne couldn't suppress came to sting her eyes. "I miss her, too," she whispered.

"Before she died..." he began, and once again they were interrupted by Bridget, who bustled across the room to set a large tray down on the coffee table in front of the long, brocade-upholstered couch.

"Shall I pour the coffee, Anne?" she asked. "Or would you like to do the honors?"

"I'll serve the coffee, thank you, Bridget," Anne said.

The tray was set with their finest silver and china, a basket full of hot muffins, butter and two types of jam. All the trimmings, Anne thought wryly, for an intimate little tête-à-tête.

Bridget was irrepressible. She turned at the door to say, "Enjoy it, you two!" then flounced back to the kitchen.

Anne fixed Timothy's coffee without asking him how he liked it. She remembered only too well that he took both cream and a liberal helping of sugar. As she handed the delicate china cup and saucer to him she saw a reddish eyebrow quirk upward, and thought ruefully that she might as well have come right out and told him she hadn't forgotten his likes—or his dislikes. In fact, she hadn't forgotten anything about him. As it was, she read an added significance into the way he said, "Thanks."

He sat down at the far end of the couch, leaving a considerable gap between them, for which Anne was thankful. She needed every inch of this separation at the moment. Being alone with Timothy Flanagan was once again proving to be much too heady an experience.

"As I was telling you, Anne...I miss your Aunt Muriel. I saw her quite often over the summer."

"So I understand."

"She told you?"

"She wrote about you," Anne admitted. "And

she usually mentioned you when we spoke on the phone. But it was Bridget who told me you'd been visiting. I want you to know I appreciate it, Tim. I'm grateful for everything you did for her. She... she thought a lot of you."

It was more of a speech than Anne had intended to make, yet she meant every word she'd said. It was true that her aunt had thought a great deal of Tim. Muriel's regard for him had grown over the summer. Anne knew this and felt an odd pang of loneliness because she hadn't been a part of any of this herself.

His tone rough again, Tim said, "I wasn't doing your aunt any favors, Anne. So don't sound as if you think I was!"

"I didn't mean to imply that you were," she countered swiftly.

"The shoe was very much on the other foot," Timothy continued, ignoring her remark. "She was... quite a lady."

Anne shifted uncomfortably. She thoroughly agreed that her Aunt Muriel had been a wonderful person, but she wasn't up to this kind of eulogizing, especially from Tim. She still felt shaky when it came to talking very much about Muriel. Now and then she was still experiencing small guilt trips of her own, because she couldn't help but feel that she could have come back to Boston over the summer and visited Muriel herself. She'd known her aunt had a bad heart, though she hadn't realized just how serious the condition had been. Even so....

Breaking in on her thoughts, Timothy said reflectively, "She told me, once, why she had never married."

Anne sat up straight. That was something she'd always wondered about. It had never been discussed within the family, and she'd never had the courage to ask Muriel herself.

"She wouldn't mind my telling you," Tim said.

"Are you sure?"

"Yes, Anne, I'm sure." He paused, then began, "Did you know that she studied piano when she was a young woman?"

"No," Anne said slowly, "I didn't know."

"She was quite a pianist," he nodded. "She played for me a couple of times."

"She played for you?" Anne interrupted, incredulous.

"She told me her fingers had stiffened up and she insisted she was no good, but I thought she was wonderful," Tim said simply. "I can see where you get your musical talent from."

"Timothy..."

"Don't worry, Anne. I'm not about to get onto the subject of your singing. Your aunt, though... well, it was when she was studying piano that she met the man she fell in love with—the brother of a fellow student, a girl named Rose. Does that name mean anything to you?"

She shook her head. "No, Aunt Muriel never mentioned anyone named Rose to me."

"Well, Rose invited her to dinner one night," Timothy went on. "And the brother was there at the house. I guess he and Muriel took one look at each other...." He glanced across at Anne, his green eyes clear and direct. "Sometimes it happens like that...or so I've been told."

Anne swallowed hard, glad that she was unable to answer him.

"Muriel's father—your grandfather—was quite a martinet," Tim said. "A very proper Bostonian and, as such, a stickler for family background. Rose's family was half Italian, half Irish. Her Irish ancestors had come to the States in the late 1840s during the Great Potato Famine. That was a terrible time in Ireland, as you may know. The potato was the main food staple, and when the entire national crop was destroyed by a blight, about a quarter of the population either starved to death or emigrated."

"Is that when your family came to the United States, Tim?" Anne ventured.

His eyes narrowed suspiciously, but at least the veil didn't descend. "No," he said, then went on, "In any event, Rose's family had been around for a while. But they were the wrong side of the track as far as your grandfather was concerned, so your aunt began to meet Rose's brother in secret."

"Aunt Muriel?" After all, Muriel had been a proper Bostonian, too.

"Love does strange things to people, Anne," Tim replied obliquely. "Anyway, the war came. World War II, that is. Rose's brother was in college in the army reserve, and he was one of the first to be called up. Before either he or Muriel knew what was happening he'd been sent to Georgia for training.

They both knew that the next step would be overseas, so one day Muriel told her father she was going to Washington to visit a friend with whom she'd gone to school.

"She didn't stay in Washington for long, needless to say. She took a train to Atlanta, and Rose's brother met her there. They had one weekend, one glorious weekend, and they wanted to get married, but they ran out of time. He'd only been able to get a weekend pass. Muriel stayed on in Atlanta, hoping he could obtain a couple of days more leave before he was sent overseas. Meanwhile, she got the marriage license."

"Aunt Muriel?" Anne asked again.

"Yes, your aunt," Tim said patiently. "Rose's brother never got back to Atlanta, though. His unit was shipped out in the middle of the night. As it happened, a friend of his had come down with appendicitis and was left behind. This fellow managed to call your aunt, and that was the only word she had that her lover had left."

Anne shivered, both disturbed and enraptured by this story. "W··· happened when he came back?"

Tim looked her s··· ···ight in the eyes and said, "He didn't come back, Anne. He was killed in France."

Tears swelled and she stammered, "How absolutely a-awful!"

"Yes, it must have been terrible for Muriel," he agreed. "It was Rose who told her, but even though your aunt's heart had been broken, she kept the news from your grandfather. Which goes to prove, I suppose, that blood ties are stronger than... anything."

Anne wanted to say something to this, but she couldn't, and after a moment Tim said, "Muriel told me there was never anyone else for her. It was as simple as that. But she also subscribed to that old theory about it being better to love and lose than never to love at all."

"Do you subscribe to that theory, Timothy?"

He set his coffee cup on the table and folded his hands. Glancing down at his intertwined fingers he said slowly, "I don't know."

Anne persisted. "Have you loved . . . and lost?"

He looked across at her. "Haven't we all?" he asked.

"Can't you just once answer a question without evading it?" she cried. "What is it with you, Tim?"

"What is what with me?" he countered.

His response infuriated Anne. "You're in danger of becoming a h-hermit!" she sputtered.

The hint of a smile twisted his lips. "Me?" he asked. "I can't see myself as a hermit, Anne."

"Maybe you can't, but I can," she insisted stubbornly. "Oh, I don't doubt you'll go on looking after your kids—"

"*What?*" he demanded, sitting up abruptly.

"Giles told me about the boys you help."

"Did he, now?" Timothy drawled in brogue, a dangerous glint in his eyes.

"Don't hold it against Giles!" she said hastily. "I . . . I was asking him about y-you, that's all," she finished, privately condemning the annoying stammer that kept tripping her tongue just when she needed it the least.

"Why were you asking Giles about me?" The glint looked threatening now.

"It wasn't an inquisition, if that's what you think! It merely...seemed to happen!" she said defiantly.

"Then why are you so defensive about it?"

"I am not d-defensive about it, dammit!" she sparked.

He paused, observing her. "You're gorgeous when you're angry," he said then, his voice disconcertingly calm, almost impersonal. "It might be fun to make you furious, just to see how impossibly beautiful you'd become."

"Timothy!"

"Ah, you see, I'm drawing fire. And I must admit I'm enjoying it, *mavourneen*."

The brogue was a cover, and Anne glared at him.

"Stop hiding!" she told him.

"Hiding? Me? What makes you think I'd be about to hide?" he asked, the brogue thicker.

Anne threw caution to the wind. "You've got two ways of retreating," she informed him dryly. "When things are not too serious, you become a professional Irishman, complete with the brogue and the blarney. But when they become really difficult, you set up this invisible shield. I call it your veil."

"My veil?" There was no doubting his astonishment.

"Yes, your veil! You used it coming back from Cape Cod, you used it..." she shrugged. "You use it all the time," she said, and could not help but feel a stab of triumph at his reaction. She had shaken him this time.

He recouped quickly, though, and said, "I think we all have protective devices, Anne. Especially when we feel the need to guard our...privacy. Call mine a veil, if you like. You stammer."

She gasped. "That's hardly a protective device! It's s-something I've been trying to overcome all my life. And I thought I'd s-succeeded...until I met you."

His eyebrows arched involuntarily, but he only said, his tone deceptively mild, "I didn't realize I had such an effect on you."

"You know perfectly well the effect you have on me!" Anne exploded, and then was horrified at herself. But she was unprepared for Timothy's.

"Perhaps I do know," he conceded quietly. "Perhaps it's the same effect you have on me. That's why I've stayed away from you as I have, Anne. Though it's taken every ounce of willpower and strength I possess."

Anne stared at him. Timothy was deadly serious. There was no levity now. No trace of the elusive giant leprechaun.

She asked carefully, "Did you really think it was necessary to stay away from me?"

He nodded, his face a study in unhappiness. "After that day on the Cape, I knew I had to put a stop to things between us. Things were getting far too heavy, and...I didn't want to hurt you."

"What makes you think you would have hurt me?"

"There is no doubt in my mind but that I would have," he said simply.

She stared at him. "Are you trying to tell me that you're a phil...philanderer?" she asked him. "Are you telling me you're unable to stay with one woman?"

Tim shook his head. "No, that is not what I am saying at all."

"Then what *are* you saying, Timothy?" she pleaded.

He didn't answer at once. He was staring down at his hands again, nervously entwining his fingers. Anne sensed that he wanted to reach out to her as much as she wanted him to, and that he literally was holding onto himself in order to prevent himself from doing so.

She moved toward him, not even realizing what she was doing. It was involuntary as the need to touch him became overwhelming, and she was startled when he recoiled, drawing even further away from her.

"Please, Anne," he said, his voice thick. "Don't make it more difficult for us than it is already."

She shook her head, puzzled. "I...I just don't understand you, Tim. When you were talking about Aunt Muriel and the man she loved, you said that...well, you said they took one look at each other and...."

"Yes?"

"You said...sometimes it h-happens like that."

"Yes," he agreed, looking away from her. "I'm sure that sometimes it does."

"Tim, you're making this very difficult for me," Anne confessed, clutching her own hands together as if trying to grasp the courage that was threatening to desert her. "I had the feeling, when you were telling me about Aunt Muriel and this man, that you saw a counterpart in...in us."

"Perhaps I did, Anne."

"Then why...."

"Why don't I take you in my arms and make love to you right now, when that's obviously what we both want so desperately?" he asked. "Perhaps it's because I think too much of you, rather than too little."

Timothy turned back and looked at her, his torment so tangible she was stunned by it.

"I'm not free to love you, Anne," he told her. "It's as simple as that."

The stillness that came between them was a vast and empty thing. Somewhere beyond it, Anne could hear a telephone ringing. She groaned inwardly, hoping that Bridget would take the call and that she would not be summoned.

But that wasn't to happen. Bridget came to the doorway and said cheerfully, "It's Mr. Winslow on the phone for you, Anne."

She couldn't look at Timothy. She stood slowly, feeling that she should test her legs before she walked on them, lest she might collapse.

"Excuse me," she managed, and made her way out to the kitchen as if she were walking in a trance.

Bridget said, "You could have taken it in the library, Anne. It would have been closer."

"That's all right," she nodded. Picking up the phone, she spoke into the receiver, wincing when she heard Giles's voice. He sounded so normal, so happy.

"I suppose Tim explained I got caught in a bind?" he asked cheerfully.

"Yes, he did."

"That's what comes of going into the office on a Saturday morning," Giles said with a laugh. "Tim got the papers out to you, though, didn't he?"

"Yes. I have them."

"He said he'd take care of getting them in the mail so they'll be delivered Monday," Giles went on. "Look, it's a magnificent day. I thought we might take a run up into New Hampshire and find ourselves a quaint country inn where we could have dinner."

Anne rallied. "I'd love it another time, Giles," she said sincerely. "But not today."

"Hey, you told me you were free this whole weekend!" he protested lightly.

"I still am," she admitted.

"Then why...."

"Please, Giles. Don't ask me to explain. Just believe me—I wouldn't be very good company."

"You'd always be good company, beautiful. And you don't have to talk if you don't want to. I'll carry on a conversation for both of us!"

"Giles, please...."

His tone changed. "Is Tim still there?" he asked her.

There was no point in fibbing. "Yes, he is," Anne said.

"I see."

"Please, Giles, don't go icy on me," Anne said, then forced a laugh. "You don't see anything at all! Tim was just telling me about some of the times he spent with Aunt Muriel over the summer. He was very kind to her and I appreciate it."

"Don't let your appreciation run away with you!" Giles warned. But there was a light note in his voice again as he said, "All right, Anne. I'll call you tomorrow and we'll plan an outing. Assuming, of course, it doesn't rain!"

"I can't go anywhere with you tomorrow, either." Anne's eyes fell on Bridget as she said this, and she snatched at an excuse. "Bridget asked me over for Sunday dinner with her family," she told him, and nearly chuckled aloud at the expression that came over Bridget's face when she heard this.

"Then I'll call you tomorrow night and we'll make plans for next week," Giles insisted firmly.

With this they rang off. Hanging up the receiver, Anne met Bridget's large pale blue eyes. "I had to say something," she said helplessly.

"Indeed you did!" Bridget retorted, smiling. "And you also accepted an invitation I've been wanting to offer for a long time."

"I wouldn't think of imposing."

"Imposing, is it?" Bridget scoffed. "It's high time you met Ben. And Peter Dwyer will be coming, too. We'll have a time of it. As a matter-of-fact, how about going to mass with me?"

"Me?" Anne echoed.

"Katharine is singing a solo, and if you were in

the congregation... well, I'd like you to hear her.''

"I've been wanting to ask her to sing for me,'' Anne said ruefully. "But I...I just haven't been completely myself lately, Bridget.''

"I know that, dear. You've had a lot on your plate, too much to handle all at once.'' Bridget's look was sharp as she said this, and Anne knew she wasn't speaking only of her Aunt Muriel's death and the complications involved with her father's will.

Her father's will! Anne stood rooted to the spot, a sick feeling seeping over her. She was having another flashback. Once again she was seeing Tim with Laura in New York, and suddenly Laura loomed larger than life.

"What is it, darlin'?'' Bridget asked.

"Nothing,'' Anne hedged. "Just...a f-funny feeling.''

"I hope you're not coming down with something,'' Bridget murmured solicitously. "You've been a bit off your feed, though it's not to wonder.''

"I'm all right,'' Anne said quickly. But as she made her way back to the living room she felt anything but all right, and shrank from the thought of facing Timothy again.

Had her initial reaction been more valid than she'd since thought? Was Laura Clarendon the reason he'd told her he was not free to love her?

CHAPTER ELEVEN

TIM STOOD UP and glanced pointedly at his wristwatch as Anne came into the living room.

"I'm sorry," he said, "but I have to get a move on. I have a luncheon engagement, and I want to put these papers in the mail first. So, if you'll sign where I indicate...."

He'd already spread the papers out on the coffee table, and resuming her place on the couch, Anne followed his instructions. When she'd signed her name for the last time, Timothy reached down, scooped the papers up, then inserted them into a rather worn leather briefcase.

He smiled slightly, but there was a reproving note in his voice as he said, "You really shouldn't sign things without reading them first, Anne."

She looked up at him quickly. "Can't I trust you, Timothy?" she asked directly. But she wasn't thinking of the papers. She was thinking of Laura.

She saw his mouth tighten, his firm full lips narrowing to a compressed line. *Have I touched a vital spot?* she wondered. *Have I hit Timothy Flanagan where it hurts?*

If so—if it really was Laura who was coming between them—then he deserved the wound. There would be more than a personal matter involved. His professional ethics would be at stake.

"I would like to think you could always trust me," he said slowly.

It was, in its way, an evasive answer. It was not what Anne wanted to hear from him. She needed affirmation, the definite assurance that she could trust him now—and forever.

She said, equally unconvincing, "I hope so."

He caught the desolate note in her voice. "What is it, Anne?"

Again she wanted to come right out and ask him about Laura. She wanted to ask him about that night in New York. But before she could form the necessary words he glanced at his wristwatch again, and the spell—for that's what it had been, she decided bitterly—was broken.

They walked toward the front entrance like two strangers, Timothy a step behind her. He was so near, she thought, yet so far away. But his presence became entirely tangible when she caught the elusive scent of his after-shave.

She wondered what would happen if she suddenly turned and threw her arms around him and pressed her mouth to his. Could he rebuff her embrace and her kiss, or would this closeness have the effect on him she was certain it would have on her? Would their problems dissolve and everything else cease to matter—if only for a short interval?

Anne had too much pride, though, to throw herself at any man—even Timothy Flanagan. Certain basics had been instilled in her long ago, she realized now. They'd become a part of her, without her ever really knowing it. She'd been taught, for one thing, that it was up to the man to make the next move in an emotional situation. And this was an intensely emotional situation, even though she and Timothy were both behaving as if they were carved wooden figures.

"I'll take care of everything," he said lamely, opening the front door himself as Anne stepped aside.

"Everything?" She couldn't resist the query.

"The papers," he supplemented. Then, already across the threshold, he turned, and Anne felt as if she'd been enmeshed in a blaze of emerald fire.

"I'll call you," he said, surprising her, and before she could answer he'd started across the lawn toward his car.

Anne went back into the house, closing the door behind her thoughtfully. That last promise, she felt strongly, had been wrung out of Timothy. She was sure he hadn't intended to make it.

IT WAS A DULL SATURDAY, a lonely Saturday. Katharine Kincaid came back to the house after her voice lesson, and she and Anne ate the supper Bridget had prepared for them. Then they played a game of Scrabble, after which Anne announced that she was tired and thought she'd go up to bed.

Katharine had not mentioned the fact she was singing a solo in church the next morning. But then she had said very little to Anne about her singing thus far. Nor had Anne mentioned that she would be at the mass, listening.

Sunday morning Anne waited outside the church at the spot where she and Bridget had agreed to meet. Bridget appeared right on time dressed in her Sunday best—a brown suit that was too tight for her and totally out of fashion. Anne was wearing a heather-toned suit.

They walked into the church together. Starting down the aisle, Anne felt a mystery in the flickering candles on the altar and the provocative scent of incense in the air.

It was not the first time she'd been to a Catholic mass, and she welcomed the experience. She was naturally inquisitive about everything, but beyond that she was a receptive person and respected religions other than her own.

It occurred to her that this must also be Timothy's religion. She couldn't help but wonder if at this very moment he was attending mass somewhere else in the city.

The time came for the choir to sing, and then for the solo. As Katharine's voice rose, incredibly pure and clear, her tones exquisite, Anne sat transfixed. Katharine sang beautifully. Her voice was almost flawless.

Then the solo came to an end, and stealing a glance at Bridget, Anne saw tears glistening on the woman's plump cheeks. She didn't wonder that Bridget had been so moved. She'd been equally moved herself. Listening to Katharine sing had put her entirely on Bridget's side. Somehow a way had to be found so that Ben Kincaid could be mollified and Katharine could make the most of her God-given talent.

Anne winced at the phrase. Twice now she'd been accused of giving up her own God-given talent. Once by Ken Phillips, years ago. And much more recently by Timothy.

As she left the church with Bridget, the September sun dazzling her misty eyes with its golden intensity, she could begin to understand why both these men had reacted so strongly to her abandoning singing.

Talent *was* a God-given thing. It shouldn't be wasted.

BEN KINCAID was a big, bluff, likable Irishman. It was impossible not to respond positively to him.

That incredible Irish charisma, Anne thought wryly, and had a vision of a tall redhaired man who possessed more than his own share of the same.

Peter Dwyer was already at the Kincaids' house when she and Bridget arrived. He and Ben were having a glass of beer and outwardly, at least, they seemed to get on very well together.

Over a dinner of ham, cabbage and a wonderful potato dish called colcannon—which was about as Irish as you could get, Bridget said proudly—the conversation centered around Peter's work at the lumber company in Maine, soon to come to an end.

"I wanted to get down here before every space in town was gone," Peter confessed, placing a second helping of ham onto his plate while Bridget smiled approvingly. "As it is, I'm late. Boston's such a college town," he explained to Anne, "that even the worst apartments in Brighton are easy to rent. I should have tried to find a place a lot earlier, but I couldn't take time off." He shrugged. "I'll get something, though. Then back to Maine for a couple of weeks, and after that...school."

"Full time this year, eh, Peter?" Ben Kincaid asked.

"That's right, Mr. Kincaid," Peter said, nodding. "I finally saved up enough for my last big effort. I just hope the degree's going to be the passport people tell me it is."

"You don't need any passport, Peter!" Bridget scoffed. "You've got the looks and the brains and the will...and that's what it takes!"

Ben shook his head. "That's what it used to take, Bridget," he contradicted. "Now you got to have a college diploma, too."

In another minute, he'd be getting onto the subject of Katharine starting at secretarial school, Anne thought dismally. She decided to venture where angels feared to tread.

"Katharine," she said, "I've never heard anything more glorious than your voice this morning. Will you be going on to study at a conservatory?"

Bridget nearly choked on a morsel of her soda bread, but Anne went on serenely, "I wish you'd been with us, Mr. Kincaid."

Ben grinned. "Sure, and the church might have fallen down if I'd had the nerve to go to mass," he confessed.

"Dad!" Katharine protested, but Ben only laughed.

"Well," he said, "I may not be that much of a

sinner. But on the other hand, I wouldn't want to take any chances. It costs a lot to rebuild a church these days!''

Everyone laughed, and Anne said jokingly, ''Perhaps the next time Katharine sings the architecture will be sturdy enough to withstand your presence in the congregation!''

Ben looked directly across at her. His eyes were hazel rather than true green, but there was a shrewdness to his expression that reminded her of Tim. And, she suspected, he was probably very much aware of what she was getting at.

When he spoke, though, his words were mild. ''You sound like quite the music lover, Miss Clarendon,'' he commented.

''Anne, please,'' she said.

''A pretty name, Anne,'' he mused, and added unexpectedly, ''My mother's name was Anne.''

He took a healthy quaff of beer and, watching him, Anne felt a prickle of tension. She wondered what she was about to stumble into. Ben Kincaid would be a hard man to brook.

But he only asked, ''Do you play an instrument yourself, Anne?''

''The piano, a little,'' she allowed, and then volunteered something she'd never volunteered before. ''Actually,'' she said slowly, ''singing was my forte.''

She saw Katharine's astonished look and was afraid to even glance toward Bridget.

''What happened?'' Ben demanded gruffly. ''Lose your voice?''

"No, I...I g-gave up," Anne told him, cursing the stammer for reasserting itself just now.

"How come?" he pressed.

"I decided to go for a business career, where I'd be sure of making a steady income," she answered, and instantly felt mortified at her response.

Ben Kincaid leaned back, a wide grin creasing his broad ruddy-cheeked face. "Wise girl," he said, clearly pleased with himself.

But Anne shook her head. "No," she said. "I wasn't w-wise at all."

"What do you mean by that?" he asked almost rudely, the grin quickly replaced by a frown. "Bridget tells me you're a banker in New York."

"So I am," Anne nodded. "I have an excellent job and a fascinating career. But...."

"But what?"

It was a moment of truth. It was something she'd never confessed to anyone, and Anne swallowed hard, realizing this. "I know now," she said, her voice very low, "that I should never have given up singing. I had a talent for it, just as Katharine does...although in all honesty I think hers is greater. Nevertheless, if I had studied at a conservatory, if I had worked very hard, I would have had a good chance for success."

She faced Ben Kincaid. "I've tried to pretend that I did the right thing," she said. "But I've been lying to myself. Actually, Mr. Kincaid, I've missed singing...every day of my life."

Silence echoed in the room. Ben Kincaid's disapproval was so acute that Anne could feel its force even though he didn't say a word. Bridget rose and said hastily, "Sit right where you are while I clear the table. I've made a real Irish trifle for dessert, Anne."

Anne was sure that she couldn't possibly eat another thing without choking. She got to her own feet and said, "I'll help you, Bridget."

"Me, too!" Katharine put in quickly.

Ben chuckled, but there was a grim edge to his tone when he spoke. "Well, lad," he observed to Peter, "it seems like they're leaving us men to ourselves!"

Out in the kitchen Anne put an empty vegetable dish down on a side counter and then leaned against the nearest wall feeling as if she were about to collapse.

"Whew!" she said. Then, glancing across at Bridget, she added, "Bridget, I'm sorry! I'm afraid I blew it."

"Maybe yes, maybe no," Bridget said mysteriously. "We'll just have to wait and see."

Nothing more was said about Katharine's singing. Dinner finished, Ben Kincaid settled down in front of the TV to watch a football game. Bridget went and got her knitting bag, saying that she'd work on the afghan she was making and keep her husband company. This left Katharine, Peter and Anne to do as they pleased.

Almost at once Anne felt like an extra cog in the wheel. When Katharine and Peter suggested she might like to take in a movie with them, she declined.

The Kincaids lived on the edge of Dorchester, as close to South Boston as Anne had been since that Sunday before Saint Patrick's Day. She had driven over to the church in her car, which she'd left in the garage at the Chestnut Hill house all summer.

She also had a map of Boston, and after driving only a few blocks from the Kincaid house she pulled over to the curb, took it out of the glove compartment and studied it. Then, with the street-maze picture fixed in her mind, she started out again.

There were steep hills around this area sloping down to Dorchester Bay, which looked very blue today. In the distance, to the left, planes were taking off from Logan International Airport, trailing vapor streams as they ascended over the city. Anne worked her way to Dorchester Avenue, found Andrew Square, and crossed diagonally onto Dorchester Street. Finally she was on East Broadway, and her pulse began to thump.

This is a ridiculous errand, she told herself. *What can I hope to accomplish by it—except to recall a lot of painful memories?*

Nevertheless she kept on driving, slowing only when she neared the Harp and Shamrock Pub.

The scene was very different from what it had been on that festive afternoon last March. Southie seemed like a relatively quiet residential neighborhood, although there were still very few parking places to be found along the curb. Anne spied one, though, and that did it. She slid into it as if she were being driven by a force outside herself. But once she'd turned off the engine, she lingered a long time behind the wheel before getting out.

She really had no business going into a place like the Harp and Shamrock. If the room were loaded with customers and they started giving her problems, she would have only herself to blame. But the thought didn't stop her.

She hesitated inside the swinging doors and gave her eyes time to adjust to the dim interior light, just as she had done once before. There was the hum of conversation, she heard the pitch of men's laughter, she smelled the strong odor of beer. Then, in an instant, everything seemed to stop, and for a frightening moment she was aware of heads turning in her direction.

I've done this before! Anne prodded herself. *I can do it now!*

She started out resolutely, heading for the bar, but it was a relief when people began to talk again, though she was sure they were still aware of her.

Perhaps they really did resent her presence, she thought dismally. After all, she was an outsider there.

She was halfway across the room when suddenly she stopped. For an agonizing second she was powerless to move. She could only stare ahead of her, disbelievingly.

Timothy Flanagan was sitting at the bar. He, too, must have been aware of the sudden cessation in conversation, for he had turned around on the bar stool so that he was sitting sideways—looking right at her.

Anne moistened her lips. She'd never felt more of a total fool. At least, though, Timothy was alone. Had he been with someone else—had he been with a woman—she didn't think she could have stood it.

He waited for her to come to him. He didn't make the slightest move in her direction. It was as if he were telegraphing the message that she was trespassing and could very well take the consequences.

Anne knew she had to keep going. She couldn't turn back now, although it was all she could do to keep on walking straight. Only when she was standing right next to him did Timothy give her any sign of recognition at all.

He asked sourly, "What brings you here?"

Anne shook her head. Then she said, in little more than a whisper, "I . . . d-don't know."

"Dammit, Anne!" he exploded under his breath. He pulled out the stool at his side. "Just what do you think you're doing?"

She climbed onto the stool numbly, aware that the bartender was heading in their direction. Tim's green gaze raked her as he asked irritably, "What will you have?"

"B-beer," she managed.

Tim gave the order tersely, but he couldn't suppress a flash of amusement as he turned back to her. "Not really your drink, is it, Anne?"

"Tim, please. . . ."

"Will you kindly tell me what brings you here?"

"I don't know," she repeated.

"That's ridiculous!"

Anne swallowed hard. "I had S-Sunday dinner

with the Kincaids,'' she blurted. ''They live in Dorchester. It...it isn't that f-far away, so I decided...."

''To revisit the scene of the crime?'' he asked dangerously.

''Tim, please!''

''You must know how you stand out in here,'' he told her bluntly.

''I'm well aware of it,'' she nodded, and added bitterly, ''People in Southie don't exactly put out a welcome mat for strangers, do they?''

''No, they don't,'' he agreed. ''But you already knew that, Anne. This is their town, and they're fine people. Most of them are hard workers, and they deserve to have their own space, if you know what I mean. After all, you have yours.''

Anne's lovely gray eyes had never seemed so eloquent. She said sorrowfully, ''And you hate it, don't you?''

''What?''

''You hate my space, don't you, Tim? You hate my...my f-family background, and everything that goes with it. You hate everything about p-people like me. You have nothing but contempt for—''

She broke off, and there was no doubting his astonishment. He stared down at her, then after a taut moment said, ''You must be out of your mind.''

''No, I'm not,'' she said levelly. ''There's something you hold against me, Tim. Something very real. And it c-comes up every time my family is mentioned and whenever we talk about homes or antiques or b-background...."

"And so," he said softly, "you think it's because I'm contemptuous of all those things?"

"I know it is," Anne asserted stubbornly.

The bartender—Mike, she remembered—slid a mug of beer across the scarred oak surface of the bar. Tim mumbled thanks, then handed it to her, and taking a long healthy swig, just as she'd seen Ben Kincaid do, Anne decided it went down surprisingly well. The cool bitterness was just what she needed.

Tim said gently, "You're entirely wrong, *mavourneen*. It isn't hate that I feel where your background is concerned. It's envy."

There was a bleakness to his face as he spoke, and she could not doubt the truth of what he was saying to her. Still, it was unbelievable. Tim was the most self-assured man she'd ever met, completely confident in a way that sometimes bordered on arrogance.

Tim Flanagan envious? she asked herself, amazed. That didn't make sense.

He said so softly that she had to strain to hear him, "You've said often enough that I have a lot of hang-ups, and I've never denied it. Time and again I've tried to tell you more about myself. But either we've been interrupted or . . . I've lost courage. I've made statements that were in themselves blatant, but you haven't taken them in the way I intended. I can't blame you for that, either. When a man tells you he doesn't know when his birthday is, or who he is, for that matter. . . ." He broke off, then after a moment said quietly, "I'm sure it wasn't easy for you, Anne, to take those things in, to realize I meant what I was saying. I could see you rationalizing, twisting the words to suit you, but . . . .''

Anne shook her head helplessly. ''I don't know what you're saying, Tim,'' she admitted.

''No, you don't, do you?'' he agreed, then added impatiently, ''Let's find a table.''

He moved away from the bar, and Anne followed. The pub wasn't nearly as crowded as it had been before, and she wondered if Tim would lead her to the same table where they'd sat on that other Sunday. But he didn't. He chose the quietest spot he could find and said, ''Now, if they'll lay off on the jukebox and the pool table for a while, perhaps we can hear ourselves talk.''

He brushed his hair back from his forehead, and the smile he gave her was so sad she could have cried for him.

''What a funny twist of fate . . . you coming back here today,'' he mused.

''What brought *you* back here?'' she asked him.

''I'm setting up a football team with some of the kids I work with. That's why I was out your way yesterday. I had lunch with another client, who also happens to live in Chestnut Hill. He owns a vacant lot here in Southie, and I wanted to propose his letting us use it on Sundays.''

''And he agreed?''

''Yes, he agreed. So I got the kids together this afternoon, but it was just a preliminary kind of thing. That's why I finished up earlier than usual. The guy I drove over with—another Boston Irishman, incidentally—decided he wanted to visit his elderly aunt while he was in the neighborhood. I told him I'd take the subway back to town, but I thought I'd stop in here first and have a beer."

"I see."

"No, Anne," Timothy corrected gently. "You don't really see very much about me at all. And... I'd about decided to let it stay that way. You've got the softest of hearts, I know. It would be almost impossible for you not to go overboard with pity for me."

"Pity for you?" She couldn't believe this. "Can you give me one good reason why I should pity you, Timothy Flanagan?"

He forced her to look at him. His green eyes seemed darker than usual and very serious. "I can give you several good reasons, Anne Clarendon," he told her. "That's what I'm afraid of doing. On the other hand, it seems wrong to let you continue to jump to all sorts of conclusions...because I'm afraid to tell you the truth."

"Honestly!" Anne sparked, annoyed with him. "You really love being mysterious, don't you?"

"I come by it naturally," he replied, his voice low again. "You see, I really *don't* know who I am. And so it follows that I don't know when my birthday is, either. Only that it must be sometime toward the middle of March."

"What?"

There was a matchbook on the table. Timothy picked it up and began toying with it slowly, his gaze fastened on the invisible pattern he was making.

"I was abandoned on the doorstep of a hospital in Dorchester, Anne. A Catholic hospital. The nuns found me and they took me in. I was, they guessed, about two weeks old. This was toward the first of April, thirty-four years ago. I've been told that I was not too far from death. Anyway, the nuns nursed me, they cared for me...I think you could say they saved my life."

Timothy kept his gaze on the matchbook as he spoke, and she could see the effort it was costing him to keep the tone of his voice even.

"Later," he said, "I was placed in an orphanage. There was a cloud over me—meaning, there were legal complexities—and I was not a good candidate for adoption. There was always the fear someone might come forward and claim me because...well, because my name had been left with me."

"Your name?"

He nodded and paused to sip his beer in an obvious bid for time. Then he said, "I was wrapped in a shawl. A hand-knit shawl. There was an envelope pinned to it. Just a common white envelope, one that offered no clues. Inside there was a plain piece of paper. Again, no clues...except that on the paper someone had printed, This is Timothy Flanagan. There was also a little pin...a brooch, I guess you'd call it. It was a silver metal of some sort, and in the middle there was a shamrock of pale green stone—Connemara marble, I've since found out. The brooch was pinned to a piece of white cardboard on which two names had been printed. Moira was the first, the second began with a K. But someone...someone had apparently cried." Timothy went on, faltering, "and a tear had splashed onto the second name, making it illegible."

Anne looked at him, aghast. "And that was all?"

"There was one other thing," Tim said. "The word Dingle. Dingle is a town on the west coast of Ireland, centering a peninsula of the same name. But I don't know which it referred to."

"Didn't the nuns check? I mean, couldn't they have asked other hospitals in this area about all the births within a period of two or three weeks?"

"The nuns *did* check," he said wearily. "As I have myself, in later years. Of course, with the passage of time to contend with, trying to uncover any clues became that much more difficult. Not that there were many clues to uncover, Anne. It was obvious that I hadn't been born in a hospital."

"Did you trace people named Flanagan?"

Tim smiled wryly. "I was an infant at the time, remember?"

"I know," Anne said impatiently. "But have you tried tracing since you've been an adult?"

"One would as well try investigating everyone in the area named Kelly," he told her. "At the time, a number of Flanagans in the area were contacted. But there was never any connection made between a local family and...me."

"Timothy...."

He shook his head. "You're already looking at me as if you want to wrap me in swaddling clothes," he told her. "And that's just what I didn't want to happen."

"You can't expect m-me to hear this without reacting," Anne began.

"I realize that," he said. "But try to understand how I feel about it, will you? I never wanted to tell you anything about any of this. I wanted to be myself with you. A long time ago I learned to stand alone without falling down. I hoped that I could stand alone with you, Anne...in a different sort of way. But it didn't work. It will never work. You know so exactly who you are, where you come from. You have a basic knowledge of self I can never have. A knowledge of your own value."

"You're wrong, Tim! People are not born with a certain 'value.' We are what we make of ourselves."

"Do you really believe that?"

Do I? Anne asked herself, knowing she was in no shape to cope with the answer right now. His information had been emotionally shattering, and she was fighting the very urges he'd just accused her of. It seemed impossible to go on sitting there by his side without reaching out to touch him, to console him....

"It's okay," he said, misreading her silence. "I'm not the only guy who was ever left on a doorstep and managed to make it through life anyway."

"But...you have some clues!" Anne countered, latching onto this thought. "You have the pin with the shamrock. You have that name, Moira K. You...you have a place, Dingle. Haven't you ever tried to f-find Moira K. in Dingle, Tim?"

He twisted the cardboard matchbook, then discarded it before he answered her. "No," he said, "I haven't. And before you ask me why I haven't, I'll tell you." He paused, then said heavily, "I'm not sure I really want to know."

CHAPTER TWELVE

"I'LL GO GET TWO more beers," Timothy said.

Anne didn't answer. She watched him make his way back to the bar. A couple of men called out to him, as they had on that other Sunday, but he only nodded and waved. This time he didn't pause to exchange pleasantries.

He was wearing sneakers, faded jeans and a worn black turtleneck, and the casual old clothes were amazingly becoming. The turtleneck emphasized his coloring, and the snug fabric drew attention to the width of his chest, his broad shoulders and arms that were surprisingly muscular for someone who insisted he spent most of his time at a desk. Yes, Timothy Flanagan could match any man in the Harp and Shamrock with his physique. And, dressed as he was now, he fit right in with the crowd.

But there was another side to Timothy. A number of other sides to him, Anne mused. Watching him as he started back toward their table carrying two mugs of beer, she was intensely aware of something else—his uniqueness. Despite his outward uniformity, Timothy was very, very different. The way he moved, for one thing, with his head held high, at just the slightest of angles. Pride, that was it. Tim Flanagan epitomized pride.

This was something he had developed, Anne sensed. Something he'd fought for. Timothy had worked hard to gain his present place in the sun. She was sure he'd gotten where he was entirely on his own. The expensive clothes he usually wore, the beautiful imported car he drove and all the other tangible assets he had, must have been gained by his own hard work. She had no doubt of this. Tim Flanagan was a self-made man in the truest sense of the word.

As he sat down and pushed a frosty mug of beer across to her, Anne wanted to say a thousand things to him but was at a complete loss for words. It would be easy, so dangerously easy, for him to misinterpret any statement she might make, any questions she might ask. He'd made it clear that in telling her what he had about himself he was paving the way for an outrush of pity from her. And he'd made it equally clear that this was exactly what he didn't want.

She did not pity him. Yet his story had made her heart ache and had aroused feelings in her that were purely maternal. She had longed to hold him close, to rock him against her breast.... She smiled at the thought.

"Share your amusement," he suggested promptly.

Anne couldn't. To suggest that he'd aroused the mother in her would be to start heading in an entirely wrong direction with Tim right now. Instead, she hedged saying, "It's nothing, really."

"Nothing, really, eh?" he rejoined, mocking her accent, which held more than a hint of a private-school background.

"Tim. . . ."

"Look, Anne," he said, cutting her off with a wave of his hand. "Let's level with each other, okay? That's the least we can do. In a way I'm sorry I told you what I did. In another way I'm glad. It was becoming such a stumbling block with me, I couldn't seem to hurdle it. Now, maybe you can understand—" he paused, his eyes narrowing slightly as he looked at her "—or can you?" he asked.

Anne stared down at the thick creamy head topping her beer and said frankly, "I'm afraid, Tim."

"Afraid?" He seemed surprised. "Afraid of what?"

"Of saying the wrong thing to you," she told him, looking back up to meet his gaze. "Anything I say to you right now is going to be. . .important. If I. . .goof, you won't even be able to consider why I might have said the wrong thing. You'll hold it against me, that's all.'

A wry smile touched his face. "What kind of a lawyer do you think I am?" he asked, and laughed shortly.

"A very good lawyer. But even so, I'm not sure you'd want to try your own case, would you?"

"What does that mean?"

"It means I sometimes feel as if *I'm* on trial, Tim. . .not you," she told him. "I'm even afraid to say that I think you've lived with a t-terrible secret," she went on, then added, "But I do think that. I don't see how you've managed. . . ."

"Yes?" he encouraged.

"Well, I can't imagine how you've made of yourself what you have!" She winced, because the words sounded all wrong to her.

"If you mean getting a good education and then going on to practice law. . . ." He hesitated, then continued, "Let's just say I was inspired, shall we?"

Anne was taken back by the bitterness in his tone, but after a moment Tim said more mildly, "Life comes a day at a time, Anne. No matter how hard we may try to look ahead—or look back, for that matter—no matter how good or bad things may be, each day still has to be lived. You can't leap over it, you can't rush it. My life came a day at a time, just as yours did. And I took it as it came. . .and tried to do with it what I could."

"You succeeded," she finished for him.

"You think so?" he questioned, then said, "In some ways, yes, I've succeeded. But when I look at myself in the mirror each morning I know that in other ways I've been a total failure."

"I don't think you really mean that, Tim."

"Don't you, Anne? I wouldn't take any bets on it if I were you."

She didn't dare look at him. She said, her voice very small, "You're t-talking about not knowing who you are, aren't you?"

"That's a succinct way of putting it," he replied, his sarcasm bruising her. But she'd gone this far, and she wasn't about to backtrack.

"Tell me a better way to put it," she said, thrusting her chin upward defiantly. "I can appreciate the way you feel."

"Can you really?" he speculated, the sarcasm intensifying.

"You won't believe it if I say yes, will you?" she challenged.

"I don't think you could be expected to understand the way I feel," Timothy said bluntly. "You haven't been through so much as a fraction of the things I've been through. You've never had people treat you as if you were just so much scum."

"Tim!" Anne exclaimed, shocked.

"It's a lousy word, isn't it? But believe me, Anne, I have been treated like scum! Luckily, though, it had a reverse effect on me. It made me get up the backbone to prove I could do something with my life. It made me really want to become someone."

He had barely touched his beer, but now he pushed the mug aside. "Come on," he said, "I've had enough of this place for today. Let's get out of here."

Anne didn't protest. She walked out of the Harp and Shamrock with him, aware of the sudden silence that trailed them. She said morosely, "I stick out like a sore thumb, don't I?"

"What?" he asked, preoccupied.

"It doesn't matter, Tim. It's just that they make me feel like such a...."

He paused and looked down at her, amused. "Such a what?"

"A...parasite!" Anne blurted. The word sprang into her mind, and even though she knew it wasn't fully accurate, it was the only way she could describe how being in the Harp and Shamrock Pub made her feel.

Tim said gently, "You're not a parasite, Anne. You have never been one, I'm sure, nor will you ever be. Parasites take without ever giving. I've known some people in my time who fit the description to a tee, but you are certainly not one of them."

He smiled ruefully. "I forgot I don't have my car with me," he admitted. "I was going to suggest we go somewhere else."

"I have mine," she told him quickly, glad to change the subject. "It's parked just down the street."

Tim hesitated, and she was afraid he was going to tell her it would be best if they parted company right there. Then he shrugged. "Why not?" he asked lightly, and fell into step by her side.

Anne handed him the keys when they reached her car, and he didn't protest. He slid behind the wheel, then smiled across at her. "Would you consider coming to my place for a drink?" he suggested.

That was the last thing she'd expected. In fact, it was a shock. She said, her surprise showing, "That would be fine. But...are you s-sure you want me to?"

"Very sure," he answered, as he turned on the engine.

They drove toward the Southeast Expressway

and Tim said, "Sometimes, Anne, I feel as if we've had nothing but a series of incomplete conversations. I'd like to finish this one, even though logic tells me it might be better to let it go."

"Why do you say that?"

"Because, *mavourneen*," he said, smiling at her in a way that made her heart turn over, "I really do want you to understand me."

TIMOTHY LIVED in a luxury apartment complex overlooking Boston Harbor. "The site of one of Boston's first and most famous wharves," he told Anne. He had a large corner living room, which offered a magnificent view of the small private marina below and downtown Boston's skyscrapers to the right, and a single large bedroom, complete with skylights and a recessed deck.

The decor was contemporary, almost starkly so with Scandinavian teak furniture, bright ceramics and near-surrealistic wall hangings in vivid primitive colors. It was as if Timothy had been determined not to let anything of the past intrude in the place where he lived.

Perhaps because his past is such a mystery, Anne imagined, and sensing the poignancy of this, felt a disturbing tremor pass through her.

There were unexpected touches, though, that gave a clue to his personality. As Timothy was fixing drinks for them, Anne spotted a collection of old Belleek tucked on a corner shelf. The lovely cream-colored china was incredibly thin and fragile, with tiny green shamrocks ornamenting each piece.

Then she was drawn to a collage of photographs he had displayed along one wall. Looking more closely, she soon discovered they were exquisite—scenic shots, all of them, devoted to various aspects of New England heritage. An old windmill, a white church with pointed steeple, a farmhouse set against a backdrop of rolling hills and vivid fall foliage, a covered bridge. In each case the color, contrasts and textures were stunning.

As Tim approached behind her with the drinks, Anne said, "These are terrific. Who took them?"

"I did," he confessed.

She swung around, surprised. "You? I didn't know you were interested in photography."

"You didn't?" he teased.

She laughed, glad that his mood was light. "I suppose I pictured you spending your time pouring over dull old law books."

"I spent enough of it doing exactly that," he said. "I only got into photography a few years ago, though it was something I always wanted to learn. It's amazing what you can do with a camera. I like to get outdoors, and since I don't do much in the way of sports...."

"Come on, Tim," Anne scoffed, surprised by this. "I thought you were forever playing baseball and football...and all sorts of things like that."

"Not anymore," he contradicted.

He paused suspensefully, and Anne joked, "Well, are you going to tell me why?"

"I don't know if I dare!" he said, laughing.

"Please...."

"You probably won't believe me."

"Try me."

Tim handed Anne her drink and said, "Once, when you and I were talking, you said you'd been a cross-country runner in college. Well, I didn't tell you then...but when I was at Boston University I was on the track team. Long-distance running, to be precise. To make the story short, four years of pounding the pavement really did a number on my knees. That's why when I suggested several places out your way where you could run, I told you I'd love to join you, but that my knees wouldn't exactly thank me."

"Yes, I remember you saying that," Anne said now, and realized this was yet another aspect of Timothy Flanagan she had not pursued to the finish.

"Anyway," he said, "taste your drink and see how you like my special Irish old-fashioned, complete with a green cherry."

"Honestly, Tim!" she protested, seeing that there actually was a green cherry in her glass. But the drink was delicious and she told him so. Then she got back to the subject they'd been talking about.

"How bad are your knees, Tim?" she asked.

"They're okay...until I aggravate them," he told her. "And unfortunately it doesn't take very much to do that."

"Then how do you handle all the sports activities with the boys you look after?"

"I don't look after them, Anne," he corrected

gently. "These are kids who need an older friend plus a little guidance. They need a chance to get out and work off some of their frustrations in healthy play. That's what I give them, and it works the other way around, too. Anyway, I don't try to participate in the different sports with the boys, I just coach them. I leveled with them about my knee problem and they accepted it. They'd be the first to push me back on the sidelines if I tried to get too involved—and keep in mind, I'm talking about some pretty tough kids."

"They must care about you a great deal," Anne said carefully.

"It's mutual."

She took another sip of her drink as if borrowing fortitude. Then she said, "It's easy to c-care about you."

"Anne...."

"No, Tim, please let me talk. It seems like... fate, my going back to Southie this afternoon and f-finding you there in the Harp and Shamrock."

"Sure now, Anne! And you wouldn't be believing in such things, would you?" he asked, his accent typically Irish.

"I believe in what I know and what I feel," she said steadily.

"In a minute you'll have me thinking that you've kissed the blarney stone," he went on, the brogue increasing.

"Stop it, Tim!" she told him more sharply than she'd intended.

"Okay," he said, sobering. Then he forced a

laugh. "I see you've downed the drink. Let me make you another one."

"All right. But may I use your bathroom first?"

"Through the bedroom to the right," he called over his shoulder. He had started back to the kitchenette where he kept the bar supplies.

Anne's pulse was throbbing as she sponged her face, then lightly touched her lips with fresh gloss, ran a comb through her hair and added a touch of perfume to the hollow of her throat. She knew that in an emotional sense she was living very dangerously just now. There was no predicting how Timothy's mood might change. The ice on which they were skating was thin, and she sensed she could be plunged into extremely cold water at any instant. Yet she was determined not to retreat. She was determined to go on—she had to go on—because she loved him. Every last vestige of doubt was swept away as Anne faced not only the reality of this love but the knowledge that she was going to have to prove it to Timothy. And she knew only too well how difficult a task that would be.

Something had happened to Timothy Flanagan, Anne guessed. Something had dented his self-confidence to such an extent that he'd been trying to prove himself ever since. And in his own mind he had not yet succeeded, nor did he believe that he ever could.

What was it he had said? That he'd been made to feel like scum.

It was an ugly word, the connotation terrible, and Anne shrank from it. Whoever had made Timothy feel like scum had done a thorough job on him. The wound—and that was exactly what it was—had never entirely healed.

And you think you can heal it? Anne asked herself now.

She was pensive as she started back through his bedroom, pausing midway to take a look at her surroundings.

The bed was king-sized with a bookcase headboard, the furniture made of a pale wood—birch, Anne thought. The decor was starkly modern. There was a huge abstract over the bed and nothing else on any of the walls. On the dresser, though, Anne spied a large photograph in a silver frame, and moving closer to it, she suddenly wished she hadn't.

The girl looking up at her was beautiful. Blond with a heart-shaped face and large expressive eyes. She was smiling a very sweet smile. She looked as if she was deeply in love, and Anne had no doubt at all who the object of her affections was.

From the other room Tim called, "Hey! Did you get lost?"

Anne backed away from the picture, trying to get a grip on her self-control. This was no time to tell him she'd seen it, she knew that. No time to ask him who the girl was or what part she'd played in his life.

Tim had told her he wasn't married and had never been married. He had made it clear that he wasn't involved with any woman, either. But he was thirty-four years old, Anne reminded herself, and

overwhelmingly attractive. Obviously there had
been more than one woman in his life. What was
disturbing her, though, was the feeling that this girl
had been the most important one of all.

He had put a cassette in the stereo and music
filled the room. He was smiling as Anne crossed
over to him and accepted the second drink.

He sniffed and said, "You smell absolutely beautiful, Anne."

"Thank you," she answered dully.

Tim stood back, appraising her. "What's the
matter, *mavourneen*? You came out here looking as
if you'd seen a ghost."

"I was thinking, that's all."

"Thinking about what?"

"A... variety of things," she replied vaguely.

"Was I included in them?"

"Come on, Timothy!"

He laughed. "I put out some cheese and
crackers," he smiled, indicating a platter he'd set
on a glass-topped coffee table. "If you're going to
indulge in Irish old-fashioneds you'd better munch,
or you're apt to fall flat on your face."

"I don't doubt it," Anne said wryly.

He looked down at her, and his face grew
solemn. He said slowly, "I can't believe you're
really here. So often I've pictured having you
here... sharing a drink with you, like this. But it's
only been a dream of mine, not reality. Just as that
day we spent on the Cape seems like a dream
whenever I think back to it." He paused and
looked at her intensely, his green eyes ablaze.

"Were we ever really there, Anne?" he asked, his voice husky.

Her mouth went dry. She moistened her lips with her tongue and answered softly, "Yes, Tim. We were really there."

"You went to sleep, and I went for a walk on the beach, and I had the crazy feeling that when I went back to the cottage you wouldn't be there at all."

Anne felt the ice getting thinner. "What finally h-happened with the cottage?" she asked.

"What do you mean?"

"Did you rent it for the summer?"

He shook his head. "No, I...well, to be honest with you, I couldn't picture taking a bunch of kids down there and roughing it. That's what I was looking for—a place where I could take some of the boys for a holiday. I planned on taking a month off and on setting up a rotation of sorts so they'd all have at least a week of it."

"But you didn't do that?"

"No, I didn't. I couldn't, actually. My case load was too heavy to go away for an entire month. So I limited our outings to day trips and weekends. The kids didn't care. They had a great time anyway."

"Has the cottage been sold?"

"As I understand it, it's still up for sale," Tim told her. "But I haven't checked lately."

"I see."

"To have gone back there would have been... too much to handle, Anne. I would have seen you everywhere I looked." He was staring at her now. "Hell," he said abjectly, "I don't have to go back

to Wellfleet to see you everywhere I look. You...
you've become an obsession.''

He was standing much too close to her, and looking up at him swiftly Anne sensed the hunger in his
eyes. Her heart went out to him. She said, her voice
shaking, ''Oh, Tim....''

He pried the drink out of her fingers and set it
down on the nearest table, and she knew exactly
what he was going to do next. She also knew that it
would be out of her power to resist him.

She moved to meet him halfway because she
wanted his arms around her more desperately than
she had ever wanted anything before. This was
where she belonged, in the circle of Tim's arms. She
never wanted to be anywhere else.

In an instant they were embracing, kissing, and
when Anne felt the touch of his tongue she invited
its exploration. It was so natural for her to respond
to him, knowing he found her own little excursions
equally tantalizing. His fingers fumbled as he tried
to unbutton her blouse, unfastening one button
after the next, and lowering his head to kiss each
place he uncovered.

She was bare to the waist now, and as Tim bent to
kiss the hollow between her breasts, Anne could feel
her nipples tautening. She shivered convulsively as
he made small circles around first one nipple and
then the other with the tip of his tongue.

Momentarily he paused, tugging off his black
turtleneck sweater and thrusting it aside. Then
Anne was in his arms again, feeling as if her flesh
was being molded against his body. He pressed her

against him, and there was something indescribably sensuous about the hardness of him thrust against the thin fabric that separated them. Anne felt her desire surging within her, her own hunger for him spiraling. And these sensations only intensified as Tim picked her up in his arms as if she were a child and started for the bedroom.

He placed her on his bed as carefully as if she were a piece of the fragile Belleek. But he did not at once come to lie beside her. Instead, he sat down on the edge of the bed and, reaching over, took her hand in his, stroking the inside of her palm in a way that set her thoroughly afire.

He said, his voice very low, "You do want this as much as I do, don't you, Anne?"

"Do you really need to ask, Tim?" she whispered.

He nodded. "Yes, I do. I know...but I need to hear you say so."

She said softly, "I want you with everything there is in me, I want you."

"You never regretted the time on Cape Cod?"

"Regretted? Oh, no, darling...."

"Anne, you are the most beautiful woman I've ever known." He was leaning over her now. She felt his fingers at her waist and lifted her hips slightly so he could slide her skirt down over her legs. His fingers were incendiary as they trailed up the inner sides of her thighs. Then he was drawing off her pale peach satin panties, and those long fingers were exploring with deliberate slowness, taking possession of her inch by inch until they reached her very core, and she couldn't repress moaning in ecstasy, she wanted him so much.

He came to lay by her side, and feeling his nakedness against her skin, she clutched him, her fingers caressing him with mounting ardor. She felt herself an empty vessel, waiting to receive him, and knew she would die without him.

Tim murmured soft endearments into her ears, and as phrase melted into phrase, Anne was aware only of the hypnotic tone of his voice. Suddenly he entered her, and her gasps were gasps of bliss. Soon she became a part of him, and they merged in a pulsating spiraling rhythm. At last, in unison, their passions exploded, binding them together in perfect completeness.

For a long time they did not speak. Finally Tim drew a blanket up over them and Anne lay nestled within the warm circle of his arms, feeling wonderfully, peacefully content.

"Asleep?" he whispered, his hot breath tickling her ear.

"No," she giggled.

"Would you believe it," he told her, "I'm starving!"

She moved her head and looked at him, smiling. "Would you believe it," she laughed, "so am I."

"How about one of my super omelets?" he suggested. "Strictly Cordon Bleu fare?"

"Sounds perfect. I'll make the toast." She sat up. "You wouldn't have a robe I could borrow, would you?" she asked then.

Tim considered this, then grinned. "As a matter

of fact," he said, "I have a short terry beach thing that might only come to your ankle. It hits me about at the knees."

This was not far from the truth. Anne wrapped the robe around her, then padded barefoot to the kitchen. Tim had put on the faded jeans again but hadn't bothered with the turtleneck. He was bare from the waist up, his skin still golden from the tan he'd acquired over the summer.

"Coffee?" he suggested.

"I'd rather have tea," Anne told him, "if you know how to make it the Irish way like Bridget sometimes does."

"And whatever is the Irish way, *mavourneen*?"

"Very strong, very dark, with both milk and sugar," she said. "Here, I'll do it."

Tim didn't protest, and after a few minutes they sat down to a small feast at the kitchen table. Strong hot tea, fluffy omelets, a stack of buttered toast and lime marmalade, which, he admitted, was more English than Irish, but still his favorite.

This is happiness! Anne thought as she poured out a second cup of tea for Timothy. *This is just what I've always wanted. If only we could hold onto it. . . .*

But happiness was indeed like a bluebird, she knew. Elusive, apt to fly away so quickly—and so difficult to recapture.

"A cloud seems to be passing over your face," Tim observed. "What is it, darling?"

Anne's smile was small and sad. "I wish it could be like this forever, that's all," she said.

His eyebrows lifted. "That's all?" he echoed. "Ah, but that would be everything, wouldn't it? Heaven come to earth. Do you think heaven ever really comes to earth, Anne? Or...if there's a heaven out there at all?"

CHAPTER THIRTEEN

ANNE LAY ON HER BACK staring through the darkness toward the ceiling. Then she turned restlessly to peer at the illuminated face of the clock on her bedside table. It was nearly three-thirty. She had been awake for hours, and sleep was as elusive as ever.

Turning over onto her back again, she remembered Timothy saying that sometimes he felt as if their time together on Cape Cod had been a dream. She could understand his feeling, for it didn't seem possible to her that this day—the previous day, she amended—had really happened, either.

In retrospect, there was an unreality to having gone back to the Harp and Shamrock Pub. She couldn't believe she'd done such a thing. And then to find Timothy there! And later....

They had shared something wonderful that afternoon. And, as important as their lovemaking had been, this sharing had gone far beyond the physical. There had been a rare fusion of mind and body— and yes, even of soul—between them. They had transcended desire, transcended pure passion. Their mutual yearning satisfied, Timothy had shown her new sides of himself. He had revealed himself to her in ways she felt certain he'd seldom, if ever, permitted himself to do before. He had been completely *himself*, natural, uninhibited and devoid of complexes—and each subtle character revelation had made Anne all the more aware of how much she loved him.

When Timothy was not trying to camouflage his feelings, when he was not trying to hide behind an invisible veil or an Irish brogue, there was an overpowering sweetness to him. There was a warmth, a terrific capacity for understanding, a gentleness, tenderness, and the special beauty of real affection in his nature. In fact, Timothy Flanagan was all Anne could imagine ever wanting in a man. All, and more!

Still, there had been a strange finality to the way they had parted. And after sharing the better part of the afternoon and evening with him, after sharing his love and confidence and an indescribably precious sense of closeness, Anne was not at all certain about what was going to happen between them next.

He had said nothing about seeing her again, nothing about calling her in the morning. He'd said nothing at all concerning the future—their future. He'd made absolutely no promises. Now, in the middle of the night, this remembrance struck Anne with chilling bleakness.

On again, off again. She didn't think she could take much more of this seesawing back and forth with Tim. After yesterday, it was difficult to understand how he could still feel he was not free to pursue a relationship with her. Yet there had been that peculiar reticence about him once again as she was leaving. Unbelievably she'd felt as if the veil had again started descending.

After she and Tim had eaten the omelets he'd prepared in a large well-tempered skillet, they'd sat side by side on his living-room couch, sipping liqueurs and listening to a Saint-Saëns symphony on his stereo. They had been as close as two people could be. They hadn't even needed to touch each other just then to reiterate this closeness. It was simply there.

Later they'd gone back to his bedroom, neither of them needing to say a word to the other this second time. There had been a different pace to their lovemaking. They had both been slower, more deliberate. They had savored every second, every caress. Anne had felt herself steeped in a heavenly languor as she reveled in Timothy's intimate touches. Then, thoroughly aroused, she had climbed with him up passion's ladder, where they had reached a blinding, shattering culmination.

They had fallen asleep in each other's arms after that. It had been nearly eleven when they'd awakened, and Tim had refused to let her drive back to Chestnut Hill by herself. Finally he agreed he would let her go—only if he followed in his own car. Anne had consented, knowing that he meant this, and that her pleas of self-sufficiency would only be falling on deaf ears were she to protest.

All the way out Beacon Street to Chestnut Hill she'd been conscious of the Saab keeping pace behind her. And independent though she was, there had been a good warm feeling in knowing that Timothy was so near.

Back at the house she'd thought he might pull to a stop behind her, but he didn't. He passed her with a farewell beep of his horn, and only then did she realize that they hadn't really said good-night to each other.

Impatiently she threw off her bedclothes and without bothering to put on a robe padded quietly downstairs in her bare feet, heading toward the kitchen. She didn't want to wake Katharine and face a possible inquisition concerning where she'd gone after she'd left the Kincaid house. Katharine was not apt to ask the pointed questions her mother would. It was simply that in her present mood Anne didn't feel like talking to anyone at all.

She made herself a cup of hot milk and took it back upstairs, and sitting up in bed, she sipped it slowly and went over everything Timothy had said that day. Most of what he'd told her about himself had been said while they were at the Harp and Shamrock. In his apartment their conversation had been more general. They'd talked about food and music. They'd talked about things they liked and disliked. They'd talked more than ever before, and he had seemed so relaxed it hadn't occurred to her at the time that he was avoiding discussing the subject closest to her heart—Timothy Flanagan.

Anne shook her head slowly. It seemed impossible that he had been abandoned on a hospital doorstep and cared for by nuns, who'd eventually placed him in an orphanage. It seemed impossible that someone, a heartbroken young mother, had not come back to claim him. The mere possibility of that happening had made him a poor candidate for adoption, she'd been told. She suspected the legal complications involved in his own life had been at least partially responsible for sparking his interest in the practice of law.

She tried to imagine what that life must have been like. She tried to imagine Tim as an abandoned infant, as a small child, and then as a boy growing up, and her heart ached at the thought.

She set her cup aside and settled down against her pillows again, finally drifting off into sleep. But her dreams were laced with episodes dealing with Timothy, and though she couldn't remember precisely what they'd encompassed once she woke up, she did know they hadn't been happy.

GILES WINSLOW called at ten the next morning. "Hope I didn't interrupt your beauty sleep," he greeted Anne cheerfully.

"No," she said rather shortly. The quality of the sleep she'd had had not been conducive to enhancing one's beauty.

"I've been talking to Bigelow," Giles went on, "your stepmother's attorney."

"Oh...yes," Anne murmured, her mind not focused on his words.

"Sure I didn't wake you up?" Giles asked again.

"No, Giles," she informed him more sharply than she intended. "You did not wake me up!"

. "Ouch!" he protested, then added, "I don't suppose I'd dare suggest you might have fallen out of the wrong side of bed?"

She laughed. "You're impossible," she told him, then realized she'd sounded a bit too affectionate. But it was difficult not to respond to Giles. He was so easygoing, so affable. There were no mysteries about him.

"At least I make you laugh, Anne," he pointed out. "But that's not what I called about."

"Oh?" she teased.

"No, Miss Clarendon. I wanted to know if you could make it down to the office this afternoon. Or would it be easier if Tim and I came out there this evening?"

"I'll come to you," she said hastily, because it was already becoming clear to her that Tim could have made this call himself instead of assigning it to Giles.

Was he going to start this business of avoiding her all over again? she wondered sadly. Or of seeing her only in the company of other people? Well, she decided defiantly, if that was the way he wanted to play, she'd follow the same game plan herself!

"Anne?" Giles repeated, and she realized he'd been talking and she hadn't heard a word he said.

"What time would you like to see me?" she asked, hoping this would cover the gap in their conversation.

"All the time," Giles said promptly. Then added, "But for today, how about three o'clock? Afterward, maybe you and I can go over to the Parker House for a drink?"

"I'll see you at three," she agreed.

The day inched by. Anne tried to write a few letters—she owed more of them than she liked to think about—but it was a fruitless effort. She wasn't in the mood to put words on paper.

She did make a phone call to her bank, though, and had a long talk with Stuart Miller, who was in a position of sufficient authority to take up the matter of her request for an indeterminate leave of absence with her superiors.

"There is so much to settle," she told him vaguely.

"I have a strong feeling you won't be coming back at all, Anne," Stuart replied, not trying to hide the gloom in his voice.

"Don't be ridiculous!" she countered. "Why wouldn't I be coming back, Stuart? I love my job."

"I don't know," he admitted, "except that you have quite a few ties with Boston. My crystal ball tells me that one of these days you may want to make it your permanent place of residence. There's no doubt you could get an excellent job there. Boston certainly has its share of banks."

"I hadn't really thought about it," Anne said, which was true. Since returning to Boston, she'd been taking life one day at a time, and even handling it that way some of the days had been very difficult to get through.

Early that afternoon she dressed very carefully for her appointment. She needed all the self-assurance she could muster, and looking her best would help. She decided at last on burgundy velvet pants, a high-collared pink crepe blouse and an off-white mohair jacket that was particularly becoming.

She brushed her dark brown hair until it shone, paid very careful attention to her makeup, and was at the door, ready and waiting, when the cab she'd phoned for arrived. Driving in downtown Boston was something she still didn't like. Trying to find a parking space was especially aggravating, and taking a cab was so much easier.

The meeting was held in Oscar Wechsler's office. It was also the first time Anne had met this senior member of the firm. He was a tall slim man with graying hair and very blue eyes, and he still limped slightly as he crossed the room to greet her.

Immediately she liked his smile, and she could tell that although outwardly he was very much the proper Bostonian, he was also humorous and compassionate. The introduction over, she turned to nod at Timothy and thought her heart would stop beating entirely.

He hadn't slept either, that much was obvious. There were shadows of fatigue under his eyes. Nor had he been able to comb his hair so that it would lie in place. It looked as if he'd been running his fingers through it.

Giles, on the other hand, was perfectly groomed, smiling and urbane. He held Anne's fingers just a shade too long as she shook hands with him, and she glanced quickly at Timothy to see his mouth tighten. He'd noticed and wasn't pleased. Anne couldn't help but feel a bit of comfort at this.

Oscar Wechsler took his place behind a massive mahogany desk, and Anne was ushered by Giles to a chair facing it on the left side. Giles managed to position himself in another chair in the middle, between Timothy and herself.

Mr. Wechsler was not one to waste his time in getting to the point, she soon discovered.

"Your stepmother has stirred up quite a hornet's nest," he said directly.

"I'm not surprised," Anne told him. "Has something new happened?"

"Not really," he said rather glumly. "Rather, a disturbing affirmation of old news that's not at all to our liking. The way matters look to us now, there's a good chance the holograph will in question would hold up in court. And according to Mr. Bigelow's conversation with Giles this morning, your stepmother is fully prepared to go to court. So the ball now bounces back to us, Miss Clarendon."

Anne frowned. "I'm afraid I don't quite follow you."

"If we go to court and lose," the distinguished lawyer told her bluntly, "the Chestnut Hill house—and very possibly all its contents—will almost certainly go to your stepmother. You, I should add, will nevertheless still be a very wealthy young woman. Your inheritances from both your aunt and your father assure that. The Clarendon affairs have been handled for years by our firm in cooperation with the First Bank of Boston, and the investments involved are extremely sound ones. Unless the world falls apart, Miss Clarendon, you should never have any financial worries.''

''Laura doesn't dispute my inheriting half of my father's financial assets?'' Anne questioned.

''No, she doesn't. Half of his estate was left to you in the holograph will, as well as in the original document our firm executed some time ago. The only difference is this matter of the Chestnut Hill house and its contents. All Clarendon family heirlooms, as I understand it.''

''Essentially, yes.''

''Well, Mrs. Clarendon seems determined to possess both the house and at least a good share of the contents,'' Oscar Wechsler said. ''I would say that it seems to be close to a personal vendetta with her. Her lawyer gives the same opinion. Frankly—and this is strictly between us—I think Bigelow wishes she would drop the suit. He's a reputable man, and this isn't his cup of tea.''

He looked across at her, his blue eyes narrowing. ''Any reason why she should feel such animosity toward you or your family?'' he asked.

Anne hesitated before answering. Then she said, ''I suppose you'd say Aunt Muriel was actually the. . . well, the titular head of our family, though I know that's a rather strange way to put it. What I mean to say is that she was like. . . well, like a dowager queen in a way. She was older than my father, and he never had the same interest in the genealogy of our family, or the antiques, or any of the other family things, that Aunt Muriel did. Also, Aunt Muriel didn't care for Laura.''

"The plot thickens," he observed, leaning back in his chair and stroking his chin. "I take it that Mrs. Clarendon was aware of this?"

"Yes, Laura was aware of it," Anne said slowly. "When my father first married her, she and I got along quite well. She's not much older than I am, and I think we really did hope to be like, well, like sisters in a way. But time changed that, and I must admit it was Aunt Muriel's fault. At least it was to a good extent.

"Aunt Muriel was very much against the marriage. She thought my father was extremely foolish to marry a young woman of a...of an entirely d-different background," Anne went on painfully, not daring to look toward Timothy as she said this. "So...she refused to receive Laura in the Chestnut Hill house."

"Literally?" Oscar Wechsler asked.

"Quite literally," Anne nodded. "You see, my grandfather had left the house to my father because he hoped the Clarendon name would be p-perpetuated. In other words, he hoped my father would have a son to carry it on. The place meant so much to Aunt Muriel, though, that my father didn't think this was fair. So, rather than try to break the will, he granted my aunt a life tenancy in the house. The house was hers until she died. It was my father's original intent that it should then be passed on to me."

Anne sighed. "I...detest this sort of thing," she said finally. "If my father really did change his mind, Mr. Wechsler, it seems to me we should go along with it. I'll admit I'd hate to see Laura have the house and all the family things." Again she did not dare look at Timothy. "I'd especially hate it if she's making trouble only out of spite. But if it's what my father wanted...."

"Don't be so altruistic, Anne." It was Timothy who spoke. "My personal feeling is that this wasn't your father's intention at all. I think he was persuaded to change his mind by something very definite."

"Exactly what are you suggesting, Tim?" Oscar Wechsler asked. "You think there might be fraud involved?"

"I wish I knew," Timothy admitted. "As of now, I don't. I am saying, though, that I don't think Anne should give up quite so easily."

"Neither do I," Giles put in. "Mrs. Clarendon certainly appears to be an opportunist. A woman who's going for something that really shouldn't be hers. Greed is one thing, but the desire to get even because of supposed slights—"

"They weren't 'supposed,'" Anne interjected. "My aunt did slight her."

"I admire your honesty, Miss Clarendon," Oscar Wechsler said. "But we still have a choice of action. Either we stand back and allow the holograph will to be admitted in the Massachusetts probate court, knowing there's a good chance it will stand up, or we start a counterattack of our own. I admit I'd be happier about doing that if we had a bit more ammunition. However, the decision is up to you."

"There is no chance of a compromise?" Anne asked.

"Yes, according to Bigelow there is some chance of a compromise," Giles put in. "Laura is not about to give up her claim on the house, he's quite sure of that. But in order to spare the trauma and the expense of going to court she might be willing to divide some of the family possessions with you."

"Generous of her," Anne said bitterly, and then raised troubled gray eyes to the older lawyer. "Can I have some time to think about this?" she asked him.

"Of course," he said quickly. "The matter's been grinding on for months. If you ask me, Mrs. Clarendon seems reluctant to take this final action."

As Oscar Wechsler said this, Anne looked directly into Timothy's green eyes, then swiftly turned her head away. Timothy was too composed at the moment. But his eyes were a giveaway.

He knows something, she thought.

"I think that's enough for today, Miss Clarendon," said Oscar Wechsler. "Give the matter some serious thought, and don't hesitate to call any one of us if you want to go over anything."

Goodbyes were said, and then Anne was standing in the corridor outside Oscar Wechsler's office with Timothy and Giles on either side of her.

Giles, glancing at his watch, said, "Nearly four. I think I'll call it a day. Ready for the Parker House, Anne?"

"Yes," she said. And she was.

But Timothy intervened. "Did you get in touch with Crocker?" he asked Giles unexpectedly.

"What?" Giles replied, obviously taken aback.

"Ferris Crocker, the attorney in that trust case we're representing," Timothy reminded the junior partner. "I left a memo on your desk. I spoke with him Friday and I told him you'd follow up today."

Giles frowned. "I intended to call him this morning but I put it aside and. . .it slipped my mind," he confessed.

Timothy glanced at his own watch. "You might still be able to reach him," he suggested. "I'll go along to the Parker House with Anne. You can meet us there."

It was high-handed, very high-handed. Giles's face spoke volumes as he said stiffly, "Will that be all right with you, Anne?"

"Yes, of course," she said, aware that she stood on the brink of a serious disagreement between the two men, and knowing it was something she didn't want to get into.

"Very well, then," Timothy said, equally stiff. "Shall we go, Anne?"

She preceded him down the corridor toward the elevator lobby, tension creeping over her. Timothy had some reason for doing this, she was sure. But what could it be?

They had only a second to wait for an elevator, and on the ride to the ground floor they maintained a silence that threatened to become icy. As they stepped out into the late-afternoon sunlight, unusually golden on this autumn day, Timothy said, "Let's walk over to the Parker House. It's not far."

"Okay," she agreed.

"Did you drive down?"

"No, I took a cab," she told him.

He nodded and started out, his long stride once again too much for her.

"Please," she said, after a moment. "Will you slow down?"

"I'm sorry," he answered, modifying his step deliberately.

"Timothy, why are you doing this?"

She saw those telltale eyebrows rise, but his tone was mild as he asked politely, "Why am I doing what?"

"Did Giles really need to make that phone call this afternoon?"

"No, he didn't."

"At least you're honest...about some things." She was going to go on, but he cut in quickly.

"What do you mean by that remark?" he demanded. "What has made you decide to limit my honesty to 'some things?'"

She blurted out her answer and knew that this whole subject had been right at the tip of her tongue all along. It was a miracle she hadn't come out with it in Oscar Wechsler's office.

"You haven't been very honest about Laura," she told him.

"I haven't been honest about Laura? Now what's that supposed to mean?" He was feigning surprise, Anne was sure.

"You're a poor liar," she said distinctly.

Timothy stopped in the middle of the sidewalk. It

was a narrow sidewalk, and passersby, having to edge around him, glared at him impatiently.

"I have never lied to you, Anne," he said firmly.

"Then let's say you haven't told me the whole truth."

"That's not so, either!"

"Then what were you doing with Laura in New York, Timothy? It's interesting that you chose to take her to one of my favorite French restaurants. I can't imagine how the two of you would ever have picked it for a rendezvous, but...."

He stared down at her, dangerously calm. "There are moments when you have a nasty way of putting things," he sid quietly. "Now you're faulting my taste, is that it? Or is it that you don't think persons like myself are capable of having good taste in the first place?"

"You're evading the issue," Anne accused.

"No," he said, "I am not evading the issue."

"Shall we start walking again?" she suggested, coldly polite. "We're causing people to trip over us."

He shrugged indifferently, but he did begin to move ahead, slowing so she could keep pace with him. But there was a darkness to the silence between them, a darkness that made Anne shiver.

"Why didn't you tell me you'd seen me in New York. .with Laura?" Tim said quietly.

"Why didn't you tell me you'd met her there?" Anne countered.

"Because I wanted to wait until I could give you a complete story."

"And it took you four months to invent something believable?" she taunted nastily.

"I'll ignore that."

"How long have you known Laura?"

"How long have I known her?" he echoed, seeming genuinely astonished. "I met her that morning in Bigelow's office. As it happened, we left together. She told me that there were, well, some things she'd like to talk to me about. She said they were rather private things. They didn't affect the case, so she felt there was no reason why her attorney should be present."

"I can imagine," Anne said caustically.

"If you want to jump to conclusions you'll just have to face up to your own hurdles," Timothy told her. "I suggested dinner and, ironic though it may seem to you, that particular French restaurant has been a favorite of mine for a long time."

"I see."

"You don't see a damned thing!" he said abjectly, then added, "Now I understand that long look of pure loathing you gave me in Wechsler's office. You do know how to give them, Anne. If I hadn't already felt like a displaced person where you're concerned, that look alone would have done it."

"Oh, please!" she sparked, annoyed. "Stop the sympathy bid!"

Suddenly she felt as if Timothy had left her, as if she were walking alone. Venturing a glance at him, she saw that his profile was rigid.

The cry came inadvertently. "Tim, don't shut me out again!"

He didn't answer and, looking ahead, she saw the Parker House on the next corner.

As they neared the entrance Timothy asked, "Would you rather I leave you here? I'm sure Giles will be along soon."

"No!" she snapped, the one short word explosive.

"I don't think we have much more to say to each other, Anne," he warned.

"On the c-contrary," she told him. "I think we have a great deal to say to each other. We t-tend to misunderstand each other far too easily."

"Have I misunderstood what you've been saying to me?" Tim asked. "It seems to me you've called me a liar and a cheat and a person with little or no taste, as well. Not in so many words, of course, but your intent was clear."

"Stop talking like a lawyer!"

"How would you have me talk, Anne?"

She looked up at him, exasperated. "Like yourself, Tim," she told him softly, almost whispering. "Can't you just be yourself? The way you were yesterday."

CHAPTER FOURTEEN

IT SEEMED IMPOSSIBLE that Giles could have covered the distance between his office and the Parker House so quickly. Yet it was unmistakably his voice calling out, "Hey there, you two!" As Anne and Timothy turned around, he hurried down the street toward them.

"Crocker's gone home for the day, Tim," he said, a bit breathlessly. "Come on, I'll buy you both a drink."

For a moment Anne was afraid that Timothy was going to refuse Giles's offer. But then he nodded, and they moved as a trio into the hotel, descending a flight of marble steps to the lounge.

Timothy ordered Bushmills on the rocks—as if being defiantly Irish, Anne thought, although at the moment she didn't find that very amusing. She and Giles decided on whiskey sours.

Giles kept the conversation going, touching on a number of things of general interest. He didn't seem aware of the tension crackling between Anne and Timothy, and Anne wondered if this was merely politeness on his part or if he simply wasn't intuitive about such things. Had the situation been reversed, she was sure Timothy would have been far more perceptive. But then Timothy was more in tune than most people to the moods and sensitivities of others.

He was such a sensitive person himself, and she'd hurt him that afternoon. She was only beginning to realize how much, and she would have given a great deal to be able to go back even an hour in time. If she had a second opportunity she would phrase her questions about Laura quite differently, for one thing. As it was. . . .

Giles suggested another round of drinks, but Anne had no desire to prolong this particular cocktail hour. Timothy, who was being unnaturally silent, looked at his glass absently, and she feared he was going to order another Bushmills. But to her relief he said, "No thanks. I have an appointment with a client before I call it a day." Then, to her astonishment, he added, "Coming, Anne?"

Giles mirrored her bewilderment, but before she could respond, Timothy said levelly, "I'm going out to Chestnut Hill, Giles, so it would be easy for me to drop Anne off along the way."

"Well. . . ." Giles began, but Timothy interrupted.

"We have a bit of unfinished business to discuss," he said.

"Okay," Giles agreed reluctantly. He forced a smile. "I'll call you later, Anne."

"Fine, Giles," she told him, but her mind was not at all on what she was saying. She had no wish to encourage Giles. The moment would come, she knew very well, when he would cease being merely a pleasant companion. All the signs pointed that way. Even now it was obvious that only Giles's innate good manners were keeping him from protesting Timothy's sudden plan to drive her home.

Giles said a bit morosely, "I think I'll have one more drink myself before I take off."

Timothy nodded and stood up, passing a handful of bills across to Giles at the same time. "Our share," he said succinctly, and Anne could have throttled him. As she'd observed before, when Timothy Flanagan wanted to be high-handed, he became very high-handed.

Giles flushed noticeably, and Anne sensed that he was on the verge of a sharp retort. But he merely remarked stiffly, "That wasn't necessary, Tim. I'd intended it to be my treat. Next time, perhaps."

"Next time," Timothy concurred.

He was right behind Anne as they left the lounge, his hand resting lightly on her elbow. There was no particular force to his thrust, yet she felt as if she were being propelled up the stairs and out of the place.

Once on the sidewalk she turned to face him defiantly. "You had no right to take over like that!" she accused.

He gazed down at her, and it was impossible not to note how tired he look. Tired...and withdrawn. He said indifferently, "I wasn't trying to 'take over,' Anne. I didn't think you wanted another drink, that's all. And I certainly didn't want one myself."

"So..."

"So I suggested we get along."

"You never mentioned you were going out to Chestnut Hill," she reminded him. "And Giles...."

"Yes, I know," Timothy said wearily. "Giles wanted to drive you home himself. I don't need you to tell me that. The poor guy's really smitten with you."

Anne bristled. "What makes you call Giles a 'poor guy'?" she demanded.

"Because I don't think you return his feelings. Am I right?"

She hesitated only briefly. "It isn't any of your business, Tim," she told him.

"Ah, but it is my business," he contradicted, taking her arm again gently. Then he said, "I left my car for some repair work this morning at a garage just off the Common. I checked earlier, and it's ready. So, if you wouldn't mind a bit of a walk...."

He didn't give her a chance to answer. He was steering her along Tremont Street, then chose a diagonal path that cut across the Boston Common. The late afternoon sunlight was touched with the ripe gold of autumn, dappling the trees, already beginning to turn color themselves, with molten beauty. Anne looked up at Timothy and saw that the sunlight had also found his hair, burnishing it to a rich copper shade. His skin, too, was bathed in bronze, and she caught her breath at the sight of him. Despite his weariness he was incredibly handsome.

At that instant he glanced down directly into her eyes, and inexplicably Anne found herself on the verge of tears. A sob, quickly suppressed, caught in her throat.

"What is it, Anne?" Tim asked gently, stopping on the footpath, his gaze concerned. "You look so... sad."

"Perhaps I am a bit s-sad," she confessed.

"You're so sure I've let you down, aren't you?" he said dully. "You saw me in New York last May, and immediately leapt to your own conclusions... which brings me to something I cannot understand. Why," he asked, struggling to find the right words, "would you go back to Southie... and then come to my apartment with me? How could you do that, Anne? How could you let me make love to you, if you think I...."

She could only manage a whisper. "I... I d-don't know, Tim."

"For heaven's sake, Anne!" he protested. "We... belonged to each other. To me, it was like... a miracle. And for you...."

"Yes?"

"I think you know what I'm saying. You know how I feel about myself, about my background." He laughed shortly. "Oh, yes," he said bitterly, "I spilled it all out to you as if you were my confessor, didn't I? But that was because I was beginning to believe in you!"

She flinched at his choice of words. Believing in someone. Trust. Faith. She knew without being told that such things did not come easily to him.

"Tim. . ."she started.

"Don't try to explain, Anne," he cut in, shaking his head. "Right now I'm not sure I'd be able to believe you. . .even if you were telling me the truth. I'm not even sure I'd recognize the truth, for that matter, so you might as well save your breath!"

He said this harshly, and Anne felt as if he'd slapped her. They started walking again, but though physically he was still beside her, it was as if the real Timothy Flanagan had suddenly moved miles away.

She said painfully, "Why don't I just get a cab, Tim. You don't really need to go out to Chestnut Hill, do you?"

He halted, his jaw tight. "Do you think I prevaricate about everything?" he demanded.

"No, of c-course not," she stammered. "But I did think that maybe you just invented having to go out to Chestnut Hill so you could talk to me, and g-get me away from—"

"Your tongue is running away with you, Anne," he said sharply. "Anyway, I have a meeting scheduled with the man I told you about before—the man who has permitted me to use his property in South Boston as a small athletic field for some of the boys. As it happens, he has become interested in this project of mine. He's even thinking of buying uniforms for the kids. I'd told him I'd stop in and see him today after our meeting with Oscar. So it was not a last-minute thought on my part, Anne. Nor was I looking for an excuse to drive you home."

He might as well tell me I'm flattering myself,
Anne thought, stung.

"I can't imagine," she managed with difficulty,
"that you particularly want to be in the same car
with me at the moment."

"Can't you, now?" he taunted, deliberately
adopting the brogue.

He had begun to walk faster, his tension manifest. Anne struggled to keep up with him only to
stumble over an uneven patch of sidewalk so that
she nearly fell. Timothy clutched her as she
wobbled, then steadied her.

"I'm sorry," he said, still holding her arm. "You
should have asked me to slow down. I suppose I'm
used to walking alone."

There was a double meaning to what he was saying, Anne knew. But as they started off again—
Timothy carefully maintaining a slower pace—she
decided not to question him. She was more concerned about where she was walking and wished her
boots didn't have such high heels.

She thought they would never get to the garage
where Timothy had left his car, but finally they
made it, and the Saab was steered onto Common-
wealth Avenue.

It was the height of the rush hour and traffic was
very heavy, so Timothy was kept busy concentrating on his driving, and for that Anne was thankful.
The less they said to each other right then, the better! she told herself.

He was not done with her, though. As he pulled
up at the Chestnut Hill house, he sat back and

looked across at her, and his eyes were as cold as Connemara marble.

"One thing," he said. "I'm not about to explain that scene in New York with your stepmother, nor am I going to apologize for that, or for anything else under the circumstances."

His message couldn't be more clear, Anne thought, her spirits sinking. He was challenging her, and the next move would have to come from her.

She waited for a moment, expecting him to get out and come around the car to open her door for her. But he didn't. He was not Giles Winslow, she told herself. No matter what the situation between them, Giles would not have neglected this sort of mannerly touch.

Timothy Flanagan did not play by the same set of rules, though. Timothy Flanagan was, in fact, different in every way she could imagine.

Anne found the door latch, her fingers trembling as she tugged it open. But before she stepped out of the car she turned to face him. "Thank you for bringing me home," she said sincerely.

He made no move to reach out and touch her. He made no move toward her at all. He merely said, as if she was a total stranger, "You're entirely welcome."

ALTHOUGH USUALLY A VERY sympathetic person, Anne was not in the mood to listen to anyone's troubles that afternoon. She intended going directly to her room, flinging herself down on the bed and very possibly crying herself to sleep.

As she let herself into the house, she was painfully conscious of the sound of the Saab's engine behind her. It was revving into action. Timothy was leaving, and she was very much afraid that this time he was going past the point of no return as far as the two of them were concerned.

If he had only reached out one finger to touch her cheek! If he had only stopped her! If he had only come around to open the door for her, and then had taken her into his arms and held her close, so close that she could feel the strong throbbing of his heartbeat!

If he had only. . . .

If she had only thought before she'd spoken about Laura.

She should have remembered his pride, Anne told herself. That dreadful all-consuming pride of his. She should have remembered how vulnerable he was, despite his self-assured, almost arrogant veneer.

But she hadn't remembered. She'd spoken her piece and had virtually accused him of deceit where Laura was concerned. This was something she couldn't take back. Nor was it something she could discuss with Giles or Oscar Wechsler.

She paused in the foyer to scan some mail Bridget had placed on the table for her. There were several sympathy letters and the usual accumulation of business mail. She dispensed with everything but a letter from the president of the bank in New York. Opening it hastily, she discovered that her request for an indeterminate leave of absence had been granted, and she was further gratified to read that her job would be ready and waiting for her whenever she wished to return.

It's nice to know that I'm successful in at least one area of my life! she thought bitterly. *If I could do half as well personally as I do professionally. . . .*

Her smile was rueful and her heart heavy as she started up the stairs. But she'd barely gotten to the second step when she heard Bridget calling behind her, "Anne, is that you?" She sounded very agitated.

A moment later Anne saw that Bridget not only sounded very agitated, she was agitated. She'd obviously been crying and was twisting the edges of her apron between her fingers as she spoke.

"Katharine didn't go to the secretarial school this morning!" she blurted.

Anne had entirely forgotten that this was the day Katharine was to start at the school. She'd been so immersed in her own problems lately that she hadn't paid Katharine very much attention. The sessions she'd planned with herself at the piano accompanying Katharine as she sang, had been deferred. More accurately they had not been mentioned to Katharine, simply because time had been so short. Now it seemed that time had run out.

Anne reversed her direction on the stairs, then followed Bridget into the kitchen, where she had disappeared.

"Are you sure she didn't go?" Anne asked, feeling very inadequate.

Bridget nodded miserably. "The school called,"

she said. "Katharine had given them the number here in case they ever needed to get in touch with me. Anyway, the woman at the school—the registrar, she called herself—asked if Miss Kincaid was ill or—"

"What time was this, Bridget?"

"Not long after you left to go downtown," Bridget reported. "I called home, but Katharine wasn't there, either. And she didn't come back here."

Bridget's voice quavered. Her blue eyes appeared faded, and her plump cheeks looked as if someone had pressed thumbprints into them. It was as if she had aged twenty years in a few hours.

Anne went into the dining room and got a bottle of brandy and two glasses out of the corner cabinet. Returning to the kitchen she poured out healthy measures for Bridget and herself, and then made the older woman sit down at the kitchen table.

"Look, Bridget," she said then, thrusting the brandy glass into her hand, "it's not going to do any good for you to fall apart. Actually I'm not surprised that Katharine didn't show up at the school."

As she said this she realized it was true.

Bridget frowned, obviously puzzled, then took a liberal sip of the brandy.

"Is Peter still in town?" Anne asked.

"No, he went back to Maine," Bridget answered. "Anyway, I don't have a phone for him there. Not that Katharine would be apt to take off to Maine, but...."

"She's probably with a friend," Anne said,

tasting her own brandy. "Let's make up a list of some of the girls she knows and I'll start calling."

Bridget shook her head. "I'm not saying Katharine doesn't have friends," she began, "but unless I'm very much mistaken there isn't anyone she would go to at a time like this. Katharine's always been one to keep her problems to herself. That's one of her troubles. She's kept it all locked up inside of her."

Bridget shuddered. "The quiet ones like her, they're the ones that get in the deepest water."

The analogy struck Anne. Timothy was also one of the quiet ones, she realized with a shock. He, too, would tend to keep the things that mattered to him the most locked up inside.

Anne forced her thoughts back to Bridget. "Does Ben know about this?" she asked, using his first name automatically. A rapport, strained though it was, had existed between them, she remembered.

"I doubt it," Bridget said. "He'll be home by now, but I'm not about to call him. Anyway, if Katharine wasn't home earlier, she won't be there now. The last person she'd want to face is her father. It would be like asking for the wrath of God!"

"Perhaps not," Anne mused.

"And what is that to mean?"

"I don't think Ben is as unreceptive to Katharine's singing as he pretends to be," she stated firmly. "He was interested when I spoke about how beautifully Katharine sang in church."

"Maybe...but he'd not darken the door to hear her for himself," Bridget countered.

"Another time perhaps he will," Anne said. "Look, Bridget, don't borrow trouble. Katharine has a good head on her shoulders. She isn't going to do anything crazy."

Anne spoke with an assurance she was far from feeling.

Bridget got to her feet, saying slowly, "I'd better fix you something to eat. It's getting late."

"Not tonight, Bridget," Anne said hastily. "Tonight you just sit and try to relax. I'll fix some soup and toast for us after a while. I'm sure you're no hungrier than I am, but we've both got to eat. Meanwhile, let's try to get some logic into our thinking. I can't help but feel that Katharine must know someone—someone she went to high school with, maybe—with whom she's close."

Bridget shook her head again. "Oh, now, I'm not saying that Katharine didn't have friends in school," she added quickly, "but not close friends. She's never been one to bring classmates home with her, and I blame that on Ben. He doesn't take to having strangers around."

"He was very nice to me," Anne pointed out gently.

"Yes, so he was. But you got on the right side of him, somehow. And you're a Clarendon. Ben has respect for your family. And I've known you, after all, since you were a wee one."

Bridget's eyes grew misty. "I knew you before Katharine was born," she said. "Back when I was still Bridget Malone, remember?"

Anne remembered very well. Bridget had been

the plump, pink-cheeked Irish-American girl who'd been full of fun. Bridget had been an ally when she had visited the Chestnut Hill house as a child. She could remember Bridget sneaking her warm oatmeal cookies—freshly made with walnuts and raisins—as a forbidden in-between meals snack.

Anne carefully measured out a bit of brandy in each of their glasses and glanced toward the clock. It was nearly seven. "Bridget, don't you think you'd really better give Ben a call?" she asked.

"He won't be expecting me yet," Bridget told her. "And if I'm late he'll put it down to my staying to tidy up the dinner dishes."

"Even so...."

"I'm not about to face Ben until I have to," Bridget insisted stubbornly.

Anne sighed. She could imagine Ben as he must have been when Bridget first met him. A big good-looking Irish lad, full of fun and mischief. She could appreciate how easy it must have been for Bridget to fall in love with him. And, if she were to judge, there was still a deep love between Bridget and Ben, except for Bridget it had become coated with a layer of fear. Ben had adhered so much to the old ways. He'd insisted that as the man of the house he had the right to determine Katharine's future. The sad thing was that he truly believed he was acting in the best interests of the women in his life, both Bridget and Katharine.

Ben Kincaid, for all of his stubbornness, had not struck Anne as a cruel man. But it was not up to her to call him and tell him his daughter had evidently taken an action diametrically opposed to his wishes.

Thinking about this she said, "I suppose the tuition at the school was paid in advance?"

Bridget nodded. "And quite an amount it was, too. I was astonished when Ben put it out without so much as batting an eyelash. It goes to show how much he wanted this for Katharine. He could see her having a good job, dressing nicely when she went to work every day, making good money without having to struggle for it. At the back of his mind I think he had the idea that maybe after a time she'd marry well—her boss, for example."

Bridget shook her head yet again. "Not that Ben has anything against Peter, I can't honestly say that. He's good enough to Peter and doesn't object to him coming to the house. Usually he shares a beer with him. But Peter's got a way to go before he'll make a good living, and Ben's not much for something like computers. He's rather old-fashioned in some ways."

"Still, Bridget, he is a good man."

Bridget raised her dull blue eyes. "Yes, Anne, he is a good man," she agreed. "But he also can have the temper of the devil—and this happening will bring out the worst in him!"

Something in Anne still doubted this. It seemed to her there was a good chance that Ben would be as worried about Katharine as Bridget was if the girl didn't show up soon.

And Katharine didn't show up. The clock never seemed to have ticked so slowly, and Anne felt as if she'd been home for days when finally, around nine o'clock, she opened a can of soup, made toast, and insisted on Bridget sharing this simple repast with her.

She followed this with a pot of strong tea—Irish tea, she thought wistfully, reminded of Timothy—and poured out a cup for each of them. Then, as she passed Bridget her teacup she was stopped in mid-motion, appalled by what she saw.

Big round tears were slowly running down Bridget's cheeks.

In an instant she was kneeling by Bridget's side. Then their arms were around each other and they clung together, moved by a mutual apprehension that couldn't be denied any longer.

Katharine Kincaid was not the kind of girl who would have done something like this merely to defy her father. Anne knew that. Katharine was an obedient girl, a religious girl, a girl devoted to her parents. Had it been otherwise, she would have defied Ben a long time ago.

She must have been troubled—very troubled—not to have shown up at the school. Thinking this, Anne knew a pang of real fear.

She got to her feet, everything forgotten now except her own concern for Katharine. She knew she was going to have to get help for both Bridget and herself, so there could be some sense put into their decision about what to do next.

It didn't seem strange at all to realize that the only person in the world she wanted to turn to when it came to seeking help was Timothy Flanagan.

CHAPTER FIFTEEN

ANNE TOUCHED HER FINGER to the telephone dial, then hesitated as a sudden vision of the silver-framed photograph on Timothy's dresser came to taunt her. She could see the girl smiling back at her and was again shaken by this. Who was she? And where was she now? Suppose she answered the phone in Timothy's apartment! Thinking this, Anne nearly choked.

Noting her hesitation, Bridget asked anxiously, "What is it, Anne?"

"Nothing," she said quickly, forcing herself to dial Tim's home number, her hand trembling nervously.

He answered on the second ring, and hearing his deep familiar tone, Anne drew in a sharp breath. The mere sound of his voice was more overwhelming than she would have believed, and for a moment she couldn't speak.

"Hello?" he repeated.

"Tim?" she rallied weakly.

"Anne!" he said anxiously, recognizing her tone at once.

"Tim, c-could you possibly c-come out here?"

"What's happened, Anne?"

"Katharine has r-run off somewhere." She sighed heavily. "At least, it seems so. Her mother is terribly worried, and...."

"Katharine?" he queried.

"Katharine Kincaid, Bridget's daughter. You know her, Tim. She's been staying here with me."

"Yes...." he said, remembering. "For a moment I almost forgot that you weren't alone."

"Tim...."

"It's okay, Anne. I'll get there as soon as I can."

Anne's eyes were swimming in tears as she hung up the receiver, and turning to Bridget she said huskily, "He's on his way."

Bridget had been watching her very closely, Anne realized. Despite her own worries about Katharine, the older woman said, "Timothy Flanagan's a wonderful man, Anne. You shouldn't be fighting your love for him."

Anne smiled a sad tearful little smile. "Am I that obvious?"

"You are," Bridget affirmed. "But I doubt that Timothy sees it. Remember, Anne, I told you that his heart's in his eyes when he looks at you. 'Tis true, provided you have your back to him! That's to say, provided you're not watching him. Oh, I've seen the both of you," Bridget waxed on. "I told your aunt, too, that I could see the way the wind was blowing."

"You told Aunt Muriel?" Anne asked shyly. "H-how did she react?"

"She said you'd never find a better man," Bridget replied firmly. "Of course, she was quite fond of Tim Flanagan herself."

"I know," Anne said wistfully. She wished she weren't feeling so confused about practically every-thing.

"Don't let him go, Anne," Bridget advised. "Surely there's something gone amiss between the two of you, but I daresay it's nothing that can't be mended."

"I don't know..." Anne said regretfully. She knew that she'd taken a step backward with Tim earlier that day. A serious step backward. In bring-ing up Laura as she had, she'd leveled both personal and professional accusations at him. They had been unspoken accusations, but he'd been fully aware of her thoughts and deeply resentful of them. Nor could she blame him. She could see now that she hadn't given him a chance to defend himself. Not that he would have cared to do so, she thought dis-mally, and she couldn't blame him for that, either.

The next twenty minutes dragged by. Bridget made a fresh pot of tea and got a pound cake from the freezer while Anne wandered through the down-stairs rooms, gazing anxiously out the front win-dows. Finally she saw a car come to a quick stop on the street. It was the Saab. She recognized its shape in the dim yellow light of the streetlamp. Then, feel-ing her heart beginning to pound, she saw the tall silhouette of a man crossing the front lawn.

Timothy! Anne raced to the front door, pulled it open quickly and literally flew at him. She felt his arms encircle her and buried her face against his shoulder. The feel of him, the scent of him, everything about him spelled sanctuary to her—a sanctuary she badly needed.

"Oh, Tim," she murmured, her voice muffled by the fabric of his coat, "I . . . I love you so!"

She could feel him stiffen. Then, very slowly, he disengaged himself from her and stepped back.

"Quite a welcome!" he observed, his voice rough, and Anne wasn't sure whether he'd heard what she said and was choosing to ignore it, or whether he hadn't heard her at all and was as rattled as she was by their sudden proximity to each other.

He followed her out to the kitchen, and Anne was reeling inside as she poured tea for the three of them and then took her place at the kitchen table.

Tim, sampling the small pieces of pound cake that Bridget had warmed in the toaster oven, listened to the story of Katharine's failure to report at the secretarial school and her subsequent disappearance.

"Two things, Bridget," he said when she had finished. "First, I agree with Anne. I think you should call Ben. In fact, it might be an idea to get him to come over here. Second, we've got to find a way to contact Peter Dwyer. Katharine may be headed toward Maine."

"Katharine? She wouldn't!" Bridget objected.

Tim cocked a skeptical eyebrow. "She loves him, doesn't she?"

Bridget looked from Timothy to Anne, and then back to Tim, her eyes wide. "Yes," she said quietly. "Yes, Katharine loves him."

"And surely she's confident that he loves her."

"Oh, yes," Bridget agreed, nodding more confidently. "I would say that's the one thing Katharine's really sure of."

"Then wouldn't you say Peter would be a likely person for her to go to under the circumstances?" Timothy suggested.

Bridget hesitated, then said, "I'd not thought about it like that. But...it's true. You do turn to someone you love when you're in trouble. If you're lucky enough to have someone."

Anne had been staring at the contents of her teacup, but hearing this she looked up directly into Timothy Flanagan's green eyes. There was a special depth to them tonight, a curiously knowing look, and she felt as if she were drowning in them, and was certain that Tim must be thinking the same thing.

She'd turned to him when she needed help.

"I'll call Ben now," Bridget said reluctantly. "Katharine's been writing to Peter, so his address should be right in her room."

"Would you rather I ran you over to your house, Bridget, so you could look for it yourself?" Timothy asked.

Bridget had a small car of dubious vintage she used for her daily commute, but Anne felt that the plump little housekeeper was in no condition to drive just now. Yet when Bridget gratefully accepted Tim's offer, she felt a pang of something she diagnosed as pure selfishness on her part.

She hated the thought of staying in the Chestnut

Hill house alone while Timothy drove Bridget to Dorchester. He would be gone the better part of an hour, at least, and now that he was with her, she didn't want him to leave.

Resolutely she shut off these thoughts. As Bridget went to get her coat, she turned to Tim and asked, "Is there anything I can do while you're gone?"

He came over to her and stood staring down at her without saying a word, and his face had never looked more inscrutable. Then he smiled faintly. "You can keep the home fires burning, *mavourneen*," he said gently. He bent and kissed her, a kiss so overwhelmingly tender it threatened to undermine the last vestige of Anne's self-control.

She reached out for him blindly, and he caught her hands in his. "Have a little faith, dear Anne," he said, his smile sad. "Have a little faith in me... and yourself."

Anne stood mute, and there was no chance to answer him. Bridget came back, and Tim shepherded her out the kitchen door, following her without so much as a backward glance.

Alone, Anne washed out the teacups and stacked them in the sink. Then she put the unused portion of pound cake back in the fridge. After that she looked around dolefully, trying to find something else to do.

She wished desperately that she'd engaged Katharine Kincaid in a great deal more conversation while she'd had the chance. If so, then perhaps she would have been able to think of something really helpful to do. Katharine might have spoken of friends that Bridget didn't even know about. Or....

Anne shook her head. There were few things in life more useless than pursuing a lot of "ifs."

She looked around the kitchen searching for any possible tasks that might be waiting, but Bridget was an efficient housekeeper. There was nothing to be done. She drifted into the library and switched on the TV, but after a few minutes turned it off again. She simply wasn't in the mood for the video world.

Finally she sat down at the piano. Her fingers began drifting across the keys, and she found herself playing a song from *Camelot*. Then she went through a series of tunes from other old musicals. And somewhere along the way she started singing without even realizing it.

She had just finished, "I've Grown Accustomed to Your Smile," from *My Fair Lady*, when she felt a prickling sensation at the nape of her neck and knew she was being watched. She turned to see Timothy standing silently in the doorway, and had no idea how long he'd been there.

She turned so swiftly, in fact, that this time she did surprise his heart in his eyes—and suddenly she knew what Bridget had been talking about. A tenuous thread seemed to spin itself between them, and Anne felt herself being drawn to Timothy. She thought her heart was about to stop beating, and somehow she was sure he was experiencing the same reaction. Yet neither of them made a move toward the other.

He said, plainly shaken, "Your voice...is so beautiful. I can think of nothing in life that would be more wonderful than...."

"Yes?" Anne encouraged as he broke off.

He shook his head. "Wishful thinking," he told her with a wry grin. "Impossible dreams." Then he added abruptly. "Katharine *is* in Maine."

"What?" The shock was sufficient to make Anne temporarily forget about what might have been a very tender moment between Timothy and herself if she could have persuaded him to say just a few words more.

"Bridget found the address Katharine's been writing to," he told her, crossing the room and coming to sit down in an armchair near the piano. "We managed to latch onto a phone number at that address. Seems it was a private home turned into apartments. The people we reached knew Peter, and they went and got him. Katharine's with him. She was there when he got home from work tonight."

Timothy thrust out his long legs and stared reflectively at the tip of his shoes. "Funny," he mused. "You can never tell about people. I should have learned that by now. I honestly wouldn't have thought she had it in her. I didn't think she had the spunk."

"She's Bridget's daughter," Anne said, which made sense to her, although she wasn't sure whether or not it would make sense to Timothy.

"So she is," he agreed.

"How did Ben react to all of this?"

"Like an angry bull at first, but he's calming down," Timothy said. "Like a lot of Irishmen, he's got far more heart than he wants to admit. He hides his softness, which he no doubt considers weakness, by bragging and blustering. But when you get down to essentials he's a good man who deeply loves his family. And he adores Katharine. He'd do anything for her. In fact, he thought that by sending her to secretarial school he'd be doing everything for her, and it would have been pretty difficult to make him see it otherwise. Now that this has happened, though. . . ."

"What are they going to do?" Anne demanded. "Peter's due to come back from Maine any day now to start school himself, isn't he?"

"Yes," Timothy nodded. "But in the meantime he and Katharine are going to get married!"

Anne was incredulous. "I don't believe it!" she exclaimed.

"Do believe it," Tim advised her. "Bridget suggested they wait and get married here, but Katharine said very firmly that they're going to get married there. By a priest, she promised. But I don't think she has any intention of delaying very long and risking the chance that her father might be able to interfere with her plans."

"Ben must have raged when he heard that," Anne said.

"Yes, he did indeed," Timothy told her mildly. "Luckily Bridget and I stopped at a liquor store on the way over and I bought a bottle of Bushmills. The three of us shared a couple of shots, and I left the bottle with Ben. I don't doubt that he will get ripsnorting drunk and have a sore head in the morning. But he'll become reconciled to this very quickly, if you want my opinion."

"And Bridget?"

"Bridget will handle Ben," Tim said matter-of-factly. "Despite all her seeming timidity she's been handling him for years. I'd venture to say that the first time she ever met up with any real opposition from him was over this matter of Katharine's singing."

"I wonder what will happen to Katharine's singing now," Anne conjectured.

"I think Peter will see that she has voice lessons no matter how much scrimping it may cause them," Tim predicted. "Katharine will have her chance, I promise you."

"When you get to Katharine's level, voice lessons can be very expensive," Anne said thoughtfully. "And having her go to a conservatory on a full-time basis might be absolutely prohibitive for them, though that's what she should do."

She looked up at Timothy as she said this, and it wasn't hard to read his mind. Obviously he still felt this was what she should have done. Possibly he thought it was what she still should do.

It's too late for me, Anne found herself thinking, but she felt no sorrow or self-pity. *I still love to sing, and I'd still like to study. But I wouldn't have the dedication to make a career of it, not anymore. It takes too much discipline, too much time, it's all-consuming. And that isn't what I want out of life any longer.*

What did she want out of life? Anne stood up and walked away from the piano. She was afraid her expression would become much too revealing to Tim if she allowed herself to continue thinking along these lines.

She asked, almost abruptly, "Would you like a nightcap before you leave?"

"I'd like a nightcap, yes," he told her. "But I'm not going to leave, Anne."

She stopped dead still in the middle of the floor. "Timothy...."

"Have no fear," he said, making no move to get up from the armchair. "I'll sleep on the couch in here. Growing up, I slept in all kinds of places, so I have the ability to drift off wherever I may happen to be. I'm telling you this just in case you start to protest that I might be uncomfortable."

"You can't stay here, Timothy," Anne said resolutely.

"Timothy, is it?" he asked, and grinned. "You are putting distance between us, aren't you? I accept that. However, I have no intention of making love to you, if that's what is worrying you. What I can't accept is the thought of you being alone here tonight. Bridget was concerned about you, too, so I told her I'd stay over."

"You t-told Bridget!" Anne exploded.

"Yes, I told her and she was relieved." His mouth twisted. "She trusts me more than you do," he said then.

"It's not a question of trusting you, Tim."

"What is it then? Don't you trust yourself?"

The question was thrust at her bluntly, and she

flinched from it. But she was determined to stand up to him and to be honest in doing so. "Perhaps I don't," she admitted.

"Then suppose you let me be strong for both of us?" he suggested. "I think that's the correct phrase, isn't it?"

She hated it when that sarcastic note crept into his voice.

She said stiffly, "I'm perfectly capable of staying here by myself, Tim."

"It isn't a question of capability," he rejoined. "And there is no use arguing with me, Anne. Call it selfish, if you wish, but I'd be unable to sleep a wink myself if I knew you were here alone. So spare me any further protests, will you?"

He was not about to change his mind. Anne knew that all too well. And it was hardly within the scope of her strength to oust him physically. She shrugged, feigning indifference, and asked, "What would you care for in the way of a nightcap?"

"I bought another bottle of Bushmills on the way back over here," Tim replied. "Do you like Irish whiskey?"

"I don't think I've ever had it."

"Well, then, you should try it." He gestured toward the piano. "Play something else, will you?" he asked her. "I'll fix the drinks."

Anne was tempted to refuse him and to say something tart in the bargain. But there wouldn't have been any point in doing so. Playing the piano would be safer than getting into deeper conversations with him tonight, she told herself. So she sat down in front of the keyboard again and let her fingers drift from one melody to another, her mind wandering.

He came and gave her the drink, bringing a coaster with him so that she could put her glass on the piano without marring the beautiful polished surface of the wood. Timothy would think of something like that, she conceded. Timothy appreciated beauty in all forms. He would protect beautiful things, things dear to him.

She found herself playing the opening chords of an old song from *Carousel* called "If I Loved You."

If I loved him! she thought, balking. *I love him so much I don't think I can go on very much longer without him!*

Tim, back in the armchair again, asked, "Will you sing it for me...please?"

Anne started softly, but her voice was soaring by the time she finished the song, her tones pure and exquisite, the words emotion filled. Hastily she reached for her drink and was glad that Tim had made it a strong one. The Irish whiskey burned her throat.

Tim said softly, "If I loved you, Anne, I would tell you so many things. I would tell you that if you were mine, each day I spent with you would make up for all the love I've wanted and never had. I would tell you...."

If I loved you, Anne.

Later Anne cursed herself for having responded as she did just then. Why had she decided to fling down a challenge at a moment when he was saying these things to her, his voice husky with emotion.

Perversity? She didn't know what it was, nor could she analyze her own reasoning. She only knew that to her horror she said, her voice very small, "But you don't love me, do you, Tim?"

She looked across at him to see that he was gazing at her in an uncomprehending sort of way, still lost in his own reverie. She pushed her point. "Who is the girl in the picture, Tim?" she demanded.

He stared at her blankly. "The picture?"

"The picture you keep on your dresser," Anne prompted, and added, "It's she you love, isn't it?"

Tim's face seemed to freeze, and his mouth went tight.

"No," he said, his voice low and angry, "she isn't. Make no mistake about it, Anne. I keep her picture on my dresser not because I love her—but to remind myself how much I hate her!"

It was a bad moment. Timothy finished his drink in one gulp and then stood, tall and remote. Once again he was a stranger.

"I'll use the downstairs bathroom," he told Anne. "If you have an extra pillow and blanket you might throw them down to me."

"Of course," she said, automatically polite, even though it occurred to her that he was dismissing her in her own house. She went up the stairs hastily, intending to carry the pillow and blanket he'd requested back down to him. But he was waiting at the foot of the stairs, and he thrust out his arms.

"Toss them!" he commanded, and she did so.

"I'll turn out the lights and check to see that the doors are locked," he told her, then added, "Sleep well."

Sleep well! As if she could sleep at all, **Anne** thought grimly as she turned toward her own bedroom. But strangely enough, she did sleep. It was a deep and dreamless sleep, and when she awakened in the morning her first conscious thought was the awareness that Timothy was there in the house with her.

She was mistaken, though. She dressed quickly and didn't even pause to bother about makeup, but by the time she went downstairs he'd already left.

BRIDGET CAME BACK to work that morning in a surprisingly cheerful mood.

"'Tis the fates," she affirmed as she bustled around the kitchen fixing Anne's breakfast. "I think even Ben admits it. He went off to work this morning in a different frame of mind, let me tell you. Though," she added, smiling mischievously, "maybe a part of the reason he was so quiet was that his head was as big as a football!"

Anne laughed despite herself. But the laughter faded when Bridget went on to say, "I'll be forever grateful to Tim Flanagan, let me tell you. He was a marvel. Ben was behaving like a lion and Tim handled him like he was a lamb. It was a sight to see. He's a great man, your Timothy...."

"You're mistaken," Anne said quickly, remembering that Bridget had said this to her before. "He is not 'my' Timothy, Bridget."

"Ah, but it's you who is mistaken," Bridget said pertly. "Just wait and see."

But there was nothing to wait and see about. That Tuesday passed without Anne hearing from anyone. Not even Giles called. Tuesday night she stayed in the house by herself for the first time, and the knowledge of her own loneliness was brought to her full force. She wasn't afraid, it wasn't that. But there was such an emptiness to being alone.

She went to sleep berating herself for having brought up the subject of the girl in the picture. Her sense of timing had been disastrous. Why was it that she so often seemed to lose total control of her tongue when she was with him?

Wednesday morning something unexpected happened that did serve to distract Anne from her thoughts of Timothy Flanagan, if only temporarily. She was scanning the *Boston Globe*, casually flipping the pages. Then, abruptly, she stopped.

It had been years since she'd seen Ken Phillips, but she recognized him instantly even though the picture she was looking at was a posed studio portrait. He was in a classic violinist's stance, his violin tucked under his chin, his profile every bit as handsome as she remembered it.

"Well!" she said aloud.

She was at the kitchen table, and Bridget was at the sink polishing silver.

Turning around, Bridget asked, "What is it?"

"An old...friend of mine is giving a concert at Symphony Hall next week," Anne said. "He's to be the soloist with the Boston Symphony Orchestra.''

Bridget came to peer over Anne's shoulder at the newspaper picture, and she sniffed. ''Good looking,'' she observed, and didn't seem at all pleased by this.

''Very good looking,'' Anne agreed. ''Ken is tall, dark and handsome. He has marvelously expressive eyes, wonderful hands. He makes a perfect image for a musician.''

''How does it happen that you've never mentioned him before?'' Bridget asked suspiciously.

''We've been out of touch for years,'' Anne admitted.

''A lover's quarrel, I suppose?''

''You're jumping to conclusions,'' Anne laughed, ''but in this case you're right.'' She paused, then reflected, ''I wonder where he's staying.''

Bridget actually seemed alarmed. ''You wouldn't be thinking of calling him, would you?'' she demanded.

''Possibly. Or I might go to the concert if there are still tickets available.''

Amazing, she thought privately, but she could face up to seeing Ken without even the slightest of qualms. In fact, it would be fun to meet him again and interesting to hear him play.

Suddenly she was possessed of an urge that was purely devilish.

''Tim Flanagan seems to have a way of finding out all sorts of things,'' she told Bridget, who stared back at her appalled as she finished, ''Perhaps he can track down Ken for me!''

CHAPTER SIXTEEN

TIMOTHY FLANAGAN was not in his office. Anne was referred to his secretary who told her that Mr. Flanagan was lunching at the Harvard Club and was not expected back until the middle of the afternoon.

Anne moved away from the telephone, acutely disappointed. She had not realized how much she'd counted on hearing Timothy's voice. The letdown because she hadn't was completely disproportionate to the incident itself, she knew. She was being childish, yet she couldn't do anything about it.

Nothing appealed to her today, and she moped around the big house for several hours, growing more and more restless by the minute. Finally she went upstairs and put on her jogging suit, then ran slowly over to the Chestnut Hill Reservoir, less than a mile away. It was a beautiful fall afternoon, the reservoir was sun-spattered cobalt, and Boston's downtown skyline, visible in the distance, sparkled in the clear early-October air.

The path around the reservoir was a well-used one, hard packed and mostly flat. Anne set a fairly easy pace for herself. She hadn't run on a regular basis for some time now—far too long a time, she conceded ruefully—and was feeling the effects of the exercise before she'd gone very far.

But then she got a second wind and with it a very special kind of concentration. Everything around her began to attract her attention—the glimmering surface of the water, the colors of the trees, the nearby Boston College campus. Noticing these things took her mind off the effort of running, and soon there was very little effort needed at all. Her breathing came more easily, her muscles were warm and loose, and she felt almost weightless, gliding along smoothly. By the time an hour had passed, and three laps around the path, she was ready to quit, but it was with the satisfying knowledge that she wasn't as out of shape as she'd feared she might be. She'd run more than six miles and was none the worse for wear.

Back at the house Anne paused in the kitchen to ask Bridget if there had been any phone calls during her absence. There hadn't been, so she showered and then dressed in chocolate-brown slacks and a loosely knit ivory sweater. After this, she curled up on her bed, feeling thoroughly relaxed and quickly fell asleep.

It was nearly dark when she awakened. The house seemed so still, everything so silent. Anne fought back the sharp sense of loneliness that threatened to overtake her, but it was an uneven battle. In this mood she was simply too aware of the bitter fact that she really was very much alone.

There seemed to be no one in the world who truly cared. Naturally she knew her mother loved her, but her mother had made her own life. In that life she would only be an intruder, and besides, her mother lived clear across the country. There could have been Laura, but Laura had turned out to be an enemy. There was Bridget, but Bridget had problems of her own. And while Anne had friends, many good friends, she wondered if there was anyone who would miss her very much if they failed to hear from her for a few months or a year. . . .

I'm becoming maudlin, she warned herself. She slid off the bed slowly and tested her legs, which were slightly sore. *What I need is to get away from this place. I need to get away from Boston, to get away from Tim!*

The impulse to escape became so strong that she itched to call a travel agent and book a trip to. . . well, to Tahiti, or someplace equally exotic. Yet in her heart she knew it would be useless. Wherever she went just now, Timothy Flanagan would be following her. Wherever she looked, she would see his face. There would be no escaping him, unless she somehow stumbled onto a formula that would show her how to wash him out of her system.

How did one go about falling out of love? she wondered, making her way downstairs rather stiffly.

Bridget was sitting at the kitchen table reading a paperback. She looked up with a smile and observed, "Well, and quite the sleeping beauty you've been! I peeped in on you, and you were as snug as a mouse."

Anne remembered something. "Isn't this the

night you were going to a bingo game with Ben?''
she asked.

"Yes, it is," Bridget nodded.

"Well, you said you wanted to get away early because Ben had never suggested anything like this to you before," Anne reminded her. "So shouldn't you have left by now?"

"I was not about to have you wake up in an empty house," Bridget said staunchly. "It bothers me, Anne, your being here alone."

"I'm perfectly all right," she insisted. Then she added a bit morosely, "Anyway, if I'm going to go on staying here I'll have to get used to it."

"It doesn't suit you," Bridget maintained, but she didn't elaborate on this. She began gathering her things together, stashing them in the big old tote bag she always carried. The miscellany she'd collected included her comfortable old working shoes, several outdated magazines that had been headed for the wastebasket, the leftovers Anne insisted on her taking each evening, saying that otherwise they'd go to waste, a broken alarm clock she planned to persuade Ben to fix, and several articles of Muriel's clothing, which Anne had gradually been sorting out.

She smiled as she watched Bridget pack. Her tote bag reminded Anne of Santa Claus's famous sack.

"I've left stew in the fridge, so all you have to do is heat it up," Bridget reported. "And there are rolls in the oven. Just heat them up, too. There's fruit salad and ice cream in the back freezer."

"I'm not apt to starve to death, Bridget," Anne said impatiently. "I'm a big girl, remember?"

"Not always," Bridget countered a bit vaguely.

Anne wanted to ask her what she meant by that, but didn't. Instead, she simply bade the older woman good-night.

Once Bridget had left, though, the sense of loneliness haunting her became pervasive. The world seemed to be full of shadows, eerie shadows. Anne shuddered, and growing restless she wandered from room to room. She was on the verge of thinking that the sensible thing to do might be to let Laura have the house after all when suddenly the front doorbell pealed loudly, shattering the silence.

She was so startled by the sound she jumped. Then she automatically went to open the door, giving no thought to who might be standing on her threshold. Still shaken by this unexpected summons, she forgot to switch on the light in the foyer, so both she and her visitor were darkened silhouettes once she'd turned the knob and swung the door inward.

Timothy Flanagan said abruptly, "You should have more sense, Anne!"

"What?" she asked, confused. His sudden appearance was playing on her nerves, raising havoc with her senses.

"You didn't know it was me, did you?" he demanded.

"No," she said, standing immobile in the doorway.

"You're alone in this barn of a place, Anne!

Doesn't it occur to you that everything in the world isn't sweetness and light? I could have been anyone—''

"About to for 'e your way in here and attack and rob me?'' she suggested, regrouping herself.

"Exactly,'' he retorted tersely. "You might at least turn on a couple of lights. It's dark out here, or hadn't you noticed?''

She hadn't, not really. She'd been too preoccupied. Now, though, she obediently switched on the lamp on the nearest table. It had a Tiffany shade, and the jewel tones glowed beautifully, radiating color against the pale cream plaster. The effect was almost melodramatic.

Tim said huskily, "I wish I had a picture of you standing there with that lamp as a backdrop. All the glory of the rainbow and....'' He shook his head as if ridding himself of this train of thought and asked, "You called me?''

"Yes,'' Anne answered. "I called late this morning.''

"I'd already left for the Harvard club,'' he said, echoing his secretary's words. "I was later getting back than I expected, and then I had to confer with Oscar and Giles. It was one thing after another today...which is why I didn't return your call.''

"You don't owe me any explanations, Tim,'' Anne said quietly. "But I...I hope that's not the reason you m-made the trip all the way out here.''

"That's not the reason...exactly,'' he said, then he frowned. He walked past her and stood closer to the lamp, but even its rainbow hues couldn't conceal the tired lines in his face.

"Since you've come this far, could I offer you a drink?" Anne asked.

He nodded wearily. "If you'll join me, that is."

"I'll join you. I think we have some of your Bushmills left. Would you like that?"

"Anything would be fine," Timothy told her and followed her out to the kitchen. He pulled out a chair at the kitchen table and sat down heavily. Anne got a couple of glasses and then went into the dining room for the liquor. She had the strange feeling there was something he wanted to tell her but had decided to keep it back.

The feeling was reinforced when she sat down across from him after handing him his drink. Yet she knew it wouldn't do any good to ask him a leading question. Timothy was an expert at dodging questions.

She waited, knowing she should let him go about saying whatever he had to say in his own way. But he did nothing toward satisfying her curiosity when he asked, "What did you do with yourself today?"

She shrugged. "Nothing too much this morning," she told him. "This afternoon, though, I went for a run around the reservoir."

He perked up and looked interested. "How did you make out?" he asked her.

"I've done a lot better," she admitted. "But to be honest, it went very well, considering I'm out of practice. I'd say I ran a good six miles—slowly, of course. But at least I didn't collapse."

"Six miles!" he exclaimed. "I'd be excited about running only one mile these days. Any aches or pains?"

"A few," Anne confessed. "Though not as much as I would have expected."

"That's great!" he said, then cautioned, "But don't overdo it."

She smiled. "I won't, coach."

Timothy grinned across at her, that heartstopping grin of his, and Anne was swept by a feeling of love for him. He must have stopped at his apartment to change clothes before coming out to Chestnut Hill, because he was wearing casual corduroy slacks in a shade of very deep green and an ivory Irish-knit sweater that was dangerously becoming.

I could look at him forever, she thought, her mind drifting. *I could be with him forever.* They would have their battles, she knew. They were both strong individuals and would never possibly agree all the time about everything. But that would only be to the good. Tim would be a challenge, and an eternal delight to live with.

He was watching her closely, and she hoped fervently that he wasn't able to read her mind, as she sometimes thought he could. The mere idea made her flush slightly, and she saw his eyes narrow.

"What is it, Anne?" he asked, his smile fading.

"Nothing," she said hastily.

"I'd give more than a penny," he said wryly. "A lot more than a penny. Sometimes I find you very puzzling. But I suppose it's not to be wondered at. We're so different, you and I.''

"Not so very different,'' she said without thinking.

"And what does that mean?'' he queried, his eyebrows arching skeptically.

"Only that I s-sometimes think you exaggerate our alleged d-differences,'' she told him, her nervousness increasing and inevitably bringing the stammer along with it.

"'Our alleged differences,'" he quoted, and smiled. "You're beginning to sound like a lawyer.''

"Association, maybe,'' she said offhandedly, and marveled that she could be light about this.

"I don't want you to become pedantic,'' he warned, then added, "not that I think there's much danger of that happening.''

"Are you saying that lawyers are pedantic?'' she teased.

"I'll take the fifth on that,'' he rejoined. He held out his empty glass. "Would you, *mavourneen*?'' he asked politely. "This has been a hell of a day.''

The simple statement shook Anne. She got up and fixed him another drink, and as she handed him his glass and resumed her seat, she couldn't help but pose the question. "What was so bad about it, Tim?''

"It was a shocker in its way,'' he said quietly. "I'd rather not get into it just now, if you don't mind.''

"Should I mind?'' she asked. "Surely your day didn't involve me...did it?''

"Yes, it involved you," he said bluntly, and Anne stiffened. Noting this, he added hastily, "It will all come out in the wash tomorrow, I assure you. I promised Oscar and Giles that I would ask you to meet with us at ten tomorrow morning. I hope that will be convenient for you?"

"Of course," she agreed, nodding. "But what's it about, Tim? Can't you give me some idea?"

He shook his head. "I'd rather not. When I left the office, which was only about an hour ago, incidentally, there were still some details to finish up. It should all be done by tomorrow, though. Time enough to go into it then."

Anne glared at him. "I could th-throttle you," she said finally. "You are the most exasperating m-man I've ever known!"

"And you, *mavourneen*, are the most exasperating woman I've ever known," he assured her in turn. "Now, what did you call me about today?"

This will serve you right, Timothy Flanagan! Anne said silently. Aloud she told him, "An old friend of mine is giving a concert with the Boston Symphony Orchestra, and I would like to get in touch with him while he's in town. You have a way of finding out...all sorts of things. I thought perhaps you could put your grapevine to work and discover where he's staying."

"An old friend?" Tim observed, his voice edged with sarcasm.

"Yes," she rejoined, expecting—hoping for—this reaction.

"How old a friend?"

"If you mean in years," she replied disarmingly, "Ken is about my age."

"Ken?"

"Kenneth Phillips," she elaborated. "He's a violinist, and quite famous."

"I know," Timothy interrupted darkly. "He played with the Boston Symphony Orchestra last year and got a standing ovation. I was at the concert myself, and he couldn't have played any better." He took a healthy swig of the Bushmills. "Where did you know him?" he asked.

"We went to school together for a while," Anne said, the words coming more slowly. "Then he... continued with music and I...."

"He was the love of your life, wasn't he, Anne?"

The question took her completely by surprise. So much by surprise that she almost answered it involuntarily. She very nearly said, *No... you are!*

Instead, she hedged. "We were... close friends."

"You lived together, didn't you?"

"Honestly, Timothy...."

"'Honestly, Timothy,'" he mocked. "What the hell is this, Anne? You're asking me to find out where your ex-lover is staying while he's in town so you can rekindle your affair with him? What do you take me for?"

Anne looked up to meet a green gaze that was pure fire. "You're misreading me, Tim," she said quietly. "I'd like to see Ken again, yes. But that kind of feeling between us burned out a long time ago."

"You're saying the flames turned to ashes, eh?"

"If you want to put it that way, yes."

"Have you any idea how long embers can keep glowing deep down inside whole beds of ashes?"

Anne smiled and spoke truthfully when she said, "There are no embers left between Ken and me. And although, as I've said, I'd like to see him again just for old times' sake, I do have another reason."

"Oh?"

"I'd like to talk to him about Katharine," she said steadily.

"Katharine Kincaid?" Tim demanded scornfully. "Come on now, Anne!"

"Katharine Dwyer by now, perhaps," Anne reminded him, then added, "and they are going to have a terrific struggle on their hands if Peter tries to finance her musical education entirely on his own."

"What would any of that have to do with Kenneth Phillips?"

"Ken must have so many connections in the music world," Anne said reasonably. "He'd know the people who decide on scholarships, for instance. If Katharine had the chance to sing for some of those people, I've no doubt at all that a way would be found for her to go on with her studies. She and Peter wouldn't have to sacrifice quite so much."

"So you plan to appeal to the better side of Kenneth Phillip's nature, for old times' sake. Is that it?"

"You don't have to put it so crassly," she told him.

"I think if I were in his position I might find it

rather crass to be approached in such a way!'' Tim
said bluntly. ''Which one of you broke off the affair?''

''I d-don't know,'' Anne stammered.

''You don't know? Do you seriously expect me to
believe that?''

''It just h-happened,'' she answered. ''Can you
believe that? Ken was incensed when I—I made the
decision to give up singing and go into a more stable
sort of career.''

''I don't blame him,'' Timothy observed dryly.
''I'm not even a musician and it incenses me when I
think of it.''

For a moment they both sat silently. Then Anne
said softly, ''It wasn't an easy decision for me to
make, Tim. It hurts even now when I think about it.
The whole issue went very deep, and it left a trauma
that lingered for a long, long time. But now....''

''Yes?''

''Well, now I'm finally beginning to feel differently about it,'' she confessed. ''I think if I'd
been meant to be a singer—to have a real career in
singing, that is—I would never have given up so
easily. Not that I really gave up all *that* easily,
because I didn't. What I'm saying is that I would
have taken the risk, even if it meant a long hard
struggle.''

''You, struggle?'' he scoffed. ''You wouldn't
have had to struggle at all. I think you know that.''

She shook her head. ''You still can't see that I
wanted to be on my own, can you?'' she accused
bitterly. ''Just because you know my family had

money, you think there was no reason at all for me to strike out by myself. Well, you're wrong, Tim. I wanted to be my own person as much as you've ever wanted to be yours. Maybe even more so!''

He gave her a level glance before he answered. ''I doubt that, Anne. But then our respective motivations would have been quite different, wouldn't you say? You had all the roots in the world—the family, the heritage, the money—and I had none.'' He broke off and shrugged indifferently. ''But you've heard enough about that side of my life, and I'm not going to get into it again. I hate people who pity themselves.''

The words came out so quickly that Anne couldn't stop them. ''Who was she, Tim?''

''What are you talking about?''

''The girl in the photo on your dresser,'' she persisted, sure that he knew exactly what she was talking about. ''Why do you hate her?''

He was silent for a very long moment. Then he said, staring down at the glass he was twisting between his long fingers, ''Because she made me so consummately aware of exactly what I was and who I was, which, in her opinion, was nothing.''

Anne could see the veil descending. ''Please, Tim,'' she beseeched, ''please. . . tell me about it.''

He didn't hesitate. ''We were in high school together. I'd been placed in a series of foster homes during those years. Foster homes can be wonderful places for kids without families, I know, but I wasn't very lucky in that respect. Except that this particular home was in a decent neighborhood—

one of those situations where you live just next door to the good side of town. It meant that a lot of kids from my neighborhood and a lot of kids from the posh section where she lived, went to the same school.''

"Yes?"

"Well...I fell in love with her the first time I saw her," he said, still staring down at his glass. "She was walking down a corridor with a couple of boys trailing along beside her. There were always boys trailing along beside her. She dropped one of her books as she went by me. I picked it up and handed it to her and she smiled. She had eyes like sapphires and her hair was pure gold. I can't even begin to tell you how she looked to me. Maybe I was young, but she was like all the princesses in all the fairy tales that have ever been written, wrapped into one exquisite package."

"Did you...did you ask her for a date?" Anne faltered.

"Of course not!" Tim said, seeming almost shocked by this. "But she asked me. The first winter dance, she asked me if I'd escort her. I was into athletics by then. I'd played football before, so they took me on the team. You can get to be a big hero fast in high school if you're into sports and a little bit better at them than most other people. She was a cheerleader at the football games, and I made my share of touchdowns. One thing led to another and she asked me to the dance. After that...."

"Yes?"

Timothy shook his head. "This must be boring you, Anne," he commented wryly.

"It isn't," she said, trying to conceal her annoyance at his obtuseness—if he really was being obtuse. There was the chance that he was goading her in his own way. "Go on, will you?" she encouraged.

"Well...." He paused to look at her directly. "In so many ways, Anne, you remind me of her."

"What?" she gasped. This was not at all what she had wanted to hear.

Timothy merely nodded. "The same background, an old New England family, wealth, that sense of belonging, that total self-confidence," he said, ticking off these items on his fingertips. "She had it all, and so do you. Needless to say I didn't tell her anything at all about myself. I didn't even want her to know where I lived." He took a deep breath, then continued.

"I rented a tux for the dance. It was too big for me, and I felt like an idiot in it. And when I tried to dance with her I was all feet. I didn't know you were supposed to send a girl a corsage to wear at a dance like that. I think she was the only girl in the whole place without flowers at her wrist or on her dress, but she didn't seem to mind.

"It went on from there. Weekends, we started meeting in...various places." Tim laughed shortly. "At that point in time she knew a lot more about some things than I did. But I was a fast learner.

"Then one night her father caught me kissing her in the shade of a tree outside her house. He came home unexpectedly, and his car headlights shone right across the two of us. We might as well have been caught in a spotlight. Her father was into politics and very influential on Beacon Hill. Well, believe me, he investigated. He found out all there was to find out about me, and after that I was dirt to her. For the rest of the year she took every chance she could find to get at me in a thousand nasty little ways.

"On weekends, after school and on Saturdays, I had a job. I had to make money to buy clothes, books, things like that. I worked in a meat market, stocking the shelves, carrying out the garbage. It's a pretty messy job, let me tell you. Anyway, she and her friends used to come by and watch me. They'd just sit there across the street in some spoiled kid's fancy car, watching me being a dirty mess wearing a blood-stained apron. Once in a while they'd shout something across at me, or snicker."

"Tim. . . ."

"As I've said," he reminded her quietly, "I hate people who feel sorry for themselves. And I admit she made me feel very sorry for myself at the time. But she also did something for me. I made up my mind that somehow I'd find a ladder in my own life, a ladder I could climb. I made up my mind that I'd see to it the day would come when she'd beg me to take her out."

He laughed bitterly. "A kid's pipe dream," he said.

"But you made it come true, didn't you?" Anne asked carefully.

"The time came when it no longer mattered, at least in one sense," he answered. "She got married to someone in her own social class. Now she's active in things like the Junior League, the proper charities. She's a sponsor of the arts. She has two daughters who look very much like her. They're both blond and beautiful."

He spoke with such familiarity about all of this, Anne was almost afraid to pose the question, yet she had to know its answer. "Do you still see her?" she queried.

"Occasionally," Tim said matter-of-factly. "These days we actually do frequent some of the same places, though I never do so deliberately. Ironically the first time we met again was at a benefit banquet, and she didn't even recognize me. In fact, she made up to me, Anne. Can you imagine that? I was torn between letting her make a fool of herself and then telling her who I was, or telling her right away to go to...."

His words trailed off and Anne asked impatiently, "What did you do?"

"I told her who I was, politely. And I must say she was shocked. This was about three years ago. A week later she called me up."

"Oh." The sound was small and dismal.

"That surprises you, Anne?" Timothy asked, quickly looking across at her. And before she could answer, he said, "She wanted me to meet her for lunch. It was tempting, I admit. But there was absolutely no point in it."

He shrugged. "So that's the story of the girl in

the photograph. I admit that long after I'd fallen out of love with her—if, in fact, I was ever truly in love with her in the first place—she still remained a symbol to me. A reminder that I had a hell of a lot to achieve. That's why I kept her picture, Anne.

"Only very recently," he added carefully, "did I begin to realize what a negative fetish the photo had become. And it may interest you to know that the other day I took the blasted thing, frame and all, and tossed it into the trash barrel!" He was looking steadily at Anne as he said this, and her pulse began to pound.

"Now," he said, "to get down to far more practical issues. About tonight...."

"What about tonight?" she asked, surprised.

"I can't stand the thought of you being out here in this place by yourself," he said frankly. "Maybe in time I'll get used to it, but right now it bothers me. So if it's all right with you, I'll sleep on the living-room couch again...."

It was anything but all right with her. Much as she disliked being in the big old house by herself, the thought of having Timothy there with her was far more disturbing. She was not at all sure she'd be able to stay upstairs if she knew he was only a few feet away.

"I will behave myself," he said. "I promise you. As a matter of fact, I'm too tired to do anything more than behave myself."

But will I be able to control myself? Anne wondered wildly.

"I appreciate your concern for me, Tim," she told him. "I honestly do, but—"

He smiled. "Are you going to tell me you're a big girl now?"

"I suppose, yes," she admitted. Then she added bleakly, "Anyway, I guess I've got to learn to be alone."

"The Clarendon heiress, is that it? Living in her Chestnut Hill mansion surrounded by her valuables. Is that how you see yourself, Anne? Repeating your Aunt Muriel's life?"

"No, that's not how I see myself!" she answered hotly, feeling herself beginning to flush. "And if you remember the story you yourself told me about Muriel, she didn't live the kind of life she did entirely by choice. If the man she loved hadn't been killed...."

"If..." Timothy mused. "Such a small but sweeping word." He looked very somber as he said this, and Anne had the feeling that he was thinking of the "ifs" in his own life. Then he shook his head and said lightly, "Come on now, *mavourneen*. Get yourself upstairs and toss me down a pillow and blanket as you did before. I'll probably be gone in the morning before you've finished your beauty sleep. So I'll see you in the office at ten, all right?"

He was already moving toward the living room as he spoke, and Anne stared at him knowing an unaccustomed sort of helplessness. He was being highhanded in a way that incensed her. Yet she knew that nothing she could say would make him alter his course just now.

Sighing, she started up the stairs and went to do as he'd asked.

CHAPTER SEVENTEEN

BRIDGET WAS VACUUMING the living room when Anne went downstairs the next morning. She glanced quickly toward the couch. There was no sign that Timothy Flanagan had ever occupied it. Obviously he'd left before Bridget had arrived.

Shutting off the machine, Bridget complained, "I was hoping you'd sleep late. The noise of this thing probably woke you up."

Anne shook her head. "No, it didn't."

"Come on out to the kitchen and I'll fix you some breakfast," Bridget suggested.

"Just coffee and a piece of toast," Anne told her. "I'm not hungry at all."

Bridget frowned. "You're getting too thin, Anne," she said bluntly, "and it's not becoming. You look better with a little flesh on your bones, and I'm not saying that just because I need to lose thirty pounds myself!" she finished defiantly.

Anne laughed. "I didn't think you were," she said, then obediently followed Bridget to the kitchen.

A few minutes later, stirring cream into her coffee, she said reflectively, "I had some of the strangest dreams last night. Mostly about Aunt Muriel."

"Dreams of the dead mean news of the living," Bridget said succinctly. "What happened in them?"

"Well, in one Aunt Muriel was getting married," Anne remembered. Then, thinking of what Timothy had told her, she asked, "Would you happen to know who Rose was?"

"Rose Mancini, I imagine that's who you mean," Bridget said. "Yes, I knew her. She was one of your aunt's closest friends."

"Where does she live?" Anne asked eagerly.

"She died four or five years ago," Bridget said regretfully. "They'd known each other a long time, and your aunt missed her very much. I guess they shared a lot of memories, because in all the time I've been working around here Rose Mancini and your aunt only saw each other a few times, but they still seemed very close. Rose lived down in Braintree. She married an Italian and had several kids. So she and your aunt were about as different as two people could be, I'd say. I always wondered at their friendship."

Anne didn't pursue this. It seemed obvious that Bridget knew very little, if anything, of Muriel's ill-fated romance, and this was a secret Anne didn't want to share. In any event, it was simple enough to change the subject by asking, "Have you heard from Katharine?"

Bridget's face lit up. "As a matter of fact she called last night. She and Peter are going to be married this morning! In a Catholic chapel, too. She wanted us to know before they did it. She wanted us

to know they're not just running away from us...
or from anything else.''

"Why didn't you phone me when you heard
this?'' Anne asked reproachfully. "You could have
gone up to Maine and been with them.''

"It was late when they called, after Ben and I got
back from playing bingo,'' Bridget said. "Anyway,
Katharine didn't suggest that I come up. I think she
was afraid her father would come with me and do
something at the last minute to gum up the works.''
She paused, then added complacently, "It's better
this way, Anne, under the circumstances. The main
thing is that now Katharine will be with Peter, and
he'll find a way to see that she goes on with her singing.''

"How is Ben taking this?''

"Better than I thought he would, to be truthful,''
Bridget admitted. Then she added knowingly,
"He'll come around!''

Timothy had inferred that Bridget had the upper
hand in her household when it got down to most
things, and Anne was beginning to believe he was
right.

Thinking of Timothy reminded her of her ten
o'clock appointment at the law office, and glancing
anxiously at the clock she saw to her distress that it
was nearly nine-fifteen.

"Call a cab for me, will you please, Bridget?''
she asked urgently. "I'm going to have to fly! I
have to be at Timothy's office in forty-five
minutes.''

She made it just on time, and hoped that she

looked more composed than she felt as she was ushered into Oscar Wechsler's spacious corner suite. All three of the attorneys were waiting for her. Timothy looked especially handsome in a tailored navy blue suit with a dark gold shirt and a narrow striped tie that combined the two colors.

Giles managed to position himself between Anne and Timothy, but it didn't seem to make much difference, she thought bleakly. Timothy had reverted to being a stranger again. He was formal and almost excruciatingly polite.

Giles, on the other hand, looked as if he was about to burst out with something. As she tried to keep her own wits together wondering what this might be, Anne began to feel anxious.

Timothy had known the previous night all about whatever it was they were going to go into, yet he hadn't wanted to discuss it with her. The holograph will and Laura must be involved, Anne thought, and suddenly she could think of all sorts of dire reasons why Timothy would have been reluctant to get into a discussion with her involving those particular subjects.

Oscar Wechsler, though, didn't keep her in suspense. Once they were settled in their respective chairs, he opened the bulky file folder lying on his desk and said immediately, "Miss Clarendon, we have good news for you."

The statement was completely unexpected. Anne looked across at the distinguished lawyer, her large gray eyes questioning, and repeated dimly, "Good news?"

"Your stepmother is not going to contest," he told her, smiling, "which means that your father's original will can now go to the probate court. She has also withdrawn any claim insofar as the holograph will is concerned."

Anne was staggered. For a moment she could only stare at Oscar blankly. Then she managed, "B-but why?"

"Mr. Flanagan can perhaps answer that best," he said, and nodded approvingly at Timothy.

"I would just as soon have you go into it, Oscar," Timothy said quickly.

"Very well. But if Miss Clarendon has any questions you'll be in a better position to answer them than I am," Oscar reminded his young partner.

He turned to Anne, his blue eyes clear and direct. "As you realize, there has been something about this holograph will that has disturbed us since we first learned of its existence," he said. "I knew your father quite well, and to me this tye of action didn't seem at all consistent with him, his personality, or his way of doing things. It was my feeling that he would have made such a will only because of a very unusual circumstance.

"He had been intending a trip north to consult with us about some of his investments—his stock portfolio, primarily. As you know, our firm has handled the Clarendon affairs for a long time. Your father wished to continue to retain us in this capacity, even after he moved to Florida.

"He died before he ever made this proposed trip, of course. So, when the question of the holograph will arose, my conclusion was that something drastic must have happened in Florida. Something of such an urgent nature that he decided to execute this document on the spur of the moment. He expected to be in Boston not long thereafter, at which time I feel convinced he would have had a new will properly drawn up.''

Anne was puzzled. ''Perhaps I'm not following you correctly,'' she admitted, ''but it seems to me that if this were the case then the holograph will would be valid. I mean...my father would have stated in it what he really wanted to do, wouldn't he have?''

Oscar Wechsler sat back in his swivel armchair, touched his fingertips together and surveyed Anne thoughtfully. ''In essence, yes,'' he agreed. ''That is, he would have stated what he wanted to do at the time. My premise is, though, that this sudden desire on his part must have been motivated by something very explicit. In other words, something happened that made him want to change his will right then and there, on the spot, so to speak. A holograph was the fastest way. It would have been adequate, let's say, until he could get back to Boston.''

Anne tried to absorb this, but having Timothy sitting just to the other side of Giles, staring out into space, didn't help keep her thoughts from whirling. She got the strong impression he didn't even want to look at her.

''Naturally,'' Oscar told her now, ''we wondered what could have happened that made it seem so urgent to your father to draw up a holograph will.

Nothing seemed to have changed in his life at that particular time. Certainly nothing he conveyed to us. . . ."

"What Mr. Wechsler is saying is that we wondered what his hurry was," Giles interjected.

"Thank you, Mr. Winslow," Oscar said rather acidly. "That is precisely what we did wonder, however, Miss Clarendon. It seemed to us your father must have had a very pressing reason for this action. We attempted to find out what that reason might have been, but for all of our queries we couldn't find a thing wrong.

"Then we went over every aspect of the will itself with Mr. Bigelow, Laura Clarendon's attorney. It was a short document, very much to the point. It stated that your father's estate was to be divided between Mrs. Clarendon and yourself—exactly the same as the provision in his original will. The only difference was that the Chestnut Hill house and its contents were to be left to Laura Clarendon, in trust for your father's heirs."

Anne frowned. "In trust for his heirs? What is that supposed to mean?"

"That's what we wondered," Oscar Wechsler conceded. "Mr. Flanagan had the thought that possibly Mrs. Clarendon might be pregnant."

"Laura?" Anne gasped. Even as she asked the question, she wondered why it should shock her so. Laura was still young enough to have children.

"It became obvious, in time, that Mrs. Clarendon was *not* pregnant," the old lawyer continued. "Nor could we find any evidence that she'd been pregnant when your father wrote the holograph. There was a chance that she'd had a miscarriage, of course, but upon investigating this possibility, we found nothing to support it.

"The will was done properly, witnessed properly. So at this point it seemed to us a pretty solid document," Oscar said then. "As a matter-of-fact, twenty-four hours ago I wouldn't have given a fig for our chances of winning if this case ever came to court. Then Mr. Flanagan...."

"Yes?" Anne prompted.

Oscar glanced toward Timothy as if wishing that he'd take up the continuance of this story himself. But Timothy was still staring out the window, seemingly oblivious to the other people in the room.

"Mr. Flanagan has felt all along that there was fraud involved here," he said. "Somewhere, somehow, there was fraud. And, of course, if we could prove fraud in connection with the holograph will then...well, then Mrs. Clarendon's case would have collapsed. That is to say, it would be tossed out of court."

"I still don't understand," Anne said, confused.

Oscar Wechsler looked at her patiently. "Last May, Mr. Flanagan had the opportunity to meet with Mrs. Clarendon in New York," he said. "It was a private meeting," he added, and Anne did not dare glance toward Timothy as the words spilled out.

"This was at her invitation," the older lawyer went on. "They'd met in Mr. Bigelow's office that morning—officially, I might say—and she suggested that they talk together later. So they had dinner. I think Mr. Flanagan would tell you he was left with the feeling that Mrs. Clarendon was a rather... tormented person, shall we say?'' He broke off and added, with some asperity, "Tim, I think you could best go on from here.''

"Very well," he said absently, still staring into space. His voice was dull, emotionless, as he began, "I felt that Mrs. Clarendon had an ax to grind. Or, better, that she thought she had an ax to grind and was bent on doing exactly that. A lot of this came out during our conversation over dinner. I discovered she'd always been somewhat... overwhelmed by your family, Miss Clarendon," he said, turning to Anne icily. "That's to say they left her with the feeling that she was inferior, to quote the word she used. Your Aunt Muriel especially, I would think. Your stepmother told me that none of the Clarendons had ever thought she was good enough for your father. However, I could tally only two Clarendons immediately involved here—you and your aunt. So I could only conclude that she was talking about both of you.''

Anne's lips tightened. She said defiantly, "I've never tried to be anything other than friendly with Laura—until now, of course. It was she...."

"Yes, I'm sure it was she," Timothy said levelly. "Her misconceptions were obvious and rather pathetic. But sometimes people from the other side of the tracks react this way when dealing with someone of your background, Miss Clarendon. The slights they feel are only imagined, but the imagined can become more real than reality itself.''

"The other side of the tracks!" Anne echoed mockingly. "Isn't that an awfully archaic expression, Mr. Flanagan?"

"Perhaps. But I consider it apropos in this case. To continue, I had the feeling that Mrs. Clarendon had gotten herself into something but didn't know how to get out of it. In other words, she'd gotten in too deep. There was no graceful exit, nor would it be easy for a person like her to ever find a graceful exit, I would say. And in this situation she could not refute her claim via the holograph will, because to do so she would have been involving herself in something decidedly...illegal."

"Illegal?"

Timothy nodded. "I did suspect fraud almost immediately," he said frankly. "When I left Mrs. Clarendon at her hotel that night, it was my feeling that she'd be receptive to any sort of overture on our part that might permit her to extricate herself from a bad situation. Yet it didn't seem to me that we had any overtures to make. I couldn't imagine the suggestion that the two of you take over ownership of the Chestnut Hill house jointly. Nor did I think it right that you agree to give up half of your family heirlooms, possessions—whatever you want to call them," Timothy said with an impatient wave of one long slender hand.

Anne ignored this, and Giles shifted uncomfortably. "Go on, Tim," Oscar Wechsler urged.

Timothy took a deep breath, then said, "Well, the phrasing in the holograph kept haunting me. That bit about the house going in trust for your father's 'heirs.' I kept thinking that your father already had an heir—you! Though I don't think he would have thought of you as an heir, but as an heiress. Do you follow my meaning?''

Anne shook her head. ''I'm not sure that I do.''

''Most men when they speak of an heir are thinking in terms of a son,'' Timothy said bluntly.

She stared at him. ''A son?'' she repeated, incredulous.

He nodded. ''Exactly. I had the feeling that your father was thinking of a son, or sons, when he wrote the holograph. So I started looking around for people he'd known—that is, people he'd known well, for years. People here in Boston. Your father went to Harvard....''

''Yes?''

''I seldom haunt the Harvard Club,'' Timothy said wryly, ''but I began to do so. Finally, yesterday...well, I suppose you could say that a number of lunches and dinners and cocktails finally paid off. I met a man named George Edgerton, who was a classmate of your father's at Harvard.''

Anne frowned. ''I've never heard of him,'' she stated firmly.

''There's no reason why you should have,'' Timothy reminded her. ''Anyway, he mentioned that he was in Europe when your Aunt Muriel died, otherwise he said he would have called on you. Then time slipped by once he got back to Boston, and he wasn't even sure that you'd still be in town.''

He paused as if considering this. Then he went on, ''Mr. Edgerton told me that he'd thought your father's death was especially ironic when his dream of a lifetime was about to be fulfilled.''

"His dream of a lifetime?" Anne repeated nervously.

Timothy looked at her steadily and said, "Your father wrote Mr. Edgerton not long before the accident happened. He wrote him a short letter to say that he and Laura were jubilantly expecting a son.''

The shock was so profound that it was impossible for Anne to assimilate what he'd just told her. She pressed her fingers to her temples, dazed. Her father and Laura, expecting a son! The idea boggled the mind.

Timothy asked quickly, "Are you all right, Anne?"

Through the maze of her swirling emotions came the realization that at least he'd called her by her first name again. She looked across at him, trying to force a smile. "Yes," she said weakly. Then their eyes locked, and Anne felt seared by that blazing gaze.

In that moment, though, Timothy showed her something he'd never shown her before. At least, not in this way. She saw his love for her in those green eyes. She felt it caress her across the distance that separated them as surely as if she'd been wrapped in a soft protective mantle. And, strangely, this brief wonderful knowledge transcended all else.

Timothy said gently, "I told you yesterday that we'd been working overtime, Anne. We had a number of phone conferences with Lance Bigelow in

New York. He contacted Laura and got back to us. It was a pretty traumatic process for everyone. But the bottom line is that Laura told your father she was pregnant. Not only did she tell him she was pregnant, she told him she'd had the necessary test taken and the result showed that she was carrying a boy.''

Timothy drew a deep breath. "Your father had always wanted a son,'' he said then, still being very gentle about this. "Not because he loved you any less, Anne, but because he wanted his name carried on. It's something inherent in most men, this business of a family name surviving,'' he told her, the words coming with difficulty. "Generation to generation to generation. That's what your father wanted. And if we attempt to guess what his thoughts might have been, we can say that he must have assumed you'd be getting married and starting a family of your own. Laura may even have convinced him that you'd never wanted the Chestnut Hill house. There's no way of knowing what she might have told him or what she might have invented.

"Your father was very proud of you, Anne,'' Timothy continued. "Laura told me this, and you were a thorn to her because of this pride. She felt you had everything—beauty, background and a glamorous independent career, as well. She felt that she fell flat in many areas. She said she'd never been comfortable with your father's friends, for one thing. Never comfortable in the role of hostess for him. That's why she'd convinced him to move to

Florida, so that they could start entirely on their own. They could make new associations, free of everything that being a Clarendon means in this part of the country.''

Tim was trying to ease the possible pain she could feel, knowing that her father had wanted a son so much. That her father might even have preferred a son over her. Anne knew this, and she knew what it meant to him to delve into this matter of heritage again. Heritage, the block between them, she was aware now more fully than she'd ever been before.

She wanted to tell Timothy that it didn't really hurt all that much. She wanted to tell him she could even understand her father's feelings and was secure in the knowledge that he'd loved her very much, regardless of Laura and everything else. She wanted him to know she'd learned to be her own person, and that had taught her how to cope with most of the things that came her way. Long since, even as he had, she'd learned how to stand firmly on her own feet.

But this was not the time to tell him any of these things. She could only look at him and say with a formality in her tone that she was far from feeling, ''Thank you very much. . . for all you've done.''

She had to be formal, or she knew she would dash right by Giles and throw herself into Timothy's arms. She would kiss away that taut line curving his lips. She would make him love her.

Oscar Wechsler said brightly, ''Well now, Miss Clarendon, with the threat of a will contest no longer hanging over our heads we can proceed to settle matters as they should be settled. It will take time before everything is finalized, I'm sure you realize that. You do plan to stay in Boston until everything has been taken care of, don't you?"

"Yes," Anne nodded. "Yes, Mr. Wechsler. I definitely plan to stay in Boston," she said, and didn't dare look toward Timothy.

As THEY LEFT Oscar Wechsler's office, Giles took over. "You owe me a luncheon date, Anne. Remember?" he said.

She didn't remember any such thing, but there would be a refuge of sorts in having lunch with Giles right then.

"No other plans?" he asked, following up on his theme.

"No," she said.

"Care to join us, Tim?"

"Thank you," Timothy said politely, "but I have another engagement."

He nodded goodbye and walked back down the hall to his office, and Anne tried not to simply stop in her tracks and stare desolately at his retreating figure. She was tempted to follow him, regardless of Giles. She was tempted to walk right in on him and say, "Look, Tim Flanagan, we can't go on this way! Seesawing up and down, blowing hot and cold. No one minute like the next. It's driving me crazy!" But Giles already had her by the arm, and she followed him docilely down the corridor to the elevators.

It wasn't the time to confront Timothy any more

than it would have been the time to throw herself into his arms in Oscar Wechsler's office. Instinct told her this.

Giles took her to a little Italian restaurant in Boston's North End. Piccola Venezia, the place was called, plain and unpretentious, and although Anne hadn't expected to enjoy herself, she began to almost at once. A smiling waiter with a towel over his shoulder ushered them to a tiny table covered with a red-and-white checked cloth, and a minute later he'd produced a pitcher of homemade red wine and a basket of warm bread.

Giles kept the conversation very light, but he also managed to exert his full quota of charm. Anne had to admit that he was a great deal of fun to be with. No complications, no tensions. How much simpler it would have been, she mused, as she twirled a forkful of delicious linguine alfredo, if she'd fallen in love with him rather than with Timothy. But it hadn't happened that way. The matter of falling in love, she concluded privately, was rarely laced with logic.

This bit of wisdom brought a smile to her lips, which provoked an inevitable question from Giles, who wanted to share the joke with her. It took a bit of verbal maneuvering by Anne to arrive on safer ground.

Lunch over, Giles wanted to get his car and drive her out to Chestnut Hill, but Anne refused to permit this and insisted that he put her into a cab instead. He did so reluctantly, and bent to kiss her lightly on the lips at the last instant. She returned the kiss, but in a spirit of affection only, and she knew that Giles was perfectly aware of her intention.

She surprised an unexpectedly wistful expression on his face as she looked up to say goodbye to him. Then he said, his voice definitely wry, "I wish it could be me, Anne."

"Giles," she began. "Don't...."

He touched her lips with a gentle finger. "I'm not going to," he promised. "I just said I wished, that's all. But it's Tim, isn't it, Anne? Every time I'm with the two of you I feel as if I've climbed to the edge of a volcano that's about to erupt."

She tried to smile. "We're not that turbulent," she protested.

"No, Anne? You're not denying that you're in love with him, are you?"

She hesitated only an instant. "No," she said. "No...I'm not."

"You don't doubt that it's returned, do you?"

"I don't know, Giles," she said honestly. "Tim is so...changeable. And...."

"Defensive?"

"In his own way, yes."

The cab driver was looking at Giles impatiently, but Giles wasn't aware of this. "Tim is as stubborn as hell!" he said bluntly. "And I've never seen a man with more pride. I don't know what it is with him. He's handsome, successful, he'll go right to the top of the ladder in the legal profession, you can bet on that. Yet I always have the feeling that he's holding back. Tim's very deep, Anne."

Giles didn't know anything about Timothy's problems with his own background, she realized, and was surprised by this. Then it occurred to her that probably very few people in the world knew much at all about Timothy Flanagan.

She said slowly, "Yes, Tim is deep."

"He could hurt you," Giles warned. "I don't know why I say that, but I get the feeling he could hurt you a great deal. In every encounter I have with Tim I feel as if he's holding back. I don't think he wants anyone to get really close to him. He's a... well, he's a mystery man in many ways."

In more ways than you realize, Giles, she thought privately. But she only said aloud, "Yes, he is."

The cab driver had turned on the meter, and Anne could not blame him for doing so. "I've got to go, Giles," she said.

"I can see," he replied, and winked. "I'll call you soon."

But it was Timothy from whom Anne heard next, not Giles. She'd barely entered the house when Bridget summoned her to the phone, and Timothy said abruptly, "Anne? I've found your violinist for you."

She'd forgotten all about her request of him to discover where Ken Phillips was staying in Boston.

Without waiting for her answer, Timothy continued, "He's at the Ritz, which is just about where I expected he would be. I didn't realize his concert was on for tonight, though."

"I must have made a mistake on the date," Anne said hastily. "I'd thought it wasn't until later in the—"

"It doesn't matter," Timothy interrupted. "It was short notice, but I managed to get tickets. . . for both of us. I'll pick you up at six, so we'll have time for a drink before the concert. Perhaps you'd like to call this old friend of yours and ask him to join us for late supper afterward, okay?"

Before Anne had the chance to answer, Timothy Flanagan hung up.

CHAPTER EIGHTEEN

ANNE DRESSED for the concert with utmost care. But it was not because she was going to see Ken Phillips again. She wanted to look her very best for Timothy. She was determined that once the concert was over and they'd had their meeting with Ken, she was going to lure Timothy someplace where the two of them could talk things out—alone.

She slipped on her favorite dress, an exquisite creation made of royal purple moiré. It was fashioned with a matinee-length full skirt, a matching cummerbund and puffed full-length sleeves. With it she wore sleek black pumps and a pearl necklace and earrings that had belonged to her grandmother. A last touch of Flora Danica and she was ready to answer Bridget's announcement that Mr. Flanagan was downstairs waiting for her.

He was standing at the foot of the stairs as Anne started to descend them, and for a moment she paused, her heart in her eyes as she looked down at him. There was something eloquent about his stance, something especially poignant about his upraised face. She cried out to him silently, Timothy, oh, Timothy! Why can't you let go?

She reached the bottom step and he moved back. "Ready?" he asked curtly.

"Yes," she nodded.

He took her light emerald wool cape from Bridget and threw it around her shoulders, then opened the front door without saying a word.

He was making his point, Anne saw grimly. There would be no togetherness tonight, if Timothy were to have his way.

As he started the Saab, he said, "I hope you had a cup of tea or something. It will be quite late before we get a chance to eat."

"Bridget fixed tea and muffins for me around five," Anne told him. "What about you?"

"Corned beef on rye and a beer," he reported as they drove around the Chestnut Hill Reservoir. Anne noted that the silvery water glittered beautifully in the early-evening darkness, and she thought it might have a mellowing effect on Timothy's mood. But he only said, "You got in touch with Phillips?"

"Yes," she answered, "I talked to Ken."

"Was he overjoyed to hear from you?"

Anne hoped the querulous note in Tim's voice denoted jealousy, but she wasn't even sure about that.

"He was pleased, yes," she commented dryly. "Though I wouldn't say he went into orbit."

"He's going to meet us?"

"He suggested we come backstage after the performance."

"What about supper?" Tim demanded.

"I didn't invite Ken to come with us, Tim," Anne said levelly.

"And why not?" he asked irately.

She could feel his green eyes raking her before he was forced to turn his attention back to his driving. She prayed she wouldn't stammer as she said, "I decided I would rather be alone with you."

"If you think I find that flattering, I don't," Tim told her bluntly. "To me it indicates that you can't face being with Phillips again. You're afraid of your own feelings for him," he went on accusingly. "You're afraid that you won't be able to control yourself."

"You're completely wrong!" she protested.

"I don't think so," he insisted stubbornly.

Anne sighed. "Timothy Flanagan," she said then, "you might pause to think that if I were afraid to meet Ken Phillips again I would hardly have gone to the trouble of getting in touch with him. If I were still hopelessly in love with him, I could have gone to his concert and sat in a back row and moped all by myself. I wouldn't have needed to bring you into the act."

"You didn't bring me into it," he reminded her. "You asked me to find out where he was staying, and I did. But I got the concert tickets and suggested we make this a . . . mutual enterprise, shall we say?"

"Call it what you will," Anne said wearily. "My prime concern in contacting Ken was to talk to him about Katharine. I did that over the phone today, and he's promised to help her. He'll be back in Boston in a month or so, and we're going to set up a meeting with Katharine."

"So," Timothy cut in, the note of triumph in his

voice oddly strained, "you'll be seeing him then, too, right?"

"Right," she agreed, and added, "It certainly will be easier for Katharine if I go with her, even though it's only an interview. Later she'll have to sing for Ken, and I've already decided to accompany her on the piano. She'll be back here with Peter very shortly, so we'll have plenty of time to work together."

"You've made quite a pet project out of Katharine Kincaid, haven't you?" Timothy observed. "You wouldn't be using her as a stepping stone, would you?"

Anne turned on him angrily. "Just what are you trying to say?" she snapped.

"You wouldn't be using her to recement your old relationship with Phillips, would you?"

"That doesn't even deserve an answer," she said icily.

For the remainder of the drive they were both silent. Then, as Timothy pulled into a parking lot near Symphony Hall, he turned to Anne to say, "It would be impossible to get a space just before the concert, so I thought it best to park here now. Why don't we walk over to the Colonnade for a drink?"

"That would be nice," Anne said stiffly.

Silence prevailed again during the short walk through the Christian Science Church Center, even though the Mother Church and the long reflecting pool were nothing less than inspirational in their beauty.

It couldn't have been a lovelier night, Anne

thought to herself, her spirits sagging. But if Timothy was going to remain apart from her—if he wasn't even going to try to be pleasant—she wasn't sure she could make it through the evening, physically or emotionally.

They reached the hotel and entered the cocktail lounge, and Anne decided to have Cinzano on the rocks, with a wedge of lemon. Hard liquor, she suspected, would put her over the brink very quickly tonight, given her present frame of mind.

Timothy ordered his favorite—Bushmills—and as she watched him take a sip, she fervently wished she could erase the constrained expression from his face. Finally she said almost desperately, ''Tim, we don't have to go to the concert, you know. I mean, if you don't want to. . . .''

His eyebrows arched. ''Are you that much afraid of seeing him again?'' he asked.

''Of course not!'' she retorted impatiently. ''It's just that you look so. . .miserable.''

''I am not exactly brimming with happiness, Anne,'' he said steadily. ''But if it's all the same to you, I would as soon not get onto the subject of *me*. This is your night to stand up to your past. To exorcise old ghosts. Or, perhaps, to pick up old relationships and renew them.'' He shook his head. ''Which is it to be, Anne?''

''Neither,'' she said flatly. ''You're jumping to all sorts of conclusions, Tim. If this was a court case, you would never win.''

''Oh?'' he snorted. He finished his whiskey without commenting any further on this, and signaled the waitress to bring him another drink. Glancing at Anne's nearly filled glass, he asked sardonically, "Not thirsty?"

"No," she said.

"Too nervous to eat or drink?"

"I wouldn't be nervous at all unless you made me so," Anne said defiantly. "And you s-seem to be trying to do exactly that."

"I'm not trying to make you nervous, Anne," Timothy told her, his weariness suddenly evident. "My mind's up to here with all sorts of things," he said, tapping the top of his forehead. "It occurs to me that we're coming to the end of the road, you and I."

"What?" she blurted. It was such a complete change of subject that momentarily she was thrown for a loss.

"You heard me. This afternoon I asked Oscar Wechsler to resume handling the Clarendon estate himself. Giles can assist him whenever necessary. After all, Giles is fully conversant with your type of . . . situation."

Anne stared at him. "What are you saying?" she demanded.

"I'm saying I stayed with all of this because I was sure there was something wrong about that holograph will," he said simply. "I felt I was in the best position to prove it, and I did so. There is no longer any need for my services where your family affairs are concerned, Anne. The estate will be capably managed by Simon and Wechsler as it has been for many years. You no longer need me."

Anne shook her head, as if trying to dispel a sudden fog. "I can't believe I'm hearing this," she said then.

"I suppose I've put it badly," he conceded. "Anyway, Oscar will relay the same information to you tomorrow, I'm sure. I got to thinking about it, though, and it seemed to me that I should tell you first myself."

"Then. . . you are withdrawing as our f-family attorney? Is that what I'm supposed to understand?"

"Yes, that's it."

"Suppose I were to ask Mr. Wechsler to have you continue handling the Clarendon estate?"

"I would refuse to do so," Timothy said gravely.

Anne was stunned. "Do you dislike m-me so much?" she asked, her voice quavering despite a mammoth effort to keep it steady.

"That's a ridiculous question!" he replied, looking away, "and hardly applicable to what we're talking about. The simple fact is that I've always been very careful to separate my personal and professional relationships. It's a rule of thumb, a very wise course to take. And it's not too late to set the matter straight here."

"I think you've said enough," Anne interrupted him tautly.

"And I think you should hear me out," he said, lowering his voice.

"I don't want to hear you out!" Anne exploded. "You've made your point, Timothy. I appreciate what you've done in regard to Laura and the will, but I get your message."

"Do you?" he asked softly.

"Indeed I do!" she assured him. "If you'll excuse me...." Anne was finding it impossible to stay at the table with him for another second. She beat a hasty retreat to the rest room, fighting back tears.

Timothy's behavior was inexplicable. She tried to make sense of it as she splashed water over a face that suddenly felt burning hot. Then she tried to camouflage her feelings by the careful application of more makeup. She added another dash of Flora Danica, as if this might give her needed courage, then walked back to him, her head held high.

If Timothy wants to put me out of his life, she told herself resolutely, *I'm not going to make a fool of myself trying to fight him!*

Her thoughts about coming to a firm understanding with him tonight had vanished. Timothy, she knew now, didn't want an understanding with her, firm or otherwise. He wanted to be his own person, free and alone. He wanted to be free of her family affairs, free of her.

He stood as she reached their table, but she didn't look up to meet his eyes. "We'd better go," he said. "I hadn't realized how much time had passed."

SYMPHONY HALL was bustling with activity. Excited patrons crammed the entrance, taxis and limousines jammed the street, and as she and Timothy inched their way inside and found their seats, Anne felt chilled with emotion. The place was just as she remembered it—the chandeliers hanging from the spacious ceiling, the marble statues gazing down from their alcoves recessed along the side walls, the massive pipe organ behind the stage.

The musicians attired in black tails, filtered onstage. Anne watched, mesmerized, as they took their places and gave their instruments a final check. Then the houselights dimmed several times, the crowd settled down and the orchestra began tuning itself to the concertmaster's A. After only a minute they, too, settled down.

In the stillness that followed, Anne could almost hear her heart pounding. Then, from a small door to the side of the stage, the well-known conductor emerged, followed a second later by Kenneth Phillips, cradling his violin proudly. Slowly the two men made their way through the orchestra and came to stand by the podium. After warmly shaking the concertmaster's hand, Kenneth Phillips turned and bowed to the thunderous ovation greeting his appearance.

Anne was transfixed as she stared at him. It was impossible not to plunge back into memory to the time when they'd been close. It was like opening the pages of a photo album and looking at old snapshots. There was nostalgia to it, true. But there was no longer any pain.

She was over Kenneth. Completely over him. Thinking this, she became painfully aware of the copper-haired man at her side. She would never get over Timothy Flanagan, she knew. He'd become hopelessly interwoven in the tapestry of her heart and would be a part of her forever.

The conductor raised his baton, the audience fell silent, and the orchestra came to life. Kenneth stood to the left of the podium, his head bowed in concentration. The moving introduction to Brahms' Violin Concerto filled the hall, and then Kenneth lifted his bow and began.

As she listened to him play, Anne forgot about everything else. The melody was so emotional, so chilling. Kenneth's technique was flawless, and the tones he coaxed from his violin gave total evidence of his mastery. Soaring and plunging, he touched upon nuances in the piece that Brahms' himself would have found astonishing, and when he'd finished playing Anne was on her feet with the rest of the audience, clapping wildly as the tears streamed down her face.

Then, as if in a dream, she became painfully conscious of Timothy next to her. He was rigid, absolutely rigid, and she realized that he was translating both her applause for Ken and her tears in entirely the wrong way.

Intermission came, and he asked politely, "Would you like champagne?"

"No, thank you," Anne said miserably, knowing she could never convince him how mistaken he was.

"Sherry?" he suggested.

"Nothing thanks, Tim," she replied.

"Then if you'll excuse me, I think I'll go get a drink for myself," he said, and with that he rose and left her.

The house lights had dimmed before he came back again, but by then Anne had begun to wonder if he was going to come back at all. She would not have been too surprised to find that Timothy had walked out, leaving her so she could face meeting Ken Phillips by herself.

The concert over, he moved silently by her side as they made their way to the backstage reception room where she was to meet Ken. It was a mob scene, and certainly a poor place for a reunion. Yet there was no doubting Ken Phillips's genuine pleasure when he spied her. Excusing himself from a throng of admirers, he moved toward her at once.

Within seconds she was within the circle of his arms, and he kissed her firmly on the lips. Then he held her away from him, gazing down into her face as if studying every detail of it, before he said, "You're more beautiful than ever, Anne. And that's something I wouldn't have believed possible."

He looked terrific, too, Anne conceded. He was tall, dark and handsome, with aquiline features and very light skin. In his black tails and crisp white shirt with ruching at the neck, he looked as if destiny had molded him to fill the particular role he was playing.

Suddenly Anne was able to smile back at him, to laugh, to joke a little, because it was exactly as she'd thought it would be. There was no more bitterness between them, nor was there love. They were two people who'd shared something once and could still be friends.

She introduced Ken and Timothy, and Tim was meticulously polite and quite astute as well in his comments about Ken's playing. It was Anne who brought matters to a close, saying, "Tim and I have to run along, Ken. And I'm delighted that you're agreeable to listening to Katharine sing. Once you've heard her...."

His dark eyes lingered on Anne's face, sparkling mischievously. "As you know," he said pointedly, "I've always had a soft spot in my heart for singers!" Then he added, "I hope you'll have lunch or dinner with me when I come back to Boston, Anne. We can work out the plans for your friend then. But first you and I have a lot of catching up to do."

"I'd like that," she told him, which was perfectly true.

As she left Symphony Hall with Timothy stalking by her side, Anne knew very well that this short session with Ken Phillips had done nothing at all toward helping the situation between Tim and herself.

He should have more faith in me, she thought, remembering that he'd once said the same thing to her about himself.

They reached his car, and suddenly the early-fall air seemed chilled. As Timothy opened the door for her, Anne shivered.

"Cold?" he asked.

"A little," she confessed.

"I'll turn the heat on once we get going."

"No, that's not necessary," she said quickly. "I...I'll be all right."

He glanced across at her, then said, "Do you still feel like dinner, Anne? Or would you rather stop somewhere for a drink on the way out to the house?''

"No!" she said abruptly, then added, "I can fix you a drink when we get home."

He didn't comment, and Anne desperately wished she could read his mind. She was afraid he might decline to come in once they reached Chestnut Hill, and decided that she wasn't going to try to persuade him otherwise if this happened. To her relief it didn't. When they reached the house Timothy walked in with her, helped her off with her cape, then followed her into the kitchen.

"I think I'll have hot chocolate myself," she said, "but there's still some Bushmill's left, if you'd like."

"Hot chocolate would be fine," he told her.

"With a shot of peppermint schnapps?" she suggested.

"I've never tried it that way, but it sounds good," he agreed.

Anne had moved to the counter, and she realized that Timothy was standing just behind her. He started to say something, and she froze. He was so close she could feel the warmth of his breath on her neck. She was almost afraid to turn around, but Timothy settled this for her. He grasped her shoulders and swung her toward him easily, and before she could say a single word his mouth descended to claim her lips.

Immediately the kiss was intense. His mouth moved as if in torment, and Anne found her own lips responding in the same way. It was if she and

Tim were silently crying for each other, trying to reach each other through an agony of conflicting emotions and mounting sensations.

His hands moved behind her shoulders, then slid sensuously down to her waist. She could feel him drawing her closer, feel his desire surge. Frantically he kissed her, then suddenly he broke off.

"Make the hot chocolate," he said abruptly, "then let's sit down and talk."

Anne was startled. Timothy sounded as if he, too, was coming to the end of his rope. She set about making the hot chocolate with grim determination, then splashed peppermint schnapps liberally into the foaming mixture, and joined him at the kitchen table.

He sipped and said, "Very good."

"Thanks."

"You're angry at me," he told her flatly.

"No...not angry," she countered.

"I'm sorry about the way I behaved at the concert, Anne," he apologized. Then he said without warning, "Phillips is a very handsome guy—to say nothing of being the best violinist I've ever heard."

"He's also a very nice person," Anne replied levelly.

"Yes, I'm sure he is," Timothy agreed, and added unexpectedly, "I'm also sure that there's no longer anything between you. I thought you should know that because...well, because I've appeared enough of a damned fool as it is. I don't want to look like a jealous idiot in the bargain!"

A smile touched Anne's lips. "I don't think

you've been a damned fool or a jealous idiot, Tim,'' she said indulgently.

His reaction startled her. "Don't patronize me, Anne,'' he warned. ''That's the last thing I need from you!''

Anger surged. "Don't be so touchy, Timothy,'' she sparked back at him. "Your complexes are hanging out all over the place!''

"Tell me about them now,'' he said, with more than a hint of the brogue. He smiled, but his green eyes were clear and cold. "And what about you, *mavourneen*?'' he asked. "Wouldn't you say you have a few complexes of your own?''

"Not in your league!'' she retorted.

Their eyes clashed, and it was Timothy who looked down first. Then, after a moment, he said very softly, "I didn't come here tonight to argue with you, Anne.''

"No? Then why *did* you come here?''

"To apologize for my sense of timing, among other things,'' he said surprising her. The brogue was gone now, and the ice had melted from his eyes. "It was stupid of me to blurt out the fact that I'd no longer be involved in your legal affairs,'' he continued. "I won't attempt to explain my reasons for doing so, perhaps because I don't fully understand them myself. It wasn't very professional, that much I know. Then. . . .''

"Yes?''

"I've already apologized for acting as I did at the concert,'' he reminded her.

"Yes?'' she repeated.

He shook his head. "Nothing more tonight," he said to her chagrin. "Enough's been said and done already. But...."

"But what, Tim?" she asked impatiently.

"This may sound like a strange thing to ask of you," he said, "but will you have faith in me, Anne? Whatever may happen, will you try to have faith in me until...."

His voice trailed off again. Exasperated, she said, "Must you be quite so mysterious?"

"I'm not trying to be mysterious," Tim began unhappily. "It's just that I...." He shrugged, then pushed aside his empty mug and stood up. "Get the blanket and pillow, will you please?"

Anne stared at him disbelievingly. "Not again!" she protested.

"For tonight, yes. But I realize, as you do, that this isn't an arrangement that can continue. Perhaps Bridget knows someone who could stay here nights with you until...."

Anne looked away and bit her lip. After a moment she said, "Perhaps she does. But then I think I'd better learn to live alone, wouldn't you say?"

ANNE WAS RESTLESS that night. She'd tossed down the blanket and pillow as Timothy had ordered, but the thought of him lying on the couch just downstairs was maddening. Things were unresolved between them and she felt so helpless. It seemed to her that every time they came to the verge of a real understanding something loomed to drive a wedge, forcing them apart.

Tim had said nothing in answer to her rhetorical question about learning to live alone, an omission she was very much aware of. But at least he'd admitted that he wasn't jealous of Ken. Anne believed him, too, and she knew there was much more significance than he'd indicated in his reasons for removing himself from involvement in her legal affairs. Yet she couldn't understand why he'd had to do this, nor had his poor job of explaining helped.

Once during the night she thought she heard a noise in the corridor outside her room, and she nearly called out. Then, in the ensuing silence, she decided she'd merely imagined whatever it was. Dreams had come to plague her, vivid and oddly tormenting dreams, and the sound had most likely been a part of them.

When morning arrived, though, Anne discovered that there had been someone outside her door. A square white envelope lay on the threshold, the single word *Anne* inscribed in deep blue across its face.

It could only be Timothy's handwriting. The lines were as decisive as he could be—when he wanted.

Anne picked up the envelope very slowly. She was afraid to open it. She knew without even going downstairs to check that he'd already left the house, and instinctively she realized that this was a message he wasn't going to give her the chance to answer.

She moved toward her bed, and sitting on the edge, she tore the envelope open. There was a single piece of lined paper inside. It read:

It's not yet daylight, but I can't stay here any longer. Nor can I further delay doing certain things I must do. Perhaps I've been a coward, I don't know. I do know I must try to prove what I have to prove. Only then will I be free to say all the things I yearn so much to say to you. Last night I asked you to have faith in me. Now I ask it again, no matter how things may seem.

The note was signed, simply, "Timothy."

Anne reread the short message several times. It was a mystery. What was it that he must do? What was it that he must prove? There was only one problem in Timothy's life that transcended everything else—the question of his identity. Hadn't he said he'd given up trying to solve the riddle of who he was long ago? He'd had so little to go on. An infant abandoned on a hospital doorstep. A shawl, a pin, a scrap of paper with a few words scrawled on it.

Now she wondered what he was about to do, and the growing suspicion came to her that Timothy Flanagan was going on a safari that could easily prove to be hopeless, one that could easily do him far more harm than good.

Anne waited, restlessly, until the hour when the law office would be open. Then she dialed the number and was put through to Giles Winslow's phone before she could protest that it wasn't he with whom she wished to speak.

But all of her questions were answered at once when Giles said, "It was Timothy you were calling, wasn't it, Anne? I wondered whether he'd told you what he was going to do.''

"No, Giles, he didn't tell me," she said dismally. "But I think I know. He's taken off for Ireland, hasn't he?''

"Dublin, to be precise," Giles said. Then he added, amused, "Are you clairvoyant, Anne?''

"No," she said shortly. "At least, not until now...."

Before Giles could respond to this she hung up, only to dial another number a second later. This time it was Logan International Airport she was calling, to book a seat on the next available Aer Lingus flight to Ireland.

CHAPTER NINETEEN

ANNE ESTIMATED she was approximately nine or ten hours behind Tim in leaving the United States to cross the Atlantic to Ireland. Beyond that it was impossible to second-guess much of anything.

Her flight on a green-and-white Aer Lingus 747 with a large green shamrock on its tail, was scheduled to stop at Shannon International Airport first and then make the forty-five-minute hop across the country to Dublin. Whether or not Timothy had followed this same plan she had no way of knowing. There was a chance that he might disembark at Shannon with the thought of renting a car and driving to Dublin, and if that were the case Anne realized she might even reach the Irish capital city ahead of him.

Giles had proved to have his own kind of second sight when it came to determining what she intended to do. He'd called her back only a few minutes after she'd made her plane reservation, and he'd been remarkably helpful. Through a travel-agent friend of his he had a room reserved for her at the Royal Shamrock Hotel, then he insisted on picking her up at her house that night and driving her out to Logan International Airport to catch her flight.

As they drove through the Callahan Tunnel under Boston Harbor, Giles smiled. "I feel as if I've been this way before," he reflected whimsically.

Anne's own smile was sad as she remembered him taking her to Logan that other time, when her first leave of absence from the bank had come to an end and she'd had to return to her job in New York. Timothy Flanagan had been uppermost in her mind on that occasion, too.

"At least you have the advantage of knowing where Tim's going to be staying, Anne," Giles said. "He'll be at the Royal Shamrock, too. It was enough of a surprise when he made the announcement yesterday that he was flying to Ireland as soon as he possibly could. But what really shocked me was when he asked for my help in making the arrangements. Business is one thing, but this was personal and... well, Tim's never approached me for anything like that before. In fact I still don't know what to make of it."

"Timothy obviously needed your help, Giles," Anne told him simply. "He does like you, you know."

"I've always hoped so," Giles admitted, "but he sure has a funny way of showing it sometimes!" He went on to say that Tim had planned to take an early-morning shuttle to New York. The majority of international flights out of Boston departed in the evening, and he had hoped that New York would offer something leaving a bit sooner in the day.

Timothy must have left New York by early that afternoon at the latest, Anne calculated silently. Otherwise he'd find himself arriving in Ireland at a most inconvenient hour. Then it occurred to her that perhaps he hadn't even left yet. Perhaps she and Timothy would be arriving in Shannon at the same time!

Once on the plane, she fastened her seat belt and anxiously awaited the takeoff, hoping it wouldn't be delayed—not infrequently the case in transatlantic flights, she knew. With the moment of departure at hand, she was rapidly losing her courage. She'd acted so impulsively. What if she couldn't find him once she got there? Possibly he hadn't been able to get a flight out of New York. Or he could have just as easily changed his mind and canceled the trip entirely.

The variables seemed overwhelming, and Anne's head was throbbing as she considered them. She was about ready to walk back down the aisle, exit through the walkway and find a good bar where she could forget this whole insane venture when the huge engines began to whir, and the terminal started to recede from her sight. It was too late to escape. Soon the plane was taxiing down the field and there was nothing left to do but try to relax.

Relax! Anne ordered herself, fighting back a hysterical laugh.

For the next several hours, after a bevy of green uniformed stewardesses had served the passengers a typical airlines' dinner, Anne tried to doze but couldn't. Then she attempted to immerse herself in the movie that was being shown, a movie she'd been dying to see, but even this was impossible under the circumstances. She was just too jittery. Then, to add to her apprehension, a nagging sense of disquiet seemed to lodge itself at the base of her throat. She kept swallowing, self-consciously, as if she could force it to dislodge.

Time passed, and eventually the pilot's voice boomed over the intercom to announce cheerfully that they would be landing in thirty minutes.

As the plane began to descend, Anne peered out the window. Far below she could see a tempestuous-looking coast stretching out into the distance. Then they were flying over Ireland itself, and immediately she was struck by its greenness. The morning was soft gray but the visibility was clear, and Anne saw that the earth spread out beneath her was like a patchwork quilt worked in multiple shades of green. She hadn't realized there were so many subtle shades of this one color, and it came to her that Ireland really was an emerald isle.

She had flown across the Atlantic three times before—once on a week's vacation during her last year in prep school, another time on an excursion with her mother before her mother's remarriage, and more recently on a charter flight with a group of friends. They'd landed at Shannon to refuel on this last flight, but it had been cloudy that day, and she hadn't been able to glimpse the countryside.

At Shannon, Anne opted in favor of staying on board the plane. She knew that the airport boasted a duty-free shop famous around the world, but she was hardly in the mood to play tourist. Then she realized too late that she should have gotten off if only to stretch her legs.

It seemed like an eternity before they were in the air again, but the pilot kept the big jet at a surprisingly low altitude. In no time at all they were landing, and it was with a sense of unreality that she realized she was in Dublin.

During the long overseas flight, Anne had fallen into a kind of mental limbo. As she went through the formalities of Irish customs and immigration, the full knowledge of what she'd done came over her, and she couldn't believe her own actions.

On the spur of the moment, without even pausing to give real thought about it, she'd decided to follow Timothy Flanagan clear across the Atlantic. Suddenly an overwhelming question confronted her.

Will he want me here? Anne paused on the sidewalk in front of the airport and wished she'd posed that question to herself last night back in Boston.

It was too late to do anything but go on. Forcing herself to act with a determination she didn't feel, she sought for a means of transportation to get to her hotel. She'd known nothing about Dublin to begin with, nor had she given herself any time to study up on it.

After a moment's thought she bypassed the various buses, some of them evidently motor coaches awaiting tour groups, and decided she'd take a taxi. Although this might be rather expensive, it would be the quickest and easiest thing to do.

The driver of the cab was young, about the same age as herself, Anne surmised. He was rosy cheeked and wore a primly tailored Edwardian suit with a white shirt and a floral-patterned flowing necktie. Anne felt sure it must be his Sunday best and was struck by the thought that this was a strange outfit for someone engaged in his particular occupation. She had to smile, contrasting his attire with the rugged garb usually worn by cabbies in both Boston and New York.

She pointed out her single suitcase, almost lost in the forest of luggage piled at the curbside, and he obligingly hoisted it up as he led her to his waiting cab.

"We'll just stash this in the boot," he said agreeably. While she watched, he opened up the trunk of the car, a small European make, and thrust the suitcase inside.

"Now then," he said, turning toward her, "it's the Royal Shamrock you wish, right?"

His brogue was delightful, a full-fledged version of the teasing tones Timothy tended to use—although his had too often been adopted as camouflage, she remembered.

The driver's smile reminded her faintly of Timothy, too, and as they started into the city, Anne warned herself that she mustn't be overly imaginative about everything she saw and everyone she met in Ireland. If she started seeing Timothy Flanagan in the face of every Irishman in Dublin, she was certain to lose her mind.

She was aware that it had started to drizzle and

wished she hadn't packed her rain cape. She was nearly tempted to ask the cab driver to open up the trunk so she could get it out of her suitcase, but he was already holding the back door of his cab open for her, and he ushered her into it with a charmingly grandiose gesture.

Then, taking his own place at the wheel, he said with a wave toward the day outside, "It's a bit of the mist we're having."

Anne nodded. "I understand you do have quite a bit of rain," she said.

"This wouldn't exactly be called rain," he contradicted gently. "We're used to the mist, here. You'll see for yourself, it comes to visit almost every day. There can be a wonderfully clear blue sky, then the clouds come suddenly and the mist falls. Gentle," he chuckled, "yet still wet."

There was a lilt to his voice that made his words seem almost poetic. Trying to prolong this so she could hear him talk more, Anne asked, "Is it seasonal?"

"The mist?" He shook his head. "Ah, no," he said regretfully. "No matter what time of the year, it's always with us. Sometimes more than others, to be sure," he added a bit cryptically.

"I see," Anne said. The Irish weather was apparently as unpredictable as she'd heard—as unpredictable, in fact, as Timothy Flanagan's moods.

Suddenly she realized that the steering wheel was on the right side of the dashboard. She'd forgotten that in Ireland, as well as in the British Isles, people drove on the left side of the road, and as her cabby started into the stream of traffic exiting the airport, her heart leapt into her throat.

They didn't go very far, however. He came to a stop with a thrust of the brakes that nearly threw Anne out of her seat, and she saw that a big tour bus was blocking their way. Evidently there was a problem with the bus, because its driver was getting out and walking around it, examining the tires. Soon several onlookers got into the act.

There seemed to be no particular hurry about whatever was going on, but there was a great deal of gesticulating and obviously lively conversation. Meanwhile the traffic continued to pile up, but Anne's cabby merely sat back and folded his hands.

He turned his head, grinning at her. "Don't worry, lass," he said calmly. "It's Ireland you're in now. You might as well just take each moment as it comes." Then he added, laughing impishly, "Over here, wouldn't you know, we do live longer than you Yanks!"

At this point the bus driver climbed back aboard his vehicle, evidently having satisfied himself about whatever problem it was that had been bothering him. Then the crowd dispersed and soon traffic was flowing freely.

Sitting back in her seat again, Anne thought about the cabby's admonition. It was true that her countrymen were sometimes possessed with chasing elusive rainbows. There was a basic restlessness to the American character. A leftover from the pioneering spirit that had settled the country, perhaps. She could already see that in contrast to the

Irish, the pace of living in the States was... frenetic? Not quite that, she told herself, but there was a definite tendency to push aside today in favor of thinking about—or worrying about, she amended—tomorrow.

We really should take more time to enjoy each moment as it comes, she told herself, and felt a certain twinge of envy toward the young man driving the cab, because he appeared to be doing exactly that.

The drive from the airport into downtown Dublin took about twenty minutes. The different neighborhoods they passed through mirrored the varying aspects of any large city, yet there was something decidedly Irish to it all. An elusive quality, ever-present. Anne saw streets lined with small stone houses, houses modest in appearance but having a trim neatness about them. She was especially impressed by the small garden plots in front of every house and was surprised to see roses and hydrangeas still blooming in abundance.

After traversing a rather rundown section of town, they came to an inner city avenue lined with gray stone houses. The door of almost every one was painted a different color. Vivid blue doors, yellow doors, green doors, orange doors, red doors, even purple and pink doors. The colors gave the somewhat grim town houses a character all their own.

"I've never seen anything quite like it," Anne commented to her driver.

He nodded. "The doors of Dublin," he said.

"Yes, they are quite famous. A unique form of expression, really. And you can be sure there's an individualist living behind every one!"

Finally they swept down a wide boulevard and through a principal intersection, and the cabby said with a wave of the hand, "That's O'Connell Street there, Dublin's main street, and wouldn't you ever know, your hotel's right on it!"

Then they were pulling up in front of the Royal Shamrock, and Anne was being helped out of the cab by a doorman resplendent in a vivid green-and-gold uniform.

As she paid the cabby, to her surprise, he produced a calling card. "If you should ever find yourself having the inclination," he said, flashing her the smile that was much too reminiscent of Timothy, "I am available for sight-seeing. Half a day or a full day, as you prefer. It's the best way to see the city, really. And I'm a Dubliner, born and bred, so I know the town like the palm of my hand."

Anne returned his smile. "I'd like that," she said. "I don't know how long I'll be here, but if I have the chance I'll call you."

She tucked the card inside her handbag, then made her way into the pleasant spacious lobby. She'd thought of first asking for Timothy but decided against it. Better to register, she told herself, and get settled in her room. She could take the rest from there.

There wasn't much unpacking to be done. Anne had worn a light wool heather-toned suit for traveling. It had a straight skirt, which she was wearing now, and a matching pleated skirt, which she had packed. In addition to this extra skirt, she'd brought slacks and a couple of sweaters and one mauve satin blouse, in case there was an occasion to dress up a bit. That, plus nightclothes and her toilet case with cosmetics, summed up the total of what she'd brought with her, and it didn't take her long to stash everything away.

This done, she hesitated to go to the white telephone standing on the bedside table. Instead, she crossed the room to the wide front windows overlooking O'Connell Street. It was late morning now, and the mist had stopped falling. Still, the scene outside seemed to be enveloped in a faint purple haze. People were crowding the sidewalks, and as she watched them she tried to picture the kind of homes they might live in, what they might be planning to have for supper, how they lived.

Awkward-looking double-decker buses dominated the traffic below her. They were a curious caramel shade and wove skillfully among the cars on the wrong side of the street—from Anne's point of view. The whole scene was difficult to get used to!

Finally, with a growing sense of reluctance, she turned back toward the phone. If Timothy was in his room, if he answered, what was she going to say to him? If he was annoyed or even indignant at her for having followed him to Ireland, could she really blame him? If this mission of his was what she suspected it was, he might want his privacy above all else. He might insist on it, no matter how strongly he felt about her.

And he had never really come out and told her he loved her, she reminded herself. Not in words, anyway. Maybe his side of this feeling between them was only chemistry. Wanting, but not loving.

It was a disturbing thought. Resolutely, before she decided to change her mind and book the next flight back to the States, Anne lifted the receiver and dialed the reception desk, only to be told shortly that Mr. Flanagan had not yet checked in.

"Are you sure?" she implored. The brogue she heard was delightful, the tone light and lilting, but the gentleman on the other end of the line said nothing to raise her sagging spirits.

"Mr. Timothy Flanagan from Boston, Massachusetts surely is expected, yes," he said patiently. "We will be holding his room for him until we hear from him otherwise, I can assure you."

All Anne could do was leave a message for Timothy to call her as soon as he got in, and as she hung up the receiver, she wondered dully when this might be.

She had no desire at all to go out, as much as Dublin would have beckoned her under more ordinary circumstances. She managed to sleep for a few hours, as jet lag had begun to take its toll, then she called room service and ordered dinner.

The food was good. She'd chosen a local broiled fish, boiled potatoes and green beans and a fruit pudding for dessert. But even if the meal had been ambrosial it would not have appealed to her just now, and she forced herself to eat only because some inner instinct warned her she was going to have to keep her strength up.

The evening inched along. Anne took a shower, keeping one ear tuned to the phone's ringing, and eventually she went to bed. It was a fitful sleep, though, and waking to a gray Irish morning was hardly an encouraging sign. To her, it seemed the mist definitely had turned to rain.

After a time, though, the rain subsided and the sun actually seemed to be trying to peek through the clouds. Unable to stand the inactivity any longer, Anne went down to the hotel coffee shop for breakfast, and then decided to go for a short walk. If Timothy rang her room in her absence he would surely leave a message.

Several imposing buildings lined one side of O'Connell Street, and Anne saw the Dublin post office among them. This structure alone was tremendously impressive. Then she passed a large department store called Clery's, which took up the better part of a block. The window displays were tempting, but shopping had no allure for her. Once she'd found Timothy, she promised herself she'd come back and buy a few souvenirs to commemorate this strange venture.

She came to a bridge over the River Liffey, and pausing midway across it she gazed down the waterway that divided the very heart of Dublin. The murky water flowed along placidly, and several boats were tied up against the quay. Anne found this a soothing and tranquil scene, especially for the center of a city. Life bustled on all around her, yet looking out over the narrow river instilled her with a sense of history, a sense of continuity. The river seemed to symbolize the tenacity of the Irish people themselves, she decided.

She realized she might as well make the best of her time and remembered that Dublin offered many things that she'd always wanted to see. One was the famous Book of Kells on display at Trinity College. She knew that this volume was Ireland's most famous antiquity, dating to the eighth century A.D., a gospel beautifully illustrated by monks. These same monks had also inscribed poems, romances and histories in Gaelic, as well as in Latin, making Ireland the first European land north of Italy to produce a literature in its native language.

She also wanted to see Phoenix Park, a verdant Dublin focal point where the Irish version of the White House and the American Embassy were both located. A friend had told her that cows were allowed to roam free in the park to graze, thus cutting down on the necessity of doing much grass mowing. In fact, her friend had come face to face with two cows serenely walking along one of the park's sidewalks, and this was something Anne wanted to see for herself.

But she couldn't enthusiastically bring herself to play tourist. Not when she'd come to Ireland with such a serious purpose in mind. Yet as each hour passed she was more and more hesitant about facing up to Timothy, and as she walked slowly back to the hotel, she found herself studying everything around her more closely, and finally she detoured into Clery's.

The salespeople were charming and anxious to please, and Anne succumbed to the temptation to buy a sterling pendant emblazoned with a brightly enameled motif from the Book of Kells. Then, as she put this memento into a special compartment in her handbag, her fingers touched another object already there.

Her heart lurched. She'd never stopped carrying the Kiss Me, I'm Irish button Timothy had given her on that fateful March Sunday in South Boston. Now she caressed its smoothness, and tears sprang into her eyes.

She was composed, though, when she entered the lobby of the Royal Shamrock, making her way directly to the reception desk. But there were no messages for her.

Frowning, she asked if Mr. Timothy Flanagan had checked in, and the middle-aged clerk said regretfully, "I fear we will not be having Mr. Flanagan as a guest, Miss Clarendon. He has canceled his reservation."

Anne felt as if she were going to faint. She must have paled, for the desk clerk leaned forward, and asked anxiously, "Would you be all right, now? Perhaps we should get you a glass of water?"

"No...no, I'm quite all right, thank you," Anne said shakily, but it took all the willpower she possessed to pull herself together. She nodded at the kindly man and forced a smile, but she didn't draw a deep breath until she was in the elevator on the way up to her room.

Timothy had canceled his reservation. Why? she wondered, panic-stricken. Had he chosen to register at some other hotel in Dublin? Or worse, had he decided once he'd reached New York not to come to Ireland at all?

Anne sank down on the side of her bed and wearily berated herself for being all sorts of a fool. What a wild-goose chase she had come on! If only she had stopped for a moment and thought this out. She had been impelled to rush after Timothy. She'd had the crazy idea that he really needed her.

Dismally, she glanced at her wristwatch. It was not quite noon. It would only be seven in the morning back in Boston, she calculated, so there wouldn't be anyone at the law office yet. Nor did she have Giles's home phone number with her.

She knew Timothy's number by heart, even though she'd only dialed it once, but she had no intention of calling to find out whether or not he'd stayed in the States. She only hoped that if he had, and had been in touch with Giles, Giles hadn't told him of her crazy transatlantic mission.

The next hour and a half dragged by. Each minute seemed like a hefty segment of eternity, and Anne was pacing the floor by the time her watch showed two-thirty.

Giles would be in by now, she knew. She drew in a deep breath and placed the call. His voice sounded so wonderfully familiar across the span of miles that Anne was afraid she was going to start crying. Then she began to blurt out everything, unable to stop stammering as she told him about the hours she'd spent waiting for Timothy, only to have learned that he was not going to be coming to the Royal Shamrock at all.

"That's right," Giles confirmed. "I was just about to phone you, as a matter of fact. Tim called the office after I left last night. I just got the message myself about fifteen minutes ago. He was in Shannon. He said he was spending the night at a motel near the airport there and would head off in a rented car this morning for the town of Dingle. That's on the far west coast of Ireland—"

"I know where it is," Anne interrupted. After Timothy had told her the story of how he'd been abandoned on the hospital doorstep, she'd found a map of Ireland and looked up Dingle.

"For some reason he decided to bypass Dublin," Giles went on. "Or at least he decided to go to Dingle first. Anne, I know this is none of my business, but... give up and come home, will you? Get a flight back here as soon as you can, and I'll meet you at Logan."

It was tempting, very tempting, to say yes. It would be so easy to fall right into Giles's waiting arms should she fly home just now, Anne knew. But it would also be highly unfair, both to him and to herself.

She knew that she sounded shaky and extremely unsure of herself as she started explaining the way she felt to Giles. But she also knew what she had to do.

"I couldn't possibly t-turn back now, Giles," she concluded bravely. "If I did, I would n-never forgive myself!"

CHAPTER TWENTY

"Would you ever be in luck!" the head porter in-formed Anne. "There is a tour group leaving for Dingle in an hour or so, and as it happens my cousin is driving their bus. I'm sure he can find a bit of space for you."

"That would be terrific," Anne said gratefully.

"The group is booked in at the Gaeltacht in Dingle," the head porter went on. "I daresay you'll be able to get a room there yourself. It's a good hotel, right on the shores of Dingle Bay."

Anne was more than willing to go along with this suggestion, and luck did, indeed, seem to be with her when, nearly two hours later, she climbed aboard the comfortable Mercedes motor coach, and they set forth.

The head porter had introduced her to his cousin, whose name was Kevin. He was a ruddy-cheeked Irishman with a delightful rolling brogue and a defi-nitely appreciative gleam in his eyes as he surveyed Anne, though he was old enough to be her father. She found an empty seat toward the rear of the bus and was relieved when no one came to share it with her.

Although the highway they traveled was the principal east-west route across the country, it was only a two-lane road. Ireland was definitely not geared to superhighways, Anne soon realized. And driving along on the ''wrong'' side of the road was an experience she wasn't sure she'd ever want to repeat. Kevin was an excellent driver but erratic!

The Irish countryside, though, was lovely. The scenery was every bit as lush and green as she'd imagined, a verdant rolling land. Even so, Anne was not nearly as conscious of her surroundings as she normally would have been, for she was obsessed with the idea of reaching their destination.

Timothy had to be in Dingle! He *had* to be! She didn't even want to think about any other possibility.

Despite the speed at which Kevin drove whenever the opportunity presented itself, it was impossible to make consistently good time on this road, and the hours passed very slowly for Anne. She was entranced occasionally by the sight of castles, some in good repair, others seemingly on the verge of falling into ruins, but though Kevin was an interesting and informative conversationalist, serving as both driver and guide, the ride seemed to take forever.

She did spark to attention when Kevin explained that the Dingle Peninsula, where they were going, was part of the Kerry Gaeltacht, one of the sections of Ireland where Gaelic was considered the principal language and English a second tongue.

Anne wondered if she might be faced with a language barrier, and managed to ask Kevin about this when they stopped at a small inn along the way for lunch. He assured her, with a shake of the head, that she had nothing to fear.

"Some of the older folk do not speak English, but most of the younger ones speak both English and Gaelic. You should have no difficulties. But if you do," he added, "I will be around and more than glad to help you!"

Lunch over, they started forth on the second phase of the journey, and Anne could not help but feel that she'd been this way before. The names of the places were all so familiar. There was Limerick, where she saw a sign on a side road that pointed to Tipperary. They entered County Kerry and then came to Tralee, where she saw another sign indicating the road to Killarney. All the Irish ballads she'd ever heard—many of which she'd sung herself—came to haunt her, the strains of "My Killarney," "It's a Long Way to Tipperary," "The Rose of Tralee," "The Kerry Dancers," and others blending in memory.

Finally, once past Tralee, they were on the Dingle Peninsula, traversing narrow winding roads as they headed for the town of Dingle itself. They'd left the rolling country behind them for a much steeper terrain. Here the mountains rose abruptly from the coastline so that everything along the shore seemed to slope inevitably toward the sea.

As they drove through Dingle town, Anne had a quick impression of streets lined with small plain houses, most of them either made of stone or with pastel stucco facades. Again she noticed flowers blooming everywhere, but it seemed to her that their brightness emphasized, rather than camou- flaged, the general impression of austerity.

Perceptively Kevin said, "Many who live here- abouts wrest their living from the sea. And as I'm sure you can imagine, it makes for a very hard life." He was pulling up in front of the hotel as he concluded this small speech, then he said with a flourish, "And so here we are!"

The Gaeltacht was a complex of two-story cream- colored stucco buildings with red-tiled roofs. There was something of a Spanish look about them, and this bit of tropical atmosphere was further en- hanced by spiky palm trees in the front yard.

Anne followed the others into the hotel and soon realized that Kevin had gone ahead of the crowd. Stepping up to the desk, she was told there was a room waiting for her—the driver, himself, had secured it for her. Kevin, she decided, deserved a good tip for this added kindness.

She climbed the single flight of stairs that led to her room instead of waiting for the small elevator already filled to capacity by the older members of the tour group. The room was small and rather sparsely furnished, but it was also modern and com- fortable. Through its picture window there was a beautiful view looking out over Dingle Bay.

It took very little time for Anne to unpack. And then came the task she dreaded the most, because now that she was in Dingle she was becoming com- pletely unnerved about the prospect of finding Tim- othy!

She picked up the phone, her hand shaking, and

asked to be connected to the reception desk. Then, when a cheery Irish voice answered, she asked, "Do you have a Mr. Timothy Flanagan registered?"

"Timothy Flanagan," the receptionist repeated. "Let me just check the register...." Anne's heart was pounding when the woman came back on the line to say, "No dear, and I am sorry. Did you think he was staying here?"

"I'd imagined he might be," Anne said dejectedly. "He's...an American."

"Well there are a fair number of small hotels and guest houses in the center of town,"·the woman said brightly. "Perhaps you'll find him at one of them."

"Perhaps," Anne conceded, and faced the fact that she was going to have to discover how one tracked down a single American in a small Gaelic-speaking Irish town, a town in which she didn't know a single soul.

But she did know someone! she remembered, after another doleful moment had passed. She knew Kevin!

Briskly Anne set about repairing her makeup and combing her hair. Then she went downstairs to find him.

"SURE AND I might have known there was a man involved in your life," Kevin said, mockingly despairing. Anne had discovered him sitting at the bar in the nearly deserted cocktail lounge.

"I decided to have a bottle of stout before your countrymen descend like the locusts," he went on, his smile taking any possible sting out of his comment. "Would you care to join me?"

"Thank you, yes," Anne decided.

"Another Guinness, Johnnie!" Kevin called. Then, once Anne had sipped the dark brew and pronounced it good, he asked, "Well, now, lass, just who are you looking for?"

"His name is Timothy Flanagan," Anne said directly. "He is tall, he has red hair and green eyes, and...well, he may be related to someone here in town."

"Flanagan, eh?" Kevin mused. "But he's an American, you say?"

Anne was forced to laugh. "Funny," she said. "Back home I always think of Tim as an Irishman. But over here...."

"Over here, unless he is most exceptional, he will surely stick out as a Yank!" Kevin joked.

"He *is* exceptional," Anne rejoined demurely.

"Ah, the lucky devil," Kevin said wistfully. "It is he who should be running after you!"

Kevin's statement hit home considerably more than he had intended it to. Anne knew this, but it was still hard for her not to wince visibly, and the stammer was returning to plague her as she said, "I d-don't know how to get s-started, Kevin. That's why I wondered...."

"If I would help you?" he finished. "Now, have you ever known an Irishman worthy of the name who wouldn't come to the aid of a beautiful lady in distress!" he boasted. Then he leaned closer to Anne and said, "There are a few of the boys hereabouts who owe me one or two, and you can be sure that I'll get onto them about your dilemma. We'll comb the whole town if we have to, though that may not be the easiest of tasks. Even though Dingle has only fourteen hundred residents, would you believe there are no less than fifty-two licensed pubs! The locals boast that a man can be thrown out of a different pub each week and still keep on drinking happily the year-round! So if you think your lad might be doing a spot of pub hopping, it could take a bit of time to find him.''

"Tim may very well be visiting the pubs,'' Anne agreed. It seemed to her that this would be a likely way for a man to get started on a trail—a very long trail—that began with only a shawl, a brooch and a piece of paper with a couple of unusual words scrawled on it.

"If he is in Dingle we will find him,'' Kevin promised firmly.

Anne hesitated. Then she said, ''Your friends will certainly want to have a beer or two to assist them in doing me this favor. I'd like to give you some money toward that.''

"And why would I not be accepting it for such a worthy cause?'' Kevin demanded reasonably.

Anne smiled, and drawing her wallet from her handbag, she produced a sheath of pound notes, which she passed across the table. ''I didn't want to offend you, that's all,'' she said.

Without glancing at the money, Kevin stuffed it into his pants pocket. ''You are not,'' he told her. ''Anyway, I shall be returning what is left—if there

is any left, that is! My friends are a thirsty bunch!"
He paused, then urged, "Now, Anne. . .leave the
rest to us. Eat a good dinner, get yourself some
sleep, and in the morning I should have news for
you."

Anne could see the logic of Kevin's advice to her,
but it was not easily followed. At dinner she
ordered the excellent local salmon the hotel
featured and she'd never tasted anything better, yet
she could only finish part of the food on her plate.

The rooms did not have their own television sets,
but there was a large "telly" in the lounge. It didn't
appeal, though, and Anne realized too late that
she'd brought nothing with her to read and that the
magazine stand in the lobby closed early.

There was nothing to do but close her eyes and
try to go to sleep, but she was very restless, awaking
through the night at the slightest sound. All she
could think about was Timothy—where he might
be, what he might be doing, and if she would find
him at all.

Fortunately Kevin did not keep her in suspense
the next morning. He came directly to her room as
she was sampling a continental breakfast of strong
Irish tea and raisin-studded scones, rapping on her
door and shouting out authoritatively, "Anne, it's
me—Kevin!"

She got up quickly and let him in. At a glance she
saw that he looked slightly the worse for wear. Obviously, she surmised, the search had required a fair
amount of imbibing!

"I wish I had another cup so I could offer you

some tea,'' she told him, but he shook his head almost violently.

"Can't abide the stuff," he said impatiently. "Anyway, I've already had coffee. Now, Anne... as to your Timothy Flanagan...."

Anne's breath caught in her throat, and it was all she could do to whisper, "Yes?"

"He was nowhere in Dingle last night," Kevin said firmly. Then, at the sight of her disconsolate face, he added hastily, "Wait now, lass! That doesn't mean he didn't come back here."

She stared at the burly Irishman. "You're saying that Timothy really is in Dingle?" she asked weakly.

"Well, he was eating his breakfast at the Crown about an hour ago," Kevin reported. "It's a restaurant not far down the road. And he has been staying at Mrs. O'Flaherty's guest house. Told her he'd be at least a week there, maybe longer."

Anne pushed aside her teacup with trembling fingers. It was too much to take in, too much to believe all at once. "Did you t-talk to him, Kevin?" she managed.

"Sorry, but no," Kevin replied. "I've not seen him yet myself, but one of the other lads spotted him and got into a bit of conversation with him. There is no doubt he's your Timothy! And as Yank as they come, from what my friend Pat told me. A big redheaded American!"

Anne choked back a laugh that could have easily turned to tears.

"He has rented a car," Kevin continued. "In

fact, he rented it yesterday. He told Pat that he drove to Killarney in the afternoon and was late getting back—which is why we missed him when we did our rounds of the pubs. Incidentally,'' he added looking slightly abashed, ''there's not a pence left of the funds you advanced me.''

''That's perfectly all right,'' Anne assured him. ''You say Tim has rented a car?''

''A blue Triumph Herald,'' Kevin informed her. ''He got it from Mr. Gallagher's garage. Told Mrs. O'Flaherty this morning that he would be gone all day, in case anyone inquired after him....''

''Oh!'' Anne exhaled, sharply disappointed by this news.

''Does he know you are looking for him, Anne?'' Kevin asked curiously. ''I thought it might be you whom he expected to ask after him.''

''No,'' she said, shaking her head. ''No, he doesn't know I'm in Ireland. At least...I don't think he knows.'' There was the chance that Timothy might have talked to Giles on the phone once again, and Giles just might have told him, but she'd asked Giles to keep secret about this, and she was sure that he would have maintained her confidence unless there was a very good reason for breaking it.

''You've gone white as the moonlight over Dingle Bay,'' Kevin observed, breaking in on her thoughts. ''Are you feeling all right?''

''Yes,'' Anne managed. ''It's just that....''

''You want to meet up with the lad, I know,'' Kevin commiserated.

''Yes, I really do,'' she admitted softly.

"Then get on some clothes!" he boomed abruptly. "And wear flat shoes, mind. You will not be wanting heels where we'll be going. Your Mr. Flanagan told Mrs. O'Flaherty that he planned to go out toward Slea Head today. And I see no reason why, with the help of the Austin Mini I plan to borrow from Patrick, we can't catch up with him!"

While Kevin went to borrow the Austin, Anne dressed with record speed. Never before had she been possessed by such a sense of urgency.

Kevin was out in front of the hotel when she got downstairs, proudly standing by the little car Anne wondered how he would possibly manage to ease his bulk inside, but he did so with no apparent difficulty.

As they drove out of Dingle, going west toward Slea Head, Anne, despite her personal agitation, could not help but be gripped by the magnificence of this glorious mountainous peninsula. The landscape and the sea were both wild and fantastically beautiful.

The area also appeared to be virtually unpopulated. There were very few houses, and only occasionally did she and Kevin pass another car.

"It is busier earlier in the season when there are more tourists here," Kevin confided. "Just now we're coming to the end of all that for another year."

Anne nodded, but she was only half hearing what Kevin was saying to her. She was more aware of the other roads branching off the one they were traveling. They were only lanes for the most part, but still they were drivable. It seemed to her that Timothy could have diverted off onto any one of them, and she wondered how Kevin could possibly be so sure they were going to find him.

Then, ahead she saw a small blue car parked to the side of the road on a narrow stretch of grass.

"Oh..." she moaned, half under her breath.

"So there he is!" Kevin exclaimed triumphantly. "I'd not thought of ever becoming a detective, but now...."

"Kevin!" Anne said softly. "Oh, my...."

Kevin's grin turned to a frown, and he asked, puzzled, "This is what you wanted, isn't it, Anne?"

"Yes," she said, nodding her head up and down like a puppet being manipulated by unseen strings. "Yes, but...."

"Now that you are here, you do not think you can face him?" Kevin ventured.

"I don't know," she confessed, her voice very low.

"Surely he would be a fool—and no Irishman at all—if he was anything but deliriously happy at the sight of you," Kevin said staunchly.

"I...I'm not so s-sure," Anne whispered. "He's s-so unpredictable."

"Would you care for me to go down and find out?" Kevin suggested, scowling. He didn't need to add that as far as he was concerned it would be a bad day for Timothy Flanagan if he didn't respond positively to Anne's arrival.

"D-down?" Anne queried uncertainly.

"This is why I told you not to wear heels," Kevin

said patiently. "The beaches all around the peninsula are beautiful, to be sure, but one must have nimble footing to get down to most of them. Do you see those outcroppings of black rock?" he added, pointing.

"Yes."

"Well, there is a footpath winding among them to the beach," Kevin told her, "and a very steep footpath it is. But it looks like your Timothy has followed it—as have many men before him when they wanted to walk by the sea and contemplate."

They'd pulled up just behind the Triumph, and Anne saw that the small blue car was empty, something Kevin had obviously already realized. It did seem clear that there was only one place for Timothy to go.

She smiled a very weak smile and said bravely, "Well...I guess there's only one thing to do, wouldn't you say?"

"I'd say that Timothy Flanagan is a very lucky man," Kevin said, then added, "And sure and he'd better know it or I'm apt to be taking the back of my hand to him!"

Anne got out of the car and started down the footpath cautiously. Kevin had not been exaggerating when he'd said it was steep. It was *very* steep, and had she disregarded his advice and worn high-heeled shoes she knew she could not possibly have made the descent.

Far below she glimpsed a tantalizing stretch of golden sand. She'd never been much for heights, and the drop was such that to look at it for very long would make her dizzy. In any event, negotiating the path required her total concentration, plus all the agility she could muster.

Midway down, though, she paused to take another overview. From this vantage point she could see considerably more of the beach. Suddenly her heart lurched and her knees went weak. Perhaps a hundred yards to her right she saw a solitary figure walking in her direction with his head bent low.

There was no trace of Irish mist today. The morning sun was dazzling, and it outlined Timothy so that he seemed burnished with gold, like a man out of legend. Anne stood very still, drawing in a deep breath and rocking slightly on her feet, small shock waves coursing through her body.

She'd seen Timothy walking alone along a beach before, she remembered, and fought back the urge to cry. She'd watched him from the top of a sandy bluff that magical day on Cape Cod, even then seeing the depth of his loneliness.

She loved him! *Oh dear God, how she loved him!*

She faltered slightly as she started down the path again, closing her eyes briefly until she'd steadied herself, and it seemed that some miraculous force had carried her this far and would keep her moving on.

Then, through a different kind of haze, she saw that Timothy had come much closer...he was standing at the very foot of the path, staring up at her incredulously.

Anne did not really know what happened next. It was as if her feet were given wings, and she flew

down the short distance still separating them. Then
she was in Timothy's arms, burying her face against
his chest, reveling in his blessed masculine strength
as everything within her crumbled and sobs began
to rack her body.

He held her very close, embracing her tightly,
feverishly, and his voice, when he finally spoke, was
so hoarse she could barely understand him.

"I thought I was dreaming," he said simply.

Anne forced herself to rally, but she was still
choking back a sob as she moved out of the circle of
his arms and stood back looking up at him, filling
her eyes with the sight of him.

"Oh, Timothy," she said.

She put everything she felt for him into those
words, and that was all she needed to do. Timothy
Flanagan's green eyes blazed as they swept her face,
and then he muttered, "Dearest Anne! Dearest,
dearest Anne!" and whatever doubts Anne may
have had about the way in which he'd receive her
sudden appearance in Dingle were vanquished.

He reached for her desperately, achingly, like a
man long deprived of food who had suddenly found
sustenance. Then he lowered his head, his mouth
closing over her lips.

The kiss that followed was more eloquent than
anything Anne had ever experienced, and pressing
close to him, she let the rough wool of the Arran
sweater he was wearing scratch her cheeks, heedless
of its irritation. She knew only that she wanted
Timothy, all of Timothy, now and forever.

He held her away from him one more time, devouring her with his eyes as if still disbelieving her presence. Then again his lips came to claim hers, and Anne felt herself being set afire and welcomed the flames that came to consume her.

His hands roved over her body hungrily, demanding more than she could give him at this moment. Much as she wanted him, she still sensed something. She sensed another presence, and managing an upward glance, she saw Kevin standing at the top of the footpath.

Anne could not read his expression, the distance was too great. But she saw him lift a hand and wave, and feeling strangely exulted she waved back, and then saw him turn away. A moment later she heard a car motor and knew that he was driving off.

"Who was that?" Timothy asked.

"I think, perhaps, my guardian angel," Anne told him, and added simply, "He helped me find you, Tim."

"It's too much for me, Anne," Timothy said, dazed. "You're here, I can feel you, but I can't believe my eyes! I don't know how you got here, how you found me...."

"You don't mind my being here?" she asked. The question came hard, because to Anne there was still a seed of doubt about his answer, despite the way he'd received her.

"Mind?" he echoed. "How can you even ask such a thing?"

"Because...." she began, hesitating. Then she looked up into Timothy's eyes, knowing there was something that had to be said before she could utter another word. "Tim," she started, then faltered.

"Yes?" he asked, his voice edged with apprehension.

"I...I love you, Tim," she said. "I love you more than anything in the world...and I would go to the end of the earth to find you...unless I thought you didn't want me to."

"Dearest Anne...."

"No, you've got to hear me out," she insisted. "When I got your note...well, somehow I knew what you were about to do. And when I called your office and was put through to Giles, it was confirmed. It hurt."

"Hurt?"

"Yes, Timothy. It hurt that you hadn't come out and told me you were coming here in search of... your p-past."

He put an arm around her and led her over to a rock wide enough so that they could both sit on it. He said, smiling slightly, "I don't know how I'm going to keep my hands off you being this close to you. I...I don't know how I can possibly hang on to my sanity! But there are things to be said, Anne."

"Yes," she agreed, nodding. "And I'd like to hear the first one first, if you don't mind?"

"The first one?"

Anne shook her head impatiently. "There's something you've never told me, Timothy," she reminded him, and knew at once that he was aware of exactly what she meant.

"If I loved you?" he asked softly.

She knew he was remembering the time when she'd sung the song with those lyrics to him.

"How can you doubt that I love you, Anne?" he asked quietly, his head bowed. "I think I've shown it in a thousand ways."

"But you've never spoken the words," she insisted.

"No, I haven't. Because, as in the song, I've never been able to tell you all the things I want to say. And I didn't think I ever would be able to tell them to you, darling, unless I could first find out...who I am."

Despite the golden sunlight that surrounded him, a shadow passed over his face. "What is it, Tim?" she asked quickly.

"I don't know that I'll ever be able to find out," he admitted quietly, looking away from her as he said this. "You see, over the years I'd somewhat gotten over it. Being a person with no past, that is," he elaborated, the words coming with difficulty. "I became successful in my profession, I had enough money to get just about anything I wanted, I was even...accepted socially. In fact, I would have said that the stigma I felt long ago had pretty much been erased. Then...."

"What?"

"Then I met you," he said. "And you had all the background and all the heritage I lacked. I suppose that's why I could empathize to a point with Laura...though I deplored her rationale for the things she was trying to do. But she never felt she could live up to your father—and I didn't see how I could possibly live up to you! How could I measure up when I'm not even really sure that my name is Timothy Flanagan. Yes, I know that's what was written on the piece of paper I was found with, but how could I expect you to understand what it's like to not even know when your own birthday is, to not even know...."

"Timothy," Anne broke in gently, so affected by the misery in his voice that she couldn't bear to have him go on.

"No," he said, seeing this. "I've got to tell you these things, Anne! I...I must! You see, I came to feel that unless I could get some sense of my real identity...I could never ask you to share my life. I could never ask you to marry me! I thought of one day being a father to your children and...."

He broke off, and Anne said, "Timothy, you are so needlessly tormenting yourself! You do know that, don't you? I wouldn't care if we never find out who you are! You are you, Tim. And that is more than enough!"

"You say that, and I believe you mean it," he said, but he was avoiding her eyes. "Nevertheless...can't you see that it might be very easy, one day, for you to become ashamed of me?"

Anne reached up a slender finger and touched his lips. "You are out of your mind, Timothy Flanagan," she told him.

"With love for you, yes," he admitted. "Do I love you, Anne? My God, I love you so much that there would not be words enough in all the books in the world to express how I feel But... I have nothing to give you," he concluded sadly. "Can't you see that?"

"On the contrary," Anne replied, and there was no stammer to mar her speech now. "You have everything to give me, Tim. You have all I ever want and more. You have yourself."

For answer, he stood up and walked away from her, looking out over the waters of Dingle Bay, a lovely shade of greenish blue. He said slowly, "I wish it were that simple, Anne. But everything within me cries out to discover who I am. I came to Ireland with my shawl and my pin and that scrap of a note, thinking that perhaps armed with these clues I could at least make a beginning. But I found that the shawl was knitted from wool you see everywhere, and there are pins with green marble shamrocks in every gift shop I've gone into, and I've already come across so many Moira Ks in the phone directories that it would take an age and a half to track them all down. I've come to realize this search of mine could take the rest of my life... and even then I might not be any closer to the answer than I am right now."

Anne moved across to him, and taking his hand tenderly she said, "It's a search I'll share with you, Tim... if you want me to. Although, for myself the outcome is not all that important. I already know who you are, Timothy Flanagan! And so nothing you could learn about your background could ever make much of a difference to me!"

"And who am I, *mavourneen*?" he asked shakily.

"The man I love," Anne said steadily. "The man I will always love. And, sure and faith, Timothy Flanagan," she plunged on, mocking a rich Irish brogue herself, "I shall have to be taking the back of my hand to you if you don't make up your mind soon to make an honest woman of me!"

"What a threat!" he teased. Then he added, his voice surging with hope, "We can honeymoon at that beautiful little cottage in Wellfleet, which, incidentally, I've decided to buy. But in the meantime, how do you think the little people would feel about it if we celebrated our love right here on this nicely deserted beach?"

"I think the little people would smile upon us," Anne told him. "If you mean what I think you mean!"

He grinned, those emerald green eyes dancing. "Is there any doubt, *mavourneen*?" he teased. And then he added huskily, "Anne, my dearest love. I want you so much. I love you so much."

Anne laughed mischievously and pulled him down onto the sand.

"You've only to reach out, my darling," she told him, "and you'll be able to touch me...and have me...forever!"

ABOUT THE AUTHOR

Meg Hudson chose an Irish flavor for the fourth book in her multicultural series. The Boston setting was already familiar territory to this East Coast author, and she drew inspiration for the Ireland segment from a vacation spent touring the Emerald Isle. Meg has written more than thirty books, including mysteries and cookbooks as well as romances. When she isn't traveling or researching background material, this prolific author can be found hard at work at her home in Cape Cod, a sprawling nineteenth century house she shares with her husband and her word processor ''Fred.''